Seth Haddon

Reclaimed

SETH HADDON

RECLAIMED

BLIND EYE BOOKS

Reclaimed
By Seth Haddon
Published by Blind Eye Books
315 Prospect Street #5393
Bellingham WA 98227
www.blindeyebooks.com

Edited by Nicole Kimberling
Copyedited by Hilary Hensley
Cover Art by Julie Dillon
Author Photo by Minna Sophia Manu
Book Design by Dawn Kimberling
Ebook design by Michael DeLuca

print ISBN: 978-1-956422-10-8
ebook ISBN: 978-1-956422-11-5

For anyone who sometimes sees a stranger when they look in the mirror.

Trigger warning: *Reclaimed* contains discussions of mass death, ableism, violence, body dysmorphia, gender dysphoria, internalized transphobia, mention of suicidal ideation, potentially triggering terms for genitalia.

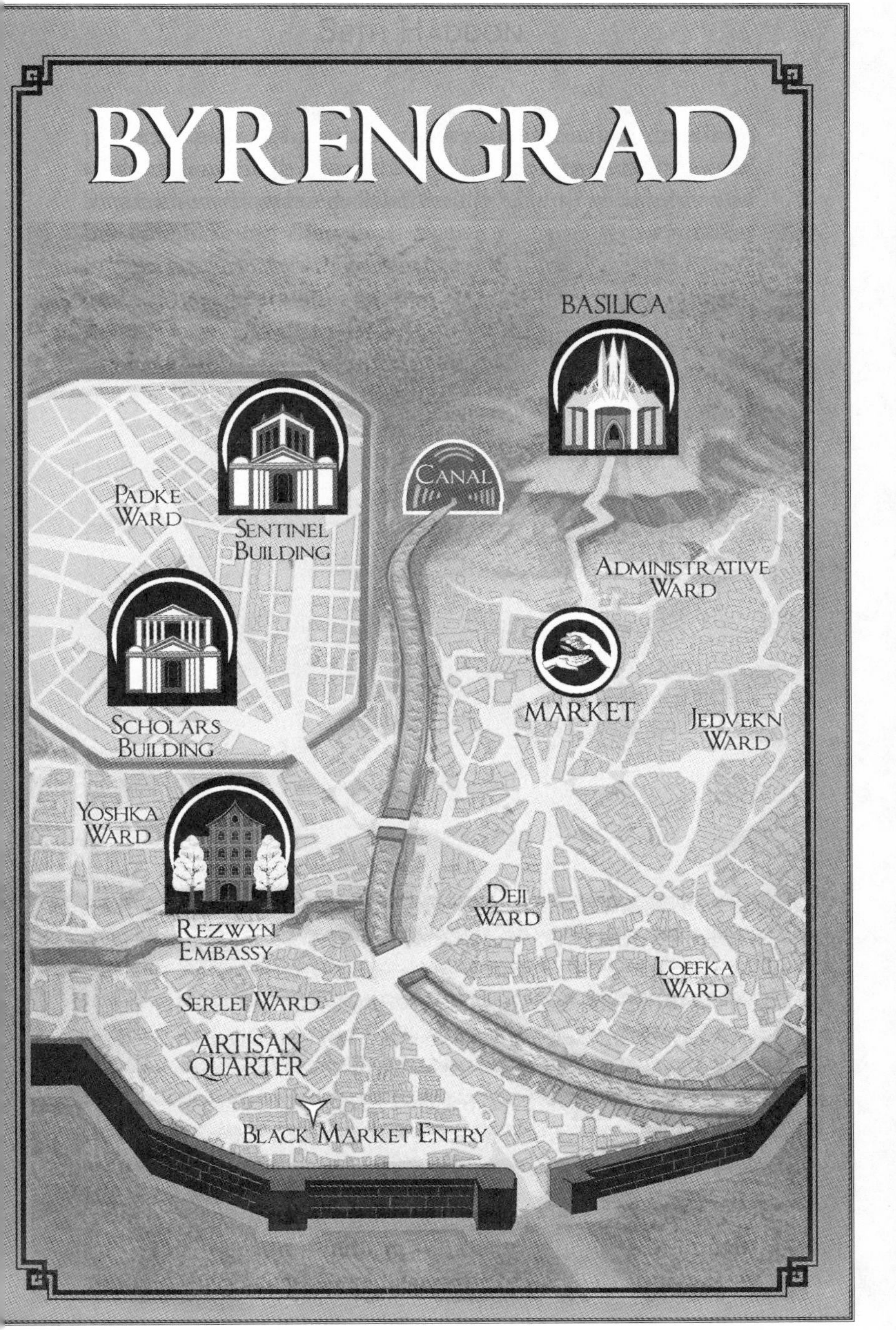
BYRENGRAD
BASILICA
CANAL
PADKE WARD
SENTINEL BUILDING
ADMINISTRATIVE WARD
MARKET
JEDVEKN WARD
SCHOLARS BUILDING
YOSHKA WARD
DEJI WARD
REZWYN EMBASSY
LOEFKA WARD
SERLEI WARD
ARTISAN QUARTER
BLACK MARKET ENTRY

Chapter One

The thing about the astral sea—that nebulous, elusive, maddening plane of existence just beyond the veil—was that no one really knew anything about it. Not in any way that was tangible. Or provable. And this meant, if one was a bit of a desperate or eccentric fellow, that one could dedicate one's whole life to answering this question: what the fuck even is the astral sea?

Discovering the nature of the astral sea had been the first exquisite obsession Saba Vasili had dedicated himself to. But the next thing he'd wanted—desperately—was to become a paragon.

In a country like Zvensia which lauded excellence in everything, exceptional people were elevated to the rank of paragon. Exalted and feted, you would be raised out of mortality, made something different by the ritual. All you had to do was be the best.

From the outside this seemed very formulaic and very achievable, but apparently it was not as straightforward as Saba Vasili had expected. You had to be the best and also not be anything but of pure Zvensian blood—no Rezwyn mother, no Uslethian great-grand-uncle, and certainly in no part grubby refugee from the vanquished state of Kerinsk.

At the top of Zvensian society sat the Grand Council, run by judges. Each city had their own judge-led Triad, and beneath that came the paragons. Nearly every vocation in Zvensian society had a paragon rank for all to aspire to. A long time in the past, paragons were elected by the community—and marked as special through masks, which confirmed rank and field. But the creation of the Triad had changed things, and now they were the ones who chose individuals to receive the paragon rank. The masks produced for each uniform now differed in material, shape, and expression for each vocation.

Saba used to think he could become a paragon too. He used to dream of it, crave it the way others might lust for food or flesh. He had wanted the title, the prestige, the relative safety that came with it, and the elaborate metal mask—two of which stared at him now.

Two paragon sentinels—people charged with enforcing Zvensia's multitude of laws—loomed over him.

Sentinels were paragons not of the mind but of the body. The soldiers and fighters and sentries of Byrengrad City, all of them were paragons of their kind. After years of training or otherwise excelling in their careers, they were awarded paragon status for exceptionality.

Though how exceptional could you be, really, when there were hundreds of sentinels in this city?

No. Sentinel was, in Saba's mind, the weakest class of the paragons, if only because of their sheer number. But sages—the paragon rank given to scholars—were rarer. Despite everything, despite where he was and what he looked like and where he came from, Saba still wanted it.

And now you'll never be one.

The damp, windowless stone jail cell was lit only by a weak torchlight. The light flickered over the brushed bronze of the masks, and the waltzing ebb and flow of the shadows made Saba feel like he was staring into a firepit, growing hypnotized by the embers.

Traditionally, sentinel masks were beaten into uncanny and terrifying shapes. One of those staring at him sported a twisted scowl, deep frown lines, and a gaping eye-slit to stare through. Saba tried in vain to squint through the dark and pick out the true human expression sitting behind the eternal fury of the mask.

Another part of him didn't want to know. What if the sentinel's real expression was worse?

He stared so long at those masks he couldn't be sure he didn't conjure them from the shadows himself, a symptom of a weak and broken mind. The Triad, those lower judges appointed by Zvensia's Grand Council who ruled Byrengrad City, had left him locked up here for—how long? Wasn't it feasible he was imagining these visitors?

Stop it, idiot. You're panicking.

Some last scrap of reasoning remaining secure in Saba's mind stepped forward to take control. It wrenched back his despairing mind, wrangling the anxious instinct back down. Saba felt emotion grow distant as he steadied his breathing and met the ever-watchful gaze of the two sentinels once more.

"Anything more you have to say for yourself?" one of the sentinels asked.

Saba blinked rapidly against the dark. The words were spat at him, and after a rush of shock—no, Saba's imagination had not conjured these masks—he straightened himself in his chair. All at once he felt the ache in every part of his body, the bruises up his arm, the open weeping wounds on his wrists from the cuffs. Ten hours earlier, his arms had been cuffed behind the chair's back; now his shoulders throbbed in protest. Disuse had made his hips ache. His tender tailbone pulsed.

And because Saba was scared and furious and relatively sure he was going to die, he looked the sentinel in the eye, clicked his tongue, and cocked his head to say, "Whoops?"

One sentinel broke from their place and punched Saba squarely on the jaw.

Crack.

Saba's head whipped back from the force. He made a sound like a dying animal—pathetic—and spent a good few seconds catching his breath as dull, deep pain pulsed along his jawbone. A referred ache started up near his temple, and he tasted salt and metal in his mouth. Bastard had split his lip. Saba's heart fluttered manically in his chest as fear flooded his veins; he wanted to scream. He wanted to go wild and thrash around like a dog, to bite and snap should they get close to him. But he couldn't let that urge out.

He laughed instead, tongue perched on his canine.

If he didn't let the wound hurt, then it wouldn't. If he didn't let himself be scared, then he wouldn't be. His mother's voice rose vividly in his memory: *You must always keep your head high, little sun.*

He flashed his most dazzling smile and imagined the blood squeezing out between his teeth. Saba craned his neck to the other side, exposing his unmarked cheek. "Give me another one—a proper one—for penance."

The sentinel's hand curled into a fist once more. His voice shook with fury. "Don't you dare be so foul. Hundreds are dead because of your machine."

Then a new voice said, "Leave us."

Saba's eyes flashed to a third sentinel who stood, only half-visible, like an apparition, leaning against the far wall. Saba's stomach dropped. He knew that voice.

Maksid had come to see him.

Why did it have to be him?

The other sentinel glanced back over his shoulder, hand still curled up for a punch. "Sir, he's dangerous."

"Thank you." Maksid peeled himself off the wall. He walked closer to Saba, so close Saba could see the familiar green of his eyes through the eye slits of the mask. The disdain, too, was unfortunately familiar. "I'm well aware."

The moment elongated. Saba stared at the sentinel, who stared back at him. And panic gave way to a more primordial type of fear—something fetid in Saba's gut, something old. An involuntary shiver rushed up Saba's spine.

The first two sentinels lingered momentarily then stepped back, giving space for the other sentinel to fill. On their way out, the three sentinels exchanged a few words.

To whatever was said, Maksid gave a nod of approval.

Saba intently watched the others leave, and when the door opened, he imagined his soul slipping out and escaping. The faint sliver of light was so beautiful Saba felt drunk from seeing it, as if he had been shrouded in shadow his whole life and was now seeing the molten beauty of daylight for the first time.

Then the door slammed closed.

Blinking in the dark, Saba came back to himself and his anger. He spit blood onto the floor and sneered up at the remaining sentinel.

"What?" Saba hissed.

The sentinel sighed deeply, as if this whole thing was just a matter of great inconvenience, and not—

Don't think about it. Don't think about it.

But the other sentinel had already reminded him of the truth: hundreds were dead because of the mechanism he'd built.

Saba raised his chin, forcing these thoughts to the back of his mind. "More ashamed than ever to have me as your brother?"

That had the desired effect. Maksid flinched violently, like Saba had knifed him in the gut. He turned back to Saba slowly, practically vibrating with rage, because beneath that mask, beneath all the trappings of his paragon status, Maksid shared the same heritage as Saba.

Of course, he shared more than that. He had the same pink-tinged skin, brown freckles, and shock of auburn hair. Maksid had managed to glean more height from their late father, but Saba still came up to his chin. They shared the same build—an excess of lank, as if every limb had been stretched and wrung out. Maksid at least could hide this ungraceful paucity beneath the heavy layers of sentinel garb. Saba, on the other hand, really couldn't escape it; what muscle he had was thin and sinewy, laid over his gangly limbs in long stretches. Now, covered in muck, underfed, and stinking, he must have looked like a starving street mutt.

Saba had at least won out with his face. Their late mother had a fine bone structure, with prominent cheekbones and a relatively wide jaw. Those same bones sat well in Saba's face, but they poked severely through Maksid's with an angry bite, as if the skin had been pulled too taut.

Which was perhaps the reason his brother had been so desperate to earn that sentinel mask.

Pettiness aside, the two of them were Kerish through and through. Only Maksid had wrapped himself so well beneath his cowl he had yet to be found out. Damn familial bonds—the sentinels were more important to Maksid than Saba now.

Maksid crossed his arms. He moved closer to Saba, whose chair had been pushed flush against the stone wall. "I really can't stand your attitude."

"*My* attitude? You're the one who can't bear the burden of admitting you're related to me. What is it, exactly, that makes you so ashamed anyway? Our heritage?"

"Stop it."

"So that certainly plays a part. Or maybe you're ashamed of what I am. Would it have been easier if I'd stayed your little sister, or were we already too far gone by that point? What about now? Do you think what's happened has ruined our chance at reconciliation?"

Maksid slammed his hands onto the wall above Saba's head. Saba jumped.

White dust and grime flittered down, snowing over Saba's hair in the tense silence.

Maksid panted heavily. "For fuck's sake, you little shit," he spat. His voice was misshapen, warped beneath the mask. It echoed gruffly. "I'm trying to help you."

Saba ground his teeth together. Heat pushed behind his eyes. *Absolutely not.* He was not going to cry. It was too late for that anyway—the damage had been done. Crying would only make his brother angrier.

Maksid shifted. He stepped away so he was no longer bearing down over Saba. In fact, he lowered himself, bringing that maelstrom expression in his eyes close to Saba's face, who stared at the mask and his brother beyond it.

Maksid reached out to put a hand on Saba's shoulder. It took every bit of restraint in Saba not to flinch.

"Why did you have to open the astral sea?" Maksid asked quietly.

Saba's stomach dropped. "Why are you so sure it was me?"

"There's no one else with your knowledge," Maksid said, like this justified his betrayal of assumptions.

The sweetness in his voice irked Saba.

Maksid took his hand away, stood, and shrugged as if all of this was done and dusted—like Saba's fate was sealed, his guilt carved into every part of this material plane.

"A small massacre," Saba murmured with a disbelieving laugh. "A fun morning for Saba Vasili?"

Maksid turned around. He muttered something, but it was lost and muffled beneath the mask. Saba half expected Maksid to give up, to walk out that door—but then the sentinel whirled around.

"Listen to me. We don't have much time, so save your act and *listen.* Your machine ripped—" he cut himself off, eyes rolling back and forth in his skull as he searched for a better word. "The event ripped a giant hole in Byrengrad, little brother. A lot of people died. Important people. Someone must be accountable for it."

Important people. Saba couldn't help but laugh at that. Important people—that's what Maksid's anger was about—not the hundreds caught up in the explosion but the one or two important enough for the Triad to care about.

Maksid kicked one of the chair legs, narrowly missing Saba's shin. The force cracked it, and the world tilted as the chair fell, scraping against the stone wall. Saba swallowed a scream as Maksid grabbed him by the shirt, shouting, "*Stop fucking laughing!*"

Saba fell quiet. He was frozen beneath Maksid's gaze, shaking from the shock of the fall and the anger.

Maksid's breath echoed dully behind the mask. He glanced back at the door and positioned Saba and the remains of the chair against the wall for balance. Then he dropped into a squat. "Kers died. A lot of them lived in Loefka Ward."

"I know."

"A judge too."

Saba inhaled. *Shit.*

Maksid gave the final blow with, "And a Rezwyn ambassador."

Saba's stomach dropped out of him. Fear in its purest form crept into his throat and curled up there in a big lump. Maksid met his eyes, and Saba knew they both felt it. They had both borne the weight of Rezwyn overreach, the legacy of imperialism that had destroyed their native country.

Saba hated the way his voice shook when he asked, "According to protocol, their emperor will send an official from Doskor to demand compensation from Zvensia, then?"

Maksid nodded. "He's already here."

An official. A Rezwyn agent. A little rat bastard come to punish Saba for this after what the Rezwyns did to his homeland of Kerinsk? After what they did to so many countries and peoples and cultures?

How dare the Rezwyn Empire have the gall to step in and berate him for any kind of violence?

But fear was in him too.

Maksid sensed Saba's thoughts. He looked down at him pointedly. "Sabina. Please, don't antagonize this man."

Sabina? No. Fuck that.

All the fear in Saba gave way to anger. He spat, "Oh, don't worry, Maksid, I'll be on my best behavior. There's nothing I love more than righteous invaders coming to admonish a victim of their own ceaseless fucking violence and murder. Really. Empire bastards. Hundreds dead are a drop in the pond for the fucking Rezwyns."

Maksid ground his teeth and ignored most of what Saba said. "New Rezwyn emperor, new everything. And don't call me Maksid. At least not in front of people. It's Justice Sentinel."

"New emperor, same history. And I'll call you that fucking mouthful when you use my name correctly."

Maksid at least had the decency to look down at his hands. "Saba," he said, enunciating slowly. "I'm sorry."

Saba tried to loosen his jaw, but it was tense with expectation. He was hit with a vision of another life. If Kerinsk hadn't fallen to the Rezwyns, if their mother had not died, if Saba was different, if he hadn't changed himself so completely, then his brother would never have dared speak to him like this. Not once.

Saba looked up. "So am I."

Maksid took a breath so large it puffed out his chest. He cocked his head. Saba watched his brother's eyes harden through the slit. Now they matched the gnarled bronze fury of his sentinel mask perfectly.

Saba tensed as Maksid said, "So then why did you open the astral sea? How could you risk everyone's safety to satisfy your curiosity?"

One tear betrayed Saba's resolve. It bubbled over the edge of his eye and ran in a warm rivulet down his cheek.

How fucking dare he? How dare he?

Maksid would throw an apology out one second then accuse him of negligence the next? Was it because Saba had changed his body? Had abandoned his name and every ounce of his heritage? Because Saba was capable of growth and rebirth and change, it made him heartless?

How could his brother think he could do this?

The door opened.

Maksid backed up immediately, putting space between them. Saba squinted toward the light. A silhouette filled the doorframe: tall, broad, and sturdy. Then the two previous sentinels moved to flank this newcomer.

Even before he stepped into the room, Saba could practically smell empire on him.

He was a big man, wide and stout, fat and strong, beautiful in that eerie way most Rezwyns were with that pale skin, though his lacked the translucent quality conventional to his compatriots. His hair was blond, he had faint lines set around his eyes, and he was bearded—perhaps in his mid-thirties. Well-groomed, too, Saba noted with almost admiration, keenly feeling the knots in his own hair and the grime caked under his nails.

The Rezwyn was dressed well in fine empire cloth, muscular arms near straining at the fabric, as well as a heavy wolf-fur cloak that was altogether too warm for this country. His boots were fantastic, ankle-length and embossed. He also carried a cane, on which he leaned heavily to stand.

The cane caught Saba's eye because it was simple in design but so obviously finely made. The wood near the handle had been carved into sharp angles, but the rest of it was smooth and rounded, polished to a shine. Saba only caught a glimpse of the handle as the man approached, but he saw the head of it was carved to resemble a hare. Not a rabbit, not that soft being. A hare. A canny and feral creature that one was. What an odd choice.

"Can you understand Doskorian?" Maksid—Justice Sentinel—asked Saba.

He knew damn well Saba could, of course, but he wasn't meant to know Saba personally at all.

You can too, Saba wanted to say. *You learned from the same tutors.*

But disgracing Maksid wouldn't earn him back as an ally—and Saba found himself willing to lie for his brother.

"Of course." Saba grinned, putting that cheerful smile on for his audience.

"Good," Maksid said curtly before nodding back to the official. "He doesn't speak Zvensian."

Under his breath Saba whispered, "Of course not."

The other sentinels—Saba didn't know their names—brought a chair in for the newcomer. The Rezwyn ripped off his cloak before landing heavily in his seat. The chair shook a little. Without the cloak to conceal him, his width and strength were obvious.

Then, in heavily accented Zvensian, the newcomer said to Maksid, "Well, you must have poor intel."

The Queendom of Kerinsk had once sat in the north at the border that used to mark the boundary between the Rezwyn Empire and Zvensia. It had been a relatively small country with a language not at all dissimilar to Zvensian. Kerish had the same lilt and cadence. Most of the grammar and the structure was the same.

But there were very few Rezwyns who knew either language unless they'd had cause to be there.

Saba stopped breathing. His eyes darted up to his brother's—he needed to see his brother, Maksid, not the sentinel. He needed the comfort of another Ker to make this horror palatable. But Maksid didn't offer his gaze. Maksid left Saba to drown.

Saba's throat bobbed as he swallowed. "You served," he said. Primal horror snuffed all calm from Saba's stomach. "You were a soldier in Kerinsk."

The Rezwyn slapped his leg. And then, to add insult to injury, he said in Kerish, "Along with many, many others."

The Rezwyn considered Saba carefully. Something about his stare made Saba shiver.

Everyone else but the two of them were in masks. Everyone else had the privilege of having their expressions safely hidden away. So this was a forced vulnerability. Everyone looked at Saba; he was cornered. He used to be smarter than this, more cautious. He never would have let himself end up alone with a Rezwyn and three sentinels who were all looking at him like he was prey.

The Rezwyn breathed deeply. He had such ease about him, such surety in his body, it was almost mesmerizing to watch. With a near dismissive gaze, he glanced at the sentinels and motioned for them to leave.

"Go on," he said in Zvensian. "He's in no position to harm me."

So you think, Saba wanted to shout. *Come near me and I'll bite.*

Maksid glanced down at Saba. His brother knew him too well. Worry laced his words. "Sir, I must insist."

"Well, congratulations, Sir Paragon, you have insisted. You may go."

Saba snorted despite himself. Guts and attitude on a Rezwyn. Funny—especially when Maksid froze. He lingered a little too long with his eyes on Saba. But everyone else retreated, and after an awkward beat, Saba showed Maksid all his teeth, like he really had gone insane.

Maksid stared back and softly shut the door behind him.

And then it was just the two of them.

Saba's eyes had to readjust to the dark. He blinked and took stock. Maksid had left his half-broken chair propped against the back stone wall of the cell. There was nothing else save for a couple of torches glowing in evenly spaced sconces around the wall. Distantly Saba was aware someone had removed his shit bucket at some point since the last time he'd used it—likely for the Rezwyn's benefit. So really, it truly was just the two of them, and there was nothing else in this cell to focus on but each other.

The Rezwyn sighed, that intense exhale, and Saba found himself inhaling in response. He was intimidating. Firstly, for his size, which was immense next to Saba's stringy form. But also for that other intangible quality, something like confidence and ease and self-surety. Saba wasn't even sure he could correctly identify it, but he felt it and wished he had it too.

"My name is Luan Zek," the Rezwyn said. He spoke with great depth, as if his voice had been comprised of that of three other men stitched together seamlessly and stripped of discordant tones. It had a weight to it, a captivating lilt. "Official title is Special Ambassador to Zvensia for the Rezwyn Empire."

Saba cleared his throat. He would have been surprised if Zek didn't know who he was already. But this name, this title, belonged to him, and he would own it every chance he got. Even now.

"Saba Vasili. Scholar and wrongfully accused mass murderer."

Zek didn't immediately reply, and Saba suddenly disliked the silence. He sat up straighter against the wall, careful not to upend the broken chair. "Sending you all the way here . . . what wealthy Rezwyn bastard died in the accident?"

Without missing a beat, Zek replied, "The Lord of Veprak."

Saba felt all the blood drain from his face. "Oh."

Zek inhaled slowly and leaned forward. The wooden legs of his chair creaked, sounding to Saba like the cawing of crows drawn out and distended.

Zek made sure they were looking at one another before he spoke. "I am here to understand who or what is responsible for the death of Krezmir Doric, Lord of Veprak. My hosts, the Triad of Byrengrad City, on behalf of Zvensia's Grand Council, have agreed to allow this investigation. The perpetrator will be taken to Doskor to stand trial. The emperor demands compensation for the loss of his countryman."

His countryman? One man lost? The sheer fucking nerve—but what else should one expect from a Rezwyn? Rage blinded Saba. He spat out, "And what of my countrymen?"

They came unbidden then, the shades of Kerinsk, in a mass haunting—not just the ones who died in the recent explosion, but the ones who were lost to the war. And here Saba sat in a cell, one of the last to survive. That alone was enough to carry the weight of legacy, the memory of a lost country. But he had so much more on his shoulders. Too much history. Too much expectation.

Zek could have slapped him for speaking like that. Shit, he could have walloped Saba with his cane without even standing up. No one would have questioned it—the walls were too thick, and what was one more bruise or laceration on a body as battered as Saba's? But he didn't. It was a kindness Saba shouldn't have latched on to. He knew better than to assign layers of meaning to action or inaction; yet he almost couldn't help it.

Especially when Zek did him the service of moving past the jab entirely, without even a verbal counterattack.

"They tell me your machine caused a lot of damage," Zek said.

Saba glanced away. "Have you seen it yet?"

"No," said Zek. "But I've been promised a tour."

Saba met Zek's gaze again. "I haven't seen it either."

Zek didn't bother to hide his confusion which Saba found interesting. Either Zek had assumed Saba had been there, or he'd been told he had—neither of which were true. Saba had been in this cell for a full week before he even knew his charge. Since then, he'd only been given the sketchiest account of the extent of the damage.

"That surprises you, does it?" Saba asked. "I told you, I've been wrongfully accused."

Zek's face returned to that sedated expression. "You're pleading innocent, then?"

I am innocent, Saba wanted to reiterate. *I haven't done anything.*

But the longer he was kept here, the less he believed it. Still he managed to say, "Yes."

In true Rezwyn fashion Zek made his face completely impassive. What little emotion he had shown Saba already was very likely put on. The display of true emotions, Saba recalled from his studies, was considered crass amongst the Rezwyns; Saba knew he would be quickly disarmed if he took everything Zek did and said at face value. But he was a scholar, for fuck's sake—a smart man.

If Zek was milking him for information, Saba could do the same thing back.

"They've told me the ground collapsed in the ward," Saba said, voice calm. "Not quite a sinkhole but a cavity. This was after the machine was activated, of course, so even if only a hundred or so died in that, plenty more had to fall to their deaths. They say it's devastating, especially for the Kerish refugees who lived there. So maybe I ought to lead that tour. Show you the devastation my infernal machine has wrought amongst the remains of my people."

Self-abasement was rarely attractive, but Saba couldn't help it. He deserved it, he felt, even if he had not caused the incident directly. A great number of refugees from Kerinsk, a country now assimilated into the west of the Rezwyn Empire, had lived in the ward that had been destroyed. His brother's words rattled in his skull over and over until they became his own, his own voice reminding him there was no one else. No one else had the knowledge to build the machine that had gone haywire, causing sudden devastation as it succeeded in opening a gateway to the astral sea.

But that was not entirely true. Two others knew enough about the device—Mossinne and Khajro, the scholar mechanics who had helped him build it. He didn't know Khajro well, but he knew Moss, and she was too damn sweet for her own good. Saba would not subject her to shitting in buckets; he vowed it right then. He would keep her name from his mouth for as long as it took to make sure she was safe.

In the weeks he'd been in prison he hadn't heard mention of either of them. This either meant they were dead or downplaying their knowledge, laying low.

Good.

Saba didn't need company to rot with.

Zek leaned back and folded his arms. His expression was strange. Where the sentinels—even Maksid—couldn't quite hide their disdain of him, Zek watched Saba carefully. Part of it, Saba was sure, was wariness. Saba had been accused of negligence and mass murder, of course, so that felt only natural. But there was a layered nature to Zek's expression, and Saba couldn't tell what the rest of the notes were. The longer Zek looked, the madder it drove him. Confusion? Interest? Disgust?

"You are not what I expected," Zek murmured finally. His lip quirked at the side, pressing up around the blond-brown beard. It might have been a sincere look, but Saba had already promised himself not to take Zek at face value.

He strained forward against his bonds. "Why's that? Too pretty to have committed negligent homicide?"

"Eh," Zek said, looking Saba up and down. "So-so."

Saba snorted, then chided himself for it. *Stupid.* Is that all it took to make Saba Vasili relax? One joke?

Zek said, "I've been told all this happened because you used illegal magic to tamper with forces beyond your station."

Saba sighed. "I'm guessing the paragons told you that."

"Judge Hirunz, actually."

Saba rolled his eyes so hard he could feel his skull straining. What a joke. "Whatever he says, I'm no witch. I have no magic in me. I'm just a scholar."

Zek cocked his head to the side. "And do you specialize in machinery or in the astrok-mer or both?"

Astrok-mer was the Rezwyn term for the astral sea. And if Zek was aware of Saba's specialization, then Saba had to wonder if his scholarly pursuits were of interest to the empire beyond the death of the Lord Doric.

For the Rezwyns, the astral sea was a rather sacred plane of being. Most of their gods resided there. For Saba, it was a source of untapped power with limitless potential. But since the Rezwyns let their so-called gods decide wars for them, Saba wouldn't put it past Emperor Dziove to conclude Saba's—or anyone's—research into the astral sea a threat to the empire.

Saba also did not like Zek bringing up the idea of a mechanic being involved.

He narrowed his eyes at Zek. "A scholar of the astral sea, yes," he began. "I study its nature. Its impact on this world. Its mythology. Relevant phenomena. For example, the magical ichor found in Uslethian gedroks and Rezwyn cajudsan flowers—does it originate in the astral sea, or is it a natural substance that merely resonates with the astral sea? That kind of thing."

Zek simply craned forward again, squinting at Saba as if trying to read him. "Tell me more."

Saba sighed and made some motion that would have been a shrug if his arms weren't so roughly locked behind him.

"I theorize that the astral sea is a state of pure possibility that has manifested a consciousness. But is that the result of being worshiped by the Rezwyns as the home of the god Suoduny? In effect did the god begin to exist because we humans needed a god to implore? Because the astrok-mer is not everywhere in the world; it exists mostly over the original Rezwyn territories. Obviously it reaches as far as Usleth, but if it ever opened before—and I believe it must have—" he cut himself off as he saw Zek's expression begin to glaze over.

One question, and you let yourself run wild.

Saba clicked his tongue and smiled brightly at Zek. "Ah, you got me rambling. Forgive me, Sir Rezwyn."

"Your thoughts on this matter are fascinating," Zek remarked. "Perhaps once this matter is settled, I can read some of your work."

Saba narrowed his eyes and smiled. Anything he'd ever written had most likely been burned by Judge Hirunz by now, and in truth, he doubted the ambassador gave a single shit.

"Thank you, but I'll honestly be surprised if I survive another night in this place," Saba said as charmingly as he could.

Zek understood the implication immediately. He glanced toward the door. "Lot of accidents in a place like this?"

Saba bit his lip. "Yes. A lot of people are angry with me."

Zek nodded. Then he returned his gaze to Saba. "I'm just here to find out what happened to Lord Doric, Saba Vasili. If I discover that you are responsible for his death, you'll be extradited to Doskor for punishment."

And without another word, Luan Zek stood. A rumble sounded in his chest, Zek grunting as he shook out some cramp in his leg, and Saba was forced to crane his neck to look up at him. At the sheer fucking size of him. Saba flushed.

Extradited to Doskor. Saba wouldn't last. They'd kill him—they'd torture him first, then they'd put his head on a pike.

"Can you do that—just take me away?" Saba asked and cringed at the way his voice quivered.

Zek turned without answer and headed for the door. *No, no*—Zek already thought he was guilty. Saba couldn't let him walk away. He threw himself against his restraints until the cuffs pressed horribly into the open wet wounds around his wrists. It stung, but it didn't matter.

"Hey! I asked you a question!"

Zek spun back around. "Yes, I can do that. Emperor Dziove is determined to find out what happened, and Judge Hirunz is happy to oblige him. Now please behave, or I'll have to restrain you further."

Saba grinned and pushed forward again. He must have looked mad, straining at the bit. *Fuck it.* Good behavior had gotten him nowhere but a dank jail cell.

"Oh, I'll be such a good boy for you, Sir Zek," he spat. "And if not, you can put a leash on me. Walk me into Doskor like a dog—I'm sure the emperor would love to see a Ker on their knees."

Zek had the gall to look amused. "What a strange man you are," he said, voice lilting.

Then he raised that red-eyed hare to the door and knocked twice to be let out. The door opened. Zek looked back at Saba, just the once, before leaving him in the dark.

CHAPTER TWO

Saba was left in the dark for what felt like eons. He stared at the muted torchlight flickering faintly on the far wall, stared until he could conjure sentinel masks in his mind's eye, until the whole room was spinning with their twisted faces. And then, because he had been left alone too long, a feeling in him woke and yawned: the guilt.

Saba wasn't sure if he was responsible, but he also wasn't certain of his own innocence. This limbo state hurt him. The scholarly part of him, the part that yearned for knowledge and had dedicated years of his life to that pursuit, thought surely not. He knew himself and his research like it was a part of his own flesh—and *that* he had inspected over and over every waking moment for as long as he could remember. So he knew his research intimately, like it was his lifeblood. And nothing he had studied could have caused the accident that the sentinels described.

Only that's not exactly true, is it? Let alone if some idiot got a hold of your notes . . .

Could he so neatly be absolved of those deaths? Could anyone unstitch the seam knitting him to the destruction? Was he even allowed to want that?

In the end, even if Saba hadn't set it off himself, he was in some way responsible.

You're alive and they're not. And you can't even live with the guilt.

The door rumbled open. Saba snapped forward just as two sentinels hefted him upwards. Saba let it happen—he saw no point in struggling—and they uncuffed him. Saba's heart sank at that. There were only a few reasons they would be freeing his limbs, and none of them were good.

Once freed, all his wounds ached threefold. His neck was tense, his shoulder blades sore. He wobbled unsteadily after sitting for nearly all of two weeks—save bathroom respites. As such, he nearly keeled over into a sentinel—into Maksid, he realized, when he met the eyes through the mask. But under no circumstances would Saba rely on his brother now. Maksid—Justice Sentinel—stared at Saba, eyes stormy and unhappy. "You're being extradited to Doskor."

There it was. They stared at each other, and Saba imagined that his brother was also experiencing the heat of burning irony in that moment. Saba remembered first the treaty the Kers had with Zvensia, the thing that had allowed them to settle here in the first place. He supposed his criminal charges meant Zvensia no longer had to render him, a Ker, aid. The other thing he remembered was that long ago, the Rezwyn Empire and Kerinsk had a treaty too—one that promised support in the form of aid; Kerinsk could call upon them at any time. The empire had eventually breached that treaty to absorb Kerinsk, and now, here was Saba, about to be disappeared behind enemy lines.

Saba folded himself into a mock bow. "So I've been sold to the Rezwyns at last."

Either out of shame or a remnant of brotherly concern, Maksid tore his eyes away and looked anywhere except Saba. He said, "I am putting you directly into the care of Ambassador Luan Zek. This extradition has been approved by Judge Hirunz."

Saba rolled his shoulders back and put his hands out in front of him. The other sentinel quickly rebound them with manacles before roughly hauling him forward. The chain links were large, swooping loops, and there was such an extreme excess of chain that Saba had to bundle half of it up in his arms just to walk anywhere. They were gaudy, impractical, and a beacon for attentive stares; anyone wearing the ceremonial manacles was marked as an obvious no-good prisoner. Saba staggered and shot a look over his shoulder at Maksid, but that spineless bastard still wasn't looking his way.

The cell door opened, and Saba was blinded by the intensity of the light. A genuine ache started up behind his eyes, and he was forced to squeeze them shut every few seconds to cope. That's what weeks of poor lighting did to you, apparently.

Grime, dank, and dark gave way to light and climbing ceilings as the sentinels escorted Saba up the stairs. They walked up several flights, moving up out of the humid underground complex to the main floor. For the first time in weeks, he saw the basilica, the physical seat of the Triad. A bloody sea of red marble spanned the floors. White marble columns struck through with red veins protruded in even divisions to the end of the basilica, arching up to the domed ceiling. It was a confection of stone and colored glass; purples and reds spilled over the basilica, fragmented through membrane-thin glass. The basilica normally lent an ethereal beauty to Zvensia's arid mountainous landscape, but to Saba's eyes it looked more like a cadaver's ribcage, not quite pecked clean of stringy red meat.

Bustling administrative peoples flitted about. They moved as if in a synchronized dance, spinning around one another, each focused on their own path through the building as they helped to run the city.

And then there were the magistrates. Magistrates and judges both held key roles in Zvensia's system, but magistrates usually dealt with less serious issues. The judges who made up the Triad were assigned by Zvensia's Grand Council.

Where paragons wore bronze masks, the magistrates wore silver, and judges were adorned in gold. Saba watched two magistrates walk in conversation. One, a woman, had her mask set in an elaborate headdress. A tall nimbus crest arched behind her head. It was heavily embroidered with thick threads and beads, and from either side of the crest's tips fell blue fabric tails all the way to the floor. Her colleague's embroidered coif was, to Saba, hardly as impressive. A silver circlet sat flat around his forehead and was somehow meant to compete with the majesty of the woman's crest. Both wore high-necked mantle cloaks with long sleeves in purple and blue. Garish gold pauldrons, more decorative than truly defensive, glinted as they passed by.

The sentinels slowed to let the magistrates pass, dropping low in a polite bow, and even Saba felt the weight of social protocol press down on his neck. He pulled his gaze away from the magistrates moments before they turned to look at him.

Fuck them. They hated you before you were an accused murderer.

But war had driven Saba out of Kerinsk at such a young age that Zvensia had raised him. He couldn't help but display the manners he had been taught.

Masks adorned the faces of most everyone inside the basilica. Saba felt the distinction like a knife opening his gut. He wore only a loose, sweat-stained shirt and black trousers with boots—he'd only been half dressed when apprehended—and was a mess of dirty, knotted hair, covered in weeks-old sweat and dirt.

As the sentinels pushed Saba onwards, dozens of eyes turned toward him. Saba made himself stare back at them, at the variations of masks, from smooth and featureless to gnarled and screaming.

The transfer of both the paragon title and the symbolic mask at once stripped you of your individuality, your weakness, your ordinariness, and it conferred upon you a title, a role, an obligation. You were awarded for giftedness by being folded back into a group—an elite group, sure, but a group nonetheless.

And Saba was the other, now and forever.

Everyone is looking at you. Everyone—everyone knows what you are, Sabina.

Sabina . . . Why did Maksid have to call him that?

Something dark and fetid in Saba's mind often equated all the immoral and awful parts of himself with womanhood. Not because women were those things, but because to Saba, womanhood itself was awful. It had been awful to him. It had shaped him one way, had been a promise of a life he had then abandoned.

And now, every time someone looked at him with disdain or disliked him, the rotten, angry part of Saba's mind told him: *It's because they know what you are.* A person who had changed his body to suit his nature or a person who had defied nature to change his body—how Saba referred to himself depended, really, on the kind of mood he was in at the time.

A person who had used illegal magic to tamper with forces beyond his station, a traitor. . . It was worse now. He knew logically the reasons everyone currently stared; he had been accused of murder, and he looked like shit.

But what if it was more than that? What if his guilt was stripping away all the trappings of manhood, every part of himself he had built up over the years? What if they could see the stitching, the learning and unlearning of behaviors and mannerisms, the parts Saba was still unconvinced looked *right*—what if they saw what Saba sometimes did when he let himself stare too long at the mirror? What if they saw *her?*

He was being ridiculous. They saw nothing except a dangerous person—a man. Which was what he was.

No false accusation could strip that away from him.

At the end of the basilica sat a small courtroom, and the sentinels led Saba inside. The courtroom was circular, and like a skull cleaved open to the brain, the domed roof above gave way to a massive oculus. Ornamental tracery arched over the window, repeating patterns of stone, so to Saba it all resembled tendon and muscle.

Why his mind made a body of the basilica, he wasn't sure, except that it was the heart of Byrengrad City.

An elevated half-moon-shaped jury box sat beneath a great window where relevant judges might sit to bear witness to some trial or the other. For now, it sat empty. Two men stood beneath the oculus. They were backlit by the far window and haloed by the light above them, so all identifiable features were blotted out to a silhouette. But both were distinguishable, at least to Saba's eyes. Luan Zek stood to the left. Saba could tell first from his size and then from the cane—and altogether from the calm, sturdy way he held himself. The other man was a judge.

Saba already knew which one. Judge Hirunz occupied a seat on the Triad, which in theory made him about as influential as either of his colleagues. For Saba, though, Hirunz had taken a personal interest. For whatever reason—sadism, or because Saba had fooled Zvensia on his Kerish heritage most of his life—Hirunz had decided to make Saba's life extremely miserable. It was Hirunz who had discovered Saba was not ethnically Zvensian but in fact a Kerish refugee in disguise. This made Hirunz directly responsible for upending Saba's whole fucking life.

The other reason Hirunz was wildly more influential than the other two was because he was the only one still fucking alive. Old age had carried off the eldest of the Triad—Judge Vilix—a few weeks before Saba's imprisonment, and the third judge—Judge Berif—had been killed in the accident for which Saba was being held accountable.

The bastard Hirunz was tall and made taller by his headdress, an embroidered coif which Saba swore Hirunz deliberately padded to give him an extra inch. Saba had never seen Hirunz's face—not his real face, anyway, not what was beneath the mask—to the point that the fine-featured gold registered in Saba's mind as flesh. Other judges had elaborate facial coverings—patterns beaten into the metal, prominent facial features, colored inlays, things to give the face a bit of life. All except for Hirunz, which said more about his personality than any customization might have. The mask he wore had delicate features, with a small nose and lips and open eye sockets for Hirunz's grey-green irises to roll around in. Those eyes followed Saba's every move as he stood and stretched. A flash of amusement made Hirunz's eyes gleam.

Truly a bastard.

The colored light meant Saba couldn't see Byrengrad, but he knew the basilica sat on a grassy cliff overlooking a canal that flowed through the city. Saba kept his eyes on the window, on the warm, red morning light bleeding everywhere. Nature might as well have been a dream to him at this point. When had been the last time he'd seen a tree?

An instant later and he was on his knees as a sentinel shoved Saba roughly down. His knees met the marble with a crack, and a days-old bruise reignited on his shin. All at once, he was again aware of every part of him that hurt. The force of the shove made him slide a little on the marble until the embossed detail on Zek's boots came into focus.

Floral details. Zek did not seem like a floral man, but what did he know?

Saba breathed deep and looked up, holding out his bound hands before him.

"Hello again," he said. Zek stared down at him with a raised brow. The light caught in his beard and set a few of those blond-brown hairs aflame with gold. Saba continued, "Be nice and help me up, would you?"

Saba swore he saw Zek's expression soften.

Zek said, "In a minute. This one has something to say." He gestured absently to the judge as if he were some interloping servant bringing trivial news.

Saba let a smile free. He hadn't meant to—thought, in fact, he had quite a tight-lipped scowl on his face. But he felt the edges of his lips turning up all the same.

The judge cleared his throat.

Because he enjoys ruining things.

Saba summoned his most dazzling smile and beamed up at him, though he doubted he could make the smile reach his eyes.

Judge Hirunz glanced at the Rezwyn ambassador then back to Saba. Though Hirunz acted as if all three judges of the Triad were present, and perhaps an audience, too, no one besides Zek and the sentinels were around to see this.

"Get up, Vasili," he hissed. Embarrassment laced his words—oh, how Saba enjoyed that.

Saba stood. He grunted from the ache of his wounds but tried to keep it from his face. He was already at a disadvantage here. He was shaking in his boots—but he couldn't let them know how much.

"I'm sure Justice Sentinel informed you of what's to come," he said, his voice gruff and displeased. Saba decided he had no energy to do anything except dip his head. Hirunz diverted his attention away from him immediately, back to the Rezwyn, and his voice turned sickly sweet as he said, "Ambassador Zek, please."

Hirunz gestured to a writing desk pushed up against one of the walls. A document had been laid out, because that was the Zvensian way. Nothing could ever be done without a ridiculous amount of paper.

Hirunz had Zek sign—for Saba, like he was property or a particularly exotic animal. Then wax was poured at the bottom and Zek pressed a seal to it. A Rezwyn seal.

And that was it.

Saba almost laughed. After years, after surviving a war and abandoning his homeland, after watching from a distance as it was subsumed into the empire, *this* was how he fell to the Rezwyns? A bit of paper, a bit of ink, a bit of wax?

Hirunz was saying, "Should you have any further questions about the investigation or what befell the Lord of Veprak, Diligence Inquisitor is the paragon investigator assigned to this catastrophe. You may write to her should anything arise; inquisitor quarters are in the Sentinel Building."

Ambassador Zek followed Saba's lead and only nodded politely.

Hirunz nodded toward Saba's favorite sentinel, who minutes earlier had shoved him to his knees. "I will have Respect Sentinel escort you to your horses."

Respect? Saba rolled his eyes at that irony.

"That won't be necessary," Zek said.

Hirunz flinched slightly. He shared a very obvious look with Respect Sentinel, almost dismissive, almost pitying. Hirunz glanced back at Zek and then unmistakably down to his leg. Saba flicked his attention to Zek just in time to see the Rezwyn's face shift an imperceptible amount.

"I really must insist," Hirunz said. His voice took on that tone, that overbearing false sweetness, thick and layered and still not enough to hide the venom beneath it.

So Saba stepped forward a little gleefully, echoing Zek's earlier words. "Well, congratulations, Sir Judge, you have insisted."

Fury flared in Hirunz's eyes, and he turned bodily toward Saba.

Shit, you fool, that wasn't smart.

Saba faltered a little, flinching and stepping back against a broad chest.

He tensed. Saba glanced up; Zek was looking down at him, bearing over him. From this angle, Saba felt beyond small. Fear and something else blossomed in Saba's stomach.

Absolutely not. You're an accused murderer. You don't get the luxury of embarrassment or whatever is bubbling up in you right now.

And guilt swarmed him, filled him up like a leaden weight. His head dropped down.

Zek stepped out in front of him, completely unaware of this turmoil. "The prisoner is in my care, and I am more than capable. Unless you think otherwise?"

Hirunz held the Rezwyn's stare, but there was a stiffness to the judge's body that even his mask and his many layers of clothing couldn't quite hide.

"Of course not," he managed. He gestured for Respect Sentinel to hand over the key to Saba's manacles. "You can return the manacles and key to the sentinel at the city gate on your way out."

Zek didn't wait another beat. "I appreciate the loan," he said. Then to Saba, "Come, we'll be on our way."

CHAPTER THREE

When they left the basilica, Saba expected to be thrown into a lockbox wagon flanked by a half dozen Rezwyn guards. Instead, Zek directed him to a very fine, two-wheeled gig pulled by a sleek, black gelding. A lone teenage girl dressed in the uniform of the Doskor Imperial Court stood alongside it, holding the gelding's reins, looking bored.

The sprung cart had a high seat and a little platform at the back for the attendant to hover on. Its top had been rolled down and secured at the back of the seat, meaning the pair of them could share in the grand majesty of Byrengrad City and perhaps briefly forget that Saba was a prisoner.

Saba would have sworn being swept up by such a pretty gig was special treatment or placation if it weren't for the distinct mark of the emperor emblazoned on the back of the high seat. The gig itself was a joyless, drab blue, but the emperor's mark—a horrifying amalgam of two gods exploding into a many-headed boar—had been painted in delicate silvery lines, the gracefulness of which did nothing to soften the confronting empire imagery.

Burdened by the frankly ridiculous weight of the ceremonial chain, which Saba had lain over his shoulder like a heavy sash, Saba stumbled over to the cart and briefly attempted to fling the long restraint over his head and into the gig. Gravity took over too early, and the chain clanked by his feet—but not before something twinged in Saba's shoulder from the force.

Weeks of disuse had affected him an upsetting amount.

"Allow me," Zek murmured. He didn't wait for Saba to acquiesce, thankfully, and took it upon himself to reach over and one-handedly heft the straggling chain into the gig. It thudded into a pile of curled chain. Zek then offered Saba his hand without ceremony, which Saba decided to take and make no fuss about since he could think of nothing worse than snubbing a Rezwyn only to fall onto his face a moment later.

He even said, "Thank you," and meant it. Zek gave him a smile—a smile Saba thought was deeply and unnecessarily self-satisfied.

Saba sat back in a Rezwyn-blue seat as Zek drove the two-wheeled gig through the vein-thin streets of Byrengrad. The groom perched at a platform at the back but had said nothing to Saba—nothing verbally, at least. She had instead given him an openly snobbish grimace—she was a servant, but she was still a Rezwyn and at least not a displaced, dirty Ker.

Byrengrad sat on a rocky outcrop. Flowering shrubs burst from cracks in the stone, while orchids, vine-like plants, and flowering weeds clung to the surface. A few umbrella-shaped stone pines and cypress trees cropped up here and there to decorate the otherwise white-grey city. Almost every building had been carved from limestone on site or dug into the bedrock itself so that everything ran on top of each other in stone layers. Some roofs doubled as streets, some walls doubled as stairs—everything felt part of an interconnected tapestry, capillaries rushing in networked chaos. And the basilica, the heart, sat above, overlooking all of it. If that wasn't a metaphor for the Triad's sense of importance, then nothing was.

The sun sat directly above them, and Saba saw the city spread out beneath him as if seeing it for the first time. Something about being outside after weeks of that dank dark made him electric; briefly he forgot about the charges, and the deaths, and the weight of his guilt. He saw Byrengrad alive with people, carts, and carriages, and he breathed in the faint scent of salt that always emanated from the limestone. Wreathed by a limestone wall and pockmarked by stone houses and salt deposits, Byrengrad glared uncomfortably bright—but Saba's heart surged at the sight of it again. A canal cut through between the cliff supporting the basilica and the upper ward to the basilica's west, veering through the lower ward. The canal was traversed by only two bridges, which were incredibly clogged at the best of times. Such few bridges were not a design flaw, but in fact deliberate. One bridge led from the poor Deji Ward to the equally undesirable Serlei Ward. The other, however, took people from Deji Ward into the richer Yoshka Ward, where embassies and other administrative buildings were housed. A gate secured the upper district from the rest, and even if the basilica sat on the opposite side of the canal, it was the most elevated point of Byrengrad and thus satisfactorily separated from Byrengrad's social dregs.

This vantage point allowed Saba to take it all in. Great gaudy buildings smeared the upper district, with several dedicated to administration or paragon business. All of them were the same exquisite limestone as the rest of Byrengrad save one—a black smudge of a thing, like untamed mildew: the gargantuan empire embassy.

He resisted looking southeast to Loefka Ward, or what remained of it, but eventually his eye was drawn to it. Saba had once looked out from up here and thought Loefka Ward looked to be nested at the city's feet like a sleeping cat. Now he could see the warped and crumpled buildings with a dark, perfect circle at their center like an eye looking back at him. Saba flinched and looked away.

"Did you really have to do me up like this?" Saba murmured. Rezwyn blue and silverwork surrounded him, making the carriage a beacon for attention. Put Saba in the front of the open two-wheeled carriage, slap a ridiculous ceremonial chain on his wrists, and he was practically a paraded attraction.

Zek barely looked at him. "Are you telling me you wouldn't have tried to run?"

Saba crumpled. What little camaraderie the pair of them had held against Hirunz, Saba had been foolish to expect it would extend beyond the grounds of the basilica. Saba shifted to stare out at the city, but too many people openly stared back at him. He squeezed his eyes shut, steadied his breathing, and lifted the chains up for Zek to see.

"Do you know what these are?" Saba said. He had tried to speak with bravado, but instead his voice sounded soft and plagued by worry. "They're basically brands. They mark me a criminal. As if I've already been found guilty."

Zek shifted the reins to one hand, briefly taking his eyes off the road to inspect the chains. Pewter and enamel bearing a Zvensian symbol of the convicted, a circle struck through with three lines in even divisions.

Saba flushed under Zek's gaze, because his mind was like that, and he found men like Zek to be equally intimidating and attractive; he was weak-willed and stupid to boot.

How many times do you have to be reminded he is your enemy?

Zek stared, which only made Saba redden.

Zek let go of the chains and whispered, "Most everyone is convinced you did it."

"And you?" Saba sounded desperate when he asked it. "What do you think?"

Why did that matter? A Rezwyn could think Saba a god incarnate, and it wouldn't change what they had done to his homeland.

Someone darted out of the crowd to spit at the ground before the open carriage. Instantly, Saba became aware of the sheer number of eyes raking over him. Disgust, fear—a lot of these people were Zvensian, by their apparent wealth, which suggested the stories spreading about Saba were—

very bad. What kind of man could murder his own people? If he could do that to Kers, what was stopping him from destroying the rest of Byrengrad? Maybe in another life, this would have made Saba feel powerful. After so long feeling weak and terrified about his true nature coming to light—both his heritage and that other thing—being feared almost felt good.

Don't let yourself feel that. You're not allowed to feel that.

Saba should only have been feeling guilt.

Zek suddenly pulled on the reins and stopped them off to the side of the thoroughfare. This only made the chatter of the onlookers worse, and Saba tried to sink into the carriage seat as best he could. Next thing he knew he was buckling under the weight of Zek's heavy wool cloak, which the Rezwyn had shucked and dropped into his lap.

"What," Saba murmured, looking down at it. The coat was ridiculous for any kind of weather in Byrengrad. On occasion it snowed in winter but never enough to warrant such thick pelts. It certainly never got as cold as Doskor. Besides, they were creeping toward summer now, which meant . . . Zek could only have been wearing this for the added effect.

Saba briefly wondered who, exactly, Zek was trying to remind of his empire status.

"Cover them up," Zek said simply as he urged the horse on again, like this wasn't a great kindness.

But Saba made himself not thank him. He rode through the rest of the city in silence.

Once they zigzagged down the slope, Zek turned them off the main road and avoided the market to take them through the poorer Jedvekn Ward, presumably to skirt too much open scrutiny. But an empire carriage drew enough attention as it was. Saba pressed himself as far back against the seat as he could and tried to focus on taking in the city.

Messenger birds flew to and from the basilica. In the wealthier part of Byrengrad, the streets were clean and fitted with beautifully carved wells every few minutes. But as they moved through the poorer city wards, the disparity became obvious. Refugees—both citizens of Kerinsk and other small nations who had been displaced by the past decades of Rezwyn expansion—occupied these wards. Zvensia had a natural boundary—a river that cut across the top of its peninsula borders that had made it a natural stopping point for empire expansion. Kerinsk had been a long strip of a country, now entirely absorbed by the Rezwyn Empire, and referred to as the empire's west. Other western towns and settlements had been assimilated, too, and anyone not willing to pay the empire's stipends had fled.

Zvensia had several treaties to honor, and Saba expected the country probably regretted ever signing a single one.

Byrengrad was just one of the many cities refugees had flocked to, hoping for more work or that more established systems would be put in place in metropolitan hubs than in country towns. It hadn't quite happened that way.

Now, a whole diaspora of exhausted people waited for Byrengrad's charity.

As they passed through Jedvekn Ward, they saw paint-smeared broken walls in rebel symbols of resistance decried the Triad. Several people worked to restore a half-collapsed building, either the result of a street clash—these were becoming more frequent as they neared the Triad vote—or the general passage of time and poor foundations.

The vote—this damned vote—would determine if any of the refugees could be considered citizens.

The vote had been postponed since the old fart's death, and Saba supposed it would be delayed indefinitely now that two judges were dead and the Triad consisted of only one person. Zvensia was all bureaucracy, all hierarchy, and only citizens could purchase food like grain at a subsidized price. Heavy-handed regulation kept the refugees poor; it kept Zvensia's ranks immutable and impenetrable.

Zek furrowed his brow at the workers, which interested Saba. What was Doskor like to warrant this reaction? What was this compared to war and broken bodies?

But then Saba realized Zek's attention had been drawn to something else. Someone dressed in Kerish colors—mauve, yellow, and sky blue—was painting. They stood on a roof and leaned over to the adjoining wall to paint—something. Someone. In a giant, gaudy mural. Saba grimaced. He could tell without even seeing the finished work who the subject was. The artist had painted the symbol of Kerish hope—a long-dead legend, someone who had never been anything more than a child. But war and desperation and hope had made that child a symbol. She was Kerinsk's lost heir: the princess.

Kerinsk had been a matriarchy, and the queen had given birth to exactly one daughter, whose body had, naturally, never been found after the country fell to invasion. This had only stoked a deranged hope in the refugees, like she might one day return to save them all.

In Saba's mind this was, without a doubt, bullshit. No one was coming, let alone their legendary princess. She—and Saba could say this with intimate knowledge—was very much dead.

Still, seeing her made him feel sick. Most things regarding Kerinsk made him nauseous, but this—the mural and the subject—made him feel markedly worse. He pulled his eyes away and demanded Zek's attention too.

"Are you here alone?" Saba asked, shifting to block Zek's view of the mural.

Thankfully, Zek turned to look at him. "Are you asking out of genuine curiosity, or because you want to know whether to try and make your escape now versus later?"

Saba flashed him a smile. "Can't it be both?"

"It would be unwise to travel alone," Zek said, turning back to the road. "Wouldn't it?"

Saba heard the implication easily and turned to see if his bodyguards were on the street beside them, but someone rushed out toward him. Zek's wolf cloak had shifted, and Saba's garish chain loped down for all to see. The refugee spat something at Saba so violently that spittle flicked onto his face. He jolted back, gasped for a good three seconds, and then let apathy kill the panic.

Saba pulled the wolf cloak over his chains again, teeth locked tightly.

Zek was saying, "I don't know that word."

"It's not Zvensian," Saba managed. "It's Kerish. I suppose you didn't serve long enough to learn it." He was taking his frustration out on Zek. Nibbling incessantly at his lip, Saba sighed. "It means betrayer."

"So you *are* Kerish. I wasn't sure."

"Allegedly, I am. But admitting such an origin divests you of all rights and privileges afforded to a Zvensian citizen."

Zek whipped the gelding into a trot. They left the refugee behind in the dirt.

Suddenly, two pairs of riders fanned out on either side of them, all dressed in Rezwyn blues. The soldiers were instantly recognizable by the insignia on the back of their uniforms—and by their swords. Zek was not an idiot, then. He had guards; they'd just been out of sight.

"Ah," Zek said, knowingly. Saba glanced back to him with a raised brow. "So that was your motive then, was it? For engineering the accident?"

"Oh, yes. That makes sense, doesn't it?" Saba slapped on his most absurd smile. "I was so wholly pissed off at Zvensia that I exploded all my former countrymen."

For whatever reason, that made Zek's face fall. He glanced back over his shoulder. "Keep quiet for now. We'll talk when we reach the embassy, after you've had a chance to wash up."

The embassy? He'd thought they'd leave immediately, head to Doskor as soon as possible. Well, Saba reasoned he smelled like shit—both literally and figuratively. The journey back to the empire's capital would take, what? Two weeks? Maybe three?

And Saba wouldn't say no to a bath.

Zek quickly turned them out of Jedvekn Ward and over the bridge that crossed the canal, toward the wealthiest part of the city. Saba frowned up at him—that detour had been not only unnecessary, but dangerous.

Zek glanced at his expression and grimaced. "I was curious about this place. Judge Hirunz mentioned you took up residence in Jedvekn Ward, just on the border of Loefka Ward," he said, by way of explanation.

Saba decided to say nothing.

An interior wall protected the upper district, consisting of Yoshka and Padke Wards, from anyone who wasn't meant to be there, ensuring the preservation of its inhabitants—both their physical safety and that of their sensibilities. Saba used to frequent Padke Ward, as the Scholar's Guild, Sentinel Quarters, and other locales central to a would-be paragon's self-actualization sat inside its walls. Saba flared his nostrils as the carriage moved beneath the great arch, which opened only once Zek flashed his sigil, a convergence of the gods Suoduny and Borviet, who represented fate and war, respectively.

If Saba hadn't been so well-versed in empire news, he might have felt a bit softer toward Zek in that moment. Of all the empire's gods—which were always strangely animistic deities—Saba had a soft spot for exactly one of them. Suoduny, who dwelled in the astral sea, was often misinterpreted as a god of fate and destiny in the most restrictive and boring way. But Saba theorized that Suoduny was actually a manifestation of possibility itself.

And Saba wanted nothing more in this world than access to all possibilities.

The new Rezwyn emperor had deliberately formed this amalgam for his personal sigil—which frightened Saba in a selfish way. Suoduny meant something personal to him. His study of the astral sea had once taken him all the way to the nomadic Temple of Suoduny, deep in the heart of the Rezwyn Empire, and even if he'd expected to feel fearful in the motherland of his enemy, he hadn't. Saba had found both kindred spirits and an antidote for his personal pain. He didn't need to fully believe in the *god* to not want it to be associated with Borviet's bloodlust.

As they moved into Yoshka Ward, Saba instantly felt small. Disgusting. Unworthy. All that learned shame rose unbidden; he felt out of place, as he always did, but worse. Usually, he could hide. He could dress the part. But everyone could see now that he did not belong behind these walls.

The building Zek led them to was nothing like the rest of Byrengrad—a dark, blue-black structure severely contrasting the sandy tones of the rest of the city. It was a heavy, square building with tall spires and large, glassed-in windows.

The stone resembled nothing of its surroundings and had to have been imported.

As was the style of the empire, two huge trees framed the structure's portico.

Zek climbed down from the carriage while the groom hopped off the back and rushed forward to take the horse's reins.

Saba pointedly refused any help and very nearly fell face first into the dirt. This he would have deserved, but what little pride and dignity he had left, he would cling to with everything he had.

Zek's soldiers came alongside them but didn't dismount. They watched silently as Zek led Saba inside.

Though it had looked small from the top of the cliff, the embassy loomed and cast an immense shadow. The structure reminded Saba of a ship run aground, its bow lodged in the sand and turned upright. The curved facade of it bowed out in a half cylinder, like he was staring at the concave inside of a rowboat. And, as if by a calenture misled, Saba felt like he was diving into madness. The belly of the beast. Diplomats or no, Saba knew the truth of what the Rezwyns were. Though their embassy was clean and well-lit with polished white marble floors, Saba saw blood staining all of it.

The entry hall bustled with activity.

Zvensian paragons rushed about; medical and administrative types, all of them somehow excelling in their fields. They laughed and chatted with Rezwyn officials, with the empire that, at the decision of a single man, could stretch and overreach and crush Zvensia the way they crushed Kerinsk. Saba scowled at them, at this whole damn scene—screw the bath. Being dragged straight to Doskor felt altogether easier than walking into this cheerful deceit.

A young man at the door spotted Saba and practically crawled out of his skin at the sight of him. He was blond, tall, and eerily thin in a brittle way that made Saba nervous just to look at him. His nose was particularly large for the rest of his face, like it had grown first and very quickly, and every other feature was still trying to catch up. He was wearing a very form-fitting tunic, which meant the thick fabric creaked at every movement.

"Absolutely not!" he squealed in Zvensian, finger wagging.

Zek, bless him, ignored the complainant entirely and kept moving.

The Zvensian official made an affronted noise and again attempted to intercept Zek—which was a hilarious sight, given the official was quite skinnier than Saba, and Zek was, well . . . Zek. At the same time, the official tried to give Saba an enormous berth, making him about as intimidating as a rat's little toe.

"Sir," Zek said, by way of acknowledgement. He gave Saba a nod to encourage him to enter, but the official—a Zvensian man—rushed forward with his hands outstretched.

"Ambassador Zek," the administrator said, laughing nervously. "We don't allow—*guests.* Of this nature."

Zek rolled his eyes. Saba glanced at the weaselly official and his pinched expression and wondered exactly what kind of person he thought Saba to be. A whore? Some sad charity case? Perhaps. Perhaps both those things at once. Saba showed him all his teeth in a wide, unhappy grin and watched gleefully as the official shuddered in revulsion.

"Here," Zek said. He waved the emperor's seal at the official. "He's a material witness in the matter I'm investigating. Good enough?"

The official deflated somewhat, drawing his arms back to his side. "I see. So he's headed for the holding cell then?"

"No. Mine." As seemed to be his nature, Zek didn't wait to answer further questions. He pushed forward and dragged Saba along with him—by the chains, unfortunately, which probably assuaged none of the official's fears.

"Don't worry," Zek called back as he hauled Saba up the stairs. "I plan to clean him up."

Two wide staircases sat on either side of the main hall. Zek steered him toward the left and lumbered up two flights of stairs, skipping the first floor where more Zvensians happily mingled with the enemy, to the second, which appeared to be peopled only by Rezwyns, and finally, to stop on the third level, where the landing was guarded by a couple of soldiers in imperial uniforms.

Zek moved past them and through a set of draperies to what looked like guest accommodations. Numerous paintings hung on the plain rock wall, most of which were Rezwyn in nature. Saba caught sight of a battle painting—which was a bit ridiculous and off-putting to have hanging in an embassy, the gall of these bastards—before Zek tugged him around a corner and the painting fell out of sight. He unlocked a door and walked them both inside.

Saba blinked. His eyes went first to the large bed simply because it was such a behemoth that it demanded attention. Four dark wooden columns sprang up to a canopy, and blue and silver curtains spilled around it.

The room was bright, with a large half-moon window with two doors that led to a cramped balcony overlooking the city. A small writing desk was squashed next to the balcony doors, and another door—presumably to the washroom—sat to the far right. A dull Rezwyn carpet covered the limestone floors, once again in blue shot through with silver thread. What was it with the empire and a tedious lack of variation?—and two faded wingback sitting chairs faced an unlit hearth.

At the sound of the door, two people jumped near vertically out of those chairs and scrambled to attention.

"Sir!" one shouted in Doskorian, going rigid instantly. She was a stern-looking woman with a broad, sharp nose and dark hair pulled flat against her head. The other was too young to be balding and yet had wispy blond hair scattered short and fine across their head. They were shorter than Saba, but their blue eyes were so unsettling that they were immediately intimidating. Saba glanced away from them.

"Did you draw the bath?" Zek murmured.

"Yes, sir. Ready, sir."

Zek either couldn't care less about catching them lounging or was doing his best to appear good-willed, which made no sense, given Saba was an accused criminal.

Having to consider the possibility that Zek might be some kind of inherently good imperialist made Saba's eyes feel like they were about to pop out of his skull.

Zek ignored the people—were they soldiers or servants—and handed the ends of Saba's chains back to him. He moved to the writing desk to rummage about in the drawers. Then he spun and, leaning his weight onto the desk, gestured at Saba with his cane.

"Let me look at you."

Saba stood completely still, frozen in something akin to terror. Zek cocked his head. Being under his gaze like that, inspected, watched, heated Saba's cheeks instantly. He was suddenly aware of—everything: the way he tended to roll his shoulders forward, the way his left hip popped since he favored his right leg when standing still. He had no bloody idea where to look or what to do with his hands.

"Spin," Zek commanded gently, making a circular motion with that hare-headed cane. Saba said nothing and did what he was told, trying to ignore the clinking of his chain and the uncomfortable tug on his upper lip as the cut from the sentinel's punch began to throb.

How much more of a dog could Zek make him? No, better not answer that question.

Zek turned to the woman, waved at her with something in his hand, and then lobbed it over. She caught it mid-air, and it sounded like a hundred bells brushing against one another. A coin purse.

"Grab the smallest size of whatever's in fashion," Zek said in Doskorian.

It was a statement that had Saba standing taller. He puffed his chest, pulled his shoulders back, and laughed defensively, saying, “Well, surely the smallest size would be for a child—”

“Go, now,” Zek told the soldiers.

Both snapped to attention, bowed, and left without another word. The door closed with a click, and the silence settled in.

All levity in Saba died. His smile fell. He made one attempt to muster up a smidge of energy to make his plea—and failed. He just looked at Zek, dead in the eyes. He chose to speak in Kerish, as if doing so might summon the shades of every war casualty. “If you take me back to Doskor, I’m dead.”

Zek remained unmoved. He sniffed and replaced his grip on his cane. Pointedly, in Zvensian, he said, “No. If I take you back to Doskor, you’ll be given a trial. Then you *might* be dead. Or you might also be free.”

Saba snorted, but Zek meant it. He really meant it. A man like him—a veteran, an experienced man—thought Saba would be treated fairly by the empire?

“You are incredibly idealistic,” Saba murmured. “The instant I cross the border, all of Zvensia will believe I’m guilty. You’ll drag me across the country and throw me before your emperor; and by that point it would be trouble for him if he did not believe it too. It is a slow, drawn out death sentence, but one all the same. I’m already dead.”

“Bath’s through there,” Zek said, like Saba hadn’t spoken in minutes. He pointed to the door at the left of the hearth. “You can lock the door. Please, by the gods, don’t try to jump out the window. We’re too high up for that to do anything good to you.”

Saba decided to give up and bathe. “And my clothes?”

“I’ll knock when they’re up here,” Zek said, and this time he wasn’t looking at Saba at all.

“Chains?” Saba murmured after a second. Zek glanced up and pushed himself from the desk. The cane hit the ground with a muted pop. Wordlessly, Zek gestured for Saba to raise his hands up, and at the same time he slipped a small key out of some hidden pocket in his tunic. Saba grimaced and raised his hands in fists, like the two of them were about to brawl—like Saba would have any chance at all against a man like Zek. Zek pulled Saba's hands toward him in one smooth motion, holding him in a cuffed embrace that seemed altogether too gentle for a man of his size. Saba let himself look at Zek up close: at the pink tinge to his skin, the sun-kissed spots on his temples, a small mole on his left cheek mostly hidden by his beard. He smelled like scented oil. His hands were warm.

The cuffs unlocked and tumbled to the ground in a heap.

Saba jerked back like he'd been slapped, spun on his heels, and awkwardly shuffled into the washroom.

CHAPTER FOUR

Fuck this. Fuck everything about it. And most of all, fuck Luan Zek!

Who decides one moment to imply their prisoner is having dramatic thoughts of his own demise, and the next to gently hold his hands?

Saba tried to avoid the bathroom mirrors as he did this, but he kept catching the misty reflection of himself, feral and messy.

What about yourself? Memorizing the details of his face like a lunatic. Bad priorities, Vasili. Besides. He won't ever be interested in—you.

This was neither a kind thought nor an infrequent one, which meant, usually, Saba could brush off feelings of physical inadequacy. Though now that he was in the washroom, and the washroom was bright, and the washroom had mirrors, his usual defense—ignore unhelpful, ratty little thoughts at all costs—was useless.

The first thing Saba did was lock the door. He tried the handle three times to make sure it remained firm before he had the nerve to move away. A large freestanding bath with bronze clawed feet sat waiting for him; the water was clear and still steaming. He'd turn that water rotten-black by the time he was done. But Saba didn't head to the bath, not right away.

He moved across the white mosaic tiled floor to the large circular window that looked out over the city. Saba pressed his face to it, scrunching up his nose against the cool glass until his skin wrinkled. Byrengrad was beautiful from here, all white stone and sun and intermittent bursts of green. He peered down at the ground, which was less pretty and more nausea-inducing—this vertical drop into nothingness. Saba hated that Zek was right. It wasn't even a window that opened. Saba would have to smash his way out (doable) and then fly (less so) if he wanted any other outcome beyond a sad, belly-flopping demise.

Unfortunately, Saba wanted to live. This had always been his misfortune. When he'd fled Kerinsk instead of dying a noble death fighting the Rezwyns it had been because he wanted to live. This time, too, he couldn't help but hope for a way to survive, even though it seemed impossible.

He peeled himself from the window and stared at the mucky shape his grime-covered face had made on the glass. Saba attempted to wipe this, just the once, with the sleeve of his equally dirty shirt, and just made a muddy mess. He quickly aborted his attempt to clean.

There was nothing else to do but bathe. Saba removed his shirt and caught the eye of his own reflection in the mirror beside the round window. The glass was unrefined, so the Saba staring back at him was trapped in mist and fog, and perhaps that's why it wasn't so startling to see how much his time in the dungeon had changed him. Saba moved forward to inspect himself. His hair, usually auburn, was a knotted nest of brown, made so by the dirt. A scraggly beard curled in unkempt patches along his jaw. Facially and bodily, he looked unhealthily gaunt, like a desperate, underfed rat, which was never something Saba expected to compare himself to. He had first started to lose weight when Hirunz discovered his heritage. In the ensuing months following his discreditation, the seizure of his research, and his general removal from all scholarly duties, Saba realized that, without his studies, he had the same intrinsic purpose as a rock might. Which was, of course, none at all.

It wasn't obsession, his interest in the astral sea. Or maybe it was—just a small one, though.

Saba wasn't insane or unhinged beyond the normal amount necessary to dedicate your life to reading dusty tomes in an effort to understand the unknowable. He had just spent so long trying to comprehend how the astral sea functioned. Without his research, without a reason to wake up every morning, things became less focused.

The underside of his thumbs grazed his chest. In the light, two crescent moon scars glinted iridescent. Saba traced them like he was trying to catch the shine imbued in his skin. The gesture was at once comforting and criticizing; he loved what these scars meant and loathed them for the same reason. After everything he did to get here, after all these years, and now, after all those deaths, could it be that his silly little dream had actual consequences?

What was your plan if it ever did work? You never thought about what came next. You only wanted to get inside it. Wanted to contact the force, Suoduny—wanted the sea to have consciousness so you could go to your knees and beg to be made different. And now Byrengrad suffers, you selfish thing.

Saba had a kind of voice in his mind—not an actual voice, just the part of him that was all reason and unflinching logic. It had started out as something boringly objective, like a puppeteer to instruct Saba and maneuver him where he needed to be. Somewhere along the way, after he had fled Kerinsk and stopped being a child, that angry, rotten part of him got a hold of it, and now, very often, that inner voice was—harsh. What should have been little more than a kernel of self-hatred tucked in a fleshy pocket beneath his ribcage had been given voice; it was a parasite at the back of his neck. Saba was so used to it he often forgot the power it could have, but now, looking at himself for the first time in weeks, an insidious, brutal feeling welled up in his stomach.

Hirunz might be wrong to call Saba a murderer. He did not kill those people gladly, happily, consciously—or maybe even at all. But if those deaths were the result of his negligence, if he'd forgotten something, if he'd let his dream fester enough to blind him to the danger his research might inflict, then perhaps he deserved whatever was to come.

He told himself to get in the bath. His body moved sluggishly to accommodate the order, heavy as if physically weighed down, which was something dramatic his body tended to do in response to complicated feelings. So he let that operative voice take over, and the conscious part of him fell away as soon as he got in the warm water. He washed himself. Scrubbed the dirt from under his nails. Dunked his head under the water and held his breath as long as he could just to make certain he really did want to live. After he was clean and the water looked like something long dead had putrefied in it, Saba still couldn't bring himself to stand. He sat in the bath hugging his knees and slowly summoning a sense of humanity back to himself. It took a long while. He made himself feel the bruises. Every time his wrists dipped below the water, the open lacerations stung brightly. He had to consciously lower his shoulders, which were so tense, a rat king of knots lodged in his upper back, it hurt to sit with normal posture.

Though he often tried to avoid looking too closely at his body, he inspected himself now. The first thing he checked—like it might have vanished, somehow—was a keloid scar raised on the back of his neck, left by the brand. It was circular and manmade with three long tails and three dots in its center.

Saba would need to make sure his hair was arranged in a way to hide it.

He really had lost weight, which was particularly upsetting when you had very little weight to lose in the first place. Saba always had to fight for every inch of bulk on him, only to have it slip away very easily. When he breathed deep, he could now see his ribs pressing against the skin, like the bones were roots reaching for sunlight beyond the wet dark of his insides. His wrists were waifish. What little muscle he had was now well-defined: bicep bumps clinging to his arms, rounded shoulders, the slightest build to his chest. He ran hands over his body and lamented the loss.

He would need another decoction soon.

Saba had a friend in the black market—but then, every scholar in Byrengrad did. Firstly, because the Triad could only provide a small amount of funding to the Scholar's Guild, after overpromising stipends to an overflowing paragon system. Secondly, the Triad loved inane paperwork, and by the time a request for materials made it through extensive budgetary constraints and Triad debates, most scholars had already found other ways to test their hypotheses.

The black market, known colloquially as the underdark, was one such way around Byrengrad's tiring processes—though Saba had long since found other things of use there. Personal things. Like a decoction of ichor flowers that, when injected, could shift what was possible in one's body. If stepping into the astral sea and exposing one's physical body to fate itself could change it very quickly, then, Saba had theorized, exposure to ichor over a long period of time could change it slowly. He had been right. His voice had deepened. He had lost the softness around his hips, had grown patchy stubble on his cheeks. On some occasions, he had found his reflection palatable to look at. It had not changed what lay between his legs, but Saba had begun to feel neutral about that part of himself. So long as he thought about the astral sea—about seizing its arcane potential and changing himself entirely—everything was easier.

Saba didn't believe in gods, but he knew the truth of the astral sea. A great power lay in it. The Rezwyns called it Suoduny, the god of fate and potential. Saba had wanted to go in and talk to it—and if it couldn't be talked to or reasoned with, he would manipulate it. Get it to change him. Get it to twist what was possible in this realm and make his body undeniably a man's.

Because even if no one had questioned Saba as a man for years, *he* did. He could look at himself and find every seam and stitch and fault, and slowly, year-by-year, this fear and this pain and this hatred of himself had started to kill him.

A knock startled him. He half jumped out of the bath, expecting, as his fear told him, that someone had walked in.

But Zek just said, "Leaving them here."

"Alright," Saba called back and waited until Zek's heavy footfalls signaled his departure. He toweled off and squatted by the door. Very quickly he unlocked it, dragged the pile of clothes inside, and slammed the door closed again as if someone might stab him if he was any slower.

Every nerve in Saba's body shrieked with a rush of pumping blood, which objectively was ridiculous. Saba still felt it, though, his heart hammering madly. He looked down at what had been picked out for him in shock.

Compared to his flimsy white tunic, this was luxury. It struck him as very odd to dress him up before slaughter, but Rezwyns had started wars for the most trivial of reasons. This new emperor could be a quick-to-anger little shit. Saba didn't know and would rather not find out.

Zek's people had picked out a green-and-gold embroidered sleeveless tunic in a jacquard style to be worn over a shirt with unexpectedly big sleeves that tapered at the wrist and would make Saba's stringy arms the equivalent of bird bones sat flush in a wing. The trousers were black with gold stitching, and the boots were ankle length, matte black with green leather lining.

Saba hadn't had a pair of boots like this since childhood.

They'd even supplied a pair of white gloves—which, unlike the boots, were enormously in fashion—and Saba could feel his eyebrows straining high on his forehead.

He hadn't noticed he'd gritted his teeth, either, until pain started up where he'd been punched earlier.

Calm down. They're just clothes.

Only they weren't, not really. Three things stood out to Saba, three things that made him deeply uncomfortable. Firstly, the graciousness of the gesture: cleaning him up, giving him privacy, buying him new clothes with budgeted coin—Saba realized he hadn't been expecting this in the slightest. From the moment they'd met, Saba had been on guard. Now he wasn't sure how to act. Ambassador Luan Zek had done something very kind to Saba, perhaps more than he'd ever realize.

He had given Saba the time and the respect to settle back into himself, to return to his humanity.

The second thing was that these clothes were of very good make—too good to hand out to someone soon-to-be beheaded.

And the third: he had not dressed this well since he had been *her*.

A vague memory surfaced from when he was four, maybe five, made spotty and confused by time; his mother and her entourage took him to pray to a god that no longer existed, a deity the Rezwyns had obliterated. Saba remembered the dress he'd worn because he had tripped in its many layers and been scolded for ruining it. The next memory Saba had of Kerinsk was fleeing it with Maksid. Little sun, his mother had called him.

You don't have to think about this. You don't—she's gone.

Only she wasn't, because Saba's fear had made a revenant of her, and the remains of her people were still painting murals, still chanting her name: Princess Sabina Vasyiluki of Kerinsk, the would-be queen, their would-be savior, dead but not gone, dead but not really. She was everything he had given up to become this. Everything he had turned away from to ensure *Saba* could live.

Shut up. Stand up. Get dressed.

He hauled himself up to stand, killed the thoughts, and dressed. In front of the mirror, he resembled himself again: auburn hair down to his shoulders, nose bumped in a way he had never been sure if he'd broken it as a child, eyes green and melancholy. To top it all off, he was wearing the exhaustion of an ancient man, not one who was only twenty-eight. But the clothes were dazzling, and they gave Saba an unexpected vivacity. In a way, they sewed him back to his body. Kept his soul from crashing out of that window.

He tried smiling at himself. His reflection returned a contemptuous smirk.

A soft knock at the door startled him. Saba spun toward it and said snappishly, "What?"

"Just making sure you haven't jumped out that window," Zek replied.

Saba glanced at the window. "I'm still considering it."

"Well, if you decide to do it, could you at least take off the clothes? We just spent a fortune, and I'd hate to ruin them with all your blood."

Saba laughed, louder than he meant to. And when he caught his reflection next, the smile was no longer inauthentic. Which was frustrating. Saba rather wanted to be annoyed and put out by his captor, and not—whatever this was.

He moved to the door and unlocked it. Zek straightened in shock and then stared at Saba, who couldn't parse what that quick widening and softening of the eyes meant.

"How do I look?" Saba said. He cocked his head. "So-so?"

"Bit better than that."

The honesty—if it was honesty—made Saba flinch. "A master of flattery," he said, sounding far angrier than he meant to.

He walked back into the bedroom only to find the two soldiers still had not returned, rendering the pair of them alone. In the time Saba had been bathing, Zek had lightly rearranged the room; the two wingback chairs now faced one another in standard interrogation format. Though as far as his recent interrogations had gone, Saba supposed this clean-and-pamper routine was one of the better ones.

"Sit," Zek said gently. Saba sat.

Zek followed suit, taking the other chair with a sigh. He laid the hare-headed cane over his lap with reverent ceremony and then gestured to a small table sitting between them.

"Hungry?"

At some point, staff had been in to bring a platter of Zvensian food. Saba's eyes glazed over, captivated first by the sheer amount of it, and next by the ravenous hunger that erupted from a sunken whisper in his belly to a growl.

Goat's milk cheese, bread cooked in egg and salt and olive oil, a thick stew, and fine cuts of meat were laid out delicately—Saba's eyes darted back to Zek. Nothing about this felt good. Or safe. Saba had gone soft too quickly; this kind of meeting didn't happen in Zvensia, not without paperwork, not without the expectation of exchange. If this was transactional, as Saba suspected it to be, then caution told him not to eat. Rezwyns could only be worse than the Zvensian interrogators he had already endured. Saba refused to owe the empire any kind of debt.

"What is this?" he asked. "Really, what are you doing prettying me up and feeding me food far too good for tastebuds like mine?"

Zek reached forward to dip the bread in the pottage. Without looking at Saba, he said, "I thought you deserved to face me as a man rather than a dog."

Saba raised his chin. "Woof."

Zek paused to consider him, just for a moment, before ripping into the bread. A flash of white teeth, a near-snarl as Zek tore into it; the bread could be skin, flesh. Saba looked away.

Zek ignored Saba's bark. "Tell me in your own words what really happened out there. Tell me what you did—and what went wrong."

This again. This is what all those niceties amounted to. Saba crossed his arms and rolled his eyes. "I didn't *do* anything."

Zek dusted off his hands and sniffed. "Well, tell me exactly what you did do the day of the incident. Beginning from when you woke up."

Saba stared out the window. Sun filtered across the apartment in a bright streak, and the vista of Byrengrad sprawled out with its spirals and cave houses dotting the rocky terrain. Mountains and plains stretched in the far distance. He breathed deep and knocked his head against the chair and refused to look at Zek, who seemed unfazed by how long Saba was taking to speak. No punch or slap across the face from his interrogator this time.

Saba was almost disappointed.

This routine—what happened on the day of the incident—had been drawn out of him again and again by the sentinels. Without emotion Saba said, "I woke, I dressed, I ate. Bread with fruit and honey if you care for the details. Then I moved all of one room over to work. The Triad had already discredited me at this point, so I was barred from the Scholar's Building. I had rented a room in Jedvekn Ward. Mostly Kers live there. It's next to Loefka. Anyway, I woke up that day, and even though Hirunz had discredited me, I kept working on my own."

"On the device?" Zek's voice betrayed him, turning somewhat high with interest.

Saba looked at him then, frowning. "No. That had already been confiscated, along with my notes. I was trying to reconstruct them. To me, they were—are—more important, at least in terms of all the theories and calculations. Everything was in there. I suppose it was my thesis, really."

Zek frowned. "On what?"

Saba paused, shifting in his seat. Guilt always made him itch with an urge to move. Saba made a low noise in the back of his throat. *Maybe I should just tell him* . . . He hadn't told the sentinels, because it wasn't really useful information, and also they'd let him shit in a bucket for over a week. Zek, at least, was nice.

"Alright," Saba sighed. "I was researching if physical observation of the astral sea was possible."

He looked down at his feet, then back up to Zek—finding himself too eager as he waited for some judgement to be passed. But Zek just sat there, waiting for him to continue.

Tension shivered out of him. To suggest in any capacity that he had, indeed, been trying to tear a hole into the astral sea large enough to crawl through would have been grounds enough for Hirunz to take him straight to trial. Zek could have shot to standing and dragged him immediately to Doskor. He didn't. He just—waited.

After weeks of it—after weeks of even Maksid, his own flesh and blood reviling him—Saba nearly lost it. Tears burned at the back of his eyes, and he had to adjust, sniff, and clear his throat to regain any semblance of control.

"Right," he said after a moment, and thought about the blast. "I don't know how exactly, but I felt when it happened. Midmorning. I just had this awful feeling open in my gut, and then I heard what sounded like a clap of thunder, and—"

One tear broke through the blockade and Saba cursed. He cut himself off to wipe it from his cheek.

Zek tilted his head. He asked steadily, "Did you see or speak with anyone that day?"

"No. No. Not until they came to arrest me, anyway."

"And this is what you always do? Wake up, eat, research?"

Saba woke from his sadness and smirked. Was that pity in Zek's voice? Saba crossed his right ankle over his left knee and swept both his arms out in a grand gesture. "The glorious life of a scholar."

Zek's eyes twinkled unmistakably. He looked so sturdy and unmoved, breathing in deep, even undulations. A faint smile ghosted across his lips, and Saba made himself look away, because his belly filled with the desire to grin madly. Saba's eyes fell to that sturdy core to watch Zek's chest expand and fall.

Mesmerizing.

Zek dipped his head to catch Saba's gaze. "Did you see or hear anything unusual?"

Saba blinked.

Boom, boom, boom.

He heard it, as he did that day: the distant rumbling, and then the screams, and then the enormous, shuddering collapse that deadened every cry beneath rock and rubble.

"Vasili?"

Saba blinked again. "Uh. Yes. I mean, I heard it happen. But so did the entire city. They said it was an explosion. Then the land opened and swallowed everything. And I don't know how I could have done that, because what I made—what I've been researching, the device I've created—doesn't have that kind of power."

His voice sounded defensive and overweening.

Not me, I didn't do anything. Not me, it's not my fault.

But if he truly believed that, then why did he feel—so—awful?

Zek just pushed forward to his next question. "Tell me about this device. In detail."

Saba snorted. "Well, no offence, Zek, but you won't understand it."

Zek raised a brow and looked Saba up and down. "I think I'm being quite polite. Bath, clean clothes, food. I can be crueler if you prefer."

Saba knew he was flushing. His heart did something frantic and upsetting in his chest, a rapid-fire beat that made him briefly nauseous. He wondered what Zek's cruelty would look like.

Stop it. Be normal.

"I apologize." Saba's eyes dropped down to the food. He picked up a bit of bread, dipped it in the pottage, and lifted it high in the same way the Rezwyns would bless an offering. "Apparently being kept like an animal for weeks has me acting like one."

His jaw ached, and his stomach demanded more, but once Zek smiled, Saba took the time to chew the bread down to a pulp, if only for the extra moments to catch his breath.

"The other thing," Saba said carefully, "is that . . . I—the device contains some components that are. . ."

Zek raised a brow. "Contraband?"

Saba pursed his lips. "Perhaps."

"I only care about the death of Lord Doric," Zek said. "And in fact, that's the only thing I have jurisdiction for. Whatever other laws you may have broken are not my concern."

"Well, in that case," Saba said with a grin. "I found an old text from an ancient Uslethian astronomer. She had claimed to use the eye of a gedrok—or an exanimate, like the empire calls it—to . . . see inside the astral sea. I thought it might work, so I found a way to get one. They're very rare, of course. And it took a while. I bought three, and the first two were probably eyes of deformed giant lizards—or some kind of glass, I don't know. They were fake."

"But not the third?" Zek asked.

Saba shook his head with a little smile. "Two of my colleagues helped me build the casing. We ended up having to imbue the structure itself with ichor, which we hand-pressed from the flowers. Huge import. I ate through most of the scholars' funding—I think a few of them are still quite angry with me about that. Anyway, the whole device is powered by ichor—ichor flowers. You call them cajudsan. They're pressed. The ichor is extracted and moves within it.

Once it's vibrating, the ichor resonates with specific astral frequencies, until they're harmonized. That's what allows the bridge to form; we align the energies between the material plane and the astral sea. And this is why the housing has to have ichor imbued in it too. This beam of energy is focused and makes a tiny hole in the barrier. Then we push the gedrok lens down, sliding it into place. It lets us look through."

He was getting excited now. He hadn't spoken about this in so long—not in any joyful way, at least. Zek's frown deepened, and Saba shot out a hand, leaning forward.

"If you're thinking 'How can that work?' then consider this. I believe ichor originates in the astral sea—that at some point in our world's past, a tear opened up, and all sorts of things spilled through. So I operated on that assumption. If ichor is not of our world, then there must be a pull to its original source. And there *is*."

It was a strange feeling, this rush of relief and joy after weeks of misery, guilt, anxiety—Saba practically saw stars. Until those hollow ghosts came again, and a violent, hysterical twist happened in his heart.

You killed them. You fucking awful idiot—you killed *them, and you still love what you made.*

Which was true and painful in its own way to admit. Saba loved his device. He loved what it meant, what it proved. Loved the potential it stored in its mechanical organs, loved what he had seen when he had used it. He loved it enough he had even named it.

The Eye.

He shifted back in the chair and stared out of the window again. Zek still hadn't said anything. Saba's insides churned in a haptic jerk of shame and sadness; he didn't want to feel this anymore.

"You must think me some kind of monster," he said finally.

Zek, who was either goodness incarnate or charmingly stupid, said, "Why should I think that?"

Saba looked at him, frowning. "Because I'm frothing at the mouth still full of passion for the thing that's killed an entire ward."

"It's your life's work, isn't it?" Zek said, like he meant it. Like Saba's lingering passion for a deathtrap machine was to be expected. "If you weren't at least a little bit in love with it, that would concern me more."

Goodness incarnate, then.

How badly Saba wanted to believe him. He felt like a plant desperate for the sun, every part of him longing to reach out to that comfort. Instead, scrabbling toward any kind of warmth, he picked up some of the meat and ate it quickly.

"Even now?" he whispered between mouthfuls.

"Even now," Zek said.

Saba sniffed. He couldn't look at the ambassador. He said, "I think you're unique in that way, Zek. I think a lot of people want to hate me. I want to hate me. I want to—I wish I could go back. I wish I could tell myself it didn't really matter."

"It mattered to you."

"But creating it obviously cost too much in human life." He said it snappishly, with real anger. This solace felt foreign and undeserved. Why was Zek wasting energy trying to absolve him? What if Saba didn't want to be absolved? What if, deep down, he knew he didn't deserve it?

"I just," Saba whispered, "wanted to know. We know some things about the arcane. About the astral sea. The empire has such a rich lore about it. Your myths, your gods, your strixes—they all seem to draw power from it. Similar beliefs extend even as far as Usleth. But Zvensia isn't like that. Neither was Kerinsk. The only thing our experts agree on that ever suggested our lands were connected to the astral sea was the existence of ichor flowers. And I wanted to . . ."

He didn't want to be absolved, but he was defending himself. He deserved the guilt, but he wanted to be rid of it. All this conflicting heartache made him want to bite down on his own arm and tear out a chunk of flesh, if only to ground himself to something more tangible than emotion.

Pain. Blood. Body.

But he was still talking, still running his mouth, still silently begging Zek to finally pass the judgement that would lift this weight from his aching shoulders. "It was just meant to make a tiny breach between our worlds, and only to assist with research. I can't understand what happened. The device—the Eye, I called it—it barely makes a temporary hole, let alone a tear. A tiny fistula, an inconsequential breach—that's it. And more than that, it was built with a failsafe. It's not meant to keep the hole open indefinitely—you have to constantly depress a small lever, or it shuts off automatically. I don't understand how activating it could have caused whole buildings to collapse. I don't know how the Eye could have even gotten to Loefka Ward to be activated again. Both the Eye and the plans to build it had already been confiscated. And before you suggest that someone used the plans to build a replica—the materials used are so rare that it takes years to gather them. This cannot be my fault."

"If you believe that," Zek said gently, "then why are you crying?"

Saba jolted. He hadn't realized, but his cheeks were wet with tears. "Because the Eye worked when I tested it. I could see inside. I saw the astral sea. But maybe activating the Eye that first time had some unintended effect that caused a disaster when it was activated again." He stared at

Zek, made sure the other man was looking at him. "If that's what happened how can I be sure I'm not the reason all of those people had to die?"

Zek glanced away and stood with a groan. He walked over to the window and stared out over the city. "How can you be sure what you saw inside was the astrok-mer and not somewhere else?"

He still spoke calmly, unbothered, like Saba and he were discussing the weather or some equally boring thing. How? How could Zek treat him with such civility?

Saba shook his head. "Because I saw a place that no longer exists thriving still—where else could that happen but the astral sea, where all possibility is born?"

"You see?" Zek turned to him with a little smile. "We both know too little about this entire incident to draw any conclusion. But if what you've said is true, and if your machine caused the breach, and the breach is still there, then your failsafe didn't work. The machine must still be functioning somehow."

The breach was . . . still there? Saba swallowed bile and clarified, "It's still open then?"

"It is," Zek said simply. "And if you were the only person who knew how to operate the device—the Eye—then who has been maintaining the breach? You've been in prison the entire time."

"I don't know. Maybe it's just broken."

"But what if it's not?" Zek wandered back over to the table and took another bite of bread. "And according to your story, you were not the person who even activated the Eye on the day of the incident that killed Lord Doric of Veprak, among others."

Saba shifted. The implication made him uncomfortable. Zek was attempting to wrangle Saba's guilt away from him, and Saba needed to cling to that, because he deserved to feel it. "Does it matter? I made the Eye, so I am responsible for what happened."

Zek turned around bodily and walked to him, cane thudding in an even heartbeat rhythm. He leaned down. Saba craned his neck to look up at him.

"That's your decision to make so long as it's only your own life on the line. But does the truth matter so little to you that you'd allow your guilt to keep me from finding who killed my countryman? To say nothing of the other victims."

"I'm scared of the truth," Saba said honestly. They locked eyes. Saba looked away first, digging the pad of his thumb into his other palm.

He could sit in this self-pity, this self-hatred; it was a familiar tarpit, near comforting to wallow in. But he had been doing that for weeks. And none of the dead were coming back.

"But that's . . . selfish of me. I know it's selfish of me. I want to know . . . what I did wrong. And I'll deserve whatever you decide, Zek, if I am responsible for this massacre."

Zek's eyes sparkled. He glanced up toward the door. "Ewir!"

The door swung open. The soldier on the other side had her sword drawn and ready.

"At ease. There's been a change of plan."

The soldier—Ewir—said nothing, but she stared at Saba with an open hostility that after weeks of sentinel abuse felt comfortingly familiar. Zek let her stand there as he moved to the letter desk. He scrawled something, stamped it with a seal, and moved back to the solider—who pointedly did not accept it.

A hissed argument started up immediately. Acerbic quips passed back and forth in Doskorian spoken too quickly for Saba to understand. Zek stepped away and said drearily, "That's an order," like he was almost sorry he had to pull rank.

The soldier sprang into position, going stiff. "Yes, sir."

Without further comment, she took the letter and closed the door. Then Zek reached into the drawer of the writing desk and withdrew a razor.

As soon as he saw this, Saba's stomach dropped out of him, like his flesh was broken and torn asunder. He wasn't sure what he felt or why he felt it, but something was—wrong. Zek turned around, and Saba stood up tensely, so quickly he shoved the wingback chair awkwardly across the carpet. Saba backed himself against the window.

Alone with Zek, who was ever calm and unshakeable, looking at him like that—well, Saba *had* wanted him to pass judgement. Only now, he was no longer sure he wanted to know what Zek had chosen.

"What's going on?" he said softly. Zek said nothing, only walked forward. What was he going to do? Strangle Saba to death? Shove him out the window? Beat him until his skull cracked open like ripe fruit and spilled blood like pomegranate seeds? Or would it be clean, that razor along his neck?

What's clean about choking on your own blood?

Saba whispered, "Please. I know I'm a little abrasive, and I know I talk back all the damn time, but I will shut up and sit on my horse and ride back to Doskor with you. Just don't—do this."

Zek stopped in his tracks, sighing, half laughing. "I told you already. I spent good coin to dress you up. I'm not dirtying those gorgeous clothes with your blood."

"Then what are you doing?" Saba wheezed. "Just trying to scare the piss out of me?"

Zek leaned on his cane and smiled. "I figure there's only so much you can tell me, Vasili—especially if you're being truthful. Maybe you can see something others can't. However, if *I'm* going to be seen with you, you're going to need to clean up that beard."

Saba knocked his head against the glass with an embarrassed laugh. "Aren't I silly," he said under his breath.

"I don't blame you," Zek said. He looked down at the edge of the razor like he could see something minute and fascinating dancing along the sharp edge. "Big Rezwyn comes at you with a sharp instrument—actually, I'd be upset if you didn't flinch a little."

Saba lowered his head and blinked at him. "You just wanted to get a reaction out of me."

"Not sure what you're implying," Zek said, tilting his head to the bathroom.

Saba grimaced. He reached up to feel the hair at his cheeks, which thinned at random points until his fingers stroked near-bare skin. This, Saba had been relieved to learn, was a family curse. Neither Maksid nor his father had ever been able to grow more than wisps, like red-brown cobweb clinging to skin. His decoction gave him a chance to overcome this, but not by much.

Saba rarely wore a beard, anyway. Zek was wrong on one front: Saba hadn't grown this during his stay in the basilica's jail. He'd given up on this level of grooming the instant Hirunz's discreditation had been publicized.

So perhaps a clean shave would be good for him. A return to—who he'd been once.

"Fine," Saba said, sticking out his palm. "Hand it over."

Zek's mouth quirked. "You understand I can't let you do it yourself, of course?"

Of course not. Naturally. Saba peeled himself away from the window with a contemptuous huff. He wanted to say: *And I'm supposed to just bare my neck for my traditional enemy?* in the most incredulous tone he could muster, but he knew the Rezwyn would answer with a dull and simple *yes*.

Saba obligingly followed Zek into the bathroom. The big man had positioned himself on the edge of the bath to stretch out his bad leg, but even sitting down he looked intimidating—in a quiet, almost soft way. The straight razor rested on his lap, and a tin can of soap sat beside him. Zek beckoned Saba closer, and for Zek to reach him, Saba had to also sit on the lip of the bath, body twisted toward Zek. Which was fine. There was nothing inherently wrong with sitting down next to someone you had technically been sold to.

Their legs were awfully close.

"To keep you steady," Zek murmured, answering a question Saba hadn't asked.

Zek smeared the cream over Saba's face, wet the blade, and got to work. He raised his free hand slowly, but surely; his eyes watched Saba's expression as his hand moved closer to cup the side of Saba's face.

Saba made a noise in the back of his throat that Zek mistook for upset. He sighed a little, and said, "I hope I didn't insult your beard," which struck Saba as an odd thing—of all things—to apologize for.

"No," Saba whispered. "It's shit."

Zek snorted. He tilted Saba's chin up and moved the sharp edge down in a smooth arc.

Warmth gathered at Saba's armpits and in the curve of his lower back. Sweat not because he was panicking, exactly, but because all of this felt radically new and strange. And—some other thing Saba didn't want to name.

Callouses grazed Saba's chin as the other man held him firmly. A distant, focused expression brewed in Zek's eyes, and concentration made him easier—or safer—to look at. Saba's eyes drifted down, and he let himself look at Ambassador Luan Zek, whose careful movements and gentle care left Saba with a conflicting rumble of emotions almost too vast for his own body. His heart felt suddenly too big.

I hate you.

Whether Saba meant himself or Zek, he didn't know. He didn't feel it either. Not really, not in any conscious way. But hate, or the idea of it, meant Saba's old convictions were still reliable. As soon as that became shaky ground, what was left of him?

After minutes of being handled, twisted, and shaved, Zek let go of his face. Saba's jaw thrummed lightly where Zek's fingertips had been. The big man tilted his head and frowned in that assessing way, the light of his eyes still focused on his handiwork.

"Mm." He nodded to himself, and then his gaze flicked up to meet Saba's eyes for the first time in minutes. "Now look at you."

What? Saba wanted to ask—but Zek made no attempt to explain himself. With a dismissive wave of his cane, he permitted Saba stand.

At once Saba went to the mirror. His reflection was still foggy, still unclear, but he looked resolutely more himself than he had in a long time.

Saba laughed. He touched his face. "Hello again," he said, aloud, momentarily forgetting where he was. He spun to Zek, who stared at him curiously.

"Thank you," Saba said finally, and meant it.

Zek's brows came together in what was probably confused surprise. He nodded and pushed himself up without any more acknowledgement.

Saba narrowed his eyes as Zek turned and nodded his head toward the door.

"Come on, then," he said. "Let's visit what's left of Loefka Ward."

CHAPTER FIVE

Sometimes Saba got this feeling, like grief, only more intense. He could describe it only like how—after witnessing something unspeakable—shock and a wet, hot fear clamped down around one's heart. Like how the memory of loss could have the same potency as the first experience. Like how the distance of years sometimes did nothing to soften the force of the bludgeon. He felt this way on occasion—and most usually about himself. His body. How others perceived it.

But now, with Zek leading him to bear witness to the calamity caused by his device, Saba felt it tenfold. He wanted to dig his hands into his chest, burrow his fingers behind his ribcage, and pop that feeling out of him. The lump just under his heart. The lipoma of guilt, self-disgust, and fear.

"Don't make me regret not putting you back in chains," Zek said. They were back in their two-seater carriage, rattling down the roads of Byrengrad with the beautiful limestone hillside in the distance. Midafternoon had crept up on him, and the sun blazed warm and bright above, making the city a glaring white. Even though it was the end of the summer, none of the foliage had browned yet; everything was green and bright. It should have made Saba feel peaceful or hopeful, or at the very least stable.

But he could feel none of that beauty when he looked at Byrengrad, not with that feeling in him, so he turned his eyes to Zek.

"I'll be on my best behavior," Saba said honestly, because he felt too tired and despondent to cause any trouble. Zek stared at him as if trying to appraise his truthfulness, and

Saba stared back, for too long, until the blue of Zek's eyes became overbearing, and he had to glance away.

They rode in silence after that. Zek turned them over the bridge and once again into the poor area of Jedvekn Ward, on their way to the now razed Loefka Ward, and Saba readied himself to shield his eyes against the mortifying mural, only to have the carriage run into a crowd. In general, this part of the city was tightly packed with hovels, the roads less clearly delineated, and the area often experienced congestion. This was natural, given the width of the roads. But this time a dozen people stood in the square around the well and spilled over the one road wide enough for a two-wheeled carriage to move through, and they shouted at one another—in Kerish, of course, which sparked a kind of juvenile fear in Saba, a remembered flinching. His body tensed at the first thunderous shout, jerking away from imagined danger. The argument was loud, brash, but not violent. Just the desperate sounds of a people extremely screwed.

As if hearing Saba's thoughts, someone cried out, "Because without Judge Berif, we're fucked, that's why."

A scoff, a sound of disbelief. "You can't possibly believe—"

"She would have been the deciding vote!"

A murmur of agreement went up, and Saba knew instantly what this was about. Maksid had told him important people had died in the explosion. A judge, he'd said.

"She would have at least tried. And now there's no way—we've lost that vote."

The vote—of course. Saba sank further back into his seat in the hope he could be absorbed somehow by the wood. It wasn't that he was against the vote—

"Kerinsk is dead," another voice said, and that snapped something significant in Saba's resolve. "It died with the princess. And now we can't even . . . "

People shifted away, and the gig squeezed through to roll forward. The voices became indecipherable babble. Saba's heart raced with unnecessary adrenaline.

Zek shifted next to him. "Vote?"

Saba blinked. "Uh," he said, and made himself turn to face Zek. "The Triad's set to vote on Ker rights . . . We're not citizens, no matter how long we've lived here. Just eternal squatters." He spun back toward the group, the ward, the living graveyard of his country. He could look at them from a distance when they were just a single fleshy body. "They're dreaming if they think it would have passed."

Berif, the judge who'd been killed during the event in Loefka Ward, had been one of the more moderate progressive minds in Byrengrad. This wasn't saying much—she was no groundbreaking voice. But she was the closest Kers had come to an ally here. There had been a great push to pull her onside, to have her convince others that Kers deserved citizenship and all the rights that went with it.

"Reliant on subsidies?" Zek asked casually, like he wasn't somewhat responsible for this outcome—for a people displaced and for the ensuing desperation.

"The price of grain is fixed for citizens of Zvensia. So long as the refugees depend on subsidies, anyone from Kerinsk is the Triad's bitch." Saba grinned wide at Zek; anger and frustration and the anticipation of seeing the site were culminating.

Stop talking, he almost told Zek.

And then the next thing out of Zek's mouth was, "And the princess? I don't recall . . ."

Saba's mind halted and then collapsed in on itself, crumbling internally. He felt raw and visceral, felt that kernel beneath his heart burst open like a pus-filled wound. "So you can invade my country, but you can't remember its history?"

Zek made a low noise, half-conceding, half-oblivious to the shuddering sack of rage sitting next to him. "Matriarchal," Zek said. "I remember that much. But the princess—"

"Was a child," Saba snapped. He made a frantic gesture with his hands, saying, "They think she'd be recognized by the Triad as a paragon because Zvensia and Kerinsk had an alliance at one time. They think that would be enough to change things. She is dead. But since no body was ever recovered, blah-blah, long-lost hope—some of the old guard hang onto the idea of her. Like she's a defunct goddess."

He'd spat the last word, fuming. His skin was hot. He had to sit there telling himself to breath in and out at evenly paced intervals before he could coax his shoulders down below his jawline. But Zek asked no further questions, and Saba couldn't bring himself to feel upset about that. In truth, he needed the silence, because as they got closer and closer to the site, the calamity, he lost all ability to control his emotions.

The world shifted with him. Everything grew eerily quiet. It felt terrible. The buildings on the surrounding streets must have been evacuated in case of collapse and were devoid even of looters. Entropy had spread like rot; Saba heard no birds, no animals. The wind here was dead. A fine sheen of sweat began to bead on his forehead, and for the life of him he couldn't tell whether anxiety or a genuine wrongness to this place was causing it.

The carriage came to a standstill when the rubble and debris became impossible for the horse or the wheels to manage. Zek gave Saba a look like he was considering saying something and nodded at Saba to get out.

"Need a hand?" Saba murmured.

"A leg," Zek said with a grunt. "And no. I'm not fragile, Vasili."

Saba shut up, swallowing the scolding. Distantly, it felt personal; it wasn't, of course, but the closer they got to the site, the less Saba could differentiate his feelings. They were converging in a soupy amalgam, and everything began to feel too much. Too painful. Too personal.

Zek climbed out and handed the reins to the groom, who took them gingerly, staring for an awfully long time at Saba, Saba's clothes, and then at Zek, like something more was at play here.

They set out, climbing carefully over the rubble of collapsed rock structures. A fine limestone dust sat suspended in the dead air, so everything appeared hazy and misted, and every breath scratched the back of Saba's throat. Coupled with the growing humidity, it was enough to make Saba sweat even in the cool air. Rocks slid and adjusted under their footfalls, and once or twice Zek cursed as his cane dislodged some vital shelf.

The instant various paragons appeared around them—sentinels, physickers, stewards—Saba began to focus on the ground, until all he could see was dried blood and dust and rubble, and suddenly he was five again, in the aftermath of one of the first battles for Kerinsk, Maksid gripping his hand, telling him: "Run. Don't look up. *Run*."

"Vasili?"

"I—I can't." Saba's voice came out thin and small, like a child's. How embarrassing. How pathetic that he couldn't even face the truth of what his own negligence had done.

There was a sigh and the crunch of rock, and then Saba was staring down at Zek's lovely floral boots, eyes fixed on the embossed pattern. He felt so overwhelmingly tired then. He almost knocked his head into Zek's chest, just for a moment of comfort.

"I'm sorry," Zek said. Saba hated that. Hated it. What could Zek be apologizing for? "Having been a soldier for so long, I sometimes forget—you are meant to feel something when you see this type of damage."

Saba squeezed his eyes shut so tightly, trying to stop himself from crying, but the motion only wrung out his hot tears from between his eyelids.

Shit. He didn't want to look up. He didn't want Zek to see.

"Hey!"

Both Saba and Zek jerked at the sound. Saba sniffled and glanced up. Two sentinels had spotted them; they clanked forward in their heavy armor, black cowled heads bobbing up and down as those screaming bronze masks howled. Both were dressed completely in sentinel gear, including heavy one-shouldered cloaks in black and lined with a warm yellow that hung from a decorated pauldron. Beyond that, they wore gorgets, cuirass, mail skirts, and greaves, as if in warfare. As if more carnage could occur any minute.

Saba swallowed. Maybe it could. But then their armor would not save them if it did either. Nothing so frail as Zvensian armor could repel the force of the astral sea.

Zek stepped in front of Saba to block his view and put a steadying hand on his shoulder. Without looking around, he fished around for his imperial seal and thrust it out to meet the sentinels' angry approach. "We'll be surveying the site, and we aren't to be disturbed."

Saba looked up, not at the sentinels, but at Zek, whose gaze had softened in a way Saba couldn't understand. Pity was one thing. This—this kindness—was another. Zek gestured his head away. "Come now."

Saba stepped forward, and in his periphery, one of the sentinels stiffened with recognition.

"That's him," she said. This sentinel was short and stout. Her body could have been beaten from the same bronze as her mask; her frame had a sturdiness to it Saba could admire. Behind her mask, she sounded surprised. Or horrified. The open-mouthed scream of the sentinel mask distorted her tone, and Saba couldn't really tell which emotion coated her words, until she stepped forward to shout, "That's the fucker—*that's the fucker who—*"

"Saba Vasili," the other sentinel cut her off with his deep, booming voice. He was taller than Zek, but leaner, and when that chesty voice emerged from his upsetting mask, it even gave Zek pause. "Stop right there."

Saba lurched to a stop. He felt sorry for himself and tired, and an order was actually rather lovely to follow when he was in a state like that. But Zek—that idealist, honor bound bastard—stepped forward.

The sentinel was saying, "You have no right—"

"I have every right." Zek's voice was quiet and firm. He needed none of the booming resonance for his power; he glowed with it, that easy, sturdy confidence. Fluidly, he slipped a folded document free of his tunic. Folded immaculately and sealed with the mark of Zvensia, triangles to represent the Triad—so Saba knew these had come straight from Hirunz. "I have every right, as these documents, stamped by the Triad indicate. Saba Vasili, suspected of causing the incident that killed the Lord of Veprak has been handed over to me, and I have been charged by Emperor Izra Dziove to bring the perpetrator to justice. But before that, there will be an investigation as well as a trial—do you understand me?"

The sentinels did not move. Saba glanced between them and Zek, practically giddy at the sight. He briefly forgot where he was and what he was here to see. Zek simply captivated his attention.

"He signed a confession," the sentinel said. Like the dead gaze of a corpse, his eyes rolled heavily to stare at Saba.

"We all saw it posted."

Saba resented that. Nuance tended to be lost in the writing of confessions after extended isolation and a few good slaps to the head. He had been asked, "Did you make the device?"

His confession had boiled down to *yes*. He hadn't been allowed to clarify. He hadn't been allowed to point out that what he'd actually made and what he had designed it to do should have meant this disaster was impossible.

Zek laughed, but his mouth sat in a hard line. "A confession is just a string of words on a piece of paper. It is not proof of anything. I have not yet seen the scene of the incident, and I have many questions."

Saba's heartbeat raced. A breeze cooled the sweat at the back of his neck, and he shivered, holding himself tense as he watched Zek who, consciously or not, was sizing up both sentinels with his considerable bulk. Zek continued, gesturing in the vague direction of the explosion site. "I want Vasili to explain what happened in detail. I will bear witness to what has happened here, and I will do so without being interrupted. And perhaps at the end of it there will be no shadow of a doubt that Vasili is responsible for this catastrophe. In that case, I will execute him myself."

He'd—*what?*

Saba stayed completely still, even as his heart dropped out of him, and bile and anger and a deep sadness welled up in his throat—what a fool. Zek wasn't defending Saba—he was only doing his job.

At least if Zek were the one to execute you, you wouldn't have to set foot in the empire. You wouldn't have to go to your knees before their emperor.

Some conspiratorial look passed between Zek and the shadowed eyes of the sentinels. Saba looked away, brow buckling.

Fool, fool, fool.

"He should be in chains!" the shorter sentinel shouted. If they were alone, Saba had no doubt she'd attempt to tear him limb from limb, that's how palpable her anger was. "But instead you've put him in fine leather."

What does she have to be angry about? She's a paragon; she's Zvensian. She doesn't deserve—

Saba stopped himself. Doesn't deserve to feel grief about this? Funny how desperately he wanted to own all of it—the horror and the death—while simultaneously still be absolved of guilt.

"Ambassador Zek, sir, *please*." She made a twitching hand gesture, not fully committing to an aggravated point; she flipped her palm, aborting the motion halfway through like she knew it would be pointless. "Put him in the chains."

Saba was surprised how sincere she sounded, how broken. Zek turned to look at him, this up and down assessment that made Saba breathe hard and slow.

Zek turned back to the sentinels. "I don't think that will be necessary."

He turned to leave, gesturing with his head for Saba to continue onward. But the other sentinel said, "Sir. I must contact Justice Sentinel and Judge Hirunz about this."

Zek shrugged and pointed at Saba to walk on. "Do what you must," he called out.

Saba followed but watched over his shoulder as the sentinels rushed back to a set of cages filled with messenger birds.

Hatefully following through with the paperwork till the end.

Saba tugged at his white gloves for something to occupy his racing mind. Zek had the power to kill him. Zek could execute him, and both the emperor and Hirunz would let it happen.

If that happened, what would Maksid do? Would he mourn? Would he choose to forget I ever existed?

"Do you really," Saba started, and had to stop to clear his throat. His voice had come out high and thin and embarrassing. Next to Zek, who carried himself so, so bloody *well*, Saba felt young and stupid. That critical, over-zealous voice of Saba's said: *Roll your shoulders back. Stand up straight. Be confident—you're a man, for fuck's sake—act like one.*

On the back of that, Saba faked a confidence he didn't feel and said, as carefree as he could manage, "Do you really have the authority to execute me?"

"Yes." Zek wasted no time. Didn't even hesitate, didn't even try to assuage Saba's fears. "But don't think too much about it."

Saba snorted and nearly slipped in the rubble. Zek's hand flew out to grab his arm. Saba scrabbled, gripping tight, and Zek lodged his cane deep and leveraged it against a stone to keep them both steady. They looked at each other, Zek with his placid, unreadable expression, and Saba with his eyebrows knitted so tightly they were practically on top of each other. He could feel them push up his forehead.

"Ha," he said with a fake smile. Behind the ambassador, Saba could see where the city suddenly stopped. The rubble disappeared, and only closer to the horizon did the debris and stone houses reemerge. This was the site of the event: what remained of Loefka Ward.

It looked like the ward had been subtracted from the rest of Byrengrad. Little could compare to it—Saba's brain struggled to comprehend precisely what he was seeing. An explosion would have made sense to him, and perhaps have been easier to swallow. But what he saw now confronted him with a nullifying, evaporating power. It was an unmaking. A disintegration. Loefka Ward was a void.

It was a circular devastation. A crater had swallowed the whole ward and with it the plants, dust, and rubble. The great horror of it was how pristine it was—even on all sides, perfect symmetry, as if a god had reached through the veil and, contemptuously and with inevitable perfection, made it so. The exactness made Saba's mind shudder. He had the urge to say: *that's not natural*—but of course it wasn't. If there were bodies here, they were hidden.

There was something else, too—a glimmering sheen on the world. Nausea filled him like a storm, inescapable and horrifying. Zek let go of his arm.

"Just keep your head down," Zek said, somehow still concerned for Saba's state of mind. "I'll tell you when I need your eyes."

Saba took the much-needed respite and stared down at his dusty boots. He went back to fiddling with his white gloves. "You aren't going to make me look?"

"Force you to confront the wreckage?" Zek clarified. Saba didn't respond, and they crunched through the rubble together for a silent beat. Zek sighed. "I don't think that ever does what people expect it to."

Which could mean so many things. Saba glanced at Zek, at his leg, and wondered exactly what the war had done to him.

What the war had done to him? *Vasili—you have too much damn empathy for this man.*

They walked a few blocks. Houses, hovels, shops, all of it reduced to rubble. Saba kept his eyes downcast, watching as he stepped over stone, tattered fabrics, what might have once been a very small shoe. Zek's footsteps halted roughly, and he shot out a hand to pull Saba to a stop.

Slowly, he looked up.

The crater was scarred. From this vantage it looked like an oily black mark on the land, but it hardly concerned Saba. His focus slipped up, above the deep recess, to the blueish, iridescent shimmer that blazed in the sky.

The tear to the astral sea.

"Gods," Zek muttered. Like it repulsed him. Like it wasn't the most beautiful thing he had ever seen.

Perhaps Saba was a bad person. Perhaps something was fundamentally wrong with him. Because when he saw that tear, every other part of the carnage slipped away and became muted by his awe. It looked like a blueish wound, a hole in fabric. Saba walked forward to the edge of the crater, and his body leaned forward as if tugged toward the tear.

Everything inside it was tinted blue—everything *inside* it. Saba paused and squinted.

Was that . . . ?

A beautiful mountain city sat inside the breach. Green and cold, highlands stretching out, ethereal and impossible, and Saba almost tumbled over the ledge, because it hadn't looked like this in years. Not since the war. More than that, he saw a silhouette of a man standing on the horizon, someone who seemed compulsively familiar.

"What the fuck?" Zek hissed. His hand was shaking. Bone-white knuckles squeezed around the hare's head.

Saba frowned and shook his head. "It's my home. From before."

"That's not what I see."

"And what do you see?" Saba turned, curious.

Zek said nothing. A master of his own face, he schooled that expression back to blank Rezwyn stoicism. Saba pulled his eyes away. He wouldn't win that fight. Zek had probably learned from birth to keep his true feelings to himself, but Saba never had. Saba spent his life wanting to scream nearly every second with how much rage and exhaustion lived inside him.

Fine. Screw this.

Saba lurched forward. "I need to get closer."

He began to make his way down into the crater, but Zek just leaned forward and hauled him back up by the scruff of his neck like a dog. Saba made a mortifying squealing noise as Zek lifted him away from the ledge with a single hand.

"You," Saba wheezed, as Zek put him down, "are unnaturally strong."

"I'm not going to destroy my leg like that," Zek replied, ignoring what Saba considered to be a significant compliment. He nodded over to the left side of the crater where wooden ladders had been built into the pit, and then he shot a stinging look Saba's way, as if to say: *You feral little man, climb down the ladder like an intelligent human.*

Undeniably, Saba felt rabid. That was the damned astral sea staring out into the world—that was everything he'd researched for years of his life. He'd only ever seen a sliver of it before now. If getting to it meant scrabbling down a particularly large crater and running madly to it, he would do it. But Zek had them walk around to the crater's opposite side, which at least gave Saba the vantage to spy below.

It took minutes to walk around it. The crater spanned most if not all of Loefka Ward's boundaries. If Saba were to launch off the side now and scramble down as the feral part of him wished, it'd be almost impossible for him not to snap a limb. The crater dropped twenty or thirty feet and then flattened out perfectly. Even from so far above Saba could see that the ground looked unnaturally smooth. As he focused, he could see that the breach to the astral sea floated in the center of the razed destruction. What looked like a small black dot from this distance floated above it. From the edge of the pit, this shining structure sat at eye level.

The Eye. Saba's device.

Saba pulled his eyes away from this distant wound and focused on getting to the ladder. It spanned the full drop, and a cream tented canopy had been set up right beside it. He couldn't see inside it, but a few people milled about, moving in and out of its cover.

A redhead and someone with long dark hair were made briefly visible before moving back out of sight.

"Ah, fuck me."

"What is it?" Zek asked.

"Oh, nothing. Just old friends." Saba tried his best smile on Zek and vaguely hoped none of the sick feeling in his gut leaked out of the expression.

Once, Saba had been close to his colleagues—inevitably close, really. Few chose to be scholars, and those that did all shared the same, slightly unhinged type of mind. Hours of studying and reading near-indecipherable tomes only to glean very little could be considered a form of masochistic trauma that bonded colleagues together. But the great reveal of Saba's Kerish heritage had undermined everything scholarly he'd ever done. With discreditation from the Scholar's Guild came isolation. Few still wanted to associate with him, and Saba couldn't blame them, not when Hirunz took such a personal interest in telling Saba what an idiot he was for attempting to fool the Triad. He isolated himself from his remaining friends intentionally, so as not to infect them with his own disgrace.

Saba had wanted to say: *I successfully fooled the Triad for over a decade, actually.* But the instant he'd been found out, his research had been discredited, and anyone else involved in his chosen topic had been marred.

His colleagues' opinion of him probably wasn't much better now he'd been accused of causing this tragedy. It probably was much worse. Very likely, they all hated him. He felt the way a prey animal might seconds before it was slaughtered—he didn't want to face them.

Hilariously, though, his former colleagues now needed him. Hirunz would never have given Zek leave to bring Saba here if that wasn't the case.

They needed him, because when it came to the astral sea, Saba was the best of them.

So he raised his brows at Zek and grinned broadly as he climbed down the ladder. "At least you made me pretty again."

“Slow the fuck down,” Zek said, as he moved himself over to descend.

Saba did no such thing. Above him, the wind ate most of Zek’s curse. The ladder would be painful for him, probably, or would slow him considerably—Saba knew this and rushed to the ground. He jumped off the last few rungs, spun toward the tear which now hovered above him in the distance, and froze. He couldn’t help but think about running—letting all that desire and fear fuel his sprint, fleeing past the scholars, running across the whole stretch of devastated crater, and going prostrate before the breach. Worship it, touch it, find some way to leap inside it . . .

Zek held his injured leg off the ladder and climbed down behind Saba with his cane between his teeth. He got down almost gracefully, cane first, good leg second, and then staggered over to Saba with an angry grunt.

“Thought you might bolt,” he murmured.

“Though you might kill me for it,” Saba said, meeting his eye. “Besides, only place I could have gone is inside the tear itself. And who knows if I could survive that.”

Zek said nothing to that, but neither did he look away. He regarded Saba with an expression not so neatly schooled as his usual. A bit of scorn had slipped through—and a bit of something else, too.

Saba glanced away. “Leg okay?”

But before Zek could reply, someone else spoke. “You have got to me kidding me,” she said. “Vasili?”

Both Saba and Zek spun toward the voice, turning their mutual attention toward the group of people sheltering beneath the awning. Several faces stared at them; the nearest was an Uslethian paladin. Her skin was flushed a deep brown as if from the cold, and brown curly hair coiled around her neck and shoulders. She wore that bright, nacreous plate armor made famous by the Gifted Paladins of Usleth. For centuries this special order had defended the small country of Usleth, far to the east, on the other side of the Rezwyn Empire. These warriors consumed ichor extracted from the bones of the massive prehistoric creatures called gedroks, a font of internal arcane power they supposedly drew upon to cast spells. It was also believed that their gedrokbone armor helped them to temper the side effects of ingesting the large amounts of ichor required to enter the order, which resulted in madness over time. Saba knew that exposure to ichor taken directly from gedrokbone, and consumed in the amounts required by the Paladin Order to develop their senses and their arcane power, would drive most people mad.

Saba couldn't help but wonder why, of all people, a Gifted Paladin of Usleth would be called in to assist in this matter. As far as he knew, Usleth's concept of the astral sea was primarily religious. All documents that Saba had read from that kingdom referenced the astral sea as a mythical space of the Rezwyn god Suoduny and concluded that the space was more of a metaphor for transcendent change rather than a real place. So what was she doing here, towering over his dear friend, the sweetest scholar, Mossinne?

Mossinne—Moss—was short and maskless, with a lithe build, auburn hair, and a face that was misted with freckles.

Saba's heart twisted upon seeing her, but it wasn't Mossinne or the paladin who had spoken.

That voice, with its neat severity, belonged to a paragon. Even with her face entirely covered by a mask, she looked close to violence. Her eyes were stormy and her body tense, and her dark hair escaped down either shoulder in straight parts. She wore a divided hennin hat in a light blue, and her bronze mask had green patina inlays around the cheeks and eyebrows. This mask marked her a sage—a paragon of the scholarly order Saba had once belonged to and the title he had always dreamed of having. Only she hadn't been a sage when Saba had worked with her.

She must have become one after he had been discredited.

Through gritted teeth, Saba said, "Giste."

Giste spun. "Sentinel!" she shouted furiously.

A shrill scrape sounded at the back of the tent, and a sentinel rushed forward, sword drawn as he ran to Giste's side. Which Saba thought was rather flattering given he was dressed like an ornamental pet and visibly lacked any noticeable muscle. The sentinel was tall and broad, about the same height as the towering paladin who at the same moment, unprompted, also readied herself. They acted as if Saba had the power to kill them all on sight.

Zek sighed so deeply Saba could hear his eyes rolling. He stepped forward and lightly pushed Saba behind him. "And you call the empire violent," he muttered, once more pulling the Triad's signed papers out for inspection. "Saba Vasili is under my care. As such, you would do well to stand down."

Zek had learned the ways of Zvensia by now. He said all this as he slipped out Hirunz's papers, raised for all to see; the Triad mark and the answering imperial seal emblazoned on the paper's end.

Giste gave no order, and so both sentinel and paladin made no move. She looked Zek up and down, gaze withering, and cocked her head to the side to size him up. Zek stiffened ever so slightly under her gaze. Was it the leg? That he was a Rezwyn? That he had any association at all with Saba? Or was it the intersection of these things? In any case, Giste's judgement was palpable—but Zek refused to back down.

"I have your own judges and the empire at my back, Paragon." Zek's voice came out as a low whisper, drawn from somewhere deep in his chest. "Are you sure you want to make an enemy of me?"

Mossinne's eyes shot toward Giste, as did both sword bearers'. They orbited her, relied on her decision, and the tension had Saba twisting his right foot toward the breach, like he could bolt there for safety, or find comfort in that terrifying beyond. Giste closed her eyes. Saba imagined her expression beneath the mask to be bitterly unhappy. She'd always looked like that when she didn't get her way.

Finally, she made a gesture. The sentinel sheathed his blade, and the paladin followed suit.

Giste glanced back toward the tent and nodded them all in. They filed in silently out of the midday sun.

Once inside and settled around a large wooden table, Giste turned and fixed Zek with a pointed stare,

"Sage," she corrected belatedly. "Paragon scholars are called sages, and I've been awarded the name Persistence."

"Persistence Sage," Zek said. "I am Ambassador Luan Zek. This man is under my care. I have been tasked by Emperor Dziove himself to understand the details surrounding the death of my countryman, the Lord of Veprak."

Giste raised her head with an irritated twitch. She folded her arms across her chest. "We already know what happened."

"Do you?" Zek sounded pleasantly surprised. He turned toward Saba with a nod of his head. "Then tell me what happened. How did this man kill the Lord of Veprak?"

Giste either didn't hear the snide tone creeping into Zek's voice or chose to take him at face value. She rolled her shoulders back and narrowed her dark eyes. "He funneled scholarly funds into his death trap of a device. Whether he wants to admit it or not, Saba Vasili designed and built a device that resulted in the deaths of hundreds—and therefore whatever his original intentions were for this research no longer matter."

Well, wonderful. Saba felt sick and infuriated simultaneously, like half of him wanted to swim forever in his guilt, and the other part urgently needed to defend itself. He couldn't move beneath Giste's hateful stare.

Zek cocked his head and looked between them. He did something with his fist and made a low noise as he shifted, like his leg suddenly felt painful.

"And who activated the device, triggering all of this?" he asked.

Saba glanced up at Zek, giddy, and then he looked back at the breach. Zek, for whatever reason, was defending him—and perhaps Saba didn't deserve it.

"Does that matter?" Giste asked.

"Yes, it absolutely does matter," Zek said. "But you can't answer my question, can you, since you don't know yourself."

Giste's eyes were mildly surprised.

Moss flinched like she expected Giste's wrath. Saba noted the tensing of her body, the way her fists balled on the table in anticipation.

The sentinel and the Uslethian paladin had varying reactions. The sentinel lurched forward and was stopped only by a near imperceptible flick of a finger from Giste.

But the paladin's face darkened, aghast with shock—though it took Saba a moment to realize she was not upset at Zek's questioning of Giste but at Giste's reaction. The paladin swiveled back toward Moss, and when she caught the scholar's eyes, she flicked her head toward Giste.

Moss bit her lip and shrugged.

After that, the paladin physically took a step back from Giste, like the realization that a sage of Zvensia could and would condemn Saba on only a feeling and without evidence was a contagion that could taint her pure paladin soul.

Though Saba enjoyed that, his cheeks burned with shame—shame that any of this was happening at all. He stepped forward past Zek's protection. "I want to get closer to the Eye. To see if I can disable it."

Giste jolted, visibly discombobulated. She seemed to register the device's name slowly. Then her eyes flashed, and she snarled, "And I want you to be very far away from the damage you've caused, but apparently, we can't always get what we want."

"Persistence Sage," the sentinel said tersely.

Giste flinched and met his gaze, then past him, where tiny little Mossinne had stood up from the table. The humidity had made her hair a little frazzled, and she was dressed in very loose, baggy pants and a three-quarter shirt. A tool belt looped around her waist and connected to her thigh. On it hung spectacles, ink, quills, and a book—she was always the scholarly archetype.

"Moss," Giste said stiffly. "Sit down."

Moss did not sit down. She didn't even glance Giste's way. With sudden nervousness, she started to wring her hands together.

"Saba?" she whispered, as if he could be anyone else.

Giste practically hissed at her. "Sit down. They're here on empire business. We let them do what they came here for, and then they'll leave."

Which was so characteristically Giste that Saba had to laugh. Even before her promotion to sage, she had been like this: tense, unyielding, always mildly furious. Saba couldn't imagine the paragon title had done anything but make her worse.

Moss slid her big green eyes over to Giste with a look of profound disgust. "You know we need him."

Giste made a very strange movement like her entire body rejected that idea. She turned away from Saba and tried to intimidate Moss once more. "Sit. Down."

"Friends of yours?" Zek murmured to Saba.

Saba couldn't look away from Moss.

"Maybe once," he whispered back, which sounded pathetic. He rolled back his tightly wound shoulders. "Persistence Sage and Mossinne were my colleagues. Khajro, too, but I don't know where he is."

Zek didn't push further, and Saba still didn't look away from Moss. They stared at one another amidst Giste's tense fury, and Saba even forgot about the silent, suspenseful observation of the sentinel and the paladin. Looking back at Saba like it was just the two of them, Moss's eyes glimmered.

"Can you show me the breach?" Saba said.

Moss peeled herself out from around the table. "Yes," she grinned. "Yes. Yes, of course. Ignore Giste, ignore everyone with a big sword." She rushed to Saba, who was still hovering near the tent's entrance, and grabbed his hand in both of hers. Emphatically, with what was unmistakably genuine emotion, she said, "It's *good* to see you."

Saba could have cried. It had been a long day, and Zek's kindness as a stranger had already felt unbelievable. But for an old colleague, after everything, to touch him, to say *It's good to see you*, made Saba feel an impossible amount of emotion rise in his chest.

"Mossinne, don't be naïve," the sentinel said, because he was an asshole. "He stands accused of *a massacre*."

But this didn't sway Moss either. She decoupled from Saba briefly and reached for the paladin to drag her forward. "Oh, Saba, you must meet Silvana. She's an Uslethian paladin." Moss leaned forward, eyes sparkling, and whispered with a wide grin, "She has untampered ichor in her *bloodstream*."

Saba flashed Silvana a look. Extremely stiffly and heavily accented, the paladin said, "Hello."

Moss held her large forearm with both hands and grinned like she'd found the paladin wandering outside the city walls and wanted to ask her mother permission to keep her.

"Judge Hirunz sent for her. She's a specialist in forging arcane weaponry and in the ichor ceremony; she's been trained by the Prime Paladin of Usleth and worked under their master forger— *and* she's one of the only specialists of ichor-driven devices to have visited the Temple of Suoduny and communed with the astral sea, *and* I'm rambling, but . . ." She tilted forward and silently mouthed, *Holy shit.*

Saba cracked a smile. Mossinne was adorable. And indominable.

But a fathomless sadness sat in his chest. He'd wanted this for years—the ability to discuss ichor and its uses, time to pick the mind of someone exposed to it, leave to study in Usleth itself, which had a large source of ichor in the gedrok skeletons found there. Now that would never happen. Paladin Silvana was only here because of Saba's mess and not for the whimsy of anyone's scholarly interest. Yet—he felt it. Agitated, eager to move, Saba said, "An honor. Truly. I would love to pick your brain, but unfortunately, I'm still in this man's custody and not at liberty to make my own decisions."

The paladin blinked at him—how much Zvensian did she understand?—and Saba repeated himself in Doskorian. Silvana gave Saba a slight nod. Desperate to move, desperate to be away from all their scrutiny, hating how exposed he felt, Saba turned to Zek like the Rezwyn could save him.

How pathetic was that?

Spineless, neglectful murderer. Your morals are as delicate as your ego.

"We need to see the device," Saba said to Zek, all in a rush.

Giste said something that became indecipherable beneath her mask. She spun to look at the breach and very unhappily said, "Ewir and I will take you."

The sentinel stiffened in response. He stood straighter and brushed a hand over his half cape.

Zek turned back to Moss. "You may ask Vasili three questions. Talk to Paladin Silvana and form them before we're back. Understood?"

Moss grinned and rushed back to the table to rummage through her papers. "Yes, yes. Thank you." Then, in very stilted Doskorian, Moss told Silvana that they needed to find a way to sum up their theories into three questions, which clearly annoyed Silvana who demanded to know why they were allowed only three. Moss related her own powerlessness in the face of Zek's arbitrary statement with a bewildered shrug, and the two of them bent over the papers, getting right to work.

Then to Giste, Zek said, "Please, lead on."

Giste spun and began to walk toward the breach without another word. Saba recognized this insufferable mood; Giste had very simply never liked Saba, and now that her dislike of him was legitimized by an arcane event, she was being far less coy about her true feelings. Ewir brought up the rear, walking just behind Zek with his sword drawn. A conversation started up between them in hushed tones, and Saba's stomach dropped when he thought too long about what they would be discussing—or rather, what exactly they were saying about *him*.

The only other things to focus on were the breach (he was going to tear his skin off with anxiety if he did that) or Giste's mask.

Pettiness won.

That mask—that title—should have been his. He had been the most prolific and widely published scholar of their group. This was his realm, his area of expertise, and he had been on track to becoming a sage. Before he'd seen her in the mask, the knowledge he could never again be recognized for his work had been painful, but it was a distant kind of hurt. More pressing pains had taken precedence, like the very real blow to his jaw. Now he was here, now that he felt so acutely the distinction between the two of them, the revelation that any scholarly efforts would always be tainted by this hit him.

Was that selfish? In the wake of all this death, Saba was thinking about his legacy.

You're walking on the ash of dead flesh. A hundred bodies lay mangled beneath this rubble. Vasili, you're a bastard.

Sometimes that inner voice went too far, but not this time. This rhapsody of emotion—guilt, longing, desire, anger, fear—pervaded Saba's perception. He felt no way to be objective about himself in this moment, and so he simply said nothing and thought nothing more, until Giste suddenly halted.

She said softly, "It's growing."

"What?" Saba said.

Giste had stopped by the beam of prismatic light that was ruptured open, a split in the world. The breach now reached all the way to the dust-covered ground. Above that, suspended impossibly in the air, rotated the Eye. It whirred furiously, pulsing prismatic ichor with every heartbeat. It seemed to feed the oily shimmer of the breach that flicked and spluttered below it. Saba tore his eyes away from the scene and made himself stare at Giste.

"It's growing larger, Saba." She sounded so despondent that it stumped him, like the walk from the tent to here had dislodged her loud fury and made room for all this sadness. Her voice went high. "I don't know what modifications you made to the device, but the failsafe hasn't worked. Nothing has."

Saba shuddered. He had to look. His eyes slid past Giste's head up into that ephemeral beyond. He saw a huge stretch of blue-tinged Kerinsk, crystalline quality to the simulacrum, and then a perfect silhouette of a familiar shimmered into view. Perfect in shape and size and as recognizable as the angry, self-critical voice in Saba's head.

He exhaled noisily.

This is your chance. Go to your knees. Beg. Pray. Ask for what you want . . .

Whatever noise he made had Giste spinning around as if excited. "You see something, don't you?"

He wasn't going to tell her, because then she would ask *what* he saw. This phantasm was between him and the astral sea, a bodiless fantasy, one possibility of an endless ocean. He pulled his eyes away from the breach and cleared his throat, attempting to look calm, but Ewir, Zek, and Giste were all staring at him. Saba's cheeks burned.

"What do you see, Persistence Sage?" Saba asked. It couldn't just be him seeing things in the undulating flow of astral power. This was untapped potential; anyone with a single ambition or dream or hope would see something.

Giste roughly turned her head from him.

Zek grunted and nodded. With his hare head cane topper, he gestured up at the Eye and asked Giste, "Why haven't you destroyed it?"

Saba nearly screamed. He whipped around, splaying his white-gloved hands out as if trying to calm a wild animal.

"We don't need to destroy it," Saba spat, far too angrily than was warranted. He bit his lip and tried unsuccessfully to stop breathing so heavily. But he needed to say this, needed to kill the thought they could just destroy his life's work. "I can turn it off. And besides, if you attempt to destroy it and fail, you might obliterate the mechanism that closes the breach. Then we're really fucked."

To his great surprise, Giste nodded in agreement. "He's right. It's a risk. Tampering with it could very well make it worse. Especially since we don't know what Vasili did to it to grow the tear this much."

Saba ignored the attitude as much as he could—he needed to talk it through with someone who knew the device. "Where's Khajro?" For Zek's benefit he turned back and said, "He and Moss built my designs. If anyone would know of a modification it would be him. He should be able to find a way to turn it off without doing anything to make the breach wider."

Quite abruptly, Ewir said, "Khajro is dead."

Saba choked. "What?"

"Not from the breach, Vasili. Not from your mess, not from the chaos you've opened up." Giste's tone came out full of scorn. "At least not directly."

Saba rolled his eyes and briefly let the urge to name call and yell fill him up. What an absolute vindictive shit Giste could be. It took another moment for him to really register what Ewir had said.

"It's not helpful for you to keep insisting that Vasili is responsible when you have no proof," Zek said drily. "Why don't we call what occurred here 'the event.'"

Saba laughed, practically barking, and Ewir moved a step closer to Giste like she needed shielding from this little challenge to her authority.

Giste sniffed and folded her arms. "Fine," she said shrilly. "Khajro didn't perish during *the event*."

She nodded up at the beam. Saba's smile fell, the reality opening craterous in his gut. He couldn't help himself. He walked closer to it, craning his neck for evidence of Khajro's demise. The earth around the beam and the open tear burned brightly, bleached white dust. It—or the tear itself—had the dank scent of a fresh grave. It smelled strangely of Kerinsk to Saba, because so much of Zvensia was dry rock. The beginnings of scaffolding had been built, probably some early abandoned attempt to retrieve the suspended Eye, and—oh.

"He didn't," Saba whispered.

"Yes. He tried to get up to it and got too close. He touched the light, and he just . . ." She swallowed and steadied herself. "He was unmade."

Saba winced. Giste spoke so nonchalantly about Khajro's death, firstly as if he hadn't been their colleague for two years, and secondly as if scholarly engineers weren't few and far between. Empathy wasn't Giste's strong suit—or at least, she often tried to hide it. But this . . . she was being so cold.

"That's it?" Saba prompted. "Unmade?"

Her eyes flashed at him angrily, and Saba realized he'd been mistaken. Emotion bubbled up in her eyes. Through clenched teeth Giste said, "He came apart. I can't compare it to anything, because it was the most unnatural thing I've ever had to bear witness to. Like a . . . like a piece of fruit rotting in the blink of an eye. All the moisture left his body. All the blood. It came out through his pores, red spots of it lifting out of his skin. And he withered. He got so small, almost flat, and then he fell apart. It was like touching an old tome and the paper crumples or breaks away. He's dead. Alright?"

Saba flinched away and squeezed his eyes shut. His head spun with the image. *Khajro. . . I'm sorry.*

But it wasn't just Khajro. It was everyone and everything in Loefka Ward. His countrymen. Children. They'd all broken apart into nothingness because of him. Without the bodies, it was almost worst; he'd carry their shades instead, carry all that unlived potential in his mind forever.

Zek walked around the breach, feet and cane crunching into the rock as he craned his neck to inspect it. Giste glanced at him, and then gestured up to the device again. "We haven't been able to get too close. Moss is too short to see anything useful. No one's been up after Khajro. . . after what happened. Mossinne and I have theorized that either the failsafe mechanism is jammed or otherwise broken."

Half whispering, Saba said, "Surely it will run out of ichor soon."

Giste, blunt and uncaring, scoffed. "Tell me, if it was fully charged with ichor at the time of the *event*, and the failsafe mechanism stopped working, how long would it take to close?"

Fuck. Alright. Saba couldn't bring himself to meet her eye, but he could feel that withering gaze upon him. Suddenly he could smell himself—sweat and dust and something else he couldn't name.

The Eye had been filled with ichor extracted from pressed ichor flowers called cajudsan. Only a little bit was required to open the puncture, and not much more was needed to maintain operation.

"Maybe a year." He tried not to sound scared as he said it. "It doesn't take much ichor to make the puncture. Even with it growing as it is, even if it was needing double or triple the amount to sustain that breach, that's still . . . months."

"Exactly," Giste spat, because she knew all this already and only wanted to make Saba feel awful.

Saba turned away from Giste. He called out to Zek, "I *need* to get closer. Zek, tell them what a good boy I've been."

"No," Giste said. "Sentinel."

Ewir drew his blade and advanced on Saba, who scrabbled back and scoffed. "Rather unnecessary, don't you think?"

Zek did him the service of once again shielding his pathetic little body with his size and brawn. Saba poked his head out from around Zek's body to stare at Giste and was sorely tempted to be openly smug about it.

"Saba Vasili is the expert," Zek said plainly.

"Saba Vasili is the reason all of this is happening!" Giste shouted. She paused and cleared her throat, schooling her voice to a much more controlled volume before she added, "And if you let him tamper with it, he'll potentially kill us all."

Could she be right? Saba wanted to believe he knew himself. He wanted to believe he could be absolved from this tragedy. But if any part of what Giste said could be true, should he ever touch the Eye again?

On the other hand, he felt furious. *Kill us all*—that kind of melodrama never helped anyone.

Zek lost his composure. He tilted his head, shot a hand out to gesture, and said sharply, "Again, I stress that you have a theory—and nothing more. Is that right?"

Giste only nodded.

Zek barked with righteous laughter. "Well, then that's bullshit."

Saba jumped and bit his tongue so hard he tasted blood. Two feelings pulsed insanely in his chest. Part of him reveled in this stranger taking his side, and the other felt revulsion. Rezwyn interference of any kind repelled him. What did it say about Saba that he so desperately needed Zek's support?

But Zek was saying, "You've had an expert on the device locked up for weeks, and you never thought to consult him?"

Giste's spine somehow shot straighter. She breathed deep and balled both hands into fists, and Saba knew she was furious at the thought of having to ask him for anything.

Her voice sounded gruff and small. "Who do you think you are to question the decisions of a sage?"

Zek's face fell flat, but his nostrils flared. "You're right," he said with a shrug. "I have no business questioning you about anything but the death of the Lord of Veprak. But I feel it is my duty also to point out that you don't appear to actually know anything about that either."

Giste didn't like that. Not at all. Her dark eyes narrowed into slits beneath her mask, and then waved a dismissive hand toward the pair of them.

"Then you have no reason to stay here questioning me," she said. "Please show yourselves out."

CHAPTER SIX

By the time they dragged themselves from the crater, the sun had taken on a burning orange hue, a solar flare of light just before sunset.

Mossinne had sent the pair of them up, promising to follow quickly with her questions. Saba appreciated the momentary reprieve. His jaw ached, partially from the growing bruise he'd acquired that morning, and next from the tension of holding his lips in a sour, angry line for too long. Giste was something else. Insufferable and challenging—and that damned sage mask had only accentuated the worst of her personality.

Saba stretched and turned in time to watch Zek haul himself up the ladder in an incredible and very sensual show of strength. As much as Saba liked what he was seeing, and as much as he shouldn't have cared about a Rezwyn's wellbeing, he had the anxious urge to apologize. He tried to stop himself. He failed.

"Sorry," he said. Zek rolled his eyes and passed his cane up. Saba took it from him and offered his arm as leverage, which Zek took without thinking. One large, calloused hand slapped down on Saba's spindly forearm and *pulled*—Saba made an unattractive squealing noise as he tried to stop himself from tumbling forward. Zek snorted at that and released him.

Saba cleared his throat. "Waste of time. You might have gotten more out of her if I wasn't there.

"Not a waste of time," Zek grunted. Saba lifted that beautiful cane to him, hands skimming over the wooden indents of the hare's head before Zek took it with a nod.

"For one thing, now I know you were telling the truth and have nothing to do with this event. And like you, I know the leader of the scholars is a bit quick to jump to conclusions."

Saba put his hands on his hips. "I'm sure there's a compliment in there somewhere."

"Of course there is," Zek said unexpectedly. "You didn't engineer the Eye to fail when activated, and yet you're honorable enough to take the fall when it did. It's a rare trait. Very uncommon—outside of aristocracy who've been trained to unquestioningly accept responsibility on principle, of course."

It wasn't wholly complimentary, but neither was it critical. Zek kept looking at Saba like he was a riddle to be unwound, a curiosity, and Saba kept looking at Zek for entirely different reasons. The sunset had a beauty to it, but nothing like Zek's gravitational pull—nothing like the power in that relaxed, grounded stance, or the surety of his self. So now, with the dying light, Zek was the only thing Saba could look at it.

And the only thing he could think was: *You inconsistent little slut.*

Saba jolted and looked away.

"*Saba!*"

Saba glanced over the edge. Mossinne grinned up at him and stared at the ladder, lips all puckered up in confusion. Her hands were overflowing with notes, loose papers, scrolls—she ended up putting half of them in her mouth and the rest under one arm as she scrabbled up after them, humming tunelessly to herself. Both Saba and Zek offered a hand as she got close to the top. She grinned again, teeth shining over the documents as she slapped her armload into Zek's hand and then launched at Saba, wrapping him in a hug.

"I'm thankful you're both so slow," she said brightly, until Zek raised a questioning brow. Moss flushed redder than blood, her eyes skirting fretfully down to his cane. “Oh—no I didn’t mean—it’s just—I *missed* you, Saba. And I don’t believe this is your fault, not for one minute. I just couldn’t say that in front of Giste, because it’s Giste.”

Moss was unbelievable. It rarely took more than a single word from her to soften Saba’s heart, attitude, or mood. Especially now. This kind of trust in him, this belief in him, made him almost nauseous.

“You don’t think I’m responsible?” Saba said.

Moss pulled a face. “No,” she said, because she assumed the best of everyone automatically and couldn’t seem to comprehend that her behavior was unique—special. “Not even if it was your device. Or rather, *our* device. You can’t bear the burden of its faulty design.”

Despite everything, Saba couldn’t bring himself to hug her. He looked down at his feet. “I’d rather bear it than you. You’re too good, Moss.”

She said nothing to that, flat out ignored him, actually. Moss turned back to Zek and grabbed her notes from his arms, saying, “You’re investigating this—and investigating it *truly*, aren’t you? Not just for your countryman but ours also, to really find the truth?”

“I am,” Zek said.

Moss glanced between them and sighed, but her eyes were bright with a kind of nefarious cunning that looked foreign on her. She stepped forward conspiratorially and stepped away from the side of the pit until no one standing below could see her.

“When Saba was discredited, the Eye was locked away. It was kept in the Scholar Building and only Giste had a key. But,” she said, “a week or two before the event, several paragon sentinels arrived and took the device with them. They said they were taking it to the basilica’s archives where the Triad could keep an eye on it. But the day of the disaster, Giste received a letter. A summons. I saw the seal, and

I read it over her shoulder, and she was being summoned by the Judges Hirunz and Berif because the Eye had gone missing."

Saba said, "What," extremely flatly and not as a question, momentarily overcome by the implication.

But Zek had more sense about him. "What exactly are you suggesting?"

Moss knew better than to be too accusatory, however. She shot up straight and made her eyes very big, shrugging as if she hadn't suggested Persistence Sage was somehow involved in the event. "Nothing. I am making no judgements; I have no assumptions. I am simply telling you what I saw." She flashed a look at Saba and her face fell to sadness. "And I want you to have all the information before you decide to condemn my friend to death."

Zek didn't answer. Saba considered Moss and wrestled with himself about whether or not to say anything. A brooding twist happened in his stomach. *Don't say it. Don't ask. You don't actually have to—*

"Why didn't you say anything earlier?" Saba's words came out petulant and churlish. Oh, Saba felt so overly young sometimes, almost like he'd never grown beyond the fears of that child fleeing his homeland. He couldn't hide the hurt.

"I . . ." Moss frowned, lips pouting. "What do you mean?"

Zek took over. "This kind of information might have led the investigation in a different direction. Away from Vasili, I mean." He sniffed and shifted his weight uncomfortably off his bad leg, seemingly unperturbed by the information Moss had given him. But then he added, "Why did you keep it to yourself all this time?"

"Well, I didn't," Moss murmured. She glanced between the two of them, pink skin flushing redder. "I told all of this to Diligence Inquisitor the very first time she asked me anything. But nothing . . ." She glanced over her shoulder again as if Giste had learned to materialize suddenly at will. "Nothing happened. Giste was summoned once, and that was it. And I don't want to think she has anything to do with it—she's distraught, Saba, truly—but I just thought you are Saba's keeper, Ambassador, so you should know."

Zek considered this with a slow, grim nod. He folded his big hands over one another on the hare's head and cocked his own. "Thank you," he said finally, before he turned to stare at the oily wound that hovered within the crater.

Saba pointedly did not look, and Moss grinned broadly, adorably, at the thanks.

"You're very welcome," she said, clapping her hands over her bundle of papers. "Now—I have my three questions. And Giste is too proud to ask you for anything, but not me, Saba. You're brilliant. You always have been. And we need you. *Please* help."

Flattery like this would usually be enough to sway Saba because he could be fickle like that, but he wanted to go his knees before Moss and beg her to shut up. *Shut up*. He didn't deserve—this.

It felt particularly strange to hear this kind of lauding, so often reserved for paragons, aimed at him. Almost ridiculous. Almost cruel.

"I want to," he said quickly. "I . . . I want to—" He choked, cutting himself off. He'd wanted to say fix things. *Fix things*. How could he? How could any of this be salvageable?

Zek's expression had moved from quiet interest to fascination as he watched this exchange.

Then Moss said, "I know." Even her smile was knowing, her chin raised high. She only came up to Zek's stomach and even Saba had to look down at her; her light auburn hair was frazzled and wispy, and her freckles buckled over the scrunch in her nose. She trusted him—and was risking her own reputation to tell him that. Saba promised himself that he'd help her in any way he could. He would claw back whatever scraps of self-respect that still lingered in him, and if he couldn't fix things, he would at least try.

Moss looked to Zek, who seemed to see in her someone readying themselves for a long explanation, because he moved aside to a pile of rubble and positioned himself against it, taking the pressure off his leg.

Moss rolled back her shoulders and seemed to slip into another part of her mind, because her voice lost all of the sweetness as she said flatly, "The device we made consists of two parts—a pin that pierces the barrier between realms and an aperture that opens so that the observer can look through a lens into the astral sea. The lens is suspended by a housing that holds the ichor that powers the spells inside, so what you're seeing there is what is being projected through the lens, not the device itself. But that projection seems to have the power to unmake what it touches, and it's getting bigger. I think the lens is amplifying and concentrating it, like when a beam of sun passes through a magnifying glass. So my theory is that destroying the device might not close the breach, and in doing so we risk damaging the lens and causing the projection to explosively refract. Thoughts?"

"That could be a danger, yes," Saba said. He turned back to look at the astral sea and the crater the device spun in; it was barely more than a blip of a hole from this vantage. He frowned. "What were you all thinking of doing to destroy it, anyway? Climbing up there and throwing a big rock at it?"

Moss went bright red and glanced down at Silvana, who had come out from the tent. The brown-skinned paladin smiled up at her with her a wave.

"I told her it was a stupid idea," Moss grumbled. She flashed Saba a sheepish look. "But I was getting desperate

. . . and paladins are always trying to solve things with giant weapons—even the smart ones."

Saba snorted. Zek shifted off the rubble and shook his leg out. White dust shifted around him as he walked, and by the time he'd settled himself again, Saba was staring.

Zek smiled at him, flashing his teeth.

"I can't figure out what's keeping it suspended," Moss was saying, and Saba was definitely paying attention to what Moss was saying. "By all accounts, it should be at the bottom of that pit, but it's just—*hovering*. Is it the ichor in the device or something spilling out from the astral sea?"

"I, uh. . ." Saba had to will himself to look away. "I'd need to get much closer to the device to know. But it's hovering in place around where the ground would have been before it collapsed, so perhaps it's in the exact location it was when it was activated, and the breach is holding it up? Like a stopper in a drain? The pressure is holding it there?"

Moss's lips curled off her teeth in a mocking grimace.

Saba folded his arms defensively. "Yes, I am pulling this out of my ass."

"Eh, that's so much of scholarship," she said.

"And what if it's being held open from the other side?" Zek asked.

Both Moss and Saba spun to look at him. What a terrifying thought—unless . . .

Saba looked down at his hands, at his flesh, and *felt it*; that possibility spun up through his bones and muscle and skin. This could be exactly what he needed. Perhaps all this tragedy, all this sacrifice, could be what finally allowed Saba Vasili to slip into the astral sea and realize himself fully. Could this wish be what kept the Eye functioning? Had someone or something on the other side heard him—answered him? Was still holding a place for him?

It's not possible, and yet . . .

"Then we would have to go inside to close it," he murmured, before really considering it.

How fucking awful was that to say? How truly selfish?

A hundred angry ghosts dead before their time howled at him, haunting him for eternity. But at least Saba could look and feel like himself.

Moss's brow buckled. Her expression made Saba feel dismal, and he worried that her determined gaze saw too much of him.

"Let's forget about that potential for now," she said. "I recall in your research you theorized the astral sea might actually feed off sentience, off emotion and memory. Or be some kind of mirror."

Zek's colorless expression repelled him. The Rezwyn stared expectantly, waiting for Saba to confirm this theory, which sounded rather stupid when said aloud. Only Saba *had* seen it, hadn't he? Seen something.

A silhouette as familiar as the dreams it sprang from.

"Can we find a way to deactivate the Eye without touching it?" Moss asked.

Saba threw his arms up. Interrogation after interrogation—he was meant to be the expert, and yet he withered further every time he had to answer *I don't know.* He had never felt more stupid in his life, and feeling stupid in front of Zek felt even worse.

Moss continued, "Or can we find a way to shield ourselves from the effects of that weird column of light long enough to deactivate it? Or even . . . to go inside the breach?"

He didn't know, and he hated not knowing. "You're acting like I've been here observing it with you for weeks," he murmured. "We don't know what the light is, except that it's deadly."

Silence spread between them. Zek stayed quiet like he wanted both Saba and Moss to forget he was there. Standing suddenly felt too much, so Saba followed Zek's lead and found a sizeable bit of rubble to shimmy onto. Moss waited patiently—she knew he'd fold eventually. Knew he'd already thought about this. Knew he'd been thinking about this for years and years and years.

He knocked his head back against the stone, avoiding a string of ants climbing happily down toward a meal buried beneath the rubble. Saba ignored them as best he could and briefly closed his eyes. The heat felt good, and he splayed his hands on the rough surface to feel grounded.

"If I *had* to guess, entering the astral sea would be like . . . exposing yourself to ichor in the rawest form." He glanced into the crater, watching as the Uslethian paladin moved about in her gedrokbone armor. "The astral sea is extremely concentrated power. We already know ingesting large amounts of ichor directly from gedroks does . . . things to the body and the mind. Unless, like our Uslethian friend, you are cased in something that can mitigate the effects. So—perhaps Paladin Silvana would be fine. Or less worse off than anyone else." He looked back to Moss. "Why risk it?"

Moss flushed. "Because this is an incredible opportunity, and I am an academic before I am a disaster specialist." Saba blinked at her. Zek shifted and leaned forward. Moss misunderstood at least Saba's reaction and flung her hands out, waving frantically. "I know. I know I should be working to close it, but a part of me—" She froze up and looked to Zek.

"Zek only cares about the death of his countryman," Saba said, hoping that was still true. Zek was being uncharacteristically quiet, so Saba turned to him and made eye contact as he said, "I'm sure he can withstand the whimsy of a scholar."

Zek looked him up and down and shrugged—bastard.

"But what if it's not whimsy?" Moss's voice went high. "What if we actually could go inside? Wouldn't you want to?"

You know the answer to this already. You just want me to say it aloud.

And something about saying it aloud worried Saba greatly, as if admitting the truth of his desire would make everything worse. He hesitated and opened his mouth, but he kept looking at Zek, who stared back with interest.

It doesn't matter what a bloody Rezwyn thinks. But it did. It did.

"Ambassador Zek!"

Everyone spun around. Two sentinels approached, and one of them was undoubtedly Maksid—Justice Sentinel. Now Saba had recognized him, he couldn't unsee the ungainly gait with which he walked. Both sentinels picked their way through the desolation, clambering over the rubble to the razed circumference of the ward's crater where walking became much easier. They were two lone figures, save for the distant sight of administrative peoples surveying the damage and laborers discussing how to best clear the mess.

Zek muttered something in angry hushed Doskorian. Then, winking over his shoulder at Saba as he stood, he murmured, "I suppose those other sentinels followed through."

Now it was Saba's turn to flush. He spun around before Moss could see and watched Zek breathe deep and ready himself for this sentinel onslaught.

The sentinels slowed, rock crunching beneath their feet.

Moss withdrew quickly back down the ladder without making eye contact with any of them.

"We thought you would be on your way now," Respect Sentinel said curtly. Smarmy little voice, that one had.

"I would be," Zek said, "if there were not some outstanding questions I thought might be answered at the site itself. Vasili's statements to me contradicted the ones in his confession, you see."

Respect Sentinel—whose name really was rather funny given everything about him—snorted and stared at Saba. "Of course, they did."

"Vasili should be in chains."

That voice belonged to Justice Sentinel. Saba steeled himself and met his brother's eyes. The things Maksid was willing to do to keep his title were astounding: Let the entire sentinel order use Saba as target practice. Never interfere when interrogations get too bloody. Tell Saba to his face he thinks his own brother a liar.

Now a Rezwyn was standing up for him. Zek only said, "So I've heard."

Maksid didn't like that. He turned bodily to face Zek, gold and black half coat swaying with the movement. With vitriol he said, "Will you be on your way soon, Ambassador Zek?"

Zek met this snappish energy with a slow head tilt. He waited, not with hesitation but with what felt like slow calculation. "You seem eager for me to go."

"I am eager for justice," Maksid said sharply. Saba rolled his eyes.

Zek smiled, but his eyes when he glanced back at Saba were dead. "As your name suggests. But I am not done here. I will not return to Doskor without a clear understanding of what befell my countryman." And with a flourish that nearly made Saba swoon, Zek added, "I am sure you understand, Sentinel, if justice truly is the value you have been named for."

The hairs on the back of Saba's neck rose, and he gripped the edge of the rubble with all his might lest he explode. Tense silence spread between all of them. Saba watched intently, eyes flitting between Maksid and Zek.

Stiffly, with a gentle tone that must have been extremely schooled, Maksid said, "Then how can we assist?"

He sounded awfully like Hirunz. Saba could hear that dick's voice all over his brother.

Zek could not have been less fazed. He sniffed, half leaning on the rubble as he gestured back to the city with the end of his cane. "I can't and won't ask much of you, Justice Sentinel," Zek said. "But do tell me where I can find a good dinner."

Chapter Seven

"I'd have thought a sentinel would've sent us to a richer part of the city," Zek said, staring out of the restaurant's cavernous opening. Night had fallen on Byrengrad. Shadows splashed across the whole rocky city, but dozens of lights from oil lamps had sprouted in the dark and flickered in open stone windows, flames wobbling in the warm, gentle breeze like luminescent spores. *Or something from the astral sea.* Saba imagined a fungal monstrosity sporing through the breach.

Saba cleared his throat hoping to dislodge this unnerving thought from his mind and said to Zek, "You wanted a good dinner, not a pretty view. Didn't you?"

Zek folded his arms and smacked his lips good-naturedly, eyes sliding over to Saba under the raised arch of his brow. "Got me there, Vasili," he said, smile charming and eyes twinkling in a way that seemed to threaten another wink in Saba's direction—which Saba wouldn't be able to handle without alcohol.

Getting to this restaurant was a bitch at the best of times, as it was tucked all the way down in one of the lower wards—both figuratively from a class perspective and literally, given that Serlei Ward sat sequestered at the lowest points of Byrengrad City. It was perhaps an hour's walk from the breach site, which Zek had said would "destroy both his body and his dignity," so they'd walked back to the gig and then seen the throng of carts and bodies on the main road.

"Too hungry for that," Zek had said with a grimace, shifting moodily. "That'll take a good hour or more."

"There are side streets," Saba had said.

Zek had nodded somewhat gratefully. "Show me," he'd said.

Saba—and the gig's groom—regretted this almost immediately, as Zek had meandered the two-wheeler across rooftops and thin streets with Saba screaming directions. Zek had been surprisingly insane about it—had put the horse into a canter and had the wind in his hair. At one point, he'd even laughed. Once they were away from the main road, he slowed them to a trot and took Saba's directions without question or comment—but that small, private smile remained on Zek's lips.

Saba couldn't stop looking at it, couldn't stop seeing what Zek looked like happy.

So all he'd managed to think about for the rest of the ride was Zek. Every interaction with him shook Saba's resolve, because it made Zek unreadable and subsequently dangerous. Even when he had spent years interacting with people behind masks, Zek remained unknowable, which only made Saba's interest more intense.

Saba wished he had a pinch of that discipline, so he wrangled the part of him that got flustered whenever Zek looked his way.

He'd made himself think about Zek in a much more boring and bland way. He asked himself questions like: did the Rezwyns send so-called Special Ambassadors for every death that befell one of their lords? This stirred the near-dead remnants of his scholarly mind, which had been packed away behind the feral survival instinct that had taken over in the jail. It was a good question. Saba had never heard of the practice, never heard of *special* being tacked on to anything the Rezwyns did. Theirs was a precise hierarchy, dominated completely by the divine emperor, and with everything ordained by gods, nothing could ever be wrong. Besides, given the violent nature of empire as a concept, he figured it was second nature for important people to go around dying. So, Saba couldn't help but worry—and worry massively, every heartbeat a persistent reminder of his anxiety—that Zek's presence wasn't about *who* had died, but *how*.

Why were the Rezwyns so interested?

Saba's stomach had finally triumphed, drowning out his anxious thoughts with pitiful growls of hunger. They had left the gig with the groom at the base of an inclined ramp and entered the eatery.

Now he and Zek were crammed into one of twenty tiny tables at a cheap staple restaurant pressed into Byrengrad's limestone bedrock. The entrance was simply a great opening, exposing all patrons to the elements. On a night like this, with the humidity dropping low and the heat still ebbing out of the stone, the breeze was welcome. But holes had been placed in a line above the entrance to slot in rods for the heavy woolen curtains used to keep out the cooler weather. A cave wall loomed overhead, a curved deformation that made the interior resemble a hollow bone with all the marrow sucked free. Garish colors and geometric patterns splattered the cave ceiling most brightly above the kitchen, which consisted of an open masonry counter with sunken terracotta pots filled with various foodstuffs. Above this open kitchen hung a single fired-clay mask. The mask was nothing like the beautiful, prestigious metalwork of the Triad's paragons but rather how they used to be. Decades ago, paragons had been community-elected people. The masks had been a ritualized effort to shift them away from individuality toward anonymously elected community members. This culture had died out, though, when the Triad had begun appointing them. The masks they still don became a remnant of a bygone time.

Tables were wedged into every nook and cranny that could hold one, which meant Zek's elbows were pressed against the patrons on either side of him. It was rather intimate, Saba thought. He avoided meeting the eyes of his fellow patrons, though the great lot of them filled up his periphery. The man next to him flirted poorly, but the woman he was with had clearly decided to laugh at everything that left his mouth. Saba found himself leaning away, leaning closer toward Zek, whose general presence enforced a bit of personal space.

Saba had snagged the seat that'd allow him to press his own back against the wall, if only for the false sense of comfort it brought him. Saba couldn't help but feel self-conscious. He was dressed deliciously—but not for this place and certainly not for someone who needed no attention drawn to him.

"I'm massively overdressed," Saba said with a grumble, eyeing the garish geometric paintings and how they clashed with his own getup. A few eyes were on him; he'd made himself a target for thieves, but at least all he had left for them to take was his life.

And for whatever reason, Zek seemed to want him alive.

"You could always take something off," Zek said, without so much as a beat passing. His unreadable expression made Saba scream silently—but he slipped out of the jacket and stuffed the white gloves in his pocket just as the waiter floated by.

Saba readied himself to call out what he wanted, which was practically the only dish this placed served: two servings of a lentil stew with baked goat's cheese, a depiction of which had been painted onto the wall above the kitchen.

But the young man froze when he laid eyes on Saba.

Saba should have known. Even if he hadn't picked out these clothes, Saba knew what wealth looked like, and most people here dressed in imitation of the clothes on his back: poorer fabrics, less lustrous dyes. He'd often visited this place with Maksid, so the proprietor and patrons knew him well. Sitting here felt like an avulsion, and he felt keenly how little he belonged anywhere. How narcissistic he must look, crawling into Deji Ward with his fancy clothes and his Rezwyn escort. He knew innately what the waiter was thinking, even before he'd uttered Saba's name like speaking it aloud might kill.

"You're *Vasili . . .*"

Saba's stomach jerked. He could never understand people who felt ambivalence toward their names, because names had raw fucking power in them. He knew how gut-wrenching it could feel to be addressed incorrectly when in itself speaking a name was a declaration. You named someone and said: *I see you. I know you. I name you. I remind the world who and what you are.*

Speaking the wrong name invoked the inverse.

Whenever Maksid messed up Saba's name, he invoked the *princess*—Maksid's idealized version of the sibling that had never truly existed. In a way Saba had grown used to that kind of discomfort. Now Saba shivered. *Vasili* was a bastardized version of his royal nomenclature. He and Maksid had decided on it when they'd fled Kerinsk, and sometimes Saba regretted that decision, because it meant Kerinsk and Saba's birthright would forever have a hold on him. But to hear his chosen name butchered by a tone of disgust?

Had Saba's selfish obsession with the astral sea ruined even this—the name he'd chosen for himself?

A few people had heard and turned around, and Saba hoped the kitchen started burning just so something else might draw their attention away from him.

Zek sighed like a man very much in need of a drink and dredged another coin from his pockets. He reached out, gently took the waiter's palm, and pressed the coin firmly into the skin. The waiter flushed but palmed it without another word—or glance—toward Saba.

"Tell him what you want," Zek murmured.

"The usual," Saba replied with his eyes on Zek. "Double it, obviously." He refused, as the waiter had, to make eye contact, but he saw in his periphery as the man shuffled off.

You're too obvious. Should've kept your hair dark . . . Should've done a lot of things, I suppose.

Zek said nothing. Saba watched him carefully, and Zek looked out at Byrengrad as relaxed as an old soldier could be. Only once in the time they waited for their food and drink did Saba catch Zek looking his way. Saba stiffened, just slightly. By some silent agreement, neither said a word until the alcohol arrived. Saba was grateful for that moment of comfortable silence.

The waiter returned with two jugs of a Kerish liquor called koranti, and both Saba and Zek nodded to one another, a wordless cheers, and drank.

Koranti was aromatic, served both hot and cold, and spiced up in the winter. He liked the way it burned. It felt cleansing, like how Saba imagined the godly faithful of the empire felt in worship. It was a poor man's comparison; all Saba had was the imitation brew of a country that no longer existed.

As he drank, Zek's face twisted. The vein at his temple pulsed with the intensity of his sudden frown. His eyes darted up to Saba's, lips pressed in a thin, sour line.

"This is Kerish," Zek said.

Beautifully understated. However, Saba could read the implication as clearly as if Zek had screamed it: *You want to make me squirm, Vasili. You want to remind us that we're not friends.*

This wasn't quite true and wasn't quite false. Saba said, "Sure is. Or at least it's how Kers remember what it tasted like. I was too young."

Zek's nostrils flared. He stared down at the contents of his jug forlornly. "Tastes how I remember it. But it's been years since I tasted anything from Kerinsk."

You want to taste something else from Kerinsk? Saba resolutely did not say this.

Zek glanced up as if he heard this lustful little voice dripping out of Saba's skull.

Shit, don't look at me like that. Saba pressed his teeth into his tongue, hoping the bite of pain could make him stay angry, could keep him from slipping into this interesting but dangerous sensation of attraction.

Very quietly, almost gently, Zek asked, "Are you trying to punish me for the war, Vasili?"

Saba squeezed his own hand beneath the table. He hoped not. He hoped he was better than that. He might want to press and prod at Zek, to extract stories and information since Zek was an untapped source, a survivor with a first-hand account, and Saba was a scholar. Perhaps the low, debased, rage-filled scavenger that Saba often tried and failed to keep in a cage wanted it. But Saba knew he *shouldn't* want that, and thus said, "No."

"But you wanted me to squirm," Zek said. His tone wasn't uncaring or particularly accusatory, just knowing, because Zek could somehow read Saba unnervingly well. Zek sighed and drank and closed his eyes. "If you want to blame me for Kerinsk, you should know I was sixteen, injured horribly, and quietly returned to Veprak before your country ever fell."

Lips pursed, Saba took his own swig out of his jug and said, "I wasn't trying to rile you, Zek." He glanced down at Zek's leg, thinking, *sixteen, injured horribly.* "I just wanted something strong enough to forget for a little while."

And because Zek was a very good man, his face softened, as if he should be the one ashamed of his tone. He raised his cup, and Saba nearly spilled half of his in his gladness to toast silently. *To the kindness of a Rezwyn.*

"Unfortunately," Zek said smilingly, "I can't let you forget too much."

Zek shifted in his chair. Leaning forward, chair creaking with his weight, Zek resembled a bear. But he had a careful, waiting energy to him that in this moment made Saba think of ambush predators. Zek had quietly and routinely collected information, and now he had something to discuss. Even if he lacked the violent recklessness of a starving predator, Saba felt him to be just as dangerous.

Beneath the table, Zek's foot lightly grazed the inside of Saba's shoe, and Saba choked on his own breath. He coughed and jerked and pulled his foot away, reeling from what might very well be imagined intimacy, as Zek frowned and said, "There's simply too much here that makes no damn sense. So I'm going to talk through it: what we know and what we don't know. Okay?"

Not an intentional inner foot touch then.

Touch-starved little freak, pay attention.

Saba nodded up at Zek and kept nodding. Zek's presence had shifted ever so slightly as he recounted.

"We know that, for some reason, Lord Doric of Veprak was here in Zvensia and was killed—allegedly in the incident. But so far, we have no reliable witnesses. I haven't seen the body. Who found it and where? What state was it in? Perhaps that will lead us to his killer."

Saba frowned. "You haven't seen the body?"

Zek ignored him, clearly still midway through his thoughts. "And this assertion that you were operating the machine at the time—it's just so patently false that it's insulting. Why would so many people go along with such a flimsy lie when numerous people state that you weren't in possession of the device at the time of the accident? Do they really think that we Rezwyns are so stupid?"

Saba instinctively straightened in his seat, realizing belatedly that none of these questions were anything but rhetorical. He closed his mouth and waited, not even sipping from his jug lest it dispel Zek's train of thought. The hulking Rezwyn had spilled forward onto the table, big hands clasped together to support his chin, brow furrowed together over his hands, which Saba found himself looking at. Staring at. Light hair curled over Zek's forearms and wrists. Zek opened up his arms and splayed them on the table, and Saba struggled to pull his gaze away to meet the Rezwyn's eyes.

"To me it seems clear that you were chosen to be the scapegoat well in advance," Zek said finally. "But why? What threat do you pose? Why send all the way to Usleth for a paladin to fix the device when they could just go drag you out of the prison? Who are you, Saba Vasili?"

Saba tried and failed to stop himself from flushing. He made himself turn away, upset by how easily he could be flustered. On the stone wall by his head, someone had carved "SURVIVE!" in tiny letters, so well-faded now that Saba had to squint to read it.

Survive. How fitting.

He had survived this long by hiding; he had wrapped himself in a shroud of it, concealed his past, and twisted himself to make sure it stayed hidden. Zek's questions were terrifying and sharp, because Zek, of course, was right. Why had Hirunz sent for someone from Usleth? Why had everyone done their best to ignore the damned expert as the breach disgorged unchecked arcane energy into Byrengrad, Zvensia, the world?

And then the quieter, more persistent fear: did Hirunz know Saba's former identity?

This was the type of fear usually classed as selfish. A large part of Saba feared Hirunz knew what he was already, even if only a few people had the privilege of knowing Saba's business. If Hirunz—or the entire Triad—did possess the knowledge of Saba's royal past, could that somehow be connected to the breach? Or perhaps it could explain why Hirunz sought help from elsewhere. Byrengrad would hate to be indebted to anyone, most especially hidden Kerish royalty. They would have to sift through old treaties to discover what they owed Saba by law . . . Saba could just imagine the paperwork.

"Look at me," Zek said. Saba clenched his jaw and looked. That ability of Zek's—the quiet commanding tone, the charisma—was a huge pain in the ass. Impossible to defend against. Zek met his eyes and said in a low whisper, "We're turning a few heads, so I'll speak quietly. You have been condemned here. Even if I can prove you innocent, I can't change that. But I can take you away from here, if you'd like."

How could he say that so casually? How could he make an offer to change Saba's life without so much as hesitating? It was like Zek was telling him: *I am willing to cause a diplomatic issue between Zvensia and the empire to help you.*

Saba felt exposed. With more venom than he intended or Zek deserved, he said, "The last time a Ker trusted a Rezwyn, our whole country was assimilated. There was a treaty once, you know, between our nations."

"Well, neither one of us are our country's rulers. I can't correct that mistake. But I could help *you*. You can start again in Veprak, or further west. Ostijan or Elkar or Banonok. Many foreigners live there."

Saba gave himself the luxury of imagining that life. What would it be like, living somewhere else, starting over again? It wasn't a novel concept, not after fleeing Kerinsk. But he couldn't find any comfort in that thought, just the horrible knowledge that if he ran, he would never forgive himself. Last time he had been a child. Last time he'd had no hope of stopping something as large and insidious as the Rezwyn Empire. But now? This was his specialty—the one thing Saba knew without a doubt he was born to do. The astral sea had breached the world, and Saba had been born to lead the people of Kerinsk, and now he was accused of killing a great number of them. Very simply, there was no way he could leave.

"No," he said with a soft, sad smile. "I can't. Zek, I appreciate the offer; I don't know what kind of relationship you have with Emperor Dziove, but harboring me in any capacity is too. . . it's too much. Not to mention—I need to know what really happened. I need to know why. Beyond my life, beyond why I was accused, I need to know who did it."

Zek opened his mouth, but Saba wasn't done yet. He leaned forward. "Besides. If I go, can we really expect the others to close the breach? No offence to Paladin Silvana, I'm sure she's very capable. But I'm the missing piece in the Scholar's Guild right now. They need me to fix the Eye."

Zek watched with eager, near-sparkling eyes. He picked up his jug and held it toward Saba in a genuine salute. "There you are." He sounded like he'd eaten something delicious. "You hadn't been overly cocky for a while there, Vasili. I was getting worried."

Saba flushed. "So you'll help me? Help me figure it out?"

"Of course, I will," Zek said, as if his help had been guaranteed from the start. "But . . . we can't go galivanting back to the site. Not yet anyway. My authority here is limited."

Saba thought for a while. Their food arrived, and Saba tore a piece of bread apart to dip into the cheesy lentil stew as he recalled his last conversation with Moss. "Mossinne mentioned Diligence Inquisitor. . ."

Zek blinked at him, chewing silently. Saba gestured impotently, searching for the words. "Inquisitors are another type of paragon. They sit somewhere between scholars and sentinels; it's really in the name. They ask questions like scholars but usually are expected to come up with solid, actionable answers, which is unlike scholars. And they have similar training to sentinels, only they don't tend to need it. In short, they investigate claims of wrongdoing."

Zek snorted. "Is paragon truly such a unique title when there are so many types?"

"It never used to be like this," Saba said defensively. Zek wasn't wrong, but he wasn't right either—and even if he spoke truth, Saba knew he'd still want it. Sage Saba. He longed for the recognition and the title and the relative security the paragon status awarded people in this city.

Zek said nothing more, eating and drinking politely; he'd probably sensed Saba's distress and dutifully shut up on Saba's behalf. *Too nice for a Rezwyn by far.*

Saba cleared his throat and tried to save face. "Anyway, Diligence. If she was the first at the site of the breach, then she might be the only one alive who knows what state the Lord of Veprak's body was in."

Now Zek looked up at him and smiled. With admiration, Zek cocked his head and nodded at Saba, which at that point was the third direct acknowledgement of the evening. Saba still lapped it up, like a dog for praise.

"Brilliant," Zek said, wiping his fingers clear of fatty grease and pottage. "Let's hope her namesake is true. Maybe you can be exonerated after all."

"You believe this traitor's fucking drivel?" Someone with a grating, nauseating voice slurred from beside Saba's head. And then pain ripped through the back of his skull as a hand laced into his curls and *yanked.*

Saba shouted. His body slammed into the wall and away as the chair clattered out from underneath him. The man next to him—a man Saba hadn't looked at twice—had stood and shoved over his own table. His short brown hair had been cropped close to the skull, and he was about double Saba's size, which said nothing, really. The woman he was with screeched, and then the whole world seemed to be roaring. Saba blinked back stars. His cheek was wet with spilled koranti, his hands scraped from an ill attempt at bracing his fall.

He heard his name, spat like a curse, and then it rumbled through the restaurant, echoed out through dozens of voices as they began to recognize who he was. No amount of coin could slow this down. He hadn't seen the aftermath of the event—whether there were riots, communal mourning, calls to kill him. Now, for the first time since the event, Saba Vasili was in public. Saba's heart sank as he pushed himself up. He was probably going to die here. His body would be torn apart by the anger of these people. They weren't even Kerish—but the event had endangered Byrengrad, and here he was, the perpetrator, enjoying a nice meal.

Coming here had been incredibly stupid. Going anywhere looking like this, so obviously himself—

A fist connected with his cheek as he was beginning to stand, and pain like fire pulsed across his face and thudded dully in his skull. Saba groaned. His arms shook, adrenaline and fear ricocheting through his blood. Then floral-embossed boots appeared beside his nose. Saba jerked away and looked up in time to see Zek grab the scruff of Saba's attacker, yank him back next to his own shoulder, and squarely strike him in the face. The punch connected neatly with a flat pop, but the man's scream came out mangled. Zek let him go, and he dropped to his knees beside Saba, both hands hovering over a bloody red nose.

Zek didn't stop there. A clean *shlick* cut across the noise. Zek beheaded the hare on his cane, unlatching some mechanism that kept it secure, and drew from the hollow base a thin, sharp blade. The air sung with the scrape of steel against steel. Bodily, Zek moved to shield Saba. He held his sword balanced against his opposite forearm, body hunkered low as he braced himself. His injured leg shook, but Zek did not fall.

"Vasili?" Zek asked.

"I'm alright," Saba said, shakily. He stood, heart racing. Saba was backed against the table. In his fall, he must have pulled the tablecloth free; the food and the empty jug of koranti had tumbled into a heap on the ground. Saba pressed himself against the clear table, and with Zek shielding him, allowed himself to catch his breath. Half the restaurant was on their feet. The silence was pregnant and deafening with its expectations.

"One zealous man I can understand," Zek pitched his voice loud. "But an entire restaurant full of them? It was my understanding that the people of Byrengrad followed the law—or at the very least recognized their Triad's authority."

Here Zek whistled to the server he had paid off. The man glanced around but stepped forward at whatever look was on Zek's face.

"Pocket," Zek said, commanding. The server gingerly reached into Zek's pocket and pulled free the pass signed by Hirunz.

"They are investigating the . . . what happened in Loefka Ward," the server said after reading it. "On the judges' orders."

Murmurs went up, but the only sound of outrage was from the man Zek had put on the ground. He squeaked when he talked, and his nose had inflated enormously, the bulbous bottom appearing like a bruised peach.

"Bullshit," he said.

Zek dropped the sharp edge of his blade toward him. "Touch Vasili and you make an enemy not only of your own Triad but of the Rezwyn Empire."

To this the man said nothing. He got very quiet, and, satisfied, Zek replaced the sword into the unassuming base of the cane. He leaned heavily against it.

"Anyone else?" he called out. No one said anything. Zek turned around and winked at Saba once. "Just what I thought."

Saba was wide awake with adrenaline. His cheek burned, and his ego was rather bruised, but otherwise he was unharmed—thanks to Zek.

The Rezwyn nodded at him and said, "As we were saying. To Diligence Inquisitor?" Saba nodded, stupefied and dizzy. They walked back to the gig in silence.

CHAPTER EIGHT

The night air was warm. Saba stared out at Byrengrad from beside Zek, holding himself with a tense poise that proved difficult to maintain. They hadn't said a word to each other since leaving the restaurant, which might have been a nonissue if Saba's mind didn't have legs. He used to like silence. Scholarly minds *enjoyed* silence—so why did this one feel impossible? Sticky? Uncomfortable? He wanted to puncture it, reach over and take Zek's hand, run his fingers along the callouses, make sure that Zek was real.

No one had defended Saba like that before. Or rather, no one had defended him since he'd become *Saba.* Womanhood and a title had made his safety a necessity, but when he'd abandoned both and chose himself, he'd never expected another soul to stick their neck out for him.

Saba looked at Zek from the corner of his eye and noted no anxiety in Zek's limbs—nothing but a quiet focus as he drove the gig across Byrengrad's precarious rooftop roads. Ahead of them, two lantern bearers lit their path with glee. Zek had paid them double their worth for the entire night just moments after rescuing Saba without question, and Zek was just that sort of man, wasn't he? Confident. Logical. *Good.*

Part of Saba kept looking for the cracks. He looked and expected he would find evidence that Zek's behavior amounted to a Rezwyn ploy to trick him into lowering his guard. But now, glancing at Zek and feeling the warmth of him, Saba could imagine himself hooking his little finger through Zek's.

What do you want from me? Why are you doing this for me? You're too good. You're. . .

"Here," Zek said, and Saba blinked rapidly as he came back to himself.

Zek handed their groom the reins and left her with the lantern bearers for safety before climbing off the gig with a groan. Saba leaped down after him.

A chorus of insects shrilled and chittered in the dark, hiding amongst the bushes and wildflowers that surrounded the Sentinel Building in a well-kept garden. A gated wall surrounded it, too, manned by a single sentinel who barely glanced at Zek's papers before letting them inside.

It looked like a lousy job.

The rest of Byrengrad was still awake, kept outside by the warmth and pleasant breeze. Saba let himself take it in, pushing away his thoughts.

Lanterns hung from stone pillars. Windchimes sounded pleasantly in the gentle breeze, and in the distance, the sounds of revelry meandered up to them. Saba could make out the muffled thumping of dancing and clapping, a tinny string instrument squealing over robust, deep drums. A woman's voice sung over it with a resonant clarity that woke Saba right up. The tune had life to it, and memory; it was so much like Kerinsk, which to Saba's faded memory was mostly brief flashes of tastes, smells, sounds.

Zek knocked and the door opened immediately onto a waifish young woman, neck-length blond hair slicked back over her skull, the ends of it curling to kiss her ears. "Humility Sentinel." She delivered her name and title with a curt, unhappy tone, even though it was her job to open the door to the Sentinel Building at ungodly hours. "Business?"

"Diligence Inquisitor," Zek said.

Humility's mask had been altered from the usual grotesque expressions of the sentinels into a softer scream, which Saba recognized as a face he sometimes made when he stubbed his little toe. He assumed Humility had it tweaked in keeping with her virtue, which she seemed to take very seriously. Saba could tell that from her posture alone. But her eyes were angry.

"It's late."

"It's urgent," Zek retorted.

She glanced between Zek and Saba with barely hidden agitation. "I will have to see if she's awake," she murmured, and then shut and locked the door in their face.

Saba laughed, breathed deep, and looked up at the Sentinel Building.

Byrengrad was a funny city, structure-wise, especially when all its soldiers were sitting pretty behind the walls of its richest ward. But he supposed that's just how Byrengrad was; the best of the best had to be lauded, applauded, marked different—even if you were one of a thousand other special individuals.

Ironic that you still want it then. Ironic that you gave up the title of princess with glee but will cling to something as common as paragon status.

"Zvensia is godless but still finds a way to worship, eh?" Zek murmured.

Saba blinked and realized the Rezwyn had followed his gaze upward. The Sentinel Building resembled the Triad's basilica—a big limestone structure with extensive additions of curved stone, iron, glass, tile, and pottery shards. Despite the motley materials, it wasn't half as ugly as it should have been. The ornate façade housed depictions of sentinels and the Triad in amongst the curved stone towers.

Saba dropped his gaze to Zek and smiled. "You've only been with us a few days and you see right through it all."

Zek's smile faded. His voice came out grave, sad. "Everywhere is the same, deep down."

Saba breathed deep as Zek continued to stare up at the

garish building. He'd misjudged Zek, probably. Perhaps it was easier to judge Zek than accept that no individual could bear the brunt of an empire's wrongdoings. Though neither did Zek shy away from the reality of the war he participated in. It felt difficult, looking at him. Nothing had really ever broken up the dense monotony of Saba's dislike of the Rezwyn empire. But Zek. . .

Zek was looking at him. Saba flinched.

"That'll be a nice bruise, you know," Zek said. He reached out and took Saba's chin between his forefinger and thumb, easily moving Saba's cheek to the light. He hissed sympathetically and let go, slapping Saba heartily on the back. "He got you good."

"Thank you," Saba said automatically. "Not for the—bruise-related commentary. For helping me."

Saving me, really.

Zek made a noise, dismissing what he'd done all too readily. He'd invoked the empire, which Saba wasn't sure he *could* technically do.

"Hirunz might regret signing that document," Zek said with a grin. "But it's been rather useful so far."

Was he being obtuse? The pass Zek had pulled out in the restaurant wasn't nearly as impressive as Zek physically putting himself between Saba and everyone else with violent intentions.

Saba shook his head. "That's not what I—"

The doors were wrenched open. Humility Sentinel floated into view and said in a voice somehow tauter than before, "Diligence Inquisitor has agreed to see you."

The door widened fractionally and Zek put his foot through as if eager to cross the threshold before she changed her mind. Saba tried to stop thinking about Zek and all that confusing business and set his eyes to the internals of the Sentinel Building instead. A new worry bloomed in him then. He didn't have the energy to see Maksid.

Let him be on patrol. Let him be anywhere else.

Inside, the stonework that made up the façade merged with glass; some lanterns were positioned behind tall panes to send brightly colored light through the interior in a strange mirror to the basilica's beautiful leadlight. This central atrium had been set up as a kind of hub, a thoroughfare with dark wooden stairs leading up, a few offshoot corridors heading to dorms or meeting rooms. Somewhere there was an armory—it had been a long time since Saba had been in this building, fulfilling a baby scholar's role of ferrying letters from the Scholar's Building that were too important to send via messenger pigeon.

Humility glided upstairs in silence, which Saba and Zek took to mean: *Follow me.*

Zek spent a moment cursing before his left hand shot out to the banister and he began hauling himself up. Saba followed behind, pretending to himself that the tensing of Zek's muscular forearm had little to no effect on him.

"You can . . . walk ahead . . ." Zek said between grunts.

"No, thank you," Saba murmured.

"What?" Zek laughed. He pulled himself up to the first landing and turned back to Saba. A little droplet of sweat beaded on his forehead. "Enjoying the view or something?"

Yes, yes, very much so. But Zek was joking—he had a testing, incredulous look in his eye, and Saba felt a bright stab of shame for thinking about him at all.

"Or something," he said finally, though Zek had already turned to haul himself the rest of the way.

Thankfully, very few sentinels were awake. They rose extremely early on a rotating schedule, so mostly whoever was awake right now was patrolling the city, save for the few left to protect the building or to open doors angrily.

The floor at the very top of the sentinel building housed the inquisitors. Great double doors divided the wing from the rest of the building. A floral incense burned and clogged the vestibule with an overbearing perfume that had Saba wrinkling his nose. A single sentinel waited at the double doors, and Humility performed a very bored handover by flicking her wrist, turning on her heel, and gliding back down the hall without another word. This new sentinel shared some of Humility's charismatic personality and uttered not a single word as they turned and opened the doors.

The room was large and simple. The original rock peeked through in limestone arches, but the rest had been covered in wood paneling. A carpet had been rolled up and leaned against a long table, and chairs were stacked haphazardly in the corner. In the center of it all, surrounded by a catastrophe of paper, was a woman.

"In," she snapped. "Close the door."

Zek obliged without a word.

The woman—Diligence Inquisitor—wore a long, sand-colored robe that billowed out at the waist. Diligence was perhaps fifty and a head or two shorter than Saba, with mousy voluminous hair that had been braided elaborately on her head. She was also unmasked, which had the same effect on Saba as if he'd seen her naked. He choked on his breath and flushed, which felt ridiculous—except that knowing her title and how few inquisitors graced Byrengrad made this visit seem suddenly intimate. Wrong. She had the window open, which at least alleviated the sharp scent of the incense, and from the looks of her—dark circles under her eyes, still dressed, papers scattered everywhere—she hadn't been at all close to sleeping. This didn't mean their visit was welcome, however.

Zek said, "Diligence Inquisitor, I presume."

"And you're Zek," she sneered. The wrinkles at her eyes crinkled as she said his name. Half rolling her eyes she added, "Only a Rezwyn would be so presumptuous as to show up this late without invitation—and with the convicted murderer himself in tow."

Saba stared at her. Her voice had a scratchy quality to it, like raw wool against the skin, and Saba realized belatedly she was tripping over vowels, voice withering as it skirted around difficult words—she had the wrong accent. She wasn't Zvensian.

"You're Kerish," Saba said, staring fixedly at her face. He flared his nostrils. This wasn't normal; no Ker could hold paragon status. This was why Saba hid his origin and why Maksid continued to hide his connection to Saba.

In Kerish, Diligence Inquisitor said, "No," sharply, quickly, almost panicked. "I gave up that citizenship before Kerinsk ever fell. I was in Zvensia before the Rezwyns invaded. But for the purposes of this moment, standing in front of you, Vasili, yes. I am one of the last Kers alive in this fucking city."

Saba snorted loudly and bared his teeth to her in a righteous, angry smile. "You relinquished your citizenship, but you claim our grief? You don't get to do that."

Eyes bulging, face suddenly pallid, her voice turned high as she squeaked out, "*And you do?*"

"Enough." Zek spoke Kerish more softly than Zvensian; the dialect came out timid, as if he felt embarrassed for knowing it. But as always, he had the surety in his tone that commanded attention. Both Diligence and Saba fell silent—for different reasons.

Saba looked to Zek like a dog might its master, because apparently that's what Saba was becoming. Diligence, however, jumped as if she'd been slapped. She spun to Zek and her expression slipped through various emotions: surprise that Zek knew the language, confusion, and then slow-blooming realization. She crumpled as Saba had done when he'd understood— Zek had served in the war.

Diligence closed her eyes with a despondent, gritty laugh. "Oh . . . what are you here for, Ambassador Zek?"

"My investigation, of course," Zek said. He'd schooled himself again into that impervious Rezwyn expression.

Saba wished more than anything he could read Zek's mind. What was he really thinking?

Zek sniffed and looked around the room. "No one here has been able to provide me with proof about how the Lord of Veprak met his end. I hoped you could, since you were on the scene that day."

"That, I don't know." Diligence shrugged, like there'd been nothing else she could have done. "I suggested that Saba Vasili should be interviewed since he built the device. But Judge Hirunz, in his infinite wisdom, perhaps rightfully decided that as a former citizen of Kerinsk I was too close to the matter. He removed me from the case."

Not before he took your suggestion and ran with it, though.

What was it Zek had said—something about a scapegoat, something about a decision being made well in advance of the incident? Zek thought Saba had been maneuvered to take the fall, and Diligence said he'd been one of the initial suspects. Because of course he was—the astral sea was his area of expertise.

"Which is when the Triad sent word of the death to my emperor," Zek murmured, finishing Diligence's story for her.

"That's right," she said.

Zek's brows pulled together. He put both of those very large hands of his over the hare-headed cane and murmured, "And who from Zvensia has been assigned in your stead?"

Diligence pinched the bridge of her nose and sighed. "Well, as far as I can tell, no one."

Saba slid his gaze over to Zek immediately, which was a stupid decision given Zek showed absolutely no reaction on his face. Instead of speaking, Zek pushed further into the room, eyes skimming over the papers scattered both on the floor and over Diligence's desk.

Saba would have been asking: *Why the fuck did you accuse me without proof, you nasty bitch?*

But Zek had been serious when he said he would only discuss that which he was authorized to. "Since you were the first sentinel assigned, I assume you saw the body. Or at least know someone who did."

Diligence glanced between Saba and Zek and then nodded. As if glad to be moving away from Saba, she sped toward her desk and began to rifle through a wad of papers, some of which were slabs of tightly-packed handwriting, while others were penciled sketches.

"I took extensive field notes. Sketches and the like. You may have access to them, and my interviews." She sounded almost eager as she pulled several free. "Whatever you need for your own investigation."

She'd been taken off the case and was still this—Saba stopped himself before he thought *diligent*.

Hah.

He walked forward and squinted at the papers around her. Several were old maps of Loefka Ward, and new sketches showed the crater and what had been obliterated. Seeing the damage laid out like that, so plainly and neatly, felt haunting.

An explosion might have been better.

He hated that thought. An event with more substance to it would have more to recover, but this unmaking tore at Saba's heart. To think parts of the world could just disappear like that . . . so much for legacy. So much for a lasting impact. So much for the hope of a body that he could recognize and love. What did any of it matter when the power of this breach could reduce so much to nothingness?

Diligence pulled out another sketch. She'd formed a circle of papers with herself at the center to mimic the placement of the device. "Close to the device, there were no bodies to speak of. Further out from the. . . effect? Incident? I don't know what to call it. Anyway, the remains became more . . . intact."

She spun the sketch around to Zek. Saba moved closer and peered over Zek's well-muscled shoulder, coming eye-to-eye with a very realistic depiction of a charred, blackened body. The corpse's limbs were intact and rigid at his side, head tilted to the left. Shadow obscured half of his face, and the other side showed his closed-eyed expression, mouth agape. What might have been grazes, bruises, or blood had been sketched onto his checks and arms, peeking out from the tattered ends of his partly disintegrated tunic.

Zek gingerly took the sketch and held it high. Saba pushed up onto the balls of his feet, conscious he was likely breathing onto the back of Zek's neck in an unsettling way. He squinted at the sketch. Diligence had diagnosed the state of the body: a broken rib, several smaller breaks in his fingers, some kind of bloody wound in his stomach.

Zek made a noise. "What was the state of other bodies in the area?"

Diligence stepped away from her depictions of the blast radius and gestured. "Take your pick."

Saba walked in a straight line, picking his way across the creaking floorboards, placing his feet in the gaps spaced between the paper. It was as Diligence described; the closer to the device, the less intact the bodies were. All the sketches stopped in an even circumference immediately next to the device to account for the sinkhole that appeared after the initial incident. But after that there were scattered dismembered limbs and odd shapes of flesh—made stranger by their neatness. Some were cut at the bone or at geometric angles. Saba had to remind himself that this wasn't a natural event; these people had disintegrated, unformed, fallen apart. The bodies came next, curled up in distress and reactive as the shock waves affected them.

And it was his fault.

Saba found his eyes welling, and he scrunched up his face in a desperate attempt to obscure those feelings. His cheeks were burning, and his chest felt heavy. Diligence stared at him curiously from afar, expression inscrutable in Saba's periphery. The comforting *thunk, thunk, thunk* of Zek's cane approached, and Zek patted him twice on the back. Saba squeezed his eyelids together. That scrap of comfort only made him want to cry more.

"Lord Doric was where?" Zek asked Diligence, voice quieter, like he didn't want to disturb Saba's melancholy.

Diligence gestured for the sketch and, with it in hand, stepped around toward the north of the site, directly west of the basilica. She placed the Lord of Veprak's sketched demise in an area with very few bodies and put her hands on her hips. Zek walked with her and squinted down at the final position.

He glanced back at Diligence, expression unreadable. "You're sure?"

Diligence frowned and gestured around the room, at the sheer amount of paperwork she'd done on this, and then made another flourish of a hand movement toward herself as if to say: *Diligence Inquisitor, it's in the name, Ambassador.*

Aloud she said, "Of course I'm sure, Ambassador."

Saba steadied his breathing and made himself pretend he felt perfectly fine. He moved forward for a better look at the diagrams, eager to know what had Zek questioning a woman whose name and demeanor suggested she was fairly infallible. But then he saw it. All of them had died in the outer rings of the Eye's effect. The bodies around the Lord of Veprak were in a similar state of charring, or disintegration, from the shockwaves. Very few, however, had any fractures—let alone the amount Lord Doric had.

Something clearly wasn't right about that. Zek must have been thinking the same thing, if his questions were anything to go by. As if hearing Saba's suspicion, Zek's eyes slid over to his. They stared at each other.

Saba gently shook his head, and Zek nodded in agreement. This felt conspiratorial and brilliant—a Ker and a Rezwyn of like mind.

For the first time in weeks, Saba felt useful, like he was more than his accusation. At once he bore the weight of the recorded destruction at his feet—and the knowledge that something was out of place.

"I wasn't told what happened to the body," Zek said, after clearing his throat. "Only that it wasn't . . . fit for return."

Diligence grimaced, her expression somehow toeing the line between disgust and apology. "Many of the bodies . . . disintegrated," she murmured. Then, almost defensively she added, "That's why we took the drawings. A team of us—artisans under my direction—sat sketching as quickly as we could."

Never mind.

Saba felt sick again. He stood rigid and feeling useless once again as Zek clarified, "You saw this happen."

"I did," Diligence said.

Which means the evidence is gone too. Saba hadn't fully considered that Lord Doric's corpse might have been a way to absolve him—but he felt the loss keenly anyway. That potential had vanished like the many caught at the center of the breach's unmaking.

Serves you right. You should never have even dreamed of the astral sea. You should never—

"So this is all that remains?" Zek's calm voice bludgeoned the anxious whining in Saba's head. The ambassador had bent down to inspect the sketch of the Lord of Veprak once more.

Diligence nodded in response, and Zek's face pinched together. He stood with a groan. "Thank you. Vasili, let's go."

"Wait," Saba said. Only one thing still had the power to absolve him. He turned to Diligence and his voice came out high. "My research notes."

Diligence's face collapsed into a near snarl. She folded her arms and looked toward the window, where the rest of Byrengrad was getting ready for sleep. "What about them?"

Saba frowned. "Do you have them? They aren't with the Scholar's Guild."

"Not that I have to tell you anything, Vasili, but no one knows where they are." She spun her head back, looked him up and down. "Is that what you wanted to hear?"

Saba fought the urge to put both his hands up. Diligence's tone was bitter and violent—and completely fucking uncalled for. Saba exhaled, impatience and anger overriding his earlier upset. The implication was unpleasant.

"They were confiscated by sentinels," Saba gritted out.

"Then show me the receipt," she said. "And I'll tell you where they were filed."

"I didn't get a receipt."

Diligence tilted her head and pursed her lips together. "Then either the people who confiscated them weren't sentinels . . . or else they weren't confiscated at all. Perhaps you've just put them somewhere very, very safe and then forgotten where to look?"

All of Saba's teeth slammed together as the dying, polite part of his mind wrangled his mouth shut. *Say nothing*, it told him. *Smile. Take that implication and deal with it later.* But he could feel his mouth twisting up into an unpleasant snarl.

Zek glanced between then and sighed. "Let's go," he said gently.

Only when Zek's finger grazed his arm could Saba move.

Chapter Nine

By the time they left Diligence, it was as if all the warmth in Byrengrad had been sapped away by the moon, and a night chill had settled through the streets. Their groom had fallen asleep, lulled by the safety offered by the two torch bearers, and Zek approached her slowly the way one might a sleeping cat. Zek rocked her awake with an apology and she smiled up at him, which was perhaps the first expression Saba had ever seen cross her face.

At the embassy, at least, a well-stoked fire had made Zek's room warm and filled with an orange glow. Saba found he could quickly brush off the cold, but even then, he still felt tense.

Zek and Saba were alone together. Which might—or perhaps should—have meant nothing. Though when he was anxious and a little feral, he couldn't really help but read into things, and thus Saba was seeing undecipherable language in everything: the emptiness of the room, Zek's silence, the shadows, the flickering of the lights.

Was Saba still a prisoner? He'd lived through weeks of guilt and nasty, unproductive thoughts, and now they had nowhere to go. Even focusing on this investigation felt hollow—not satisfactory to that gaping wound guilt had carved into his gut. Absolution couldn't be so close. But if he still remained a prisoner, then why had Zek brought him back here?

It was because he had nowhere else to go, of course.

Doubt sat in his gut and managed to break through the tipsy barrier alcohol had gifted him. It was beginning to feel like he could never be absolved from this, regardless of whether he had activated the Eye or not.

A dozen or so candles burned softly, which, along with the crackling fire, doused the room in a flare of sunset colors. In this low light, Zek shucked his outer jacket and threw it rather forcibly over one of the wingbacks with a sigh.

Despite the emptiness, the dim lighting worked in Saba's favor, draping Zek's strong form in a bold silhouette. The room smelled like Zek, which Saba could only identify through vague comparisons: a bit like salt spray, a bit like leather and dirt. Sweat, alcohol, wood—nothing that on its own should have elicited any kind of response from Saba. Yet he found himself breathing in. Deeply.

Fucking embarrassing.

"Not sure I like that woman," Zek muttered gruffly.

This startled Saba, because they hadn't said a word to each other since leaving Diligence Inquisitor to her almost-ritualistic spread of papers. Saba cleared his throat. "No?"

Zek pulled a face and seemed to think for a moment. Without looking at Saba, he wandered to the bar, popped the stopper, and decanted himself a drink. "Perhaps that's unfair of me," he said in the same murmuring tone. He threw the drink back with a sharp bite of a breath and poured two more drinks. He held both glasses in one hand, strong forefinger and thumb pressing the insides of the glasses together, and he walked over to Saba tiredly, as though his body ached. Saba gently pried one of the glasses from Zek's grip only to realize the ambassador was completely in another world. Brow furrowed and voice low he said, "She's close to it. Everyone is very close to it. It's difficult . . . knowing who to trust."

"Back to thinking I'm the culprit, are we?" Saba murmured with strained laugh. He grimaced.

Why did you say that? You shouldn't have said that.

At best it gave off an air of desperation, as if Saba was a feeble abandoned dog scrounging around for scraps.

Which, alright, fair. Given his current prerogative—follow Zek's orders without question—perhaps that assessment wasn't entirely off the mark. But at worst . . .

Zek was looking at him, and Saba's thought withered in his head. That stare lingered for a long moment, the Rezwyn's expression inscrutable, searching. Saba's smile slipped. What was he looking at? What did Zek see?

Zek only broke the stare to walk over to his wingback chair and slowly lower himself into it. The movement must have hurt; Zek face twisted with pain, and he arched his body this way and that to get comfortable. Whatever ached—and from the look on Zek's face, it was more than just his leg—hurt enough for him to swear loudly.

Saba hated that.

This was the longest Saba had been privy to Zek's pain, which felt at once a privilege and a burden of sorts. Zek was obviously used to this experience, but Saba wasn't sure where to look, wasn't sure how to react. Zek didn't want Saba's pity, he'd made that clear enough. But the emotion curling up in Saba's stomach was something else altogether. He didn't have pity for Zek. He had concern—out of place, uncomfortable, out of character concern. *Not only is Zek a Rezwyn*, Saba reminded himself, *but the bulk of those injuries were sustained in the war that destroyed my homeland.* Each time Saba's subconscious reminded him dryly of Zek's involvement in Kerinsk's collapse, Saba expected the knowledge would stick.

Well, it hadn't stuck yet.

Zek's pain, for lack of an eloquent way to put it, fucking sucked. Both for Zek, who had dealt with it for over half his life, and for Saba, who selfishly found it upsetting to bear witness to.

He sat down in his own chair without another word, just as Zek said, "I can't tell if you're flattering yourself or just trying to get my attention with these claims of your terrible evil."

Saba snorted. *Both*, he wanted to say. *Neither*. Some of this confusion inevitably came from his own guilt—he felt he should be seen as evil, felt himself helplessly holding his remorse in both hands with nowhere to put it.

See? I feel terrible. Take it from me—absolve me of it.

Only Zek couldn't do that. No one could.

Zek swirled his glass. "I think I can trust you, Vasili."

Saba jolted and flushed. Why was that enough to make him flush? *Embarrassing*. Saba sipped his drink and loosened his flamboyant outer jacket, right fingers working a few buttons free. He caught Zek watching him and wished he knew why Zek was willing to give him the benefit of the doubt.

Saba murmured, "I think I can trust you, too."

Zek smiled, an amused twist to his mouth and eyes.

"But don't make me regret saying that," Saba amended, because it felt too vulnerable to trust wholeheartedly.

Zek chuckled over his raised glass. "Likewise," he said. He sipped and his expression buckled into somber contemplation. "Tell me what you thought about the sketch of Lord Doric."

Saba thought back to the look he and Zek had shared. "I thought something seemed off. But I don't know what."

"The other bodies," Zek said quietly, as if coming to a realization, "were twisted up."

Saba had his own realization. "Oh. Because they reacted—to the device. Or the shockwaves."

Zek slapped his thigh and jabbed a finger excitedly in Saba's direction. "Exactly! Every other body showed signs of distress. Fighting back. Shielding their face. Reacting to the intense light."

"Except for Lord Doric," Saba said. He narrowed his eyes and drank deeply from his glass. He already had a buzz going from the Kerish liquor, and this drink mellowed him out even further. A gentle, buttery feeling began to spread in his chest. With his anxiety softening, he could mull this over more wholly. The Lord of Veprak had not reacted. He had not fought back. "Was he unconscious?"

Zek raised his brows as high as they would go and his whole forehead crinkled together. "Did he die there at all?" he asked irascibly.

Saba frowned, absorbing some of Zek's frustration as he considered the implication. The complexity of Lord Doric's demise only reinforced the mystery of the situation. Something about the question chilled Saba to his core. He ran his fingers through his hair as best he could with all the curls, and asked, "Well, if he *was* moved, does that mean whoever killed him is . . . responsible for the incident as well?"

Zek continued, oblivious to Saba's anxiety. "I don't think it can be unrelated," he said solemnly. Then he sighed, despondent, and added, "But then there are two mysteries: someone murdered the Lord of Veprak—and someone destroyed Loefka Ward and framed you."

Saba forced himself to look back at Zek. He shifted and leaned forward in his seat. The pair of them locked eyes.

Saba bit his lip. "Can it be the same person?"

Zek made a doubtful face. "Is anything ever so simple? It could be. But it could just as easily not be."

They lapsed into silence, into a banal, near-comforting quiet. Which agitated Saba further, because a great many people had died, and the astral sea was still bleeding into the world. He wasn't allowed to feel things like good or rested or peaceful until that was dealt with.

He scratched at his face and downed the rest of the drink, placing the glass on the ground. Then he doubled over and leaned on his knees, which were both vibrating with his anxiety.

"I need to get to the Eye," he whispered. Almost like a prayer. "I'm the only one who has any chance of closing the breach. No offence to Giste or Moss—but it's my design."

Zek, as always, looked serene. He gently knocked his head to one side. "You asked Diligence about your notes. Your research."

He did not sound concerned, but Saba still reacted poorly. His vision swam and the animal part of Saba leapt forward with its teeth bared in a snarl. Distantly, Saba knew he was being needlessly aggressive. He had the urge to defend his life's work and at once divorce himself from it. Because the truth was that, in among his own personal musings, the potential to expand the breach had been explored.

He'd written about it. And here was that destructive consequence.

"They've been stolen," he said hurriedly. His next words flew out before he could stop them. "Think about it. No way could someone create an opening capable of expanding at all, let alone from a fist-sized hole to man-sized breach, unless they read my notes and realized the Eye could do more than make a tiny puncture."

Zek frowned. His grip tightened on the arm of the chair as he leaned forward, breathing slowly. "What?"

Shit.

That rabid animal in Saba's gut fled from the forefront of his mind, leaving only an empty gap. Horror filled it, a great deluge of panic that pulsed through his body. What had he done? Why had he—said that?

Sternly and with precision, Zek said, "Vasili, you're keeping something from me."

Beyond the din of Saba's heartbeat and thick breathing, Zek's voice pierced through. He still didn't sound concerned, but his tone had taken on a sharp edge to it, scalpel-thin, precise. It made Saba want to cut his own stomach open, to bare it all to Luan Zek.

"No," Saba whispered nervously. "No, actually, I told you I was researching the astral sea to see if it was possible to get to the other side. The Eye—the hole made for *research*—was the start."

"But not the end goal," Zek clarified.

Saba scoffed and rolled his eyes. "Of course not."

Saba slammed his mouth shut. He'd wanted to say more. *What kind of scholar would I be if I stopped there? Why would Byrengrad offer us any financial resources for such a project if we only wanted to peer inside?*

This was the true crux of it. Trying to wrangle any funds free from the tight grip of the Triad proved consistently difficult. But framing their research as something with potential—either for expansion of the breach, the potential collection of ichor, or research that could aid in diplomatic relations, namely with the Rezwyn Empire—had been the thing to get their grant approved.

Looking back, it seemed a dangerous thing to offer anyone, let alone the Triad. But Saba had been desperate.

He was tense and lashing out, and Zek probably didn't deserve it. Saba had to be cautious; his reasons for opening this wound in the world were his own, and Zek could very easily find fault in that. The absolution Saba craved could be torn from his feeble grip.

You wanted to change your form so badly you have doomed an entire city.

If his own voice could turn to self-hatred so easily in response to the truth, he wondered what a Rezwyn might think of him.

Zek watched him carefully. He appeared concerned, like he was wrangling all his fear back behind the calm mask of his eyes. Was he giving Saba the benefit of the doubt?

He tilted forward, placing his empty glass on the carpeted ground beside the curled foot of the wingback. His right hand clenched around the hare-headed cane, and all the while, Zek did not dare look away from Saba.

"Everything in me is concerned about the expansion of an unstable breach. Why are you trying to get into the astral sea?" Zek asked carefully.

Whatever righteous defiance was left in Saba's body dwindled to nothingness. He still didn't speak, but not out of resistance; he just found he couldn't, that the muscles along his jaw wouldn't respond. The ache from the two punches he'd received that day began to thrum as he gritted his teeth. Speaking would be the equivalent of opening himself up, letting Zek see inside.

He didn't want to be that vulnerable. Not now, not ever.

Zek was saying, "You're not a stupid man. You know the nature of the place well; you're an expert. Rezwyns have never tried to get there physically because we've seen how it affects souls. They get corrupted—broken down or lost. You must have theorized the same thing to be possible, or expected, for the physical body. And based on what we saw in Loefka Ward, that theory is correct. Humans can't survive in there."

Saba closed his eyes very briefly. With his voice thick, sticking in his throat like paste, he managed to say, "I know."

Zek's brows came together. He shifted a fraction in his seat. He wanted to speak—Saba watched his jaw shift and open and close again as he thought better of it. Zek waited with patience—a foreign thing for Saba to bear witness to.

But what could he say? *Zek, I so often want to take the skin from my back and open up my ribs and rip the very core of me free just so I don't have to bear this body.*

Zek, if I could give half my life for the body I crave, I would do it in a heartbeat.

Zek, there's a part of me that almost does not care what's happened to Byrengrad if it means I have even half a chance to crawl into the astral sea and remake my whole body as fully male.

Desperation and panic and everything ugly spewed to the forefront of Saba's mind. He couldn't speak; he feared how Zek would look at him. He couldn't avoid speaking for much longer—Zek waited still, watching with concern.

Finally, Saba gasped and cleared his throat. White-lipped, he looked to the floor, since Zek's gaze was so blue and piercing that meeting those eyes might have spurred Saba to tear them out.

"Have you—" Saba started softly. He raised his voice a pitch and began again. "Have you ever wanted something so much that you became violent? To yourself, or to the world? You'd do anything—you'd bludgeon the logic, and you'd ignore every scrap of happiness until all you could feel was that *want*? And the feeling wasn't as simple as regret, but it hurt the same way, like you were grieving something you'd never had?" He glanced at Zek even though his roiling insides urged him away. "You ever felt that, Zek?"

The Rezwyn blinked at him. He cast a look at the ceiling and seemed to genuinely ponder Saba's question. "Perhaps not exactly as you have," he said, in the tones of a jaded soldier. "But I do know grief."

Right. Of course. The leg, and perhaps as well the loss of purpose, or a young man's expectation for his life beyond war. Different from the innate, intolerable hurricane of Saba's existence. But still grief.

They locked eyes. The severity of Zek's stare, or perhaps the sincerity of it, had Saba shivering as if left outside in the cold. When Saba felt this anguish—which was immense and sharp and aimed always at himself, with nowhere else to go—he could only ever describe it as complicated. He sat at the intersection of suffering and desire; what he craved was also the source of pain, what he longed for could never come to pass. Not in this plane.

Now, after telling Zek in simple terms what anchored his soul, what gave him purpose, the impossibility of his situation hit him. Sudden exhaustion, sudden pain, sudden embarrassment—all of it coalesced into a lump in his chest. And sitting there before Zek only made it worse, like he was on display, a grotesque curiosity to be ogled.

Stop it. Zek doesn't even know what you are. Does he?

Saba couldn't contend with the possibility Zek had seen through him, and so he launched up, ready to pour himself another drink.

"Would you mind?" Zek tapped his own glass with the end of his cane, and the gentle tinkling of wood on glass became aggravating daggers at the base of Saba's head.

Pick it up. Pour a drink. Calm down.

"Mhm," Saba said, rushing over to the bar. His hands shook as he decanted the liquor, and he took a quick shot before properly pouring out the glass. He exhaled and tried to get a hold of himself.

You're overreacting. You're being stupid.

If that thought was right, then this panic was ego and vanity grappling for the throne of Saba's mind. He cared so much about what he looked like, and sometimes he was afraid that he was ungrateful. Plenty of bodies ached, or were sick, or needed help. Saba squandered his able body with his longing to change it.

But then why did the very flesh of him react as if to a threat?

There was no threat. He was safe. Nothing was happening.

Saba pressed a hand to his chest, firmly massaging the balls of his fingers against the fleshy muscle above his heart, then lower, where he fancied that he could feel the crescent moon scars through his shirt. Part of him thought about telling Zek—but why should he? It was his business. It was irrelevant to the investigation.

And part of him didn't want Zek to look at him any differently.

"Alright over there?" Zek mumbled.

Saba jumped. "I'm sorry," he said, rushing back to press the glass into Zek's hand. Their fingers brushed together, and Zek's were rough, warm, made scratchy from labor. Saba hesitated before relinquishing the glass to him. *Idiot.*

"Whatever your reason, you don't have to tell me," Zek said. He looked up at Saba as he spoke, exposing the long, taut muscles in his neck. Shadows undulated over the prominent bump in his throat, which was positioned delectably, like a firm unripe fruit. Saba wanted to reach out and press the pad of his thumb against it—wanted to push, to feel the resistance, the rumble of Zek's sonorous voice as he responded to the pressure.

Something else was fruiting in Saba's body; he shuddered and stepped back until he was in his own chair and cradling the liquor-filled glass in both hands. Zek, whose head had tilted to watch Saba's retreat, said, "But I'd like to know this. *Why* do you think your research has been stolen?"

He wasn't going to press Saba further. How kind—how suspiciously kind.

Saba answered, "Because getting into the astral sea would require a hole much larger than a pinprick."

A flicker of vague panic cross Zek's face. "You wrote down how to make a larger breach?"

Saba gripped the glass more firmly and took a few aggravated sips from it. Earlier agitations had been blunted by Zek's kindness, but Saba felt himself grow defensive. If Zek spoke to him like Diligence Inquisitor, in that same near-disgusted tone, Saba was afraid he might cry.

"I wrote how it might be possible," he said curtly. "I was researching it. I've *been* researching it for years. I've tried everything from ichor-infused looking glass, to prayer, to Suoduny. The Eye is the culmination. But I didn't write out a handy step-by-step on how to destroy the city. I did . . .

discuss it, though. We made mention of the possibility when we applied to the Triad for funding."

If Zek noticed Saba's tone, he didn't acknowledge it. His gaze dropped down to his drink, which he swirled casually. After a beat he asked, "Are you suggesting part of *why* you were discredited was to gain access to your research?"

What other reason could there be? Zek had been the one to plant the thought that Saba had been scapegoated. But Saba, really, was a nothing scholar—so long as the status of his birth was kept under wraps too.

"Well, think about it. If someone found out I'm Kerish, the arcane research would only be icing on the cake." He swallowed hard. "I'm not Zvensian; I have no legal right to anything in this society."

"And the official reason for the confiscation was what? Dangerous research?"

Saba shrugged. "Pretty much."

He hadn't looked too closely when his access to scholarly privileges had been revoked. His physical access to the building made sense, as did anything financial. Technically, though, his own research should have been his to keep. Except, in the flurry of activity after his heritage was revealed, it had all happened so fast. Moss and Khajro had been formally censured, but Saba had been the one to take the legal fall.

Saba looked down at his hands and ran his finger over the indented lines in his palm. His mother had divined them once, and only once: A lifeline splintered, branches withering. A life marked by difficulties and constant struggle.

If Kerinsk had never fallen, if he had done what he'd been told and learned to be a princess and a queen, if he had ruled Kerinsk, would his palms have showed anything different? Or had this life always been his, from the moment he'd been born?

Saba shook out his hands. "The other thing is that Giste only became a paragon recently. After I was discredited."

"Ah." Zek's voice had a primness to it. He leaned back in his chair and raised an arched brow in Saba's direction.

Saba sighed. Giste might be innocent—her promotion down to chance. "It could be coincidence," he said.

Zek choked on his snort. "But how often do we get those?"

Saba laughed dryly. They lapsed into a relaxed silence Saba felt grateful for. The day had been paradoxical, at once dragging and speeding. Exhaustion—several months' worth of it—pressed dully at the back of Saba's eyelids. Sitting in such a large chair felt absurdly close to affection; the wide back and the high armrests comforted the animal of Saba's mind. *Relax*, it said, and he did. Even as anxiety pushed his heart rate higher, he could feel his body giving in to sleep.

But then Zek said, "I can't fully understand it. Why your heritage means you can't do well here."

Saba rapidly blinked sleep from his eyes and pushed himself more upright in his chair. A vision of Maksid came unbidden. Not the version he was now, cinched up in that stuffy sentinel garb, but how he'd been in Saba's youth: Scrappy, determined, deep hollows withering the fine skin beneath his eyes. His ruddy brown hair plastered to his face, dirt and blood and tears streaked down his cheeks, Maksid saying, "*We need to run. No, no. Mother's gone. We have to—*"

Stop thinking about that.

Time had changed Maksid, and he'd beaten himself into shape for Zvensian society like the bronze of his grotesque mask.

"You can do well if you lie," Saba said eventually. To give himself credit, too, he added, "I think I did quite well with lying."

Until he got caught, of course.

Zek snorted—perhaps didn't quite understand. Saba flexed his hands. Complications arose whenever he spoke about Kerish-Zvensian relations. Nationalists called for Kerish eradication or removal. They'd overstayed their welcome, apparently. But centuries ago, Kerinsk had been settled by the same people who settled Zvensia. They were sister cultures, with sister languages, only Kerinsk had been matriarchal and Zvensia had cooked up their Triad meritocracy.

Had it been reversed, could Saba say for certain Kerinsk would have accepted Zvensians with open arms?

His throat felt thick. "Zvensia never wanted us," he murmured. "So many of us spilled into their country. And a lot of us, myself included, wanted to get as far from our old country as we could. We pushed deep into Zvensia."

Zek wasn't snorting now. The mood was shifting, all the air in the room growing cold with it. A moment ago, Saba might have looked across at the chair opposite him and seen beauty in Zek's hulking form, warm desire clouding reality. Now, with the veil torn back from his eyes, Saba reminded himself exactly what Zek was. What he had done.

Don't say anything. Don't say—

"I'm not sure I can forgive you for it, Zek." Saba's tolerant, well-trained tongue gave way to a much more scornful voice. He flinched in surprise at how much heat flared in his words. "I can respect you, I can think you honorable—but you were part of the reason I never . . . had a home."

Zek's dreamy eyes did not flare in a tempest. In fact, he looked barely shaken at all. He opened his mouth, breath exhaling sharply as he started speaking and aborted the attempt. The Rezwyn breathed in deeply. "Should I tell you about it?"

A vague sick feeling flared to life in Saba's gut. This information was something he wanted, something he craved; half of it desired by the scholarly creature in his mind, and the rest by the child that had fled his homeland. Could Saba handle this information?

"Maybe," Saba said aloud. "But I'm scared to know, I think. I was nine when we fled. I wasn't even in the country when it fell to Rezwyn hands; twelve, I think I must have been. Thirteen? I don't know. We heard about it via town crier maybe a week after it happened."

"If it makes you feel any better, the man who ordered that invasion is dead," Zek said, with a tone that implied it certainly made *him* feel better.

Nio Beumeut had been emperor most of his life. He'd died a year earlier, replaced by Izra Dziove, though the circumstances regarding the late emperor's demise were . . . questionable at best. Wrapped in arcane scandal. For a long while, the empire's hold on its many acquisitions had been slipping. Some had been empire holdings in name alone and had operated with their own gods and language and cultures. The empire had abandoned its gods-given right to expand, perhaps only because the body of it became so bloated that any further expansion would make the whole overripe thing pop with soft rot. Toward the end of his life, Nio Beumeut had been smart enough to turn the focus internally.

But it didn't matter. The betrayal had happened. The treaty—the thing that Queen Deinah Vasyiluki had assumed protected her country—had been breached. It still didn't matter, even now that Dziove was apparently different, or better, or working somehow on unstitching the complex grasp the empire had on all its holdings.

It would never happen, not in any meaningful way, because without the empire's presence, Dziove would be out of a job. Besides, places like Kerinsk had been near razed. Absorbed wholly into empire borders. It was ethnocide, genocide, and all that had been left was a wound of a place, ripe for infection. And it was gangrenous now. Too late. Nothing could be done to wipe it clean of empire.

"So Nio Beumeut is dead." Saba scoffed loudly. "He's not dead in a way that matters."

Saba paused, expecting Zek to grow defensive, as most Rezwyns did when confronted with the truth: empire was a contagion. Instead, Zek gave no reaction except a slight smile.

Saba had no idea what that smile could mean.

"I have to disagree," Zek said. "Not just because Emperor Dziove is a good man, but because when Nio Beumeut finally died, I felt the most genuine relief I had in years."

It was like something you'd say to deliberately lower the inhibitions of a man destroyed by empire. Saba bit the soft flesh of his tongue and folded his arms, refusing to say anything. He should have known this sentiment of Zek's by now. Especially if it was true.

"Calm down, Vasili, I am no traitor."

Saba showed all his teeth. "Would make you more interesting."

"Gods," Zek said, voice airy. He pushed his thumb against his temple and glanced at Saba from under the shield of his hand. Saba thought he saw Zek's gaze drop low, skimming over his lip, or his chest. "You can't help yourself, can you?"

Saba smiled. Couldn't help the spread of that grin, couldn't stop his cheeks betraying him like that.

Zek sighed deeply and made a gesture in the air to summon his thoughts. "It's a complicated feeling. I was a soldier; I fought for the empire. You would think that'd make me a patriot, but this concept of Rezwyn superiority—it's bullshit."

Fuck. Whatever was happening felt better than flirting. It had the same dangerous quality as a confident proposition, and Saba's heart fluttered as if that's what Zek had asked him. He looked at the Rezwyn in the low light and found all he could see now was the stout bulk of him, the strength and the softness.

You're meant to be seeing an enemy.

Somewhat breathlessly, Saba said, "Does the emperor know you feel this way?"

Zek got up to pour yet another drink. Without looking at Saba he answered, "Of course. It's why he made me an ambassador."

Saba frowned. "What does that mean?"

The liquor trickled into the glass. Zek surveyed him now, over the top of his drink. "When Nio Beumeut died a year ago, there was dissent. A great number of people wanted to return to the old ways."

"Expansion?" Saba said hurriedly.

Zek nodded.

Saba knocked his head back against the wingback. Horrifying. The great conquering power of the Rezwyn Empire terrified him. Rightfully terrified a lot of people. The effects of their decades-long growth was still apparent; the displacements, the cultural clashes, the suffering of people still scrabbling to recover. All for gods that either did not exist or, at best, should have been too powerful to give a single shit about human worshippers.

"Emperor Dziove was determined to not let this happen. He allowed several western city-states their autonomy."

Which was exactly the kind of lukewarm take only a man raised in empire could offer. Saba rolled his eyes to the point they strained in his sockets. Zek could be kind, thoughtful, intelligent—and about as stupid as a log.

"I have a good reason to hate the empire," Saba said. "You can't . . . think I can excuse it all for the paltry offerings of your new emperor?"

Zek walked back over, but he turned to stare at Saba instead of sitting back in the wingback. "About my part in the fall of Kerinsk, I'm ashamed, Vasili. I admit it."

Saba blinked. It was a simple statement. It made Saba's heart lurch. He could barely parse Zek's expression from the shadows, but the Rezwyn's eyes glinted as firelight reflected off something wet.

"I . . ." Saba started. He had the urge to apologize—for what?—and stopped himself, because empire had never apologized to him. He sighed and squirmed and eventually gestured for Zek to sit back down just so he could avoid having that big form standing over him like that.

Zek continued, unperturbed, "Nio Beumeut sent me off to war at thirteen."

And the guilt was instant. Saba had judged him so quickly and wholly, assumed him a willing agent of the empire. Saba squeezed his eyes shut and pressed the tips of his nails into his palm. "Zek . . ."

"I was a loyalist then," Zek said, cutting off Saba's half-formed apology. "Raring at the bit. But that changed almost instantly. Why are you looking at me that?"

Zek's tone had an eerie calmness to it. He furrowed a brow at the look on Saba's face, which Saba himself felt pulling all his skin taut. Everything in his face went tight. He didn't know what to do with his hands, especially now that they were starting to grow clammy. What should he do? Comfort Zek? Stand up and drink a whole bottle of liquor in the hopes it numbed him?

Zek's tone grew dark. "Vasili, if you are pitying me—"

"I'm in awe of you," Saba said hurriedly. He sighed, rubbed at his temples where a bright pain had begun to spark. "It's not pity. I just—you were a child."

Zek stared at him, then dropped his gaze to his drink. He swirled it in the glass. His voice came out soft. "I told you—I felt the greatest relief of my life when Nio Beumeut died."

Saba watched the firelight ripple along his cheekbone. It was funny, how quiet and contemplative Zek truly was. The size of him, and Zek's innate confidence, had Saba expecting a different sort of man. But the very core of him was good, as if immune to disease, resistant to rot.

Saba had to ask. He finally answered Zek's first question with, "Will you tell me what happened?"

Without looking up, Zek nodded solemnly. "There's not much to tell. Not really. I fought. And people kept dying. A lot of friends. Lots of young people. But not me. I was Squadron Leader at fifteen, for all of six, seven months. Horse trampled my leg. I was lucky I got to keep it." He paused to sniff, and haltingly drank from his glass. Eventually he said, quite softly, "Then Kerinsk was officially annexed. But I had already been discharged."

Saba stayed silent. It wasn't that he didn't know what to say. Instead, it was becoming difficult to think of Zek as an enemy, in any respect. Yes, Saba's life was still on the line. And yes, Zek looked like he could crush Saba without a second thought. But the reality of who he was seemed to be constantly shifting.

Then, after meeting Saba's eye, Zek murmured, "I don't want you to look at me and see empire, Vasili."

Saba shivered.

Zek nodded toward the bed. "Get some sleep."

Saba flinched and looked back at the bed, then toward Zek. The conversation hadn't finished naturally. Clearly Zek no longer wanted to talk—or no longer could.

"Where . . .?" Saba left the rest of his question unasked.

Zek gently shook his head and closed his eyes, closed them as if to block Saba and the room and the whole world out.

"Chair's good enough for me," he said. "Don't have to get up again."

CHAPTER TEN

Saba woke at sunrise curled on his side and cradling himself fetally, muscle memory supplanting sleepy relaxation in his muscles. He woke sharply with an aggressive intake of breath; he was curled up near an embankment, dewy grass melting the dirt across his face to mud, with Maksid looming over him, maskless, a decade younger, forefinger pressed to his lips.

Be quiet. Don't move.

Only when Saba blinked again, Maksid wasn't there. Sunlight bubbled over the window as the sun rose, casting strangely amorphous shadows on the wall. Saba bit his tongue—at least he hadn't cried out, at least he hadn't woken weeping—and waited for the rapid beat of his heart to settle.

There had been an awful time, after he and Maksid had fled, where Saba had expected to die. Not from the war, not directly—not from a Rezwyn spearing him through the heart. But wartime made dogs of men, curdled good hearts, made people desperate. The townships around the capital of Kerinsk had been raided first. Pillaged, ravaged, destroyed, both supplies and people alike. It meant that anyone escaping Kerinsk proper had no immediate haven to flee to. It meant anyone running blindly along familiar paths like well established roads were often running into trouble. If not Rezwyns, opportunists. Bandits. Rapists. Thieves. People desperate enough to lose themselves to violence.

Saba didn't have to wonder why he was thinking about this. He only had to shift a fraction, skirt his leg down an inch, and he could see the blond head of a Rezwyn squadron leader sleeping peacefully in the wingback chair—facing away from both Saba and the door.

Saba's fingers pressed into the sheets. Disappointment and anger scorched at Saba's heart—where had all this softness come from? Had years poring over tomes weakened him to this? Here he was sleeping in nothing but a frilly shirt in the bed of the enemy; Saba hadn't felt so close to being a princess in years.

You should go. Get up, get dressed, and just—go. What would the queen say if she'd lived long enough to see you now?

Despite himself, Saba jolted.

The Rezwyns had a sprawling pantheon, a real, heartfelt belief in deities swirling just beyond human comprehension. When he'd been younger, still fighting to remove himself from that aching ruin of his new life after the war, Saba had wanted to believe. The existence of a god like Suoduny tempted him, blurred the edges of his reality to the point where Saba used to fancy that the veil between the astral sea and the material plane was little more than a water bubble—something he could press against until it popped. This was back when he believed he could brute-force his way into another plane of existence. Suoduny—fate, destiny, every possibility, like a condensed ball of choices and consequences—lured Saba out beyond the confines of dreary logic and proven theories. He had wanted the magic of a god to lift him from the truth—that even if magic existed in this world, it was just another chaotic force. Another thing that wouldn't bend to the whims of humans, simply because it didn't have the sentience to care.

But he'd always had a niggling fear that his mother—the queen, the dead woman, face opened in a half scream—would know. That his faith, or his interest, counted as betrayal. Saba had already left girlhood behind, and with it the promise of ever ruling matriarchal Kerinsk.

To be lured in by Rezwyn fancy was just another betrayal.

And now you're being lured in by a Rezwyn you fancy.

Saba's eyes flitted over to Zek's head. He gnawed on his

cheeks and sheathed his anxiety as best he could. The sunlight shone well over the windowpane now. It wouldn't be long before the other man woke up.

So what was Saba doing?

Either get up and run, or get up and stop overthinking.

He found he couldn't do either. He couldn't obey that aggressive, logical little voice in his mind. His eyes were drawn back to Zek, who at that moment was little more than a floating half head of blond hair. Nothing that should have caught Saba's attention. And yet.

Saba swallowed, reasoned himself out of this ridiculous, longing stare. All that talk with Zek the previous night had unsettled him.

I'm in awe of you, Saba had said. He'd meant it then; maybe the alcohol had been the thing to wear his defenses down.

Goodness in a Rezwyn doesn't eradicate the bad. It doesn't mean he can be absolved.

But who was Saba to think so earnestly about absolution, when he craved it like a starving, emaciated street dog, and snarled and gnashed at the man who had done nothing but help him?

You are that fucking little girl cowering in the grass while her brother protects her. You are still that stupid little girl, no matter how much you try and run, no matter how much you try and change—

Saba got up. Sweat pricked at his lower back and neck, and his skin itched. He had the urge to run, or fly, or smash through the glass and die bloodily in a mess of limbs—anything for this discomfort to stop. Standing up had done nothing to help obscure Zek, either. From this vantage, Saba now had a half view of his big form. He'd removed the tunic at some point in the night, probably warmed to sweating by the now dwindling fire. But this meant, of course, that Luan Zek wasn't wearing a shirt—which coincidentally was the only thing Saba was wearing.

A thick even down of brown hair covered Zek's chest and stomach. He was barrel-chested, broad, and fat, with one arm slung over the rise of his belly as he breathed deeply. Saba stared for too long and then shivered. All the heat from the previous day had been sapped out overnight, and he was shivering because of that. Certainly not because he liked what he saw.

He stumbled over to where he'd discarded his pants the previous night, roughly pulled them and his fine boots on, and went to the door with his hand outstretched.

He paused.

Leaving seemed very stupid, now that the sun was properly smiling on him, and the fog left by sleep had dissipated. Even the anxious chattering in his mind had faded.

Where would he go if he left? More so, why should he go? Zek had already offered him an escape and he'd refused it, specifically because he hadn't caused the event.

Saba Vasili was the only one who could close the breach.

A knock sounded. Saba flew backwards at the same time Zek cursed and peered around the back of the chair.

They met each other's eyes, and the look on Zek's face brought with it such reproach that Saba felt savagely stupid. Zek knew why he was up and creeping around by the door. Saba closed his eyes. He tried to will away from the flush from his cheeks, but there was no stopping the embarrassment of being caught.

"I'll get it," he said stiffly.

Zek grunted with permission.

On the other side of the door stood one of the embassy officials, who looked utterly perturbed that Saba had answered instead of Zek. Which either had something to do with knowing Saba's face, or what the official assumed about Saba's presence in the Rezwyn Ambassador's room. Most likely that weasely man from the main hall had started a rumor—one which Saba was almost painfully sorry wasn't true.

The bewildered official stood a head taller than Saba, with his brown hair slicked close to his scalp. His skin held a reddish tint to it, and he puckered his lips in an obvious show of distaste before he flicked the note he held up to Saba's face.

"For Ambassador Zek," he said.

Saba, feeling petty, leaned against the door frame and plucked the letter out of the man's fingers.

"Why, thank you very much," he said, scrunching his face up awfully. Then he slammed the door shut in the official's face.

Saba turned on his heel and marched the letter over to Zek, avoiding as best he could the rise and fall of Zek's large chest, the sheen of sweat tangled in his hair, the size of him—*for fuck's sake, Vasili, just hand over the letter.*

"Here." Saba glanced away as he passed it over, but when Zek didn't take it immediately, he found himself glancing back. The Rezwyn's fingers grazed against his. He edged the letter out very slowly, achingly slowly, from Saba's grip.

Zek frowned at him. "You weren't going to escape, were you?"

"Of course not!" Saba grinned automatically, even as the lie felt rotten in his gut. How could he explain the feeling to Zek?

I want to be done with this, but I know I can't. I had a moment of weakness. Yes, you offered me escape just last night—I'm just being silly.

It turned out he didn't need to defend himself at all. Zek gave an amused, all knowing smile before he opened the note. Quickly, though, that sweet, gentle expression—curved lips, twinkle in the eye, warmth that made Saba's chest seize—evaporated.

Shit.

Zek sighed loudly and stared out the window.

"Diligence Inquisitor will accompany us to Loefka Ward."

Saba made a little uncomfortable noise in the back of his throat. He'd wanted this, and also wanted it to be anyone other than the woman who'd been responsible for him shitting in a bucket for two weeks. "I thought she had no sway anymore," he said. "I thought she'd been removed from the case."

Zek shook his head and slowly stood up, making the whole very large and mostly naked thing impossible to ignore. "She was never replaced. They removed her after your accusation and assumed that would be the end of it."

And perhaps it would have been, if not for Zek. If not for the empire's strange interest in a horrible event occurring well outside their jurisdiction.

Where has suspicion gotten you thus far, Vasili?

Zek passed the note to Saba, and Saba took it carefully. It read:

> Ambassador Zek,
>
> Will accompany you and Vasili to the site to inspect device. Persistence Sage will allow this under my guidance. If Vasili is unable to turn off the device, Persistence Sage has forbidden him from any further tinkering in case of nefarious designs. Sentinels will be alerted and asked to mediate. Meet midmorning.
>
> Diligence

"*Nefarious designs?*" Saba wheezed, lips curling away from his teeth in a snarl. "Seriously?"

He couldn't quite tell if he should be flattered by her suspicion, which seemed to craft from conjecture an entirely different, far more bloodthirsty Saba Vasili. One who perhaps despised Zvensia for its treatment of his people. One with a little more backbone, a flair of personality. It was almost a disappointment for Saba to know he wasn't that person.

"Better find a way to shut the Eye down, Vasili," was all Zek said. He'd gotten up and, thankfully, had begun to dress. Saba could not stop himself from a final stolen glance at Zek's chest, large pectoral muscles stretching as Zek pulled his shirt over his head.

"I'll find a way," Saba murmured, pulling his gaze back to the letter. "But how does this relate to our Lord Doric? Won't Giste drive us away?"

"We know his injuries aren't consistent with the other casualties of the event. But I doubt Judge Hirunz will accept that at face value." Zek rubbed at his face and ran his fingers through his short hair, which felt strangely hypnotic to watch. Zek suddenly pointed at him. "And no serious inquiry can begin while the Eye is still operational. You are the only one who understands it well enough to disable it, and it will be integral that you do that if we're to inspect the area—not to mention ensuring the safety of the citizens who live there."

Saba pulled a face. He had—concerns—about the breach. More concerns than the relatively simple matter of it being there at all. Opening the breach, as a deliberate act, involved sigils. But given the expanded size of the existing hole, were the sigils used to open it the same ones Saba had been attempting to generate for his own plans? Never mind that he also lacked any knowledge of the sigils required to close it if the failsafe couldn't be relied upon. Either this breach was the result of a freak accident, or Saba's experimental research had, indeed, been used to open the tear by someone other than him—an idea that was terrifying in every respect.

Zek was saying, "Which is what you want, I assume, Vasili—to see what went wrong and to help people?"

Saba jolted and stayed very still. He nodded, because of course he wanted that, even if it was a rather reductionist summary of his desires.

Zek's face flickered. He sighed deeply. "I'm flattered you didn't walk out on me just now. But I'm not so naïve to think you're staying for late night talks about the complexities of empire. I offered you an out; you said no. You want to know what went wrong."

Perhaps it's not the only reason. Perhaps there are other reasons I want to stay. Saba did not say this. Saba could not even comprehend saying that. What he wanted could never come to pass, because Zek was Zek—a Rezwyn, an ambassador, and probably not a man who would be interested in someone like Saba.

"Yes," he said finally. "Yes, of course, I do."

Zek nodded at him and grabbed his coat. "Then let's find out what went wrong."

They arrived before Diligence or any sentinel, just as the sun had reached a comfortable height above the skyline. The heat felt liquid-thick today and carried a promise of sweat, to the point that Saba needed to shuck the beautiful outer coat and unlace his billowing shirt to endure it.

Once again, they left the gig a decent walk from the site itself. The groom passed Saba on her way to the front and grunted out an acknowledgement—the first bit of acceptance he'd gotten from her.

They picked their way through the rubble in silence, and Saba averted his gaze from the hundreds of specters his guilty mind conjured.

All this suffering, all this death, was because of him. Now he had a chance to prevent more of it from happening.

Overnight, Loefka Ward had changed only slightly; the crater was still razed, empty, and charred. But wooden scaffolding had been raised beneath the Eye, built upon from the early work Khajro had put together before his demise. The breach shimmered at him as if in greeting, and Saba could have sworn it looked—bigger.

As they began to descend into the crater, Giste saw them coming and shot out of the tent, folding her arms with animated disdain. But Moss—sweet Moss—grinned and waved, flanked by the ever-stoic Paladin Silvana. That one was a mystery, but her fondness for Moss endeared her to Saba—and her armor certainly made Saba want to get close to her, for his own selfish reasons. He climbed off the ladder and glanced toward the hole where the breach shimmered.

If one was clad in gedrokbone armor, sealed in, protected, could they survive actually entering the astral sea?

Zek grunted as he climbed down. His bad leg had flared up overnight, based on his cursing. No doubt sleeping upright had done nothing to help. At the bottom, Zek handed Saba his cane once more in what was rapidly become a ritual.

Saba took it carefully and felt the intimacy between them. He wanted more. More than this casual exchange; more than touching this cane. His mind started to wander, and a thought emerged unfinished: *I wish. . .*

But the object of his wish never came to him.

"You're back?" Giste seethed, just as Zek slipped the hare-headed cane from Saba's hand. "Remind me again how inspecting the device has anything to do with a foreign lord's death?"

Had she received no notice?

Saba wished he could act wild toward her. Gnash his teeth, growl, bark—make her just uncomfortable enough that she might turn this fetid attention elsewhere. He couldn't, of course; partially because he was a coward, and partially because Giste was now a Sage, and that had to mean something. If Saba wanted the title so badly, then it had to mean something.

Fortunately, Rezwyns had no qualms about sticking their noses in other peoples' problems—or even sovereignty, for that matter.

Zek's grip on his cane tightened. His mouth hardened into a thin line. "We won't disturb your work, Persistence Sage. But we do have reason to believe that Lord Doric's death may be a separate incident, and we need to inspect the area where Lord Doric's body was located. Vasili is here to see if he can deactivate the Eye so that we can do that safely."

Saba had to force himself not to smile.

Giste flinched, hunching into herself. Her masked face turned slowly between Zek and Saba. Even with her features covered, her disdain was palpable; the air grew thick with it, like an unpleasant fetor was being exhaled through the eye slits.

"*We*?" she hissed. Revulsion curled around the word. Saba flinched.

"You're a sorry looking lot."

All of them spun up toward the sound. Wrapped in the majesty of the morning sun and a dazzling high-necked dress, Diligence Inquisitor stood surveying them like royalty might their subjects. This wasn't an entirely apt description for someone like Diligence; she was more a predator, a carrion scavenger, waiting for her prey to tear itself apart.

A thick belt wrapped tight around her waist, and her dress had been gathered beneath it, bunched up to keep it dragging on the ground. Long, beautifully embossed leather boots peeked out from underneath the sandy-colored pleats. Unlike the previous night, today she wore a mask—a bronze so pale it shone like silver with black iron inlays. Her mousy colored hair had been tamed into intricate braids pinned across her head. Again, Saba was struck by how delicate she could make herself look, but she climbed down the ladder with ease and leaped off the bottom rung, dusting her hands off and placing them on her hips.

"Right." She sighed, dipping her head immediately to Giste in a paragon-specific acknowledgement. Giste's arms unwound from one another as if a sliver of respect was all it took for her to soften. Both Moss and Paladin Silvana introduced themselves in haste, and Diligence turned her attention to Zek.

"Ambassador Zek," she said, voice sagging with what Saba recognized as preemptive exhaustion. She obviously didn't want to be here—or rather, not here under these circumstances. Not beholden to the man she accused.

Zek half nodded in deference. "Inquisitor."

A beat passed—a deliberate, silent moment no one filled—and Saba bristled slightly, since the only person whose existence wasn't acknowledged was his own. Saba's nostrils flared.

"You've called me here. Ask me your questions."

Zek turned toward Diligence. "The wounds on Lord Doric's body were inconsistent with every other body that survived the initial blast. Correct?"

Diligence narrowed her eyes, and her neck sank into her shoulders. Zek had put her in an uncomfortable position, and her body couldn't seem to hide it. "Correct. There were gouges in the flesh. They could have been caused by rock shrapnel," she said unsteadily. "But . . . there were several others that were deeper. Those could have been caused before. But it's impossible to tell. The body didn't survive for long. It was right there—on the edge of the crater."

"So quite far away from the breach." Zek's eyes were warm, a summer storm over ocean. He pressed, "Were the wounds deep enough to be caused by a knife? Some other kind of sharp weapon?"

At this line of questioning, Diligence shot up straighter, like she'd wiggled onto the very knife Zek was referencing. "Well, yes, but—"

"I am trying to find the truth," Zek said through a tight smile. "That's all."

Diligence made a noise, but its meaning didn't escape her mask.

"Well," Diligence said dryly, "shouldn't we all be smiling? Vasili is here to close the breach, so you can dig around in the dirt for even more *truth*."

They all turned with the same amount of enthusiasm as Diligence allowed to coat her words. The rippling form of prismatic light had allure for Saba, at least. His heart clenched.

Don't, don't, don't. Don't close it. This is your only chance.

How horrible a person would he have to be to keep such a thing open for a chance at a life that had only ever existed in his mind?

"Let's do it then," he practically shouted. Zek looked at him, and Saba looked back, damn near praying the Rezwyn took his enthusiasm at face value. If anyone questioned him, if Saba had to, at any point, explain himself, then his resolve might buckle.

They walked out in silence. Diligence made a low whistle as they got close, which she did not elaborate on no matter how long Saba stared at her. Had it changed? Was she surprised by something? These would all be good details to know before he was to climb up awfully close to the belly of the proverbial beast.

Giste shot her arm out, superficially blocking the way to the scaffolding. Ewir, her sentinel guard dog, wasn't around this morning.

Giste's eyes were dark and her voice thin. "We wait for the sentinels."

Saba glanced at Zek, who looked very much like he wanted to speak. He did not, however—prevented by his lack of jurisdiction.

Which Saba figured did not *really* limit *him*.

"How much has it grown?" Saba asked quickly.

Giste scoffed. "I don't see what that has to do with—"

Bullshit. Even if it would cost the whole of Byrengrad, Saba doubted Giste would ever admit to being wrong. They didn't have time for this level of pride. He spun around.

"Moss?" he said.

Moss jolted, eyes darting between Silvana, Giste, and Saba.

Giste said, "Do *not*—"

"An arm span or so," Moss said.

Giste cursed for all the wrong reasons.

"An *arm span?*" Saba balked. His throat grew heavy, and everything inside him—the thick wet mass of his innards, the bones that made up his ribcage, the heart protected and fluttering beneath it all—burned in him as if infected. This wasn't right; it had only been a day.

Moss looked to Silvana, who nodded.

"Well, it's hard to be accurate, because it's rippling, but—yeah. A decent amount." She sounded so carefree that Saba thought he might be going insane. Where was the outrage? The fear? The hysterical insanity? They were scholars, like Saba. Surely they knew what this meant?

If Saba couldn't turn the device off now, how far could the breach go? Would it rupture through all of Zvensia? Or farther than that?

Silvana said, in the most amount of words Saba had ever heard from her, "There is. . . abundant ichor in that deathtrap device. Feeding it." She turned her eyes to the breach, and her lip curled away from her teeth in a snarl. "And it fluctuates for no reason we can fathom. Larger and smaller. A big flare came this morning, just after daybreak."

Her accent clipped several of the vowels, but her Zvensian was good enough that Saba couldn't pretend she didn't know what she was talking about.

Saba looked to Giste. Without a word, he tried to communicate that only he could stop it.

"It's your call," he murmured after a moment. "You are the sage."

Giste ground her teeth audibly then ran her hands through her hair, backing away. She turned to Moss and jabbed a finger in the little scholar's direction. "Watch him carefully. And Paladin Silvana, look out for any changes in the breach. I suppose it would be inconvenient if Vasili were to disintegrate." She then spun to Diligence, both her hands raised beside her head like surrender. "Inquisitor, I want your sign off on this. I will not endure the sentinels' wrath should they decide to show up and take offence at my decision."

"In regard to the Eye, Vasili is unfortunately the expert," Diligence drawled. "I have little sway, Persistence Sage, but I'll defend the action. The sooner we can stop this, the better." Seemingly satisfied with this, Giste turned back to Saba and raised that sharp-nailed finger in his direction. She punctuated every order with a jab at Saba's chest, seething, "Do *not* touch it. Do *not* tamper with it. Stay out of the beam of light. You will look *only.* You will look, and then you will report directly to me. Do you understand?"

Saba folded his arms and stepped back out of her aggressive range. "I'm not stupid, Giste."

Giste's eyes went wide beneath her mask. "*Persistence Sage*," she hissed. Then, "Saba, if you fuck this up, your life will be forfeit."

Zek stepped forward. Saba's heart swelled with the imagined defense until Zek said, "His life is the empire's first. If anyone kills him, it will be me."

Fantastic. Ideal, even.

Saba smiled as wide as he could manage because it felt like the appropriate response to Zek's little betrayal. He headed over to the scaffolding beneath the Eye and began to climb up, still smiling.

He said, "Maybe I'll let gravity do the job, if it'll save me coming back down to this horrible standoff."

Moss jumped forward and whispered, "Be careful." Her gentle smile was so sweet that Saba stopped shaking for a moment. He climbed up further, and then the world below him shrank until the hulking form of Luan Zek finally appeared manageable. "Try not to fall," he said.

Fuck Luan fucking Zek.

The palms of his hands clammed up with sweat as he climbed carefully up the makeshift ladder. He had climbed a good fourteen feet up before he came onto the platform within range of the Eye. The scaffolding had been built well away from the beam of ichor reflecting through the gedrokeye lens, and this meant Saba's range to access the Eye itself was poor. But he could see it clearly. It spun and whirred loudly, emitting a soft halo of the prismatic light associated with ichor.

It was made mostly of metal and looked like a distended cube. The gedrokeye lens, bowed and transparent, stared directly up at the breach. It concentrated the ichor being churned within the device itself so that an iridescent beam of energy flowed upwards. From afar, it appeared somewhat peaceful—a delightful, beautiful display of light and color locked in a dance. Nothing in Saba's mind screamed danger, but if he were to touch it, the skin of his mind might bubble up and melt, or wither away into nothingness. There was never any telling what exposure to large amounts of raw ichor would do to an individual, except that Saba could say with confidence that it might not end well.

The beam pulsed with mesmerizing consistency. Occasionally, tails of prismatic light would flare out, licking at the air. Saba attempted to count the intervals between these surges but found no consistent pattern. So be it.

Saba squinted at the Eye, attempting to discern how it sat in midair, whether anything helped it remain hovering like that. He came to no conclusion.

His staring revealed one other thing: the device was rotating, ever so slowly. As far as he could tell, a balanced equilibrium existed between the device and the breach; the ichor fed the open wound, but the astral sea itself was spilling out into Byrengrad, and Saba's device had been caught in this emanating energy.

He crouched lower and stared at the bottom of the device. The metal casing extended down, giving the device four feet to stand where the ground had once been. The bottom of the device showed Saba the innards of his creation, which were exposed for airflow to prevent overheating. And thank past-Saba's ingenuity for that.

He had to crouch down even farther to get beneath and find the failsafe. The mechanism was nestled to the left of the Eye's outer casing. It was a very simple valve made of gedrokbone, the only substance that could withstand and close off the flow of ichor, forcibly stopping it from reaching the gedrokeye lens. Closing the valve would close the breach.

If the failsafe had been there, of course.

But it wasn't. A conspicuous gap existed where the mechanism should have been. The failsafe wasn't broken; it had been removed entirely. Someone who knew how the Eye worked, who knew the importance of that mechanism in preventing all-out disaster, had tampered with it and pulled the mechanism free. This someone had gutted Saba's work, had doomed the whole ward to destruction.

Saba's body shook, fury and fear setting his veins alight. He pressed his head against the rough wooden platform, pressed until he felt the delicate skin of his forehead begin to strain. He had the urge to smash his head against it.

Do it. Just do it. Do everyone a favor and turn your over-zealous, ambitious mind to a pulp.

The pain would feel almost like a reward. The oblivion it promised had never looked more desirable than now. What was stopping him? Why shouldn't he just—end it? Step into the prismatic light and get unmade like everyone else?

You idiot. You idiot. *You made something more dangerous than any weapon, and you are surprised that it's been used as such*?

The guilt and the panic and the despair—it was too much. How was he meant to climb back down and face all of them now?

"Vasili?"

Saba flinched. He crawled to the edge of the scaffolding and peered down through bleary eyes, wiping tears from his dirt-covered cheeks. It was Zek. Of course it was Zek.

"Yeah. Yeah, I'm fine!" Saba called back, but his voice cracked with the strain of the lie.

He turned back to the device for another inspection. Saba had told Zek the truth about wanting to get into the astral sea, if not the reason why, and now he had to make sure his hunch was correct. Had the Eye been weaponized deliberately to destroyed Loefka Ward? Up until now, it could have been passed off as a mistake. An accident

Don't be a fool. This wasn't an accident.

But if it was—if it *could* have been—and Saba could be absolved of a sliver of this enormous and ever-growing guilt, then he needed to know.

The device rotated above him. Carved into the metal casing were sigils, symbols he had etched by hand with intention and ichor. These sigils kept the device stable. One sigil kept the flow of the ichor at a steady rate, feeding the breach at a sustainable pace to keep it open. For the original intended size of the rift, this would be a very small amount.

But with the size it was now, more ichor had to have been funneled through the Eye to grow it.

It's already bigger than it should be. You know what you're going to find.

As the device rotated, Saba caught sight of an additional sigil. Of course, he had been right. This sigil, a curved, bow shape struck through with three perpendicular lines, had been designed by Saba to grow the breach. But as far as Saba knew, it had not initially been etched into the Eye. Yet there it was.

A chill passed through Saba's body. He saw stars, felt the blood drain from his face and the cold settle in his feet and his stomach.

Someone had Saba's notes. Someone intentionally wanted the breach to grow. Zek had been right all along; Saba had been the scapegoat from the start.

But why?

All he had ever wanted, all he planned to do, was get to the other side of the astral sea. For himself. For nothing more nefarious than making true a fantasy he'd had for years, to become an ideal version of himself, a man whose vision he had been fostering in his head since he'd been a child. He had never wanted—this.

Rage burned in him. How dare they! How dare anyone take this from him, how dare they twist it like this. How dare they make what could have been a beautiful realization of self and make it selfish and guilt-laden and murderous? It was a violation of something deeply personal, and he felt at once stupid and horrible. To use his research like this was one thing. But to corrupt his dream? To take that—albeit flawed—wish of his, and taint it with the blood of his own people?

A breadth of conflicting emotions burned in his belly.

You can't stay here. You're upset. You need to breathe—get out.

That logical mind stepped forward to puppet Saba out of his panic. Sick with anxiety he began to climb back down. But then—the breach—*reacted.*

Saba shook, horrified. Dazed. A prismatic flare flashed from the column and curled around Saba's body. Saba felt it grasp something, strip away something vital; not to steal, not to absorb it or erase it—but to share it with Saba.

Every logical thought faded away, and Saba craned his head to stare at the breach, which seemed to respond to his stare with a light pulse. The flares around the glowing Eye ebbed, vaulting up through the air, and the more Saba stared at them the more convinced he became that they were sentient. Perhaps not like he was, not with blood and breath and soul. But they moved with purpose. For some reason he put his hand out, and the wisps erupted toward him with avidity, snaking around his arm, pressing into the pads of his fingers, edging his fingernails up to slip under them. Nausea rumbled in his belly, but it was dampened by a woozy haze. All fear, all self-concern, fell away into nothing. The breach's flares beckoned, and Saba felt as though he might willingly slip off the ladder to the ground below—as if he might crawl into the astral sea and let it take him.

A vague voice resisted in his mind, straining to get out. *You are touching the astral sea. You are a fool, Saba Vasili, and dying might not be the worst that could happen to you if you go in completely.*

He should be flailing. He should be pulling his hand away. The power of the exposed breach could unmake things; if he stayed close, if he let it curl up his body, he might simply cease to exist. But the tendrils of ichor pulled back when the breach pulsed again.

Saba sucked in a breath. Sweat pricked at his forehead, making his temples slick and his eyes sting. He blinked rapidly, and before he could understand it further, a vision resolved in his mind.

It had the consistency of a memory painted over with a dreamlike fog—a silhouette stood before him and phased ever so slowly into someone familiar. Saba's chest seized. He had a brazen thirst for the male body he saw; it was everything he had ever wanted. This fantasy of who he might be, this dream of the man he longed to become, was a lure he wanted badly to follow. He saw the idealized version of himself standing in the ether, tall and broad shouldered, strong and handsome.

The astral sea is showing you what you want. That's all that is happening.

But then again, he used to theorize about this: that the astral sea might actually feed off emotion.

Saba squeezed his eyes shut against the image, shaking and embarrassed that the core of him—a pathetic *character*, an impossible ideal—might be the loudest thing in his mind, so loud that an entirely different plane of existence recognized and reflected it.

Saba's stomach dropped, and the breach blared in response, as though it was listening to him or responding to him. He had gone and done something irrevocable by touching it. After a life filled with stupid moments, he still managed to feel surprised at this one. Something in the astral sea had connected to him.

But that made sense, didn't it? The Rezwyns called this sentience Suoduny. They prayed to it, asked it for intervention. Wasn't making the Eye just a different type of prayer? A mechanical request to petition this force for help?

The force of the pulsations from the breach made the scaffolding sway. Saba flattened against it and yelped, his heart hammering as he almost lost his balance.

"Vasili?"

The voice echoed. Saba looked down to find Zek staring up. The Rezwyn was leaning on his cane. Shadow obscured his face, hiding his expression. Saba tentatively stepped toward the ladder. The breached sparked and pulsed again.

Zek jolted forward like he'd been pushed. "Vasili, get down!"

Saba shook—shook with fear and distress. But he scrambled down—just as the bottom legs of the scaffolding collapsed.

Shock rushed him. The ladder he clung to went careening off at an angle. The ground hurtled up to meet up.

"Jump!" Zek yelled, eyes blown wide.

Saba's body moved before he registered Zek's voice, and he leapt from the collapsing scaffolding—into Zek.

A dizzying moment passed where Saba was in the air and Zek was on the ground, arms around him. Then time caught up and they fell together. The landing felt dull and sudden, knocking both sense and air out of Saba's body as they sprawled back in the dust. Saba's face rested against the soft rise of Zek's chest. He thought about crying, burying his face into the other man's chest and hoping for comfort, hoping Zek would embrace him.

His shame would be too strong, though, if he did that.

Saba felt very weak. Exhaustion and despair had a reek to it, a putrefying, sweat-coated scent he was certain leaked from every pore. On the other hand, Zek smelled somehow familiar. It was all Saba wanted to fall asleep right then and there. Weakly, he pulled back from Zek's chest and rolled off into the dust. Tears had gathered at the corner of Saba's eyes—would it be such a bad thing to sleep?

"What happened?" Zek mumbled. He shuffled and grunted as he sat up. "Vasili, look at me. What did you see?"

Giste stepped forward with her arms crossed. "Well?" she snapped.

Diligence, Silvana and Mossinne all waited, pinning him down with their eyes.

Saba had to report. He gulped back his shock and the adrenaline shake that was making him unsteady on his feet. He had to report—though perhaps not everything. Perhaps not the kiss of the breach. He would keep the image he was shown in the astral sea to himself. The sigils, too. But the rest he had to say aloud.

"The failsafe mechanism isn't working." His voice sounded barely like his own, croaky and flat.

"What?" Moss whispered.

"As in," Giste said slowly, clarifying, "it's broken?"

"As in," Saba said, rolling his achingly dry eyes toward Giste, "it's been removed."

"So you cannot close it today?" Diligence asked.

Saba shook his head. He wanted to say more. Did she not understand the severity of what he was saying? There would be no closing it today, tomorrow, or the next until they remanufactured the failsafe. Saba felt certain there would be no finding the old one.

But he said none of this. Diligence sighed heavily and looked around. "Then there is no reason for me to stay. I will be reporting these events to Judge Hirunz."

No one bothered trying to stop her. She left quickly, and Saba was grateful for it, because he had to contend with Giste and Moss staring at him—staring in horror.

He couldn't bring himself to speak. The failsafe had been removed, and the breach was expanding. Both Moss and Giste knew by now about the nature of his research; he had never tested the sigils he'd designed on anything, let alone an open breach. Without the failsafe, what did that mean for the Eye? If the sigils had been designed to grow the breach rather than contain it, disrupting the gedrokeye lens might make things worse.

So how was Saba meant to stop it? And what had it been attempting to communicate by showing him that vision of his wished-for self? Most importantly, how had he survived that light that had unmade so many others?

"*Vasili!*"

Saba twisted around in the dust and pushed himself up. Gravity dislodged a few tears from his eyes, and they drizzled slowly down his face. He had to blink them away and squint; the morning sun illuminated four bronzed figures. Giste's sentinel protection had finally arrived. But that voice, and the leader of the pack, could only be Maksid.

Either his brother kept being assigned to him by chance, or Maksid kept asking for it, which Saba felt to be quite flattering, especially when his brother was so clearly filled with rage.

Maksid tilted his head as he got closer. "And Ambassador Zek." Maksid crossed his arms. He ignored the others entirely and kept his rancid, righteous gaze on Zek. "I thought we agreed you were only authorized to investigate the circumstances surrounding the Lord of Veprak's demise."

Zek made a noise under his breath—a Doskorian curse, Saba thought—and took his time standing up and brushing dust from his trousers. He stretched with his eyes closed and murmured nonchalantly, "And I recall asking if justice truly is something you value."

Zek opened his eyes and struck Maksid with dazzling blue. His mouth twitched in a barely contained sneer, and the muscles in his jaw tensed and untensed in unison with his hand flexing on the hare-headed cane. "I *am* investigating the circumstances surrounding the Lord of Veprak's demise. Diligence Inquisitor's diagrams of his injuries are inconsistent with every other body recovered from the unmaking event. How can that be? Conveniently, of course, the body disintegrated—the inquisitor's drawings are all that remain of my charge. But this overbearing bureaucracy is doing neither of us any favors—except that the Inquisitor's meticulous paperwork reveals an extreme inconsistency in the condition of Lord Doric's body and the other victims of the incident."

Maksid narrowed his eyes. "What kind of inconsistency?"

Zek didn't miss a beat. "When the Empire is ready to show its findings, it will. But not before every avenue has been explored. Perhaps Lord Doric's condition was indeed caused by the device. But perhaps not." He had stepped forward as he spoke, walked until they were chest to chest and he could tower over Maksid with a dignified, unspoken superiority that made Saba somewhat flustered to bear witness to.

Maksid said, "Vasili should not be so close to the Eye."

"I allowed it," Giste said, which surprised Saba. "But only after Diligence Inquisitor gave *her* allowance. And Vasili has identified our problem with ease. The failsafe mechanism is not incapacitated. It has been removed entirely."

"Meaning what?" Maksid asked. He sounded dismissive, aggravated. The other three sentinels swayed behind him, clearly attempting to match the volatility of his mood. Tension clogged the air; the wind seemed to avoid the dead ward entirely, and somehow, even with the sky above, Saba began to feel suffocated.

He faced Maksid head on and said slowly, "Meaning someone with knowledge of the device tampered with it. Not me though. I was in prison. Everybody knows that."

Maksid stared at him. Saba wished he could see his brother's face and instead imagined it—the clammy, pale realization leeching blood away from his cheeks, the dawning horror of this new reality they had to contend with.

Shakily he asked, "What does that mean for the breach?"

Saba didn't answer.

Instead, it was sweet, tiny Moss who cleared her throat and said, "Well . . . we've already established it won't go away until the ichor runs out . . . if it runs out."

He wished it was still that simple. Now he'd seen the sigils, now he knew they were scratched into the surface of the device, made one with it, instructing it to expand, Saba longed for the simplicity of merely waiting for the ichor to run out.

"The plan hasn't changed. We must destroy the device," Giste said slowly. She waited a beat, breath catching like she'd expected an interruption. She frowned and turned bodily to face Saba. "You're not fighting me on that, Vasili?"

Saba stared at her. What could he say?

No, I still want to transmogrify into the version of myself I've been keeping in my head like a pet since I was a child. Don't destroy the device that will unmake the world.

Besides, who else knew about Saba's research?

He shrugged, attempting to play off his hesitation as contemplation. "We don't know what will disrupt it. If we don't wholly destroy the lens, we could make it worse. We could try to remake the failsafe device, but that would require getting close, dismantling it, and reinserting it all without upsetting the breach further."

"What if we try to move it?" Paladin Silvana asked.

Without a word, Moss and Saba glanced at one another.

Giste said, "Well, we can't ensure equilibrium. We can only control our side of the breach. Who knows what's happening in the astral sea? Moving it could make it worse—we should destroy it."

"And if we end up with an imperfect or shattered lens that refracts ichor in a hundred directions?" Saba spat. To hell with this. His body ached, and the device of his creation was probably going to eat the city.

It was clear that Giste desperately craved to appear in control of this situation, but they needed to work together. He stalked forward, hoping Giste would see his sincerity in the sweaty, pained expression on his face. "There's no failsafe to shut it off before the ichor runs out. Are we equipped to deal with the possibility of dozens of tiny breaches all across the city?"

Let alone the sigils! One breach was bad enough, but a dozen of them, all operating under the same instructions as the first? All of them growing exponentially, consuming all of Byrengrad, unmaking the city itself?

Saba blinked rapidly. He probably looked insane. Zek stared at him, not unkindly, and mouthed, *Are you alright?*

Saba felt himself flush. His shoulders ached from the hunch in which he held them, and the persistent pulsing pain in his fingers had begun to refer to the base of his skull. Sweat dripped down his neck. He needed bandages. A bath. A drink. Not the raised brow of a very handsome man, not the questioning cock of his head.

Saba nodded, just the once. But Zek did not look away.

"The small one is right," Silvana said gruffly.

Saba turned to her, aghast. "Moss is *two heads* shorter than me."

Silvana ignored this outcry and murmured something to Moss in a low voice. Moss responded immediately, jumping into action to rummage at her belt. Quickly she tugged out a tiny, well-worn manuscript and relinquished it to the paladin.

"From Usleth," Silvana said. She drummed her fingernails on the leather cover. "Very old."

She quickly flipped to a page, attempted to translate, and then made a frustrated noise.

Zek stepped forward. "May I?"

"You speak Uslethian?" Moss asked in awe. Her eyes went very wide, and Saba recognized her expression as one of respect. Learned people had always resonated with her.

"Rather poorly," Zek admitted.

Was that shame? Saba supposed he'd only needed the language during his time as a soldier.

Moss rolled her eyes. "Oh, better than me, I bet. Vana?"

Zek said something to Silvana then in stilted Uslethian, which earned him a smile so dazzling it almost rivalled the paladin's nacreous armor. She handed over the manuscript, and Zek stood for a moment, mumbling to himself as he parsed it.

Then he said, "Ah. Gedrok Ach Meedin, the Mad King who consigned his eternal soul to the astrok-mer in the hopes of being reborn."

Silvana smiled and nodded.

Zek returned to the manuscript. He cleared his throat. "I'm no scholar, but this is an . . . old treatise on the creation of the Uslethian Paladin Forge. About the forge's creation. What went wrong, what went right," Zek said, not understanding that this was material worth frothing at the mouth over. "Old stuff."

Moss scooted closer. Gazing at the book, her eyes lit with something close to lust.

Silvana leaned over Zek's shoulder. She was barely shorter than him, and so could easily meet his eyes as she said, "This part is about exposure to ichor. Some people can endure it. No one knows why. But most cannot and go mad."

She turned the page. Zek swung the manuscript around for everyone to see. Giste leaned forward, and, rather comically, all four sentinels leaned back. Saba snorted, and at once, unbidden, Moss and Saba moved to either side to inspect the manuscript. Saba turned the page back to the sketch showing how the Uslethian Paladin Forge shielded the surrounding city from the ichor that they used when crafting gedrokbone into their shining armor. He ran his fingers over it, accidentally skimming the rough skin on Zek's index finger. Saba flinched as if burned.

Focus. What do you see?

He turned his attention back to the page. The wisps of smoke bore a striking resemblance to the wisps of ichor that had swirled around him in the breach, and so Saba understood immediately.

"The Uslethians imbued the building with ichor," he said wonderingly. "The sketch shows that, even if the forge was exposed, the ichor would be refracted inside the walls. And if only paladins worked there, they'd be relatively safe. The ichor wouldn't spread. Is that right?"

Silvana nodded and pointed to her armor. "Perhaps if we cannot dismantle the Eye, we can seal it away."

"Seal it away?" Saba said, and then sighed, because he understood what had to be done.

"You're suggesting we build another casing for the device out of gedrokbone. Then we can enclose and safely move it, keeping the breach inside until the ichor runs out?"

Silvana nodded. "That's right."

It could work. But it would require a lot of gedrokbone.

"Two plans," Saba said. "We make a failsafe device to replace the one that's missing. For whatever reason, if we fail in this, then we need to contain the Eye. Still, the only people I know of who can access illicit gedrok materials are. . . well, I'd rather not add another crime to my name."

He looked to Maksid as he spoke.

His brother sighed heavily, raising a hand to the back of his neck. "Does the Sage concur?"

Giste had her arms folded. She turned to Moss, then Silvana, then back to the breach. Eventually she spoke. "I see no other way. Mossinne and Paladin Silvana, please accompany Vasili and the ambassador; you will inevitably need to be consulted on how to build this."

Both Moss and Silvana nodded enthusiastically. Moss made an excited face and silently vibrated when Saba looked her way—this felt like old times. Saba could almost be excited if not for the growing dread in his gut.

But Maksid had to ruin things by asking, rather cattily, "And why, exactly, should the ambassador accompany you? Surely this is beyond his jurisdiction."

Zek smiled. "It has nothing to do with jurisdiction. Saba Vasili is still my prisoner. If I don't consent to his involvement, then he's not going anywhere or doing anything."

Giste opened her mouth, clearly outraged by Zek's arrogance.

Zek continued, "However, as a representative of the Rezwyn Emperor I would be happy to render assistance in this Zvensian domestic matter and accompany Saba Vasili wherever Persistence Sage requests he go."

Stiffly, Giste nodded. "I request it."

Maksid sighed. He turned to the other sentinels and sent them away wordlessly.

In the time it took them to scale the crater, Maksid waited, and everyone waited with him. Saba watched his craned neck and the way the sunlight spilled over his bronze mask, which, from this angle, gave the amusing impression that the gnarled, screaming face was directing its ire at the sun. But as soon as the sentinels had climbed out of the pit and disappeared from view, Maksid turned to Saba and grabbed him.

"You mean to go to the underdark, don't you?"

The tenebrous underdark was an underground labyrinth of natural cave systems and tunnels beneath the city. It had been co-opted years ago by less scrupulous folk, who had outfitted it and made it the site of a bazaar for black market goods and hard to find wares, perfect for scholars unable to successfully research anything on a Triad budget.

Maksid's tone held a close approximation of brotherly concern, though a sentinel's disapproval undercut it. Saba folded his arms. Waiting for Zvensian bureaucracy would kill them. He said bluntly, "If we did it Zvensia's way, we would write to Usleth, petition the king, beg for some legally acquired gedrok material, ship it back, build it—months would go by." He stared at his brother. "We don't have months."

To Saba's great surprise, Maksid said, "I know."

Saba flared his nostrils, shocked into laughter. He narrowed his eyes. "Justice Sentinel," he said playfully, "what has gotten into you?"

"Nothing," Maksid said, voice growing hard and defensive.

"Oh, don't nothing me. You're skirting bureaucratic protocol," Saba said. Dizziness whirled in his mind; this behavior felt as dazzling to him as some grand scholarly discovery might. He kicked Maksid in the shin. "Are you feeling quite alright?"

"Stop it," Maksid said.

Saba smiled. "No. I don't want to."

Maksid mumbled something that sounded like, "*For fuck's sake,*" and turned with a heavy sigh to Zek. "If you're recognized, ambassador, it would be . . . undesirable. But if I accompany you—"

"Please," Saba scoffed. "If you show up, paragon mask and all, the whole market will implode in on itself. We'll get nowhere."

"So, we wear disguises."

Everyone spun toward Moss, who blinked innocently at all of them.

"What?" she said, shrugging. "Saba's recognizable right now, especially because of his hair. The ambassador is too, in a way. A few changes, some different clothes for Zek—all anyone will see is some random hunk with really good shoulders."

Everyone continued staring at Moss.

Saba mouthed *really good shoulders* at her with a raised brow—a raised brow in agreement, because Zek's frame truly was quite impressive. A look of horror dawned on Moss's face as she registered what she'd said.

"Sorry," she said, hands out to assuage Zek. "Sorry, was that weird?"

"Not at all," Zek said, and he smiled this gentle, warm smile that had Saba's hand flexing and unflexing.

Moss visibly unwound. She put a hand over her heart and looked up at Silvana, who, Saba noticed, had been watching Moss the whole time. "Good. *Good.* Then—it's decided? There's plenty of materials at the Scholar's Building. You'll need some less pretty clothes, but otherwise, we can do everything there, and—"

Giste said, "Well, now, I never said—"

"Oh, but please?" Moss asked, with no small amount of sweetness.

No one was immune to Moss. Giste looked up at the sky, as if in prayer, and then dropped her head to look at Maksid. Dryly and quickly, she said, "I would need an assurance from Justice Sentinel that the Scholar's Guild will in no way be held accountable for this."

Maksid balked. "I—I can't assure—"

"I'm saying that if they're caught you will take the fall," Giste clarified.

Maksid stood still, frozen in discomfort. He shifted from foot to foot, made a half-aborted motion with his hand, and then slackened in acquiescence. "Fine. Fine. But hopefully—if Judge Hirunz sees and understands that we have closed the breach, he may be more forgiving."

"Well, we'll do our very best," Saba said with a grin. They stared at each other, and something about Maksid standing there, hiding behind his sentinel mask and his sentinel title, infuriated Saba so wholly he realized he would never be able to castrate that fury. Seeing his brother's face obscured by that gnarled bronze only made the feeling worse.

Oblivious to this, Moss clapped her hands together. Saba was shaken from his animosity.

"Wonderful!" she said. "Shall we?"

Chapter Eleven

They split up after that, all of them crawling out of the razed ward like dusty vermin and skittering off. Giste went to work on acquiring the extensive funds necessary to make any kind of purchase at the market, and Maksid sulked off to his quarters, presumably to lie in the dark and hope he never had to make good on his promise. This left Saba, Zek, Moss and Silvana to make their way to the Scholar's Building.

Zek and Saba rode in the gig, and Moss rode at the back with the groom. Silvana rode alongside them on a horse, but noticeably hung back. Saba heard Silvana and Moss conversing, and then a third voice—the groom. Within a minute, she was laughing—the hilarity of the contrast between how the girl reacted to Saba and how she reacted to Moss almost made Saba laugh.

Though his mind was on other things.

He directed Zek toward the building, which he hadn't visited since his exile. But otherwise, he was contending with half a dozen loud thoughts clamoring for his attention.

It felt good to have a purpose again; Saba reveled in the certainty of his own importance, which made ignoring the death and destruction that much easier. But each time he let himself feel it—let the true despair of those deaths flood his system—he felt, too, the tug of the breach in response. Like his ligaments had been pulled taught, a fishing line hooked into the tendon and tugging. Ignoring it felt impossible. Made him feel insane with confusion. How could he have touched the breach and not been unmade?

The first explanation was more denial than truth. He'd imagined touching it—he must have, or he wouldn't be here next to Zek.

You touched it. You felt it. And it felt you.

He knew if he were to look at the breach, he would see it react to him. He knew, too, that he should tell someone. Giste was out of the question. But Zek . . .

Only, Saba didn't want to. Not because he was particularly worried about Zek's reaction, but because he had imprinted on the astral sea the way small children do their toys, and now he felt a companionship to the open bleeding wound of it, like the impossible, inhuman energy could understand him more wholly than anyone made of flesh and blood.

Illogically, he thought maybe that could be why he wasn't unmade: that the raw power in the astral sea had seen the core of him and found him worthy.

The truth—developed by his scholarly mind—decided on something more sober. Something about him had protected him or at least made him briefly immune.

But what?

Saba tried to clear his mind. The closer they got to his old haunt, the harder it was to keep his mood from slipping low. If it wasn't what happened to Loefka Ward, then it was the mystery of the breach. If it wasn't that, it was his exile. And if it wasn't that, it was something else. Too many things were making him feel low lately.

These emotions were different to the more overwhelming guilt he felt about the razed ward—thankfully Saba's emotions had their priorities straight. But the sheer enormity of that tragedy made it difficult to swallow. His feelings numbed out eventually, leaving him hollow and distracted. In the grand scheme of things, returning to the Scholar's Building he had been rejected from was a much smaller wound—but that made it far easier to feel it keenly.

The building itself had never hurt Saba; he had wanted very much to be welcomed into its halls, to lose himself in tomes and study, and to smell always vaguely of burning candles and the slight pungent scent of old books—which sounded rather dire now, for a life goal, but that was who Saba was. Perched in the eastern part of the Padke Ward and carved from the white rock of Byrengrad, the Scholar's Building was a series of small cave-like rooms for study, stone arches, a simply unnecessary number of candles positioned in nooks in the wall, and the space was filled always with some of the most pedantic people in the country, Saba included, naturally. An interlocking web of ivy festooned strips of the exterior white rock in inconsistent bursts, forming an awning of green above the entrance where the vines were most concentrated.

Moss led them inside without ceremony, but Saba hadn't returned here since his discreditation. He refused to show it on his face, but his body lurched as he stepped over that threshold, and the meaning of his return settled in him. He came back not as a scholar by title, but as an accused criminal, and everything he had done to be worthy of this place once again felt out of reach.

But Saba was no stranger to feeling like an interloper everywhere—even in his own skin. He balled his fists, accepted the bite of his fingernail into his palm, and let Moss lead him through his old home.

"So, we have to go upstairs, right up to the top. You remember—of course you do," Moss babbled. She glanced sheepishly at Zek and said, "Ambassador, for someone of your standing, it'll be best if we make you less recognizable. The best place to do that is right up top. There's, uh . . . there's stairs."

Zek nodded. "I'll be fine, Mossinne. Thank you."

She smiled at him, then up at Silvana, and said, "Right," suddenly definitive and certain as she began to lead them.

Though much of the building was humble, heavy embellishment decorated the central atrium. It consisted of a large communal space for study, an array of regularly referenced books and scrolls stored in stone walls, and large wooden tables spanning wall to wall. Young scholars chattered and scribbled furiously, and a great many looked up to watch Saba pass—which started a whisper immediately, like the chittering of summer bugs, an incessant and aggravating noise that might as well have been outright mockery.

"Ignore the children," Moss said. She shot them all a look as she passed, her expression uncharacteristically dark, and she said loud enough for them to hear, "Half aren't even real scholars yet. They have entrance exams to worry about."

This earned a few outraged shouts, and when Moss turned around, Saba flipped the whole catty lot of them off just to hear the sweet dulcet tones of teenaged fury.

Once a wall swallowed the open study hall, and they were left in the embellished hallway, Saba slowed his steps. Moss seemed to subconsciously recognize his need to linger, since she slowed, too, and nodded at him, as if to give him permission to wander slowly. She and Silvana walked ahead, and Saba imagined himself here a year ago, two, three, always desperate for a future where he might be different. Where had that gotten him? How much had he missed by wishing it all away?

The sounds of Zek's footsteps slowed behind Saba. "It's very beautiful," he said.

"Yes," Saba said, smiling. He turned back to Zek. "Though it doesn't seem your style, Zek."

Only when Saba turned, Zek wasn't staring at the embellished hallway at all. He was staring right into Saba's eyes.

Saba flushed.

Ridiculous. Saba pulled his eyes away—the movement of his head had drawn Zek's attention, obviously, pulled it away from the beauty of the architecture. His desire felt childish and inane; he craved the attention of his enemy, his keeper.

Stop it. You're only going to hurt yourself. He doesn't want you.

"Oh, I can appreciate beauty," Zek was saying. The *thunk* of his footsteps and cane started up again, and Saba swallowed a shaky breath. He had more important things to worry about than his own damnable lust, which needed to be leashed and collared in the bowels of his mind.

Saba blurted, "Wait. I need to tell you something."

And Zek, bless him, leaned in conspiratorially without question.

Saba murmured, "There was something else different about the Eye. Something I didn't tell the others. Only someone with my notes, or with their own similar knowledge, could have done it."

Zek frowned but didn't press, allowing Saba to fill in the gaps. Moss called out, "Are you coming?"

Saba glanced up to find both her and Silvana staring. He waved in affirmation and began walking forward. Without notice, Zek slipped his free arm into Saba's and pulled him close, so they were walking abreast like old friends. Saba's heart flew to his mouth; his tongue swelled with a desperate yearning, and he grew too flustered to speak. When he chanced a look at Zek, the Rezwyn was smiling down at him, eyes crinkled. His warm breath tickled Saba's neck.

Shit.

"Um," Saba said. He shook his head, pulled his attention to Moss and Silvana walking ahead, and said quietly, "I told you I wanted to—get to the other side of the astral sea. And I told you my notes were necessary for the Eye to become a breach. Only—I didn't explain how."

Saba continued, "I made sigils. With Moss and Khajro. They're imbued with ichor, and they're meant to keep the opening stable. Except, it's easy with the Eye; that hole is tiny, and the sigils are there to stabilize it. But my hypothesis needed the hole to grow. So, I designed a sigil that could make the breach larger. Only I never . . ."

Shame made him trail off.

Zek made a low, gruff noise in his chest and said, "Never got around to figuring out how to stabilize a much larger breach?"

Guiltily, Saba nodded, then added, "But the thing is—I didn't etch the symbol for expansion into the Eye. Someone else did that."

Zek patted his arm and said, "The same person who removed the failsafe, no doubt. So the sigils are making it grow?"

"Exponentially," Saba said, and his voice lost coherency and crumbled halfway through the word.

"And all of Byrengrad could be. . . unmade," Zek concluded sullenly. He shook his head. "The Rezwyns believe the soul is different. It can enter the astrok-mer unscathed. But there's never been any talk of a body entering—since it isn't a physical plane. It's immaterial, so how can you exist materially there?"

Saba sighed. Zek prompted him with an elbow nudging into his ribs. "What do you believe?"

"That it's possible to enter," Saba said. This wasn't quite the same as Zek's statement, which told Saba the Rezwyn perspective. This concept belonged wholly to Saba, who had cared for it and fostered it for most of his life, who still wanted madly to prove it. "But it's not possible to enter and . . . stay the same. That the material, the body, would shift and alter—perhaps even if the person was wearing protective gear like the gedrokbone armor of the Uslethian Paladins to mitigate the effect."

Speaking it aloud embarrassed him, since it wouldn't take much for Zek to understand the reason Saba wanted so badly to enter the tear was because he so badly wanted to be different.

Quickly, Saba added, "History suggests there have been breaches before. Slips in the makeup of our worlds, like a thinning membrane. Things have passed through. But they have been natural, and as far as I can tell, the breaches . . . sorted themselves out."

Zek said plainly, "What are you thinking?"

Which was a simple question for the amount of thoughts Saba was keeping in his head.

He listed them all out as they came. "Who killed the Lord of Veprak? Who stole my notes and used them to alter the device? Who destroyed Loefka Ward and framed me? And *why me*?" Saba grimaced. This was the one question that he might know the answer to: because of who he used to be—but how could he tell Zek that? "Whoever did this intended to destroy Byrengrad."

"Did they? Or did they only intend to destroy that part of it that was destroyed and then couldn't shut down the Eye once they'd accomplished their goal? Or are they intentionally keeping the Eye open for some other reason?" Zek's tone was flat; he remained equanimous. His eyes slid down Saba's face, and he blinked rapidly for a moment before sighing. "Nothing has been solved, Vasili. There could be three or more separate parties involved. They could have destroyed your research. They could still have it. It could even be another scholar conducting their own research."

"I know," Saba admitted. Then, because something about this conversation felt like it had wounded their camaraderie, he said, "Are you sure about this? Coming with me, I mean?"

"You're meant to be in my care," Zek said.

"And you're meant to be following Zvensia's laws, ambassador."

Zek smiled. Saba breathed in, smelled sweat, leather, and a scented oil wafting from his beard. Which Saba was staring at, or past, at the pinkish tinge to Zek's lips.

"If Moss is to be believed," Zek was saying, "we'll be in and out without anyone the wiser. Besides, you *are* right.

We can't keep letting this thing grow. And it's hard to concentrate on finding a murderer when the city is at risk of simply ceasing to exist."

"Yeah, a fair point," Saba said, and Zek and he grinned at one another.

They rounded the corner to see Moss and Vana stalking up an incredibly beautiful, very tall staircase. Carved from the rock, it wound around itself four times, making four flights of stairs to lead up to the attic where Saba had often worked. Saba had never really given this staircase more than a cursory glance, perhaps other than a sad little cry when he was feeling lazy about having to climb it. But Zek said, with a little moan of his own, "Oh, fuck me."

Saba startled and looked at Zek—who was not looking at Saba this time, but the staircase. Naturally.

Saba started, "Are you—"

"It's fine," Zek said. His voice was flat and steady, though Saba saw him silently considering the great number of steps. "It will just . . . take a while."

Zek inclined his head, and Saba could see that his cheeks were flushed, perhaps from embarrassment or a preemptive exertion. The big man walked to the banister, gripped it tightly, and began hauling himself up. His cane clacked against the stone steps, and each stair earned a low, deep grunt from the belly and then a ruminative pause once the step had been achieved. But Zek quickly found a rhythm, one that mesmerized Saba—grip, haul, rest, repeat—a method which involved a great deal of bicep flexing, or straining really, as Zek hefted himself up. It took very few leaps and bounds from this view to picture the mental image of being pushed around by Zek's weight, which was inconvenient and distracting. Saba decided to schedule that image for another, more private time.

"What can I do?" he said, after coming to the realization he'd been trailing Zek like a dog.

"Nothing to be done," Zek said gruffly. "Except one thing—don't look at me like that, Vasili."

Saba flushed and laughed. "I'm not looking at you with pity, Zek."

At the next step, Zek paused and turned to Saba, panting hard. "No? Then what?"

Saba dropped his gaze to Zek's lips, then lower, then away. He made an abortive gesture for Zek to continue. "Something else," he said weakly.

Saba couldn't bear to look Zek's way, but his peripheral vision caught the subtle shift anyway, a softening in Zek's face, a prolonged stare. But then Zek turned his attention back to the behemoth task ahead, and Saba could safely beat himself up in his mind for a few silent minutes.

Zek did not complain once, but Saba could recognize pain. He fought the urge to console Zek, who did not need consoling, who did not need to comfort Saba in turn for a pain he had also lived with for most of his life.

"Tell me more about your work," Zek said. "It will entertain me on the journey. Why do you know so much about forging exanimate bones?"

Examinate was the Rezwyn term for the colossal fauna whose bodies dotted the landscape of the Kingdom of Usleth. Saba rather liked the sound of it, but on principle said, "Gedroks, you mean. My interest in them has to do with tracing ichor back to its source. My theory is that there have been tears between this world and the astral sea before. It's likely that ichor flowers like those used by the priests of Suoduny, and ichor itself, originated in the astral sea. And so the next logical step for us to consider is that the gedroks must have originated there, too."

Zek nodded at him. "And so?"

"If it's true, this revelation—that entire world, the geopolitical makeup of it, Usleth's ability to survive empire expansion and Kerinsk's inability to avoid assimilation, comes down to something as awful and simple as the bodies of gedroks falling where they did." Saba gave a short laugh. "Usleth had discovered the gedroks. Usleth had formed the paladin order which protected it from incursion. What if it had been Kerinsk? Is it selfish to ask that question?"

"What if things were different, you mean?" Zek asked. "I don't think so. Then that's your real interest in the astral sea? To see if it's possible to . . . make things different?"

Was it?

Zek had laid it out so bluntly, it was hard to be sure, so Saba simply said, "Perhaps." He thought again of the silhouette he'd seen and its distinctly familiar shape. Saba cleared his throat. "Do you mind telling me what you saw when you looked into the breach?"

Zek halted then, glancing back at Saba with a half frown. He sighed before he hauled himself onward. "An old dream. What I might have been like if I had never been injured."

Saba felt himself flush, not with embarrassment or shame or desire, but with an unnameable feeling. Almost like kinship, almost like understanding—the difficulty of having a desire that at once conflicts with your reality and has the potential to harm your happiness. Hypocritically, Saba wanted to say: *You shouldn't give those kinds of thoughts any life*. But that was hardly his place.

"And?" Saba prompted instead.

"Unrecognizable. Still in the army. Unchanged, in many ways, from that sixteen-year-old boy I was when I went in. But also . . . unchecked imperialism."

"How could you tell? I only saw an image."

Zek snorted. "Perhaps I'm . . . projecting. Or maybe, I know how I would have ended up. Confidence, loyalty, and praise. I'd have lived in that vacuum and I wouldn't have been . . . a good man."

Saba thought this a stretch, because Zek was an inherently good man.

"I don't think it was just your injury that made you reassess the empire, Zek," he said. "I think—if you care what I think—that you're a good man."

Zek thought about this and grunted. "I aim to be." He sniffed for a second and looked back Saba's way. "I think you're a good man, too."

Zek's words made Saba's chest seize. Saba glanced away; he couldn't revel in that feeling for long. His mind had caught on the whole reality of Zek, and even Giste, admitting to seeing things in the breach. For Zek and Saba alike, both visions aligned with some kind of ideal self, however flawed those ideals might be in truth.

The flares had touched Saba and not affected him. What if the breach had. . .recognized him?

Saba had spent so long constructing the Eye, what if his intention—to find and become that man in his dreams—had affected the breach?

What if he and it were connected?

"You alright, Vasili?" Zek called. Saba had paused on the stairs, mulling it all over.

Maybe you are connected—but no one needs to know that right now. Not until you're sure.

Saba sped up to join the others.

At the top of the stairs sat an airy, loft-style room, with open, glass-free windows carved into the limestone. Painted floral scenes adorned the stone roof, the color faded with age like everything else up here. The wooden floor had faded, too; small sections of it were rotting and creaked in protest every time a foot went near the dying boards, but they'd been like that for as long as Saba could remember, and so far no one had fallen through. A wide, long desk took up the center of the room, but only three rickety chairs were still up here. Several shelves packed tight with scrolls and wooden crates lined the far left wall, along with other odds and ends like vials, compounds, and dried ingredients. A door sat to the far right, and a small reading alcove with a dusty red carpet sat in the other corner.

"Oh, I'm sorry, Ambassador," Moss worried.

"It's the stairs' fault, not yours," Zek huffed. "Might need a minute, though. Before we start." Then, with embarrassment, "Sorry."

Saba locked his jaw together. Zek should not be embarrassed.

Saba stepped forward and gestured to the door with his head. Moss caught his gaze and nodded.

"Of course," she said. "We have hours. Take your time. In the meantime, Vana and I will prepare for the underdark."

"Can you do me a favor?" Saba asked. "Could you figure out how much gedrokbone we'd need to make another failsafe, and how much we'd need for the container?"

Moss grinned broadly and pulled out blueprints from under the table, which she then spread with great flourish. "Consider it done."

"You're the best." He turned to Zek. "Come," Saba said, leading the way to the door.

Both he and Zek were breathing hard, and both for entirely different reasons. Saba opened the door to a tiny limestone room, unevenly shaped, with a bumpy arched ceiling curving overhead. A bed, desk, and chair were crammed practically on top of each other.

"Sit," Saba said, gesturing to the bed.

Zek went and lowered himself to the bed with a groan. He lay down fully. Sandy hair smeared across his forehead, tangled with sweat. The dewy shine to Zek's cheeks did not stop there. There was a shine to his beard, and a soft gleam to the skin of his neck, which Saba realized he'd been staring at. He blinked and cleared his throat.

Zek asked, eyes closed, "What's a bedroom doing up here?"

Saba folded his arms and leaned against the wall, hoping the cool stone might calm him down. Zek took up most of the bed. His feet dangled off the edge. Saba imagined sitting on the bed with him. Lying down. Which he could not do, and should not do, and had no right to do.

"The whole building is filled with little rooms like this," he said eventually. He had to turn his gaze upwards to the uneven ceiling to say it without his voice shaking. "Some scholars stay here permanently, while others are more transient. But people get obsessive. We work late, we rise early. Sometimes you need a place to put an exhausted scholar so they're not asleep at the desk."

Zek laughed, but a twang sent his voice high-pitched. "Then I am thankful for exhausted scholars."

"As am I," Saba said, far too quickly. "How's your leg?"

Zek made a noncommittal sound. The cane clacked against the ground as Zek positioned it upright, and then he pushed himself up on the bed until he was propped against the bedframe.

"Aching," he said. He sounded despondent but resigned, as if there was no other way to be. "The knee's the worst part of it. Shifts too much—it's too unstable. But I'm grateful to have a leg at all."

Zek pushed his big thumb into the knee and began to massage it over his clothes. Saba felt pressure in his hands, a twinge, a pulse—his hands were empty, and he could not bear it. He pushed himself from the wall in a rush, feeling preemptive heat burn his cheeks as he said, hesitantly, kindly, desperately, "Let me."

Zek looked up at him with a slight frown.

Before embarrassment undermined him, Saba added, "You're in pain. And . . . I have nothing else to do."

Zek stopped massaging his leg. The room seemed so small, suddenly, and Saba's skin felt sticky and hot, set to burning by the furnace of his heart running rampant in his chest. He forced himself to move, to get closer to Zek, which only made him consider sitting next to Zek on the bed or going down on his knees.

Absolutely not.

Saba was too much of a coward for that, and *this*—this offer, this intimacy—already felt overwhelming.

He did not know what he was doing. For someone as obsessed with the body as him, Saba had very little immediate knowledge of the science behind flesh. He knew pleasure, and pain. Desire. Grief. But the mechanics of movement were a foreign beast.

He couldn't meet Zek's eyes as he pulled the chair closer and positioned himself with both hands hovering over Zek's leg. Very gently, he began to press around the knee, and further up into the upper thigh. Zek exhaled sharply. The sound wasn't quite pain, but his whole body tensed under Saba's touch as if resisting it. Saba tentatively pressed higher into the muscle, then down into and around the knee itself, each touch a question, a clarification.

Here? Here? Is this okay?

And the only response he got from Zek were half-swallowed grunts and eye twitches. The leg felt stiff beneath Saba's fingers, the muscle a convoluted tangle of knots and inflammation. After a few minutes, Zek's hand moved to rest on Saba's. Without question, Saba slowed his massage, and then stopped, his stomach dropping not from fear or worry but from a great rush of lustful anxiety. Zek's hand completely enveloped Saba's own.

Saba swallowed. He wanted to take his other hand and hold Zek. Apologize for any pain he'd caused. Ask if it had helped. Ask if he might lie down next to him and close his eyes. He said nothing, of course; he simply waited for Zek to come to his senses, remove his hand, and sit up.

But that didn't happen either.

Saba's cheeks were red. His fingers hovered over Zek's hand. Each finger was nearly double the width of Saba's own. A white puckered scar cut across Zek's index finger. Four freckles were interspersed across his hand, and blond hair curled in a fine down to half obscure them.

Something caught Saba's eye: a pale line around Zek's wrist, too pale and neat to be a scar. Bravely, Saba reached out to skim it with his finger. "What's this?'

Zek's eyes flickered open. He frowned down at his own wrist and made a low noise in the back of his throat. "Hm. Adolescent folly."

Saba just stared at him, until Zek added, "A binding ceremony. Though I wore the band for years afterward. Hence the tan."

Saba flinched. He drew his hand back slightly. Cold doused his insides. Stiffly he asked, "You're married?"

"I was," Zek said, closing his eyes again.

"To a woman?"

Slowly, Zek turned and looked at him. His brow buckled slightly, since he couldn't possibly understand Saba's tone, or the reasoning for it. "Yes," he said carefully.

Saba heart flew to his throat. Foolish. He had never felt so fucking *foolish.*

His interest in Zek seemed not only silly, but childish; Luan Zek was not interested in men. Luan Zek would certainly not be interested in a man like *him*. But even worse—the thought that if Zek did, in fact, take an interest in Saba, would it be because he saw Saba as a woman?

"Oh," Saba's voice emerged embarrassingly stiff. "Was she . . . very beautiful?"

Zek made a face, and then shot his brow up. "In her way she was. Is. But in the end, that didn't make us work."

Saba's voice stopped working, arrested on his tongue, which refused to move. Thinking felt difficult and sluggish; or rather, any coherent thought was impossible to hear over the whispered cacophony of questions thrumming in his head. Suddenly, imagining Zek touching him in any non-innocent way felt both ridiculous and wrong, like Zek was not his to fantasize about. Saba squeezed his eyes shut. A thick nausea filled his stomach, like fat, bloated intestines wriggled about in there.

Oh, shit. You really wanted him to like you.

"You can ask," Zek said.

Saba flinched, as if surprised that Zek still had something to say to him. Saba did not ask a thing, which only made Zek smirk. He rolled his eyes quite dramatically, the way Saba always did, which probably meant Zek was mocking him.

"We met before the war," Zek said, like that was obvious, "and married as soon as I was discharged. Hadn't seen her in years. And we were both different. I was . . . worse."

Saba's brows buckled at Zek's interesting choice of word. He cocked his head and pressed, "Worse?"

Zek's stormy blue eyes grew soft with pained nostalgia. "Unpleasant," he said carefully, tongue tiptoeing around the word. "To be around. I was unhappy about the leg. About my body. I was mourning who I used to be, and who I imagined I'd become. It's—we were too young." His expression changed, scrunching up dismissively. He waved a hand through the air as if to dispel fog. "We had changed too much. That's all."

A dozen things passed Saba's lips before he found the right thing to say. He could have said: *I'm sorry,* which was both insufficient and simply incorrect. *I think your body is very beautiful,* which was far too selfish for this moment. *I can understand grieving a body,* which, though true, wasn't quite what Saba wanted to say.

"And now?" he actually asked. "How do you feel about your body now?"

Zek met his gaze. The lines around his eyes crinkled; he seemed pleased—or interested. He made a soft snorting noise and repositioned himself on the pillows, staring up at the faded painted ceiling. "What a question. In two minds, I'd say," he said lightly. But then Zek took his time. His expression softened. The smile drifted from his lips. He sat in silence for a moment and mulled it over, and when he looked down at Saba next, he had a tiny furrow in his brow. Saba wanted to lean over and smooth it away with his thumb.

"I feel like my body is a vessel I am in, and it's not really me," Zek said. He shrugged, adding, "When it hurts, anyway, I think like that. The bitterness is still there. But more and more, I feel . . . peaceful. No longer angry." His posture softened as he said it, the tension in his muscles unravelling and unwinding. "It's my body. I've been injured for as many years as I haven't been, now. Why dwell on a possibility of recovery that will never come to pass? Why squander what happiness I can find? I am *this*. I can be happy about that."

Saba exhaled, and his lungs expelled every worry and wish and shaky, desperate jealousy. He wanted that same emotion for himself, in a way: Acceptance without grief. If not happiness, then the kind of neutrality that meant what-might-have-been no longer hurt him.

But a part of him shivered in revulsion at the thought of accepting himself. Letting go felt like losing. He longed for the potential of himself, craved a version where he not only recognized his body, but loved it—even if it meant changing himself completely. Even if the desire and the dream was, very simply, unhealthy.

Zek said, "What is it?"

"Nothing," Saba lied. He ran his hands down his face and shifted in his chair, gesturing to Zek, "Except, well . . . I wish I was anything like you. When it comes to how you feel about your body, I mean."

Zek pulled a face. "You don't like yours?"

An understatement, and somehow also not quite right. Saba laughed and swung his arms out wide. "Oh, something like that."

Zek tutted. He leaned forward, shifting so he could look Saba in the eye. And he winked.

"It doesn't have to mean anything. But for the record, Vasili, you are very easy on the eyes."

Saba flushed and, instinctively, reflexively, rolled his eyes. "Liar."

"You can't do that, you know."

Saba balked. Zek's tone had dropped low and firm.

Saba tensed. "Do what?"

"Control what people think of you," Zek said. "For better or worse."

Saba stared at him. It was one thing to dislike his body, to see the movement of the skin around his scarred his chest and grimace, to touch the width of his hips and feel a visceral, aching disgust. To feel all that, and to have someone else—*like* it?

Zek continued, oblivious, saying kindly, "What I mean is you have no right to assume I'm lying. No matter what you think of yourself, you don't get to dictate what someone thinks when they look at you."

If Saba could be attractive to someone else, then his dislike of his body moved from an immutable truth—something he has considered tearing holes in the seams of the universe to change—to something much less all-consuming. Saba's natural response was to reject the idea outright. But Zek was looking at him, staring, really, with those piercing blue eyes, and Saba's body reacted when his mind could not. He relaxed—somewhat. His shoulders dropped an inch away from his ears. The lump in his throat began to fade.

He wanted to control what other people thought of him. He wanted them to see him as Saba Vasili—and not the lost princess of Kerinsk, for one thing. But it was almost more difficult to accept that others might not share Saba's view of himself—including the self-disgust.

Zek sat up and patted him on the shoulder, seemingly aware he'd dropped something quite profound into Saba's lap. "Don't worry. I had to learn it, too, for better or worse. Are they looking at my leg? Do they pity me? Do they see what I used to be? Are they just being polite? How much of all that is what other people think, and how much of it is really me?"

Saba leaned into Zek's touch like a dog. "How did you manage to learn how to handle it?"

"You could start by taking my compliment," Zek grinned.

Soft laughter ripped through Saba's chest. He squeezed his eyes shut and said, "Thank you, Zek." He reached up and replicated Zek's motion by patting his shoulder. "You're . . . easy on the eyes, too."

Zek smiled, and Saba smiled, both leaning over to clasp the other. Eventually Saba had to clench his jaw to stop the stressed, anxious feeling in his gut from bubbling up. He blinked rapidly and was the first to pull away.

"Uh . . . you should rest. Take a nap," he said, getting to his feet.

Zek smiled again. "I'm strangely not tired anymore."

Which meant what? Which *could* mean—so many things. Saba's insides flipped and danced, and he couldn't help but glance at Zek's lips.

"Right," Saba said as calmly as he could. "Okay, then. Shall we?"

And then he turned and sped out of the room.

CHAPTER TWELVE

It probably said a lot about Saba that he left that offshoot room sweating, with a keen ache in his chest he knew to be fear. How quickly comfort could be corrupted the second he was out of Zek's orbit.

He tried to keep it from showing on his face, walking confidently out of the small rest room and back into the attic, but his body shook. Of course, there wasn't anything to fear: Nothing physical, anyway. No immediate threat. Nothing that might tear the life from him.

But what had scared him was the way his body reacted when he and Zek had stared at one another. Past the lust or the general attraction he felt toward Zek's body, looking at Zek, meeting his eye and truly seeing him, sparked a rabid, panicked emotion in Saba's gut. A small eternity had passed in the few seconds they had locked each other in that stare, and Saba's heart had cracked open like the shell of something raw and beautiful, soft and fragile.

It was going to hurt. That was the conclusion his mind had come to: *whatever this is, if you entertain this feeling in any meaningful way, you will be vivisected.* Maybe not for a while. Maybe the cuts would be small and neat and barely there. But the act of caring—of caring beyond the physical—felt intensely intimate.

His heart felt both heavy and warm, hope and fear competing for his attention. As the emotions burned brightly in his chest, he sped out of the small room and back into the scholar's loft.

Ignore them. Byrengrad might unravel. Focus on that.

But at least if Byrengrad went, so too would Saba's heart.

Saba slipped his hand along the stone wall of the corridor before the attic's ceiling opened upward. The room blushed orange with afternoon light, and dust motes danced high above the window. Blueprints had been spread across the enormous worktable, and crates had been shifted and removed from the shelving to the left of the attic.

And there, by the open window, with a little breeze tousling her hair, Mossinne leaned up on the tips of her toes just as Paladin Silvana leaned down and kissed her.

Saba halted so violently that Zek walked into him.

"Shit, sorry," Saba said, spinning back to apologize to Zek. But he'd spoken aloud, of course, and he whipped his head back around to find Moss and Silvana had pulled away from one another.

"*Shit*," he hissed, cringing. "Sorry."

A heavy flush had exploded across Moss's face, turning all her brown freckles scarlet. The short scholar stood shaking, vibrating with embarrassment. Silvana nodded to Saba and Zek as if nothing were the matter, because that's what Uslethians were like when it came to things like kissing.

Zek's breath warmed the side of Saba's neck as he slipped close. Zek's jaw grew in Saba's periphery as he edged his face over Saba's shoulder, and whispered, "Why does Mossinne look like she might cry?"

"I caught her kissing the paladin," Saba explained, but this was an unsatisfactory answer for Zek, who turned to stare at him with a raised brow. Rezwyns were perhaps closer to Uslethians than they might realize, at least in matters of the heart.

"It's Zvensia," Saba said. "They're a little more . . . proper. Kissing is not something you do in front of people."

"Hm," Zek said. Silvana looked at Moss eagerly, but the scholar refused to turn to the paladin. Zek smiled. "From what I recall of Usleth, it is not like that at all."

Moss murmured something, and Silvana nodded, moving to the mess of shelves and bottles. She climbed the ladder, and Zek slipped past Saba to help her, but not before firmly squeezing Saba's shoulder.

Moss watched Zek stiffly and then, icily, snappishly, turned to Saba, who gave her a wide smile. This was not received well. Moss rushed toward Saba with her finger held accusingly, until she could crowd close to his face and jam it against his chest.

She hissed lowly, "Don't say anything."

Saba put his hands up. "I've said nothing at all."

"Well, keep saying nothing," Moss said. She dragged her finger back through the air, gaze squinting and searching.

"Okay," Saba said with a smile.

Moss deflated. Her eyebrows shot up high, and her brown eyes welled again with shame and panicked fear. "*Saba,*" she pleaded. "You're saying things with your eyes."

The look on her face stopped making it funny. Saba clasped her hands, really held her, let her know through touch how sincerely he meant it when he said, "Moss, I will say nothing."

"If Giste found out—" Moss began, stuttering. She bit her lip and moved her hands further up Saba's arms, until her nails were digging sharply into his upper arm. "It's just. It's unprofessional. And I have no permit."

Saba frowned. Moss blanched, mouth agape. Frustration crept into her face. She said, "For *fraternizing.*"

And Saba loved her, he really did, but he couldn't help but roll his eyes.

Permits were technically required the moment one gained any kind of relationship status in Zvensian society. It was, simply and transparently, a way for the Triad to keep track of who was involved with whom, and thus a way to track breaches between divisions or levels of society. If some damaging conspiracy were to be leaked to someone outside of the city operatives, the first place to look would be at everyone's lovers. Of course, half the time permits were used in other awful ways—like preserving Zvensian purity, discouraging fraternizing with refugees, or punishing undesirable matches.

But this? A scholar and paladin? This was early and sweet, just a bloody kiss.

"Oh, you dummy," Saba said, caressing her cheek. "She's not even Zvensian."

This did not have the intended effect. Moss's green flecked eyes bulged in sudden horror. She gently slapped Saba's hand away and cocked her head with her mouth agape, staring like she was waiting for him to register how stupid he sounded. She made an abortive, frustrated gesture.

"Which is even worse!" her voice strained high, straddling the line between a whisper and a scream. "I'm in a professional capacity. I am a member of the Scholar's Guild. If I want to fraternize with anyone of equal rank, I need a permit. But if I want to . . . *kiss an Uslethian paladin?*"

She ran her hands over her face. Saba stood there useless; whether or not Saba found the whole Zvensian bureaucracy laughable didn't matter when it made Moss this stressed. But then she betrayed his good will by saying flatly, "It's different for you. You don't have the rank to worry about anymore. You can flirt all you want with the ambassador, and some people—Giste—might frown on that, but there's technically no reason you couldn't—"

Saba put a hand up. She shut up.

Saba could feel his cheeks, pricked red with sudden heat. The boards beneath his feet creaked as he shot a flustered look over his shoulder. Zek was preoccupied, bulky arms outstretched overhead to carry any boxes Silvana passed down.

"I'm not," Saba said stiffly. He swallowed and stared right at Moss. "Flirting with him, I mean."

Moss stared at him and said nothing, but the stare itself had a grim finality to it, like she had buried him and now stood above his grave. It was so withering and felt so unjustified that Saba flared his nostrils and swung both hands out in an exaggerated shrug.

"What?" he said. "Stop looking at me like that. You're insane."

"*You're* insane," Moss grumbled. "You're eating him with your eyes."

"I absolutely and resolutely am *not doing that*."

Moss rolled her eyes and kicked Saba in the shin. She smiled at him. Her cheeks dimpled, freckles scrunching up over her nose. "It's alright, you know. One good thing to come out of your discreditation is you can fraternize with whomever you wish without any consequences ever landing on you."

She meant it nicely. Sweetly. That's always how Mossinne meant things. But when Saba was Sabina—when Saba had once been in line for the Kerish throne, and Zek had been a soldier at the end of the country's life, consequences had more weight to them.

Because how could he ever forgive himself? Even if all evidence thus far pointed to Zek being a good man, on principle alone, on behalf of everyone ever hurt by the Rezwyns, Saba should not look at Zek and feel—anything. Except hate. Except disgust.

"It's not that simple," he said. He imagined, in a runaway thought, Zek kissing him. Rough hands pulling at his hips, firm and forceful, crowding their bodies together. He imagined himself—properly. What the sensation might feel like if his body was different, if Zek unlaced his trousers and slipped his hand low and felt something that Saba only wished was there. A fantasy like that had an inherent safety, an impossibility that made it permissible. He could let his body grow hot in wanting and desire for something that would never happen. But if Saba imagined Zek kissing him as he was, lithe and perhaps too skinny, under-muscled; if Zek were to slip his hand in Saba's pants, if he could touch Saba and find any commonality with his former wife—

Disgust and panic reared up inside Saba, a distressed wave of emotion that encircled his heart, his stomach, his intestines. A thick paste of it made his insides grow sticky and uncomfortable; he wanted Zek but could not bear to be wanted by him. It made no sense. It scared him. He wanted Zek to want him, wanted to be had by him, and at the same time had the urge to eviscerate himself. Scrape out all the organs, the wet mess of them, the blood, the fat, the bone. He wanted to be empty. He wanted his body to be empty; he wanted to evacuate it, leave it completely, run for the hills. For the astral sea itself.

"Saba?" Moss murmured. She had reached out and laid her fingertips on Saba's shoulder.

Saba gasped and met her eye, but then Zek called out, "Any more crates to get down, Mossinne?"

Moss pulled her hand away and spun around. "Nope," she said. She looked back to Saba, who nodded at her tightly, just the once, and hoped that would be enough to move her on. Discussing this muddle here wouldn't be possible.

Her face buckled, but she said loudly, "Let's get to work."

Both of them moved close to the desk where Silvana and Zek had laid out a variety of vials, substances, and clothes.

"Remind me again what's scholarly about this?" Zek said, crossing his arms.

Moss shrugged and began unloading items from one of the boxes. "Well, it's easier to have young scholars playing around with these kinds of compounds than ones that can do a lot of damage."

Saba, whose thoughts had turned resolutely dark, forced himself to be present, which required beating back the tar-like anxiety in his gut with sheer force of willpower, and then pretending to like himself. With energy he did not truly feel, he winked at Zek. "Plus, some excursions require a little subterfuge."

Zek snorted and asked no follow up questions. When Saba glanced at Moss, her eyebrows were in danger of shooting off her forehead. She might have mouthed the word *flirt* at Saba—or perhaps *slut*—before she sighed and ran her hands through the pile of clothes strewn across the big table.

"Obviously, we'll start with the clothes. You're both dressed far too well. So even if they let you in, they'd charge you triple."

Becoming someone else, even in clothes alone, felt like a reprieve. Perhaps too eagerly, Saba shucked the outer layer of his tunic. "What do you have for us?"

He kept undressing, pulling his undershirt off before she even had a chance to reply—and froze. He hadn't been thinking. Locked in a moment of fear and shame with the shirt above his head, Saba thought: *Oh, fuck.* He hastily took it off. But now he was exposed, and it shouldn't have elicited this feeling—shame, worry, a sickness in his gut. He waited, waited for Zek to say something, to comment on his scars or linger too long with his stare. Zek did none of these things, but that didn't stop Saba's mind. Zek might draw his own conclusions about what these scars meant. And if he did, then how could Saba ever be sure that Zek was being sincere again? He could never know if Zek was just being kind, if this changed how Zek saw him.

It shouldn't have mattered. Nothing as simple as his own nakedness should sway him so easily into that awful, complicated feeling. It shouldn't have mattered what Luan Zek, little more than a stranger, thought of him. Saba's logical mind knew that his scars shone beautifully, and they meant he had chosen himself. Saba had chosen himself a long time ago.

So why was his heart in a flurry?

Moss was saying, "Absolutely nothing pretty, for a start. Vana stepped on them a bit, too, for good measure. Thank you, Vana."

The paladin shrugged. "They were not—" she stumbled through the sentence, picking her words carefully "—bad enough."

To keep his mind off Zek, Saba rummaged through the clothing and picked something up. The style in Byrengrad, even for the poorer classes, tried to emulate the complex layering and draperies worn by the Triad; an attempt to shroud oneself in the trappings of status. Saba sifted through and picked up a high-necked blue shirt with long sleeves. Ties hung loosely from the back. It looked well worn, creased with several holes eaten through the material. Saba went to put it on—felt his heart hammering with an almost gleeful urge to be covered again—and Zek lurched forward. His cane clattered against the table.

Saba startled. All of them turned to look at the ambassador. A soft pink had bloomed across Zek's cheeks.

He cleared his throat. "I'll, uh . . . help."

Saba didn't look away from him, for fear that the hole Moss was currently boring into the side of his skull would go through his eyes next. As such, Saba didn't move.

"Oh," he said, very quietly, and very high. He rushed to pull the shirt over his head. Zek came up behind him and gently helped tug it down, but as he did, his warm thumb brushed against Saba's chest—against the comet-flare mark of his right scar. Saba's heart raced and he knew from the sting on his cheeks that he'd flushed. It took immense effort not to turn around, took almost the same amount of bravery as it might have taken him to ask Zek outright what he thought of Saba.

Zek's lips pressed close to Saba's ear, his breath tangling in the red curls gathered at the base of Saba's neck. He murmured so only Saba could hear him, "So that's how you know of Suoduny. You've been to the empire."

Saba's blood ran cold.

He rounded on Zek. Saba's jaw tensed—he was scared instantly into a protective posture, a hunching of the shoulders to hide what used to be the twin mounds of breasts. This was a habit he sometimes still slipped into, for there was comfort in making himself smaller.

So that's how you know Suoduny . . .

"What," he said flatly. Speaking felt difficult. Thick shame and fear bludgeoned him from the inside, which felt similar to being punched repeatedly, or eviscerated. Zek had seen him and now was flaying him, peeling back the skin, the tendon, the muscle, and squinting at the viscous mess inside. Saba hated this vulnerability. His bit his tongue so hard his whole head stung with referred pain, until the regret and embarrassment were buried beneath the sting. He bit until he could focus on Zek without feeling the urge to cry.

Zek nodded down at his chest. "Your scars," he whispered. "The shape of them, the way they healed—I've seen them before."

Zek spoke so casually, seemingly without understanding of the weight of his words.

It was true. Saba had been to the empire. Saba had bartered his way there in exchange for half of his worldly possessions: the last of his royal Kerish jewelry, blue ceramic struck through with gold and pearl, and the mud-encrusted shoes he had fled in, a dusty pink turned the color of dried blood after his escape.

A collector had snapped those up, a man with an obsessive interest in Kerinsk. Saba had walked into his house—which had stretched large into the bowels of the Zvensian cliffs—and been bombarded with the history of his country hanging from the halls, covering every inch of space. Shoes, scraps of clothing, jewels, trinkets. Terracotta jugs, prayer beads, half a statue that had survived some battle or another. The culture and the life of an entire people suspended at the moment of the country's destruction.

The horror of it had not been lost on Saba, even as he handed over those shoes, even as he took the coins and pocketed them. He had bartered his heritage with someone's morbid curiosity for coin, and he would use those coins to step even further away from who he had been when he'd fled Kerinsk.

It was a protracted betrayal of his birthright—his obligation. But he couldn't help it.

If Saba hadn't bartered those shoes, he would have killed himself.

Once he'd gathered the coin, he bargained his way into the empire. Perhaps this was the only time Zvensian bureaucracy had been of use to him. The falsified identity, Saba Vasili, had at least lived a few years in Byrengrad before applying to the Scholar's Guild, and no one had looked too closely at the small town to the west he'd claimed to be from. Getting into the empire had been relatively easy, but finding his destination had proved difficult. He had gone to the nomadic temple of Suoduny, the empire's god of fate, in search of their priest—who was the same kind of man as Saba.

Selvik.

The priest had been young, about the same age as Saba, and covered in fine, dainty scars, self-inflicted as part of his worship. He had bindings across his chest, which had scared Saba at first—Selvik had not undergone the same surgery Saba wished for. It made it difficult to trust him. But this type of thing—the fluidity of the body, of expression, of being—was common in the empire.

So Saba had taken off his shirt, and even without the shared language, Selvik had understood.

Saba recalled the bitter taste of tea derived from ichor flowers and other herbs, a hallucinogenic and makeshift anesthetic. He recalled woozy anxiety and then a balm of unconsciousness. Part of him even recalled the feeling of being in a kind of dance, slipping in and out of the astral sea, hands interlaced with his idealized self and spinning together—though that was very likely a fever dream. Upon waking, though, with great clarity, Saba remembered sweat, pain, and blood. Healing took time. The ache was made worse by gravity, which seemed to pull on phantom breasts, made laden the wounds pulled together by ichor-imbued silk thread. And despite all this, despite the pain, what Saba remembered most was relief.

He had expected euphoria, joy, something rabid shooting through him. But when he'd looked at himself and saw Selvik's handiwork, twenty years of tension had unknotted in his shoulders. He relaxed—perhaps for the first time in his life.

Good, his body had seemed to say. *Correct.*

For the first time in his life, Saba had felt right.

"You wear them well," Zek was saying, in reference to Saba's scars. His hands dropped from the laces at the back of the shirt. "Finished."

Zek stepped away.

Unsteadily, Saba murmured his thanks. No disgust or fear or uncertainty sounded in Zek's tone. Instead, Saba heard admiration. Awe. He looked up and met Zek's eyes, and that damn bastard had the audacity to wink at him like this conversation wasn't something profound. Like this wasn't something Saba had hoped for or worried himself into knots over for years and years and years.

He sees you. And he—appreciates what he sees.

"Fuck," Saba said sharply. The rest of the room jumped.

He'd cursed unexpectedly—but internally, a thousand emotions had flooded his system, emotions that had been dredged up from an ancient, primitive part of his brain. That part was screaming, whooping, crying. The inherent vulnerability of being recognized or seen was one thing. To be appreciated? To have Zek look at him, acknowledge him, and still look at him with a gleam in his eye?

It was too much.

Moss drummed her fingers against the stone windowsill. "Alright," she said. "Let's hurry it up."

Saba turned and grabbed the rest of his clothes: a grey mantle capelet, trousers, boots, a belt. He shuffled off awkwardly to the room where he had massaged Zek to finish changing, but once inside, he leaned his forehead against the closed door, covered his mouth, and screamed.

A crack like thunder sounded in the distance. Saba rushed back out just as Moss spun toward the window and gasped. Distance and the stone muffled the noise, but Saba watched as prismatic light flared in a starburst over the horizon—exactly over the growing breach. The city reacted, too; faraway alarm bells rang out.

Saba's heart raced. He stared at the plume slowly dissipating in the sky, like the breach itself had screamed, like the breach had been unable to contain a surge of emotion and become unstable.

Like it was human. Like it was Saba.

Had he done that?

No. No. Don't be ridiculous.

But he made himself breathe slowly all the same and got hold of that runaway heartbeat, and curiously enough, the breach had no further spats.

He stole a moment for himself, and it was this brief, quiet breath that stopped Saba from snapping in half. Two days since he'd been dragged from his jail cell, and too much had happened already.

"What happened?" Zek asked, pushing closer to the window. "Do we need to go to the site?"

"No," Moss said with a sigh. She rubbed her face and turned to Silvana. "No, we have a better vantage up here. What was it you said earlier?"

Silvana tilted her head and said, "I am not sure why it happens, but each time it grows, it, uh . . . does that."

She gestured to the window where the bright light was already fading.

"We need to get to the underdark," Saba said seriously. He ignored the horrible feeling that the breach had reacted to *him* and focused instead on getting ready. "The sooner we can craft this failsafe, the sooner we can close the damn thing."

This spurred everyone into motion.

Zek moved back to the table and quickly removed his shirt to rummage through the pile of clothes for anything that would fit. Scholars tended to be a lanky breed, and evidently Zek was struggling. But this meant Saba had time to stare at him, to take in the size of him.

He felt guilty, somewhat, for taking his time after such an obvious show of the breach destabilizing and expanding. But he couldn't quite convince himself to pull his eyes away. He scoured Zek's body and saw the muscle under the fat, the hair over his chest and belly and back, the white scars. Heat rushed through him. Zek leaned both hands on the table with a heavy sigh, and Saba allowed himself the fantasy of being beneath him, right there, belly down. How would it feel to have that weight bearing down on him? To feel the edge of the table jutting into his hips? Zek's warm breath on his neck, or fingers gripping Saba's hair, wrenching back his head?

Zek turned, not sharply or accusingly, but slowly, as if he could hear Saba's thoughts. He smiled knowingly at him. Saba wanted to eat his own hand. He walked forward and looked at the ground where it was safer, eyes following all the flowing patterns in the woodgrain. In his periphery, Zek continued to dress. He tugged on something heavy from the pile. It burst free suddenly, and heavy coattails swept across the table, sending Zek's cane clattering to the ground.

Before he knew what he was doing, Saba was on his knees. Too quickly he had picked it up and had it balanced over the palms of his hand, like he was offering his sword up to a king.

Really? On your knees immediately? Don't you dare look up, you slut. Nothing good can come from looking up at shirtless Zek from this angle—

He'd already looked up, of course.

Zek looked down, face appearing over the rounded rise of his pectoral muscles, his belly rising and fallen with steady breath. Saba could put a hand out, run his fingers through the down of hair, but the city was in danger of imploding, and Moss had her mouth open in Saba's periphery, and Zek was staring at him and smiling gently, probably oblivious to what this sight was doing to Saba's wellbeing.

"Everything all right down there?" Zek murmured. His voice rumbled through his belly.

"Oh," Saba murmured, finding it impossible to look anywhere for too long. "Wonderful."

Zek flinched. "What was that?"

"Nothing," Saba said. He stood hastily, and as he rose, a flicker of something indescribable crossed Zek's eyes. He cleared his throat and glanced away, tilting his head from Saba

"You'll still need something for your hair," Zek said conversationally. "The color makes you too striking."

Saba, who at this point was feeling overly brave and overly ruttish, said, "Just the hair that does that, is it?"

Zek laughed. He scratched the side of his cheek and shrugged. "I think you know you're very handsome."

Saba flinched and froze.

"Here," Moss said. She practically slammed one of the wooden crates down between the pair of them and pulled a vial free. Then she grabbed Saba's hand and pressed it into his palm, not letting go until she mouthed, *Flirt!* at him.

Saba didn't want to stop it. This was the most fun he'd had in months. But now that he suspected the breach was connected to his state of mind, he worried about experiencing any kind of strong emotion—not when the whole city could be consumed by those fluctuations.

He took the bottle and raised it to her.

"All you have to do is—"

"I know," he said, and his smile faded. It was a temporary salve-like dye. All he had to do was smear it over his head, and it would turn the color a muddy brown. So long as he wore his hair down, he could hide the brand on the back of his neck, too.

There it was—that old feeling of nostalgic shame welled up and replaced the nervous, blushing joy.

The last time Saba had covered his signature redness, he had been fleeing his homeland.

So hold onto that horror. Think of nothing else.

You cannot afford to be distracted, Saba Vasili.

CHAPTER THIRTEEN

The underdark was a known secret.

Saba didn't know the truth about its origins, but like many things in Zvensia, it had about half a dozen myths surrounding it. A result of the war, it was a preemptive tunnel system created with multiple entrances beneath shopfronts, taverns, and houses so that entire wards could be shuffled to safety. Saba had heard other stories, too: that it had been a shrine to a god long dead, a theatre, a natural wonder—none of which accounted for the tunnels, but some of the best stories made little logical sense.

What the underdark had become, though, was something altogether different. It functioned like a black market, but its greatest attraction wasn't just its illicit goods.

It was the lack of bureaucracy.

Half the wares it housed could be accessed in Zvensia proper, just not easily. Saba had once requested ichor flowers for the purpose of study—not for use, or consumption, but to pick apart and stare at. It had taken two months of requests, documents, proceedings, and begging to be granted.

Thus, the underdark provided a crucial service to Zvensians wanting to do anything in a timely manner. As far as Saba knew, it was communally run and deliberately unregulated by the Triad. There had been brawls, scraps, even a stabbing once. None of the victims had grounds to report these incidents or to expect justice, since these dealings had occurred outside of the Triad's jurisdiction. Saba suspected the Triad encouraged shady and unsavory types to stir trouble in the underdark, if only to convince people slowly but surely of the necessity of bureaucracy.

But sometimes, like tonight, it was not only worth the risk, but also the only option.

Saba was accompanied by Moss, Paladin Silvana, and Ambassador Zek. They hoped to find gedrok material—in their dreams, enough for the casing that would contain the Eye until it simply burned itself out, and likely in reality, at least enough to refashion the failsafe device that Saba, decked out in paladin armor, could then replace in the Eye.

They'd waited less than an hour in the attic before leaving the Scholar's Building and walking to the Artisan Quarter which sat in the southwestern Serlei Ward. Their little party entered through a staircase at the back of an artisan shop, which led down into a gloomy, naturally damp tunnel. Dirty mosaic lined the ground, and the tunnel went on for a long, dank while before it split open into a large underground grotto.

Immediately there was chatter. A thrumming constant noise filled the air. Silvery stalactites ruptured through the bowing cave ceiling like tiny daggers, all of them lit up by the stream of moonlight that leached in through the small natural skylight at the far back of the cavern. The underdark itself had been set up on a raised formation that meant no one had to slog through the ankle-deep water that served as a moat. Coming back to this place felt almost familiar. To be amongst thieves, collectors, academics—those who knew the value in skirting Zvensia's bloated processes—was to be among like minds. Even now, when disguise was necessary, Saba felt calm douse him.

Everywhere was awash in a warm golden glow; dozens of lanterns and candles burned in stone nooks and crannies. Decorative cages hung from the ceiling, their bottoms drowning in wax as candles burned and bled within them. Stalls were crammed so close to one another that half the time it was impossible to tell where one ended and the next began. Trinkets and foreign herbs, tinctures, scrolls, books, stolen goods, an incredible carved wooden chest made by the renowned Uslethian woodworker Szargrid—all things spilled over one another. A few bruisers stood about—hired hands meant to intimidate—but otherwise the mood was light. Airy. How odd that the greatest sense of community Zvensia could muster was only allowed to manifest in the dankest, darkest depths of the city.

Then he spotted trouble.

KERINSK'S LAST HOPE:

PRINCESS SABINA VASYILUKI OF KERINSK, DAUGHTER OF QUEEN DEINAH VASYILUKI OF KERINSK, MUST BE FOUND!

RETURN THE MATRIARCHY OF KERINSK TO ITS FORMER GLORY AND DRIVE OUT THE EMPIRE!

For all intents and purposes, the leaflet was very well made. It took a moment for Saba to acknowledge, to vacate his mind and let a hard patience take over—a dissociative power that could allow him to ignore the very personal horror of seeing that many feminine titles referring to him. The Kerish girl who was handing out the leaflets was one of three, all of them wrapped up in makeshift Kerish flags—five alternating stripes of mustard yellow and magenta and a crest in cyan blue, which on these were represented by a bloated blob of blue felt—and all standing at the various entrances to the underdark. Saba had gingerly taken a leaflet and then thought about all the ways to destroy it, particularly because it had contained a beautiful portrait of the imagined princess. Long, curly red hair, tiny nose, big doe eyes. What pure dedication, to carve that wooden block for this purpose. Saba imagined rolling the inky dabber over the block and then smoothing the printing paper with the baren a hundred times, just so everyone could own a copy of the princess's likeness.

They need the hope. They live off it. Of course, they'd draw you. Laud you—her.

Guilt swarmed Saba as he backed away like a coward, unable to meet them in the eye, lest they see him for who he was.

You abandon your people, you let them suffer. But Saba couldn't be their princess. He couldn't be their leader in any capacity. He had forged a home in Zvensia as best he could; the empire was never going to loosen its grip on Kerinsk.

They must move on. Like you've moved on.

Saba shoved past, breathing hard, but no one seemed to notice his reaction. He dropped the leaflet into the muck and walked forward into the underdark itself.

"We'll split up," Moss said. "Cover more ground that way. Meet at the northern entrance?"

Saba ignored how eagerly Moss had said that, but he couldn't quite ignore the impatient twitch of her hand as it edged closer to Silvana's.

Saba swallowed a snort and clarified, "The tunnel next to the bar?"

Moss nodded and dragged Silvana off without another word. Immediately, their absence made Saba feel exposed. He stepped back toward the comforting bulk of Zek and cleared his throat.

"Try to stay close. It's easy to get lost."

Zek only nodded at him, though he wasn't looking at Saba at all. His eyes were fixed on his own leaflet. Saba thought about snatching it out of his hands. *Don't look at it, don't look at me*—that was the rabid anxiety in his mind. But then Zek shifted and glanced at him expressionless, ready to move.

The Rezwyn had been quiet, more so than usual. Perhaps he disliked less than legal activity—which wasn't an explanation that fit well with Zek's character, but Saba's anxiety told him the only other reason Zek hadn't spoken was because he now felt uncomfortable in Saba's company.

He called your scars nice.

But who did that? What kind of compliment was that?

Saba smothered the thought. They were here to find gedrok material. Enough to build a casing, and failing that, another failsafe. They were here to stop Byrengrad from disintegrating into astral nothingness. When Saba considered the weight of that, it became easier to ignore his own ridiculous fears. They moved between the stalls together, searching for that signature prismatic sheen of gedrokbone and scale, finding nothing.

Hoping to get lucky, Saba planned to go to the stall where he'd bought the working gedrok lens, but everything had been shifted about. Every stall owner wore a mask, but few were recognizable—not in the way the Triad or the paragons were identifiable. These masks were made of composite materials: wood, ceramic, fabric. Some were theatrical and dramatic, others plain facial coverings. All of them lacked the symbolic language Zvensia's official masks featured. The result, for anyone who had lived in Zvensia for any time at all, was disorienting—and deliberately so.

As such, they moved slowly. A few merchants attempted to peddle pretty iridescent shells as gedrok material. A few others lifted animal bones they'd painted an unsettling, gummy pink.

"The skin's like that," Zek murmured. "Not the bone."

"And when have you seen a gedrok?" Saba asked with a laugh. But Zek did not respond. Zek didn't even smile.

"Come on," Saba said. He tugged Zek away from the stall and moved to a quieter part of the market, and it was there, finally, that Saba spotted someone he recognized.

"Would you mind. . .?" Saba murmured, gesturing to the stall with his head. And Zek, impossible and kind and understanding, left him to his business without a single question.

The stall in question was small and neat, with scrolls, trinkets, and concoctions arranged in a meticulous system.

What had drawn Saba to this stall initially was a fresco—completely intact, half a wall laid haphazardly against one of the curved cave walls. Its seller claimed that the fresco originated in Usleth, which Saba honestly didn't doubt. But it was so expensive that it had sat untouched in the underdark for nearly three years now, and Saba considered it part of the underdark's off-market décor.

It depicted a gedrok. Saba had never been fortunate enough to ever see one in person, though he had dreamed of them. First, he had dreamed of calling one to rescue him from Kerinsk when he was still a child, asleep in his bed, thinking: *Come to me. Help us.* He hadn't understood at this age that the gedroks were ancient and long dead and far to the east of his homeland.

He stared at the fresco now. Gedroks were oddly catlike: a malformed, lengthened cat skull, nimble form sitting back on haunches, but then lizard features took over in the eyes, the reptilian fingers, the tapered tail. In Usleth, he knew the preserved gedroks reeked of brine, their brittle translucent skin pallid and sickly. An account he'd read described the gedrok's skin as sac-like, like it could be popped, like all its innards could spill out. Which wasn't true, of course—the gedrok's exterior was iridescent scale. The fresco tried to show the skin's translucence by painting an aura-like glow around the body. Veins ran labyrinthine in blues and reds, moving from limbs to organs, creating a detailed cartography of the flesh.

Saba pulled his eyes from the fresco to the front of the stall. A large tome sat open at the front where the merchant kept track of every item and every sale. It looked like an apothecary, and on the surface it was.

"Zolaise?" Saba called.

The person behind the stall flinched. Their mask consisted of a patchwork layering of leather, black fabric, and ceramic charms sewn over the top, which clacked together when they turned their head.

They were, perhaps in the way of all masked people, androgynous—but Zolaise had accessed a new kind of androgyny, where no matter their body, they seemed to walk that thin line between presentations. Saba had never seen them maskless, but he had guessed at their age—older than him by a few years, but certainly no more than a decade. They had strong bulk to their legs and lank in their arms, and they moved with a secure ease in their flesh that Saba envied.

In a way, Zolaise was like Saba. They had talked about it once or twice: What their bodies meant to them, or didn't mean. What change would look like. Zolaise hadn't felt the same as Saba about most things; in fact, they'd announced they loved their body the way Saba hoped to one day.

So Zolaise had slipped away from confidant and friend to something else, something other: someone with something Saba coveted, and also a stranger he could never hope to relate to, and at the same time a compatriot by the very nature of their similar experiences.

But at the basest level, their relationship was professional—transactional, even.

Zolaise leaned forward, and their eyes narrowed into a scrutinizing squint.

"Are you a new face, or a hidden one?"

Their musical voice thinned as it seeped through the mask. Saba waited under their scrutiny, listening to the indistinct caroming chatter of the market. In the beat of silence, Saba planned. He had bought the gedrok lens from Zolaise, which suggested, at least, that Zolaise was somewhat reliable. But they had a unique hold over Saba in another, more pressing way.

"Ah," Zolaise snorted. With a trace of satisfaction, Zolaise bolted upright and mock bowed. "The great scholar gracing me with his presence again. What are you looking for?"

Saba's disguise had failed him, but perhaps that was for the best. He came close to the stall and leaned his elbows on the only empty space on the table.

"Two things," he said. "Gedrok material being the first."

"Nope," Zolaise said, lips popping over the sound. "I only had the lens."

"Really?" Saba said.

"Yes. You think everyone and their dog has access to the bodies of rare, long-dead ancient creatures?"

"Of course not," Saba said with a tight-lipped smile. "But I had high hopes for you, Zolaise."

This weak attempt at flattery had no effect. Zolaise tilted their head. "Anything else I can help you with?"

Saba sighed. "A bundle of leather-bound notes whisked out of the Scholar's Guild weeks ago."

"Best of luck finding that," they said, which was fair enough. Something as indiscriminate as a pile of notes would be impossible to find in this place—if they were here at all. It was an eager dream at best.

"I do have your usual decoction," Zolaise said. Their voice softened slightly, which made Saba tense. "Want it?"

He did. He slipped some coin onto the counter. "Need a new needle, as well."

Without further ceremony, they made the exchange. Zolaise supplied him with his decoction—that which helped his body edge closer to his ideal. Selvik had been the one to mention Zolaise to him and provide the recipe that extracted the minute dose of ichor from the cajudsan. He'd find time to apply it later. Saba stepped away from the stall and hoped Moss and Silvana were having better luck.

As he stepped away, he saw Zek propped up against the cave wall. He'd managed to find a quiet spot, and when he saw Saba he smiled and gestured with his head behind him. Saba followed and found the cave wall curved around to a damp, sequestered nook. Someone had lit a candle and balanced it haphazardly on part of the jutting wall, but otherwise it was the emptiest part of the underdark, a hidden nook Saba was surprised no one had laid claim to it with their overflowing wares.

Zek turned to make sure Saba had followed. Something glinted in his hands.

"You found something?" Saba asked, excited.

Zek nodded. He opened up his hands. Resting in his palm shone a pearlescent pendant, uniquely veined with shining red. It was a necklace—a gedrokbone pendant on a golden chain.

Saba glanced up at Zek. "Beautiful," he said. "Rather small though, isn't it? And a bit sad to destroy such a pretty thing for the failsafe."

Zek's nose wrinkled as his looked down at the necklace. Almost sheepishly he said, "I wasn't intending on destroying it."

Saba snorted. "No? Then what?"

Zek said nothing, but he took his other hand and eased the dainty chain over his finger, raising it up so the pendant dangled and danced in the light of the single ebbing candle flame.

"I intended to liberate it from this drab setting," he said. His voice sank low, and he leaned in, leaned so close Saba's stomach convulsed with sudden anxiety, so close he could feel Zek's heat. "Such a pretty thing deserves an equally pretty place to sit, don't you think?"

Saba blinked at him. His mouth ran dry. "What?"

"Turn around," Zek said.

Saba stared for a moment in blank incomprehension before he turned. Zek's words hadn't quite made sense to him. They still percolated in his mind, fermenting slowly like an aged wine or perhaps more like a thick, inedible soup. His body knew Zek's meaning before his mind did, because his heart had begun to race, and his palms were growing clammy. None of this felt good or right. Instead, he felt—strange. Unsettled. Before he knew it, Zek's big arms appeared in his periphery and lowered down over him, gently brushing the hair away from the base of Saba's neck to better place the necklace.

Saba went stiff. The Kerish brand sat raised at the back of his neck. Could Zek recognize it? Had he been told to kill the princess, marked by the brand of office?

It was another thing to worry about, but it floundered beneath the weight of his heart, which began to stretch painfully in his chest.

What a uniquely complicated feeling. And in this rising panic, the action of Zek leaning over him made Saba feel strangely, uncomfortably feminine, to the point that when he looked down and saw the pretty pendant sitting in his clavicle, he blurted out, "I'm not . . . a girl."

Zek's hands flinched against him just as he did up the clasp. Bravely, Saba turned around to look Zek in the eye.

The ambassador frowned at him. "That much is obvious."

A very loud silence spanned the second after Zek shut his mouth, but the anxiety in Saba's gut gave way to a rabid and very likely misplaced anger. He steeled himself, balled his hands into fists, and spat, "Is it?"

They stared at each other. Zek blinked, a slight pink tinge reaching his cheeks. He backed up against the grotto wall. The register in his voice shifted defensively low. "You think because of my history . . . my previous marriage—"

Yes, that was it. It didn't matter if it was fear speaking now, or some other more sensible thing. Saba said with confidence, "I think you saw the scars and thought that made me . . . easier."

Affronted, Zek said, "In what way?"

In every way, Saba wanted to say. More palatable, to a man whose romantic history included a woman prominently. Or easier, in the sense Saba might be desperate enough to be courted by anyone at all.

But Saba knew how panicked he could get over this. On the off chance that Zek meant it, had bought this necklace in good faith, was telling him he liked Saba not in stolen glances and imagined fantasies, but through a gesture like this, Saba chose to say nothing.

Zek stepped forward and closed the distance between them. Saba flinched, teeth cutting hard into the sensitive, fleshy center of his tongue.

"Whoever has told you that a man like me might be uninterested in a man like you is an idiot," he said. "Because I can say, without reservation, that I like you very much."

Anxiety blared in Saba's skull, like the death cry of a wounded dog.

"I don't think it should matter," Zek said, "but I can see it matters to you. So I'll tell you this much: I have been with women and men of all configurations. You are not some easy mark. In truth, Vasili, you are, for many reasons, not easy at all. But I like that about you. I like a lot of things about you. Let me show you how much."

Saba exhaled noisily and did not move.

Say something. Thank him. Or better yet—just kiss him.

It would be easier without words—easier to show how he felt with his body, or the way his body reacted beneath Zek's touch. It would be far simpler to open himself for this man, or to say *prove it* and hope Zek did. But Saba couldn't. He just couldn't.

Zek could say in no uncertain terms he liked Saba, and even if it was what Saba had wanted, or craved, or longed for, it didn't—make sense.

Flushing, stuttering, he said, "If you are . . . joking with me . . . "

The flush on Saba's face must have been mistaken for something else, something close to anger. Zek jerked back. His voice went high with concern, and he shook his head emphatically. His lip curled up, and suddenly he looked so much younger than his thirty-something years. "What part of this reads as a joke to you?"

He sounded disbelieving. Saba yearned to tell him: *There has almost always been a caveat. I am attractive in certain lighting. I am attractive until I take my clothes off. I am attractive when someone is desperate, or until they realize what I have or what I lack in the way of appendages.* Or worse: *I am attractive because I am unique. I am attractive for all the things I dislike about myself.*

And there were cases where this wasn't true, where people—men—liked the warmth of him, the ease of the fuck, or where they liked him despite what he had. But he wanted to tell Zek that caution had so often saved him, that anxiety to the point of paranoia had preserved him, and that anytime he had accepted things so readily, it had never done him good.

Saba wanted to be wanted. Not *despite* his body, and not *for* its uniqueness. Which perhaps made no sense, which perhaps was a line so thin it could not be walked. He wanted to feel desirable. He deserved that. But part of him knew, too, that Zek could say every right thing, and it would still snag on the burrs in his mind.

So eventually, all Saba said was, "The part where you say you're attracted to me and mean it."

Zek stepped forward again, as if tugged by an invisible force. Experimentally, he reached out and gently touched Saba's waist.

"I thought it was obvious," he whispered.

Giddiness and fear doused Saba. He shook his head and let humor save face, let humor cut through Zek's effusive sincerity and bleed it out, to make it easier to swallow.

Saba scoffed. "Well, I think you're delusional." He couldn't meet Zek's eyes. "Clearly. Look at me, I'm covered in dirt."

Zek was not dissuaded. He frowned. "I met you covered in dirt. Now I'm spending my coin on pretty trinkets for your neck."

Saba's hand shook as he touched the necklace. "As far as accessories go, it's a marked improvement from cuffs."

"Saba," Zek said, almost chiding. He reached up and swept a hand through Saba's hair. His fingers caught in the thick curls and the dye, which made Saba laugh, and once he laughed, it all came out—all that giddy, anxious energy, all the sharp, uptight resistance.

You're a fool, part of him thought. And so what if he was? So what? He had known Zek a handful of days, and for weeks before that Saba had been in a cell, and for months before that shunned by the city he had come to know as his home, and before that, before that, before that—

Saba realized with great and profound clarity he had spent so much of his life wallowing in guilt about what he wanted. About how he wanted to live.

What kind of life was that?

The air between them felt thick and electric, like the waiting pressure of Byrengrad before a thunderstorm. Zek's eyes were heavy. With his heart in his throat, Saba took in the sheer size of him, let himself revel in the thrill of being so much smaller. And then he pressed up on the tips of his toes and kissed Luan Zek.

Zek didn't hesitate. He wrapped his arm around Saba's waist and pulled him close, grip forceful and full of intention. His cane clattered to the ground, and they stumbled back together, crashing into the grotto wall. Zek moaned as his weight shifted onto his bad leg, the sound turning into a short, airy laugh. He didn't let Saba go, just ran his hand up to the back of Saba's head, fingers clenching tightly in his thick hair, and now free of his cane, Zek dug the palm of his left hand into the sharp rise of Saba's pelvis.

Their display was too heated for polite Zvensian society—but just another shadowy exchange in the underdark. Saba silently thanked this natural nook as he pressed himself close to Zek's warm belly.

Someone cleared their throat.

Saba and Zek pulled away from one another. Backlit by the dozens of lanterns, Paladin Silvana stood leaning against the wall with her arms crossed. Saba slowly lowered himself down from the tips of his toes.

"Don't tell Moss," he said.

Silvana promised nothing, just grinned and peeled herself off the wall. "We found the materials," she said slowly, stilted. "You two did not come to the meeting point."

Zek cleared his throat. "Momentarily distracted."

Silvana grunted and waved her finger overhead before spinning on her heel. She didn't wait for them, so Saba took a moment to recover. He and Zek met each other's eyes, and Saba found the Rezwyn was looking at him differently. Not worse, or indeed, in any way negatively—but his gaze was noticeably different. A new kind of weight sat in the way he regarded Saba—but there were things to do.

"Come on," Saba said. He returned Zek's cane and relished in the stolen touch of their fingers. "We should—"

Zek grunted and walked ahead, cane clacking on the stone. He glanced back at Saba and winked. "We *should* continue this later."

Is that a promise? Saba almost said. But Zek had already turned away, and Saba needed to spend the minutes it took to reach the northern exit calming himself down in more ways than one.

At the exit, Silvana and Moss were talking animatedly—which Saba took as a very personal betrayal, given he'd just asked the paladin not to tell Moss, and she clearly was telling Moss everything. The small scholar spun to Saba with a ridiculous grin on her face. Saba tensed and walked ahead of Zek in the hope he'd somehow miss it.

"Stop it," Saba hissed.

"No," Moss said with a playful twang.

Saba shot her a deliberate look and, manifesting Moss's anxiety from only a few hours before, said, "But I have no permit."

Moss scrunched up her face scornfully. "Oh, don't be a bastard."

Saba grinned at her. "You love me."

"Yes—which is why I know nothing and have seen nothing." Her scorn had been replaced by a fractional, conspiratorial smile. She put up both her hands.

"Good," Saba said. He glanced at Silvana who shrugged at him.

"My Zvensian is bad," Silvana said, by way of explanation. Only sometimes was a good ally a silent one.

Moss began, "But I was thinking—"

"Stop thinking," Saba said.

"—that it's actually really late and you look tired, like really tired, the kind of tired where if you don't get horizontal in the next hour you might die. So, you know, Vana is strong and she's already carrying the stuff. Which is only enough for a failsafe, by the way, so I'll have to make the failsafe but not the casing, and, well, *basically*, there's a few hours, or even days, before we'll need you anyway. So, you should, you know—sleep." Moss patted him on the shoulder.

Saba stood there, mouth agape, and he could feel Zek's eyes on him, boring into his skull, while the two women looked at him with their devious little smiles. Stupefied, Saba stayed silent.

Moss leaned around him and said to Zek, "What do you think, Ambassador? Does Saba maybe need some rest? In a bed? Maybe in your bed—not because it's *your* bed, exactly, but because I'm sure the embassy gives you really big beds—"

Silvana put a hand on Moss's shoulder, which caused the smaller woman to quieten instantly.

"Too much?" Moss asked.

"Much too much," Silvana answered.

Zek exhaled softly and stepped closer until Saba could feel his breath on the back of his neck. He tensed in a kind of expectation, wondering if Zek might steal a touch of his waist again.

Instead, Zek said, "Well, I could certainly take a rest."

Apparently, this was all Moss needed. She perked up, still grinning ear to ear, and waved emphatically at the pair of them. "Great! Good. Okay, goodbye!"

She grabbed Silvana by the wrist. The paladin had only a small sack of gedrok material, presumably enough with which to build the failsafe. Together they exited rather rapidly, leaving Zek and Saba staring after them.

CHAPTER FOURTEEN

In the end, they hadn't done what Saba wished, nor what Saba presumed Zek wished. They had ridden back to the embassy in tense silence, legs touching and bumping against one another as the gig rolled over uneven rooftops. Saba had clenched his jaw so hard it had begun to ache, and then Zek casually slipped one of his massive hands over Saba's thigh and squeezed, which meant Saba's jaw tightened to the point he expected to crack three teeth.

But his teeth had remained intact, and Zek had walked him up the stairs without a word.

Except when they got there, a letter was waiting for Zek, and suddenly Saba realized they wouldn't be doing anything unclothed together that night.

"I'm sorry," Zek had said gruffly. His voice had gone deep and dark, and he flashed Saba a hungry look that bordered on fury. "Something requires my attention."

Me, Saba had thought about saying. *My body. Take me to bed, Zek.*

But he hadn't said anything—hadn't even kissed Zek. After that, the tension in the room had doubled; the air felt thick to breathe. Zek had left, and Saba had done the very polite thing of going straight to bed, hoping he would dream.

Zek's business, whatever it was, had taken more than the single night. Which was fine. He was an ambassador—this kind of work was to be expected. Saba's incessant and pulsing desire, as all-consuming as it felt, simply did not take precedence over empire.

But fuck empire. Saba felt insane.

For the next three days, Saba sheltered in the unlikely sanctuary provided by the Rezwyn embassy. Freed of duty, obligation, and with nothing to do but wait, he let himself sleep. Sleeping felt safer. It created less chance of emotion, less chance of the breach flaring exponentially. Only with this framing could Saba allow himself to heal. Gradually his bruises faded, and his muscles relaxed. But never, really, his mind.

Moss and Silvana did him the kindness of building the failsafe. They sent notes and questions about the blueprints and the design, which Saba answered rather glumly. He thought vaguely about how he would do it—how he would need to build taller scaffolding, how he would need to approach the device, perhaps using Silvana's armor. But all of this was distraction, a way to ignore what his body wanted.

Zek came and went. His time in the room was spent mostly writing letters back to his superiors in Doskor or sleeping—which he still did on the chair.

The unspoken thing sat between them, and with each day that passed, Saba wondered if it would ever be addressed. He still wore the gedrokbone pendant. But Zek's hands hadn't wandered over his thighs or up his chest again. He hadn't kissed Saba, not on the forehead, or the neck, or the lips.

Until—

Saba was laying stretched out on the bed in nothing but a robe. The bath had been hours ago, but he hadn't felt like dressing. Anxiety made Saba speak—about anything at all, which Zek allowed, or welcomed, with an amused smile. Zek had gone out and met a rider from the empire and had returned half an hour ago, sweaty and tired. Saba hadn't asked questions. He'd received his own letter that night. Moss and Silvana had done it.

The failsafe was completed.

Night had fallen, and a fire was going, warming the room. Saba had just started speaking, hoping to hear Zek's voice, or to edge a laugh out of him.

"They said they'll head to the site with it. Final checks, or something. But tomorrow morning—"

"—We'll attach it." Zek folded his arms and nodded at Saba. "Or, I suppose, *you'll* attach it."

For some reason, the knowledge that the failsafe was done only made the tension between them much worse.

This is it. Now is the time.

Tomorrow the world would be different. Perhaps Zek would realize there were prettier and more attainable men to pursue back in the empire.

Zek, as if hearing him, said, "What will you do afterwards?"

Saba didn't know what to say, or rather, found it difficult to think about. He clicked his tongue and stretched back on the bed and thought instead of Moss and Silvana's nascent romance, which, like Saba and Zek's, couldn't possibly have a happy ending.

"Forget me. What about Moss and Silvana? I can't see an Uslethian paladin making much of a go of it in Byrengrad, but would Moss be willing to go live her life in some nowhere town like Piron? They barely know how to read there, let alone *study* anything. I've heard they have dirt roads in Piron. *Dirt roads* . . . how can a place like that be called the capital of a country, let alone of Usleth? Any way you look at it, they're doomed."

He didn't know why he was saying any of this. He spoke with a conviction he really didn't feel—he didn't want them to be doomed. Silvana and Moss were quite sweet together. But he felt this kind of growing certainty that it would be. That any kind of romance that happened here and now would be doomed inevitably.

"I've been told people will do amazing things for love," Zek said. Zek sat back in the wingback chair and pulled off his boots. “Get their shoes dusty in foreign prisons, or risk all sorts of nasty diplomatic complications. Even help clear the name of a beauty falsely accused.”

Saba stilled. He almost sat up on the bed to look over at Zek but managed to control himself. Was it happening now? Could he hope for it? Days of waiting had only made him simmer more, and he found Zek so difficult to read that he worried Zek had changed his mind, had grown bored of the idea, or thought better of it.

Instead of anything coherent, though, Saba just said, “You don’t love me.”

Without missing a beat, Zek said, “Well, I’ve hardly had time to.”

“You’ve been busy,” Saba said. A quiet aggression laced his tone, but Zek only snorted.

“You’ll forgive me, won’t you?” Zek said. He shifted in the chair, hips grinding back as he got comfortable. His legs were spread. Saba thought about—*stop thinking about that.* Zek grinned like he knew what kind of fantasies were dancing in Saba’s mind. “I didn’t want empire on my mind when I finally took your clothes off.”

Saba pressed his face into the sheets and exhaled. When Saba didn’t turn around—because turning around would require some other action to come after it, such as talking, or flirting, or being vaguely normal—Zek moved himself toward the sideboard.

Saba felt ridiculously anxious, like he was being hunted for sport, or perhaps like he’d been plucked from the streets and brought here specifically for an encounter—like Zek was a stranger.

“Drink?” Zek asked, oblivious.

“Please,” Saba said, voice twisting in a way that was almost begging.

Zek walked over and passed him a drink. Saba pushed himself up to standing and took it off him. He stared at the glass's contents, then up at Zek. The hearth light haloed him, made his bulk intimidating and fiery, and suddenly Saba felt like he was eighteen again, fumbling around with another boy for the first time and apologizing for everything: for the way he kissed, the way he touched, the way he was.

His heart ached with the memory. *You are not eighteen anymore. You are different now.*

But he felt an apology bubbling up all the same.

Saba blinked rapidly and took a sip. The liquor burned, but he would need three of these, or four, if he wanted to bludgeon his fluttering heartbeat into something steadier. Saba went rigid.

He'd had days for these dark emotions to flare up, but of course, they could only happen now, right at the precipice. Blood pumped in his ears. He wanted to touch Zek. Kiss him. He wanted to be held, fucked, loved—and simultaneously didn't want to be touched.

"You are allowed to sit, Saba," Zek said. Amusement laced his words; perhaps he thought Saba's anxiety cute, simple. "These are your quarters, too, at the moment."

Saba spoke without really thinking. "I feel like standing."

"Alright," Zek said, shrugging.

Saba watched him and threw back the rest of his drink, which made Zek snort as he lowered himself into the chair. He considered Saba in silence, eyes grazing up and down, gaze so sharp Saba could feel Zek's desire prick over his skin. A foreign thought—a near impossible idea: Zek wanted him. Zek felt it, too.

The Rezwyn swirled the contents of his drink around in the glass and nodded back toward the bed. "Vasili, if you're tired—"

"No, I've never been more awake in my life," Saba said seriously.

"Saba."

There was a question there, hidden behind his name. It made Saba shiver, because he could hear what Zek meant in the flat tone of his voice: *It's been days since the kiss. Since the suggestion of doing more. Why are you nervous? You say you want this, but you're hesitant. If you want to forget this, if you want to sleep, you're allowed to.*

I hear you, Saba thought about saying. *I know what you're asking.*

More than anything, Saba didn't want to fuck this up.

Saba said breathily, "I want to walk over there and climb into your lap."

A flicker of something raced across Zek's face. He shifted, slipping the hare-headed cane off his thighs and moved his legs apart. "You're more than welcome to."

Saba flushed. "Well, don't tempt me. I should tell you—I should try to talk to you."

He knew he was rambling and knew, too, he wasn't making much sense. He went and poured himself another drink, just as Zek asked, "About?"

"Myself." Saba's hand shook as he poured. "And what I'm like. I suppose three days of thinking endlessly about you, about this, has . . . dredged something up."

"Gods," Zek said, not wholly devoid of frustration. "If you need it said plainly, I will say it: I am attracted to you. And if you'll let me, and if you desire it, I want to take you to bed tonight."

Saba stopped pouring and leaned on the small table with half his body weight. There it was, exactly as he'd wanted it: straightforwardness. But, shit, is that all it took for his body to react? The honesty, the plain desire, the gruffness in Zek's voice, the look in his eyes? Saba turned and watched him sitting there, filling out that chair, legs open. Zek was confident. The poise and the surety wafted off him, and it had an intoxicating power to it, perhaps made more potent by the sheer number of months it had been since Saba had last done this. Or his reaction intensified because of *who* he would be doing it with.

"No, it's not—I mean," Saba picked up the glass and walked back over to him. "Zek, you are precisely my type. Precisely."

Zek raised a glass to that, and Saba laughed, then sighed, then sipped his drink. "But I don't think you understand. Or at least, I think it's easier for you to forget. Or ignore it."

Zek thought for a moment. He shifted in his seat, crease appearing in his brow as he considered. "I know what it's like to have a body not . . . function how you want it to."

Saba bit his lip. That wasn't the same. Defensively he said, "But it's not—it's different. And I don't mean that dismissively. I mean that . . . at least you had it. Before. Not in the sense you should be grateful for the years you had before your disability, but I'm jealous, in a sense. I'm just—I'm tired. I'm angry. All the time."

Zek said nothing.

Saba swallowed; he was fucking this up, but he needed to say it. He needed Zek to know what happened in his mind, the buzzing noise of his thoughts and self-doubts. He needed Zek to understand the weight that came with his desire for sex—and exactly what he was overcoming.

He finally allowed himself to sit down again. Halfway through sitting his robe shifted, briefly exposing his upper right thigh. Zek's eyes darted down unabashedly. Saba let him look. But then he covered himself and curled his feet up on to the chair. "Would you change your body?"

Zek looked up at the ceiling and exhaled. After a beat, he looked back down and met Saba's eyes. "No. Would you?"

"Yes," Saba practically shouted. "A thousand times, yes."

Zek stared at him in a way that made it difficult to keep his gaze. Saba looked over toward the fire. It wasn't this simple.

"And I know I shouldn't want that," he murmured. "I know wanting that makes me miserable, and I know there's nothing good in dwelling on something other than my reality. But I crave it. I grieve not having it. I grieve something I never had! At least your feelings make *sense*, Zek. Yours feel legitimate, and mine feel—insane, yet also inevitable. I've met people like me who are truly happy with themselves, and I don't know how they do it. I don't know if they lie to themselves until they feel it's true, or if it's genuine. Or if I'm broken and should be happy with what I have—grateful I can at least be *this*. But my body feels like a stopping place. Halfway between destinations. And I'll never quite get to where I'm meant to be going. If I think too long about it, about my configuration, or about how I move through this world, how I feel I should have been—it hurts. You could say anything, and it would still hurt. Because I know what I should have been, and I will never—"

The wingback chair released Zek with a creaking groan. He came over.

Fuck—how embarrassing. How stupid. Saba felt suddenly unsure of himself, but he made himself look up. And something about Zek's presence, and the look on his face—which was neither disappointment nor disgust, but a lovely, controlled grace—made Saba calm.

"I have never once thought as badly about you as you think about yourself," Zek said plainly. "And I met you in a jail."

Saba caught his breath and snorted.

Zek attempted to lower himself, but his leg clearly ached from the days of activity. He sighed down at Saba, leaning a big hand on the rise of the wingback above Saba's head and towering over him. But Zek's presence had stopped feeling intimidating. The Rezwyn worried at his lip.

"I don't want to make you upset. We can forget what happened in the underdark."

Idiot. Saba looked up and made sure Zek saw him—really saw him. "I don't want to forget what happened in the underdark."

Zek raised a surprised brow. "No?"

"No. But I wanted it to be clear that I—that sometimes, my body and I aren't friends."

"Well, we don't have to do—"

"Shut up, Zek, you're not listening." Saba shot up from his chair and kissed Zek on the mouth. They stumbled back, completely off balance.

Zek managed to keep a white-knuckled grip on his cane.

Saba pulled away, put both hands on the side of Zek's head, and knocked their foreheads together. "I am telling you I am anxious, but I want this. I am telling you I rarely feel good about my body, but that I want—you. To touch it. Me. And if you see me, and you want me, then you should take me. Okay?"

Zek tugged Saba back and took his chin between forefinger and thumb. He pressed firmly against Saba's jaw and pushed his head back until Saba had to crane to meet Zek's eyes. Something fundamental was different, now. Not worse, or better, but Zek looked at him with the import of someone swearing allegiance to a monarch, with the severity of the waves in a brewing storm.

It made Saba comprehensively insane.

Saba had engaged in trysts before, stolen moments in beds, moments where his lust had flared up and he had fucked near-strangers with eager glee. But so rarely had anyone wanted him so openly, had wanted him before they knew what kind of man he was, or because of it, or despite it.

"Bathe," Saba said, the closest thing to a command he could muster. Zek snorted, because neither of them was under the illusion Saba was in control here.

"Cute," Zek murmured.

"Bathe," Saba said again. "And then . . ."

Zek raised a questioning brow and forcibly maneuvered Saba's chin higher in the same moment. "And then?"

Saba exhaled breathily and let himself rest his chin more wholly in Zek's grip. In answer, he slid his hand down Zek's body, palm brushing lightly over Zek's cock, twitching through his pants.

Zek's knuckles turned white over his cane. He let go of Saba's chin, grabbed his waist, and tugged him close. Their bodies crashed together. Saba opened his mouth; their lips pressed against one another, and Saba pushed forward eagerly, seeking a deeper kiss. Zek, the teasing bastard, pulled away.

He regarded Saba with a knowing, dastardly smile. "Won't be long," he said, before heading to bathe.

Breathlessly, Saba laughed. He moved to the bed and collapsed onto his back, pressing the palms of his hands into his eyes. He had the urge to convulse somewhat violently on the bed; his mood had just shifted completely. The open honesty of Zek's desire and the fact it matched Saba's own had set him afire. He could feel himself throbbing. Months of languishing had suppressed all this; the discreditation, the shame, the Eye, the event—his libido had become a shadow of its former self, beaten into submission. Now it reared hot and alive once more.

He reached down to touch himself, grinding a few times against his own hand, just grateful for the pressure, and then sat up with a frustrated exhale. He had to keep himself busy. It would be at least ten, twenty minutes before Zek had scrubbed himself clean, enough time for Saba to completely lose what little grip he still had on his mind.

He moved to the side of the bed where he'd abandoned his dirty clothes. In the time they'd been gone, a new set of beautiful clothes had been bought on empire coin and lay folded up on one of the pillows. Saba moved those to the ground in preparation and then squatted, rummaging through the clothes he'd worn to the underdark. He found the pouch he'd bought from Zolaise, pulled it free, and then stood.

The decoction, derived from ichor and infinite possibility, synthesized in a way that shifted his body toward the masculine. The vial had been sealed with wax, which he needed to cut open, so he moved to Zek's desk and found the fancy, jeweled letter opener to slice the wax free. Administering the medicine involved an intramuscular needle that Zolaise made. A bulbous glass flask sat on one end, which Saba filled with the decoction. It connected to a goose quill canulae that Saba had to insert into his skin, pressing firmly into his thigh until the skin shuddered open and the needle could sink easily into the muscle. Saba took the weight off his left leg as the decoction entered him. It took a full minute to be drained. Starbursts popped behind his eyes as his body adjusted to the rush of power, and he had to sit down as his heart rate increased and prickles darted down his limbs.

And suddenly, outside the window near the desk, he watched as a flare of prismatic blue light burst overhead. The breach seemed to be reacting to his injection. Saba frowned at that; reacting to moments of negativity or extreme emotion made sense to him, as far as this impossible connection between him and the breach *could* make sense. But to respond in this way to his medicine?

It's the ichor, the scholarly part of his mind said. *It must be. It all comes from the same place, from the astral sea.*

And Saba had been microdosing himself with the substance for years. Was that why he was connected to the breach?

He turned back to the desk and sighed, and his eyes fell to something peeking out from underneath a pile of papers.

His stomach convulsed. It was his handwriting. His handwriting was on Luan Zek's desk, half covered by stray notes written in Doskorian.

He already knew what he'd found. Saba pushed the other papers aside. Lying there—liquor-stained, corners curling up from exposure to the elements—were the notes Saba had spent the last days desperate to find. He bit his lip. No cohesive thoughts came to him, only emotion, and those he found he couldn't name. Nothing felt distinct except a low, pulsing anger at the betrayal.

Saba opened the first page. It had been stamped with the symbol of the Rezwyn empire, that blend of Suoduny, the god of fate, and Borviet, the god of war.

What a fool I am.

Saba should have known. His whole country had been obliterated by Rezwyn interference, and even a treaty had not been enough to stop empire, and here he was, so quick to let his guard down because an attractive man gave him a necklace? Was that enough to wipe away decades of war? Colonialism? Suffering? The trajectory of Saba's whole life had been changed by this fucking empire, and he—

Saba stopped his panic and shot up from the desk, notes in his arms. He didn't know what to do. He wasn't sure why they were there. But he knew, more than anything, that he couldn't stay.

Saba hurried over to the bed and pulled on his new clothes. There were too many damn laces, so he left most of them undone, letting the jacket hang loosely as he did up his trousers.

And then the door to the bathroom cracked open, and Zek was standing there, glorious, slightly wet, with only a towel around his waist. The fire glinted off his skin. It hurt to look at him—for a multitude of reasons. Saba wanted him so badly.

Why did it have to come to this?

Zek saw the look on Saba's face, and his brow buckled. He hurried over the threshold, leaning forcibly on his cane.

"What?" he said, voice high with concern. It sounded genuine—but Saba knew better now. Never trust a Rezwyn. "What is it?"

Saba started organizing himself, bending down to fish his boots out from the end of the bed where he'd abandoned them.

"Saba? Has something happened with the breach?" Zek called. The floor creaked as he moved toward Saba.

"No," Saba said. He squeezed his eyes shut and picked the notes up off the bed. "Yes, kind of, but no, that's not. . ."

Saba could hear Zek's measured, even breathing. Something changed when Zek got close. His register lowered. Almost disappointed, Zek asked, "What do you have?"

Saba spun and brandished the fat wad of his notes in Zek's face. He waved it so aggressively the thing groaned as pages pulled at the aged binding.

Zek just stared down at them, then glanced up at Saba, completely impassive.

Heat burned across Saba's face. His nostrils flared. "Nothing?" he hissed. "Nothing to say?"

Zek blinked at him and tilted his head. "What am I meant to say?"

Bastard. A helpless outrage filled him. Restlessly, he laughed and ran his hands down and over his face. Had he gone insane? Is this what complete and utter hysteria felt like?

"These are my notes," Saba said slowly, as if Zek was stupid and hadn't realized. "The notes I have been desperate to find for days. Your empire's mark is upon them. So tell me this: How? Why?" But he didn't let Zek speak, because some other awful thought sped ahead of him. Before he knew what he was doing, Saba said, "Or better yet, Zek, just tell me. Are you really here to investigate Lord Doric's death?"

Zek opened his mouth, then closed it. He took a slow, deep breath. "No," he said.

Saba stuttered. He hadn't expected such honesty. He'd wanted to be wrong. In response to these emotions, another flare went up. The whole room went briefly white as the breach screamed the way Saba could not. What a color, for the dark, impossible horror he felt roiling in his blood.

The blinding light illuminated Zek's face. He turned to stare. "What . . . ?"

Saba ignored both the breach and Zek. He needed air. He needed to—

Well, that was it, wasn't it? There was nothing else to be done. He needed to get to the breach. He yanked open the door.

Zek spun back around. He dropped his towel and began to wrench on his own clothes. Saba moved out into the hall. Halfway down the stairs, Zek's voice echoed over to him. "Saba, let me explain!"

"Don't call me that!" Saba yelled back. The few administrative people still awake at this hour turned to look at him, three or four inhumanly masked faces. He squeezed his eyes shut. What had he been thinking? How could Zvensia ever be his home? How could a Rezwyn ever be his lover? "It's Vasili to you."

Or worse: it was Princess Sabina Vasyiluki of Kerinsk, a name Saba had long ago tried to sever from himself. But the way his body ached, the severe and screaming shudder of his heart, felt like the whole of Kerinsk was inside his skin. All of their ghosts shouted for his attention, every person his negligence had dissolved through the unmaking power of the astral sea.

Saba rushed out of the room and made it to the end of the hall before a guard stopped him. His gut dropped. Here was the truth, the awful reality. After all this, he was still a prisoner.

The floor creaked behind him. Saba glanced back, tears in his eyes. Zek stood there wrapped in a robe.

"Let him go," Zek commanded. The guard stepped aside.

It was the kindest thing Zek could have done for him in the moment.

Saba turned around without looking back, running out of the embassy toward that beacon in the sky.

The astral sea was calling.

Chapter Fifteen

Sweat pooled at the base of his neck and dampened his hair. A black haze—this amalgam of fury, fear, and great upset—darkened Saba's vision as he stumbled through Byrengrad. He had the notes stuffed under his arm, but he was so damned skinny that even that small weight was enough to unbalance him. Saba ran at an angle, shifting himself and the notes constantly, his mind a swampy, suffering cacophony.

Don't think about it. Don't you dare think about it. Just get to the site.

He didn't know quite what he meant to do. Or rather, the logical part of him, the scholarly part of him, pretended Saba's most base desires weren't currently spurring him on. Blame it on his dashed arousal, or the vulnerability born of betrayal; he had been wrong and hated himself for it.

Nothing could comfort him quite like obsession could.

The night was in full swing, which worked in Saba's favor. He was scuttling across the ground and climbing up stairs to dart across the paved roofs of stone houses, running alongside gigs, and shouldering his way through revelry. Any affronted shouts went nowhere, earning little to no attention—but even if they had, Saba wouldn't have stopped running.

As he crossed the bridge from Yoshka Ward into Deji Ward, the moonlight withered above the blazing light of the breach. From here, he couldn't see the Eye, but Saba could see the glow of pearlescent flares emanating from the wound-like tear, softly pulsing. His emotions must have caused the breach to grow.

It looked oddly like daytime, but more like day at a distance, like he might be able to walk from dusk to dawn in seconds. Revelry died out the closer he got, but the chatter and noise from the crowds stayed the same.

"What's going on?"

"That light, I don't think—"

"The Triad should be—"

Agitated discussions and fearful cries resounded. People moved away in large groups as he walked through Deji Ward. And the closer Saba got to the breach, the more he felt it—the astral sea stretching and waking, pressure like the pads of fingers pressing with intention against his temples. This pressure hadn't been there before, not in any noticeable way.

Something in the breach had shifted. Something had changed. Saba's emotions—which currently were an indistinguishable soup in his gut—must have flared too hotly and affected the breach. Or Moss and Silvana had done something in the days he had been separated from them.

You should have gone straight there instead of waiting around for Zek to bed you.

If his emotional connection affected the breach, Saba should never have been so selfish as to put himself in any situation where his emotions could run high. Romance, affection, love—these were some of his greatest fears. Greatest desires. He should have told Zek: *I won't do a thing with you until the breach is closed.*

But he hadn't. And now . . .

He was still minutes away from the razed portion of the city when a horse whinnied behind him. Saba had clambered up onto the risen road that ran across the houses in Deji Ward before it spilled abruptly into the crumbling ruins of Loefka Ward. Beneath him, the crowd had started to thin, repelled by the proximity to the breach. As he thought of it, it flared, just for a moment: a plume of light spraying into the sky like water from a spiracle. The wind howled in his ears.

Could it . . . hear him? Was it calling to him now, beckoning him from across the city?

Could Saba forget all this and drop into the astral sea and let it unmake him, let it pull the flesh from his bones and remake him from osseous matter, from the smallest bit of cartilage? Could Saba come back *different* and *better* if he let himself be changed?

Saba finally reached the edge of Deji Ward and followed the rooftop road down to the abandoned outer ring of Loefka Ward. He walked with determination toward the site.

The crack of a whip whistled sharply through the air. Saba's stomach dropped on instinct. He picked up the speed, not bothering to chance a look behind him, but *shit*—he hadn't run in months. In years, probably. His lungs were scorched, and the very particular pain of disuse had begun to pulse in his hips. Involuntarily, he began to slow down.

"Saba!"

Zek's thick voice spread thin when he shouted; half of its depth was wicked away by the air. Saba made a pathetic noise and stumbled forward. Another gig rumbled toward him, and he skidded to a stop and stepped aside to let it past. Now he allowed himself to look back. Zek was up front, urging the horse onwards.

"Saba!" he called, much closer now.

Half-defeated, Saba turned and stalked forward. He didn't bother to run, which probably made him look really pathetic. "Stop calling me that."

". . . Vasili," Zek conceded after a moment. The gig rumbled to a stop. The horse stamped, kicking up dust. "Please."

"Leave me alone, Zek." Saba kept walking. He shifted his notes to his other arm and gripped them tightly.

"I have secrets. But so do you."

Saba's walls shot up. He bit his tongue so hard he tasted blood and spun back to face the Rezwyn bastard. Fire raged in him.

Girl, girl, girl—was that what Zek meant? Was that how Zek had always seen him? How dare he. Saba stalked back and spat blood and saliva in Zek's direction.

"Fuck you!" he screamed. "You can't possibly be comparing the truth of what I am to whatever you've been hiding."

Zek blanched. He shifted, half shuffling off the gig. "No—that's not—" He sighed and looked up at the sky. Saba looked past him, over the rubble and the stretch of a hundred paces to the pit. The Eye spun, sending columns of prismatic light down to frame them. Zek said, "I know you have personal reasons for wanting to enter the astral sea. And it's not my business to prod or dig into that, so I haven't. I've wanted to, and I haven't. But you're right. I have . . . kept things from you. Namely . . . that I am not an ambassador."

Saba turned fully to stare at him. A warm breeze rustled through his hair, cooling the sweat on his skin. Sounds of panicked chatter and some haunting, worried cries floated up to the road. Saba said nothing at all.

All those nights Zek had left on business. The way he spoke to Zvensian officials. The way he spoke to Judge Hirunz. Or perhaps, the most telling, the way he treated Saba.

Saba wasn't sure what sort of person he'd expected, but Luan Zek had never really fit neatly into the role of diplomat.

Zek cleared his throat. "At least, not in the usual sense of the word." And then, "I'd stand up and walk with you, Saba, but my leg is killing me."

"It's fine," Saba said, sweeter than he meant to.

"Come and sit with me."

They were about as close to the site as they could get with a gig, which still put them a hundred paces from the edge of the pit.

Wordlessly, Saba walked back toward Zek. His limbs felt leaden. He shook with fury and exhaustion, but his eyes strained in their sockets, sharply awake. The gelding snorted and rummaged for tufts of grass in amongst the destruction. From this vantage, the city spread out labyrinthine above them.

No one jumped out of the back to help—Zek must have left the embassy in a hurry, rushing after Saba. In any other circumstance, it might have been a sweet gesture.

Specks of firelight stippled the houses and taverns. The moon cast everything in a silvery hue. Zek gave Saba a few moments in complete silence, which Saba took gratefully. He thought of nothing but the landscape, tried to see nothing but its beauty.

Then Zek spoke to him. "I'm not an ambassador," Zek repeated. "I'm . . . a different sort of agent for the empire. When Dziove was named emperor, there was still a great deal of dissent. A younger emperor to many meant . . . a return to the old ways. But Dziove had made it clear he opposed the push to return to the empire's initial purpose."

Saba blinked. Dubiously he asked, "He opposes expansion?"

Zek's lip curled off his teeth. Exasperation seeped into his voice. "Do you really think, after everything Nio Beumeut did, after everyone I saw die, after my leg—that I would so gleefully serve a colonizer?"

An easy thing to say. Saba wanted to reply: *Kerinsk is still occupied. I know a dozen city-states who can no longer stand on their own without empire assistance.* Zek's question was a nice thing to say, but it was just words.

"Empire is insidious," Saba said gruffly. "I don't know what to believe."

Zek looked disappointed. His jaw tightened. He kept his eyes firmly on the road ahead. "I regret what happened to your homeland, and my part in it," he said, which meant Zek had clearly read Saba's mind. "And I swore from that moment on I would never let myself be cajoled into something as brutal as war ever again. I am like you, Saba, a self-made man—in another way. I would never have served Emperor Dziove if I didn't believe he could be . . . better."

"That's idealistic," Saba said reactively. He sighed and worried at his aching temple. "But I'll let you have idealism. Explain why you have my notes. Explain why you're here at all."

Zek shifted. Saba bit his tongue again, angry at himself for his own vulnerability—for the fact this was happening at all.

It isn't even your fault Zek's a liar—but that didn't matter. If he hadn't gotten close to Zek, he wouldn't be feeling so awful now.

Another flare shot up into the sky. Zek flinched. His eyes dropped to Saba beside him.

"Answer me truthfully—are your thoughts connected to the Eye? Or your feelings?"

"You owe me an answer before I owe you anything."

The air turned tense. Zek straightened in his seat. His shirt was half-undone, and he had rushed after Saba, practically chased him, and yet still seemed so intimidating. When he rolled his shoulders back and let his gaze harden, Saba shivered.

Luan Zek said, "Lord Doric deserved to die."

Saba's breath caught in his throat. "What?"

Something fundamental shifted in Zek. The easy exterior, the unflinching calm with which he held himself, fell away to expose something far less comforting. Zek seemed older, more jaded. He looked despondent as he said, "In fact, it was my duty to ensure he died. He was an old relic—a threat to Dziove's rule, an expansionist. He wanted to annex Zvensia. He wanted to reignite the war with Usleth. And he could have kept his life if he'd minded his own business. But he didn't."

This was too much. They'd been searching—they had been deciphering this mess together. Hurt, Saba said, "*You* killed him?"

"No," Zek said quickly. "No, that wasn't a lie."

"And me?"

Here Zek took his eyes off the risen road and looked at Saba. His gaze softened fractionally. "I've known you were innocent from the start, Vasili."

Zek took one hand off the reins and pulled something from the inner pocket of his jacket. It was a folded piece of paper. Saba plucked it from his fingers and watched Zek cautiously, but the Rezwyn had already returned his attention to the roadside rubble.

Saba shivered with sudden proximity to Zek, to the breach, to the truth. He opened up the paper.

The note read:

> The target has been eliminated, but not by me. Seen something. A judge killed Doric and did something. On purpose. There's a breach between worlds. Saw object in the basilica and thought nothing of it. But found it with this tome, which I took: ichor and unnatural manipulation of the astrok-mer. The tear has caused distress. I will investigate closer tomorrow. Will send report to embassy also. —Hulik

Saba stared at the letter. *A judge killed Doric and did something. On purpose. There's a breach between worlds.*

Blood crowded into his ears until he could hear nothing else. *What?*

The elderly judge had died weeks before the Eye had been activated. Judge Berif had been unmade in the event itself during a visit to Loefka Ward.

Which meant Judge Hirunz—

Saba laughed, because he didn't know how else to react. The horror blinded him. He curled over himself and laughed and laughed, until he was crying. Then he rubbed his hands against his eyes, letter still clutched in his hand.

"On purpose," Saba wheezed. "On fucking purpose."

The Kers at the site of the breach had been murdered. Not unmade by some uncaring, preternatural force. Killed—deliberately—by a man who thought Saba's countrymen were little more than a waste of space. By a man who could not comprehend that they had lives and hopes and dreams, that they were worth as much as anyone else in this city.

He pulled his hands away. Zek's face scrunched up in concern, and the Rezwyn nodded carefully at him. "But I have no proof."

Saba flinched, rubbed his face and handed the note back to Zek. Anxiety made his hand jitter. Furious and scared, he said with as much control as he could manage, "I'm guessing your agent never sent that follow up report?"

"No," Zek said simply.

They glanced at each other. For once, it was Zek who looked away first. Saba didn't want to say anything, but if this Hulik had been investigating the breach . . . if he'd touched it, entered it, then he had been unmade. Nothing would be left. Had he wandered in after the Eye's initial activation? Had he been positioned somewhere to see the murder of the Lord of Veprak and the powering up of the Eye, writing a letter to his superior, avoiding that initial explosion only to touch it on a whim and die anyway?

"You don't have to say it," Zek said glumly. "I know."

They both climbed out of the gig slowly. Saba clutched

his notes to his chest and realized with solemn clarity that Zek had possessed them before ever meeting Saba. He'd read them, and he'd already known who killed Lord Doric, but he was still in Zvensia.

Why was Zek still here?

"You've sent a copy of my notes back to Doskor, haven't you?" Saba asked.

"A summary of them," Zek confirmed. He stretched with his eyes squeezed together, and then regarded Saba carefully. He clicked his tongue and began to walk toward the site. "You seem more concerned about that than anything else."

Saba's grip on his notes tightened. "It's my life's work."

"And look what happens when it's in the wrong hands," Zek snapped. Saba flinched just as Zek cursed in Doskorian. There was such a distance between their bodies now that Saba could hardly stand it. Zek spat over his shoulder and turned back to Saba. "Quite frankly, this breach is Zvensia's problem. If I was smart, I would have left already. Marked Hulik as dead, returned with the notes, perhaps monitored the Eye to judge its impact from afar. Maybe getting this involved was a mistake. Staying here means involving the empire even further in Zvensian politics."

"Then why are you here?" Saba spat.

Zek said nothing, and Saba stopped fidgeting to turn bodily towards him. Zek did him the courtesy of facing him fully.

Saba knew how he must have looked. He was hunched forward protectively over a bundle of pages, sweating and upset, a mangy dog at best.

"Don't make me beg my own colonizer for help, Zek," he pleaded. "You have the power to destroy my life. To let Byrengrad be unmade. Let me close the breach before you do whatever you mean to."

Would the Rezwyns want to punish him for his work on the astral sea? Would Saba still end up there, in chains, a prisoner?

Would Zek do that to him?

Zek turned around to face him. His expression changed, buckling violently, but when he spoke it was clear and strong. "Tell me what you think. Why am I still here, Vasili?"

"Fine," Saba growled. He gestured to Zek's pocket, where the Rezwyn had returned his agent's note. "If a judge did this—if Judge Hirunz did this with no care for his own country, then there's no telling how he might apply his new knowledge to, say, a traditional and long-standing enemy."

"Sure," Zek said. "The empire must be careful. Anything regarding the astrok-mer demands we investigate, and if Judge Hirunz truly subjected Zvensia to this, then you are right—the empire must contend with the potential that he could do the same to us. That is, of course, if he knows how to wield the power of the open astrok-mer—and this chaos suggests he doesn't. But I still could have left by now. The emperor is waiting for me. I need to report; I really should have left by now, Vasili. I didn't, I haven't, because of *you*."

Saba swallowed. "Why?"

Zek shook his head, like he couldn't bear to answer. "The Triad said that a foreigner had been arrested for the death of Lord Doric as well as for activating the Eye. So at first I went to the prison hoping that I'd find Hulik there, still alive. Then I saw you. At first, I thought I should find out what I can. Get you to wax lyrical about the arcane device of yours. Then you spoke, and I recognized the anger in you, and the fear, and the urge to live. The fire. I saw you, and knew I should leave, but I couldn't. You were innocent. They were going to destroy you, one way or the other. I didn't want that to happen."

Saba shivered. *Don't go. Don't leave.* His mouth felt gummy, voice thick in his throat, and he couldn't speak. But he reached out, just enough to slip his pinky finger into Zek's. The Rezwyn squeezed back.

Zek cleared his throat. "But one thing still puzzles me—Hirunz targeted you specifically. He framed you for this. Why? What could he achieve by doing that?"

"I don't—" Saba said. This was too much. Zek had stayed for him. Hirunz had probably opened the breach. Accidentally? On purpose? Lord Doric of Veprak—well, who knew how he was involved in all this, except that Zek's agent Hulik had seen him killed by a judge. But if Judge Hirunz was responsible for it all and had scapegoated Saba specifically . . .

Saba's laughter came out like a bark. This was too much. He pulled his hand free of Zek and doubled over in sudden pain.

"Fuck," he said. "*Fuck!*"

Zek said nothing, waiting patiently for Saba to speak. And Saba, from his squatting place on the ground, looked up at Luan Zek with dead eyes.

"I didn't think he knew," Saba said.

Zek raised a questioning brow, but nothing else about him shifted.

Well, why not tell him? Zek already knew about the configuration of Saba's body. He knew Saba was Kerish. What would one more revelation do?

He's practically a stranger, Saba's mind told him. But whether that thought came to him because he was worried who Zek would tell, or because Saba worried how Zek would see him, he couldn't be sure. The more sensible thought—that Zek, regardless of his kind words, was an agent of Emperor Dziove—barely crossed Saba's mind.

Let them know. Let them all know.

"I was rather important in Kerinsk, Zek," Saba said. He pushed himself up to stand. "And if Hirunz knows about me, eliminating me makes sense. He hates the refugees. We're a drain on his resources. And if it were to ever come out—who I really am—he might not be able to control the Kers any longer."

Zek was still frowning. Saba's throat clammed up.

Do it. Do it. Just fucking say it, you coward.

Saba said, stilted, awkwardly, "I was their princess."

Nothing shifted in Zek's expression. The moment stretched out between them. Saba's heart ached, anticipation gripping the pulsing organ, squeezing it, making it hurt. Then Zek cocked his head, exhaled, and he asked, "The one the Kerish refugees still laud?"

Saba nodded. He brought his hand up to the back of his neck, hesitated, and then moved his hair aside, turning so Zek could see the raised mark. Fingertips pressed gently against the keloid skin. Zek would know this symbol. Perhaps he had been tasked with finding the princess—making sure she died.

Saba dropped his hair and glanced back at Zek, who pressed a finger to his forehead, eyes closing. "Gods, Saba."

Something happened to Zek then. If Saba had ever misunderstood the term dawning realization, he saw it play out now on Zek's face. His pale skin went pallid, eyebrows shifting fractionally upward, angled for minuscule despair. Saba found he could read Zek with ease.

"Yes, that's right. You and your country took my birthright from me. And in a twisted way, you also saved me. Kerinsk was a matriarchy. I was Kerinsk's heir. Changing myself the way I have, becoming who I am—I don't know. I am selfish enough, sometimes, to be grateful the whole country collapsed, just so I never had to find out what my people would think of me."

"Don't," Zek spat. "I hate that, Vasili, I hate hearing you speak of yourself like some great burden. Don't think of yourself as selfish, or a disappointment—you chose yourself. You don't know how rare that is. You don't know how brave you are."

It felt patronizing. Stupid. Made Saba feel small and brittle. And at the same time, he had never had anyone say that to him, not for years and years.

Barely above a whisper, Saba said, "I only did it so I could live."

"And live happily," Zek said firmly.

They stared at one another.

Can I live happily? Can you help me?

What Saba wouldn't give to go back an hour, to take his clothes off, and go to Zek's lap when he offered it. Saba wished for the oblivion.

But would Zek touch him now? Did Saba want that? Zek had betrayed him—let Saba run around like a headless chicken searching for notes he already had. But even if Zek had no obligation to stay or to help, he had.

Even so, Saba had to say, "If you think of me any differently, I don't want to hear it."

"I don't," Zek said too quickly.

Sometimes, Zek could be too idealistic for his own good. How he had survived war, injury, and empire with his idealism intact, Saba might never know.

Somewhat sadly, he shrugged at Zek. "But you do. I was royalty, even if that title is now defunct. I was a girl, briefly, even if I really never was. I am a big problem politically, and a bit of a problem bodily—even attraction to me isn't simple or straightforward."

Zek briefly closed his eyes. His jaw tightened. When he spoke, his voice was stiff, like it was squeezing itself through the gaps between his teeth. "No, the attraction part is as simple as it gets. Inevitable, even. I see you and can barely—" He sighed. "You're putting words in my mouth."

Maybe. Maybe I have to. Maybe every time I don't, I get hurt. Saba scoffed and looked down at his hands. His heart hurt with a very particular ache; sometimes it was easier to kill your own hope before something else did. He felt himself edging toward the cliff in his mind, ready to shove this kernel of growing affection off and watch it dash its brains out on the rocks below. "I am bracing myself for the inevitable."

Zek had the gall to ask, "Inevitable what?"

"Time when you leave."

"Am I leaving?" Zek asked. "Why should I do that now, of all times?"

He gestured to the breach, which had begun flashing a blinding white. Horrified, Saba realized the light matched the beat of his heart. Zek kept his hand out as if this was enough to justify everything—him staying, him wanting Saba.

Saba ignored it and said, "Because it's too much now, isn't it?" Zek watched him with wary curiosity, and Saba had to turn away. "It was already too much—a breach with the potential to unmake the city. I'm the scholar accused of unleashing it. Your role here—your fleeting role here. It's been a handful of weeks, and I've been fantasizing about touching you when all this insanity was happening, and I just think, if I wasn't so desperate all the time, that maybe I wouldn't be so upset when nothing I hope for comes to pass, and—"

Zek turned to him and pulled Saba across the seat and into his arms.

That was all—there was no kiss, no words, just the embrace. Zek's arms held a crushing power to them, and at the slightest bit of pressure, Saba exhaled.

"You need to breathe," Zek murmured calmly.

Saba breathed. Over Zek's shoulder he could see the prismatic light previously blooming over the city begin to fade.

Zek said, "You're affecting the breach. Your fear, your upset—negative emotions, right?"

Saba reached up and touched the outside of Zek's arm. He pressed his face close to the bulge of Zek's bicep, briefly relaxing against his warmth. "I think so," Saba whispered.

"Fear is the worst. It started when I went into the pit, I think—I felt the astral sea touch me. I saw . . . the man I've always envisioned myself to be staring back in the breach. And I just—"

"Breathe," Zek said again.

Part of Saba fought the instruction. He wasn't used to relaxing so easily, especially around men—let alone men who had a different kind of effect on Saba's body. But two things existed simulatenously in Zek's embrace in that moment: the desire for him bodily, and the other, warmer, far more unsettling thing that danced far too closely to genuine care.

But another part of Saba found it easy to do what Zek said.

They both pulled away to stare at the pit. The Eye rotated as evenly paced as ever and below it, the breach had settled.

Zek put a hand at the back of Saba's head and squeezed. He pressed his lips to Saba's forehead. "That's it, good boy."

Saba's eyes fluttered closed, and all the fear and exhaustion and anger rushed out of him. He wanted to be angry at Zek. Perhaps it would be easier or better if he was. But Zek had risked much to help Saba, and continued to risk much, and Saba could feel the necklace against his neck, and it didn't matter that they'd only known each other a few weeks—Saba wanted him.

But Zek's words calling him *good boy* fired in Saba, low and hot, like he could not bear to hear them spoken unless Zek meant them.

"Don't," Saba whispered.

Zek pulled away and said, sharply, "Oh, I didn't mean—"

"Don't call me that unless you plan to follow through."

Saba had mumbled that against the bulge of Zek's bicep, still staring toward the site. In front of the rubble, where the only bit of movement came from the wind moving dust and ash along the ground, Saba's guilt should have reignited. It didn't.

He turned to look up at Zek. His heart raced. And then something pressed under the soft part of his chin. Hard wood—the hare's snout of Zek's cane gently urged his head up. Saba craned back, eyes heavy. Zek leaned forward and kissed him.

A scream erupted nearby.

No—not just nearby. From the direction of the pit.

Saba pulled away. Something felt wrong. He felt all the color drain from his cheeks; this was not the breach. This sound was distinctly human. And the only humans at the site, as far as the letter had said, were Moss and Silvana.

He met Zek's eye. "Go," Zek breathed. And then—louder, half shoving Saba away, he shouted, *"Go!"*

Saba shot out of the gig. He spun away from Zek and buckled, foot catching on upturned rock and rubble, then righted himself and kept running.

The edge of the pit lay a hundred paces away. He pushed himself as fast as he could to the ladder. The warm night air crowded into his ears, muffling everything but the ragged sounds of his own uneven breathing. Another scream went out, and then, very distinctly, a flood of "no."

"No, no, no, no!"

Saba skidded to a stop moments before he toppled over the edge of the pit. A few lanterns were lit at the base of the ladder, and one near the open tent, the awning of which struggled and flapped madly in the wind. He saw the gedrokbone Moss and Silvana had collected from the underdark, now fashioned into the new failsafe. It sat glinting prismatically every time it caught the glare from the breach, like a mirror calling to itself. But no attempt had been made to attach it, and no one was there—no one was by the tent. Then shadow ate most of the site, and Saba could see nothing for a stretch until the place where the astral sea spilled into Byrengrad. Above that flaring, pulsating wound spun the Eye that had caused this whole mess. At eye level, Saba stared at it, and regretted ever making it.

Pulsing prismatic light ebbed weakly from the breach, and from that light he caught sight of silhouettes gathered beneath the beam. Two? Three? Something shone, metal catching light—someone wearing a mask.

Was a paragon with them?

Or a judge?

If it was a judge—

He nearly threw himself down the ladder. He scrambled down it awkwardly, mind racing ahead of him, dozens of panicked thoughts coalescing into a single one: *Mossinne*. Because who else could that scream belong to?

And if it was a judge—if Hirunz was here, after everything Saba had just learned about him—

When he had five rungs left to cover, he jumped and ran toward the breach—which, at the rising chatter in his head, bloomed overhead in iridescent brightness. The whole site lit up like it was daytime. Now the Eye spun above him, and the breach bloomed from the lens all the way to the ground of the pit, a prismatic wound blaring down into the dust. Inside, standing like a servant might, waiting for an order—was Saba.

Or a version of him: the ideal, the dream, flesh perfected.

Saba felt like he might throw up. But unnatural power burned off his anxiety. What he felt wasn't just adrenaline. Something more took control of his limbs, his heart rate, his emotion. Saba tried in vain to control at least his breathing, knowing he affected the size of the breach, but there was too much fury in him.

That was it. Rage. Fury. A desire to finally take control. In the brightness, he could now see the rest of the figures gathered around the pit.

Giste with her arms out placatingly, and Moss kicking the air violently, kicking the *air* because Hirunz had hefted her from the ground by her hair. Silvana had her sword drawn. Two sentinels—Maksid and some other—flanked Hirunz.

"Put her down," Saba called.

The breach stayed bright and flaring. He could level his voice, keep that part of him calm and flat. But everything else brimmed with rage. It felt half-anxious, part of him futilely clinging on to sanity. If he let himself go, he'd become fury incarnate. No matter his size, no matter his morals; he wanted this to hurt. Hirunz had gone too far now. That was Mossinne. That was his *friend.*

And Hirunz—Hirunz knew too much about Saba. Hirunz was threatened by him. Saba didn't have enough knowledge to drag Hirunz down, but he could let his fury do the work.

Wispy arms of opalescent light flared off the body of the breach and whisked dangerously close to Hirunz. He flinched away and dropped Moss, who landed with a screech. She ran straight into Silvana's arms, and then pulled a dagger from Silvana's belt.

"You *bastard!*" she screamed. She half lunged toward Hirunz, but the sentinels jutted forward with their swords. Silvana flinched and put a protective hand on Moss's shoulder.

"Arrest them," Hirunz said hoarsely.

"Sir?" a sentinel said. Saba wanted it to be Maksid.

Hirunz turned. "Unapproved tinkering on a device that has killed a great deal of people and continues to threaten the safety of this city. Illicitly acquiring gedrok material. We have a bureaucracy for a reason. What will Usleth say when it learns Zvensia has engaged in illegal acquisitions? Let alone the—the *fraternizing!*" He ran a hand down the back of his neck. His eyes glinted behind his golden mask. "I'm disappointed, Giste."

Giste said nothing. She seemed frozen in place, like she wasn't sure who to align herself with.

"This is what is going to happen," Hirunz said. "The Triad will supervise the construction of the casing. We will contain the breach and move it out of the city. We will make an exchange with the empire, and this problem will go away. But we will do it properly! With processes!"

No one had turned to Saba yet.

Because why would they? Everyone looked at Saba and saw a scholar. The greatest threat he posed was his mind, and even then, the danger Hirunz had tried to align with Saba had been entirely manufactured; Saba hadn't opened the breach. Somehow, for some reason, *Hirunz* had. Saba was little more than a mangy, underfed scholar, someone Hirunz could throw to the wolves.

No one was looking at him now and expecting he could or would fight back.

Well, Saba wanted attention now. He wanted to be seen, as he really was. And the breach, that quivering open wound, that energy, a port in the storm of Saba's life, heard him.

And he let his rage slip out of him.

It happened slowly—or that was how Saba perceived it. None of the movement was tremulous or aching; the breach flared smoothly, peeling apart the sky more so than cracking through. It was like the sky wanted to open for it. With the impression of old and rotting wallpaper, the world sloughed away to reveal the tear and its view into the astral sea. Saba, somehow, made it grow, coaxing that distant and blurry silhouette closer.

The silhouette of his own desire stepped forward, and the whole site—perhaps all of Byrengrad—drowned in impossible brightness. Then the light dwindled, not like a flame but like a sunset, and the breach returned to its soft glow, drowning all of them again in darkness. Only it was bigger now—big enough for a human to slip through.

"You," Hirunz spat. In the dark, only the wild whites of his eyes showed, alight with a frenzied fury. His wiry form seemed leaner, stripped back; distantly, Saba registered that he wasn't wearing his usual judge's layering. This peeled back appearance made him smaller, but stranger, too, like a fine knife had flayed all the skin from him, and a good bit of muscle and tendon, too. This ill-formed, disproportionate body suddenly threw itself at Saba.

Saba darted back, but he was too slow. Hirunz scruffed him like a cat and dragged him forward, shaking him violently.

"You did this," he spat—pointing at the breach. The new shape was less clean, a broken tear into the world. Hirunz's grip on his neck sent referred pain twinging down his back and shoulders. "You just made it bigger! Worse!"

But when Saba looked back, Hirunz was smiling, a dusty, carnivorous grin that chilled Saba to the core. Was he seeing that correctly? Saba twisted against Hirunz's grip. His heart was racing. Then Hirunz laughed—completely devoid of humor. He sounded exhausted.

Ridiculous. Selfish. Hirunz had killed Lord Doric, had framed Saba, had etched the sigil from Saba's notes into the Eye, had removed the failsafe, had started this breach and wanted it to grow. He had no right to feel tired. No right to be smiling. Judge Hirunz had no right to feel anything but crushingly sorry—and Saba knew he didn't.

"I know what you did," Saba whispered hoarsely. "Everything."

"What do you think you know?" Hirunz asked on the end of that eerie, hysterical laugh. But before Saba could reply, the judge let go of him. Saba grunted as he landed and tried to straighten himself. In this moment he heard the cry of someone else behind him, a voice exploding in the open expanse of the site.

"Saba!"

Saba turned. Zek had found him. He limped forward, evidently in pain, but with a determined eagerness that made Saba shiver. The breach's glow illuminated the Rezwyn's face. All his features twisted with worry, anguish knitting at his brows. It happened slowly. Saba turned, saw Zek, and thought several things at once: that Zek had a beauty to him even when he was worried, that he was glad Zek was here, and one more thought, a little crueler.

Damn it, Zek. Why couldn't you have told me sooner that Hirunz was responsible?

Saba knew the answer intrinsically, even if he didn't like it.

Because Zek had correctly assumed that Saba couldn't always keep a grip on his emotions. Because now, standing here before the judge somehow responsible for the death of Kerinsk's legacy, a massacre of the people who had sidestepped a genocide, Saba's fury and fear were crashing heads, competing for his attention. Flares of prismatic light, beautiful but deadly, licked out toward them, and the silhouette inside the breach cocked his head.

Saba stared up at Hirunz and said, "I could ask Suoduny to unmake everyone here right now if I wanted to."

"Stop it," Hirunz said. His voice wavered. "Stop it now."

But Saba didn't know how to stop it. Perhaps he didn't want to. He marveled in silence as that blurred, shadowy figure he knew to be himself but *better* shimmered in the astral sea. It knelt down and extended its hand to him.

"What," Saba said quietly, transfixed.

Hirunz made a noise of agitation. "You can see something?" he spat. "Why don't you go to it?"

Someone sucked in a sharp, brittle breath.

"*No*!" Zek cried, seeing something Saba couldn't. "*No, wait!*"

And then two hands pressed against Saba's back and pushed him into the breach.

Chapter Sixteen

By all accounts, there should have been nothingness. Not the nothingness associated with sleep or death—both of which were closer to different states of being—and not the black expanse of night that Saba sometimes thought felt like a vast emptiness.

Nothingness, really, was an absence of anything recognizable or knowable; a paradoxical thought, since acknowledging nothingness would suggest it was both recognizably nothing, and knowable enough to pass comment on.

As it was, the place where Saba Vasili ended up was about as knowable as his own flesh.

This was how it happened: He fell—was pushed—into the engorged wound of the astral sea. His flesh had touched it, and dozens of sparks had lit up along his body, electrifying his organs and his tendons and his bones. But he had not been unmade.

He realized this only upon waking, and even then, it took several minutes of dazed confusion for his mind to parse his new reality. Saba gasped like he had never drawn breath before. His eyes watered, and a briny odor crowded his nose. Faintly, he could smell rot, like a fish baking in the sun, but that came and went. With vertigo-like dizziness, Saba sat up. Tall grass itched at his legs, which were bare apart from socks, one tight around his calf and one so loose it bunched up around his ankle, half slipping inside his shoes. These were impractical and dainty. His hair was longer than ever, an intensely curled nest that fell below his chest—which still had breasts.

And he was in a dress.

"No," he murmured, in sudden panic. He thrashed and tried to stand, but gravity felt stronger than normal. Weighted and unbalanced, he toppled back down into the grass. Pain throbbed in his head and his heart raced as it slipped into the throes of a true panic. "No, no, no."

"*Quiet*," a voice hissed. Something tugged at his hair, not unkindly, but with enough force to pull his head back down. He landed flat so that he was now framed on either side by tall green grass that shimmered with prismatic morning dew.

Breathe. Calm down, the rational part of him said. But everything was alight with the realization: *You're a girl again. You're a girl. You stupid fool—you can't escape it.*

It hurt to breathe. He moved from panic to a kind of distant, aching pain, something that didn't stop the adrenaline in his body but numbed him enough that he stopped hyperventilating. Part of Saba vacated the front of his consciousness and left it blank and empty, retreating further into the keep of his mind. The dress felt scratchy. Vaguely he realized he was dressed incorrectly; he wasn't wearing an underdress. He wasn't in stockings. He had no gloves, no hair pins, no veil, which the women of Kerinsk were meant to wear.

His mother used to tell him: *You're the sun of this country. Too beautiful, too bright. You'll blind them if you let them look upon your face.*

In Saba's mind, he'd replace the 'u' of sun with an 'o' and imagine his mother calling him that. *You are the son of this country. You are my son.*

She had never said that. She'd never had a chance to. She had died, and Nio Beumeut's forces had swooped in to take Kerinsk. Saba had let them, because he was only twelve and he wasn't ready. He'd never wanted it, anyway. *Make Maksid the heir*, he had said once to his mother. *Make him the princess.*

It doesn't work that way, little sun, she had replied. Saba didn't know why he was the way he was, but he felt like vomiting every time someone referred to him as princess.

How silly it all seemed now.

Saba breathed slowly and came back to the moment. The sky above had the appearance of a mottled bruise, purple smeared with a horrific yellow. The wispy clouds glimmered, flickering and pulsing against the sky. A man—a boy really—shuffled into view over Saba's body and pressed himself close, hand over Saba's mouth. Instinctively, Saba seized up, but his body quickly unwound. This was a familiar touch, a familiar memory.

Maksid.

His brother looked young. He had a softness to him at this time, before age and war and Zvensia had snuffed it out. These days he did everything with a kind of tired duty, to the point Saba couldn't be sure if Maksid was trying to protect him out of brotherly love or Kerish loyalty.

Saba was, of course, heir to the throne.

He remembered this moment well. They were on the road, fleeing Kerinsk and the invading Rezwyn army. There were still two years to go before the city was absorbed completely.

"What—" Saba began, but Maksid clamped his mouth shut and put a forceful finger to his lips. Saba focused on breathing. The world fogged with mist.

Chatter warbled nearby. Saba couldn't pick out the words; not then and not now. Maksid pressed low and hovered there for an amount of time Saba thought to be unnecessary. Then he pulled away and said, gruffly, "You should shut your mouth more."

Saba remembered the feeling that bubbled up for him then: affronted shock. Maksid had never spoken to him like that. Not once.

It's just a memory. You can't change it.

Saba didn't want to change it anyway. It had happened. He barely remembered it. If this was the astral sea, then it was sorely disappointing. Where was the vision of his idealized self? Where was Suoduny, multifaceted and looming?

"They broke the treaty, you know," Maksid said unprompted. Saba ignored him and stood up. He walked for a bit, pressing against the air, trying to find a seam in this memory. He was still, inevitably, thinking of this place physically, and he found it near impossible to consider that it only appeared this way because his mind wanted it to.

Maksid said again, "They broke the treaty, you know."

"Yes," Saba called back absentmindedly. "I remember."

The vision shivered and split. The sky dissolved into blackness. Saba closed his eyes.

Before the invasion, Kerinsk and the empire had been shaky allies. They'd had a treaty, similar to the one Kerinsk had with Zvensia, but the one with the Rezwyns specified that Kerinsk could call upon the empire for aid.

When the queen had died, Saba had been about to be crowned. But he'd been a child. Everyone had known it. The Rezwyns had known it. And Nio Beumeut had invaded right in that moment of vulnerability.

Saba hadn't really felt it back then: the distinct emotion of being torn from his birthright. He hadn't understood it. He hadn't wanted it in the first place. Even now he had that extensive emotion of separation from his title, because it was bound up so entirely in gendered weight. But standing in the astral sea, standing amongst undiluted power, with his mortal mind scrambling to make sense of a place that existed wholly outside time and space, Saba felt—sad.

He took a shaky breath. Now that he could stand upright without falling, he saw that the scene had broken apart. He now stood on a little island in a sea of blackness. Sharp flashes of iridescence cut through the expanse at random intervals, and other archipelagos of light wobbled in the distance. Beyond this, nothing else stood out to him.

By now, he simply should have stopped existing. Every second he spent here, incredible and unknowable power was affecting him. He was being exposed to dangerous levels of ichor.

According to every account, when the Eye had been activated, everyone in Loefka Ward had simply stopped existing. Radiant beams of astral power had engulfed them, unmade them, evaporated them into a mist or briefly preserved their bodies in ash. But not Saba.

Why not Saba?

Perhaps you're already dying. Perhaps your flesh is pockmarked and sloughing off from the ichor, perhaps the pain is so intense your mind has retreated here, to some childhood moment. Perhaps you have seconds to live and it's all stretching out impossibly long in this part of your brain.

Or perhaps . . .

Saba's hand flew up to the gedrokbone necklace. Could this little bit of gedrokbone be enough to mitigate such unmaking power? Or was something else at play here?

He turned around. Maksid sat poised in the grass, locked in the memory of their departure from Kerinsk. His youthful face stared blankly at Saba, who hated everything about this. After knowing himself for so many years, to be back in this version of his body was a cruelty. Agitation spiked in him every second he thought about it, so he tried and failed to not give it any attention. The softness around his hips, the slight pull of breasts, the constraint of the dress as it hugged his waist—*I will go insane if I am made to stay like this. I will go insane.*

Maksid stared like he was waiting for Saba to return so they might continue the memory. Saba didn't move. He said, instead, "I came here for a reason."

He spoke with confidence, even if that wasn't quite true, assuming Maksid was some agent of the astral sea, assuming there was order to this primordial chaos. Perhaps if he spoke his will into the world it would change for him. Saba had been pushed in, but underneath that small betrayal sat a kernel of something else. Saba was horrified when he recognized it.

Relief.

Relief that he hadn't actually thrown himself in. Relief that it had been someone else, that he might pass the blame to Hirunz, who was already so easy to hate. Because if it had been Saba—if he had been the one to leap willingly into the embrace of this impossible plane—he would have to contend with the knowledge that still, after everything, the desire to be different meant more to him than any desire to live.

For Zek, Moss, Silvana, Maksid, even Giste—embracing the idealized version of his body by choice might very well have condemned them and all of Byrengrad to the astral sea's unmaking power. Without Saba, how would they close the breach? Especially now that he was so resolutely tied to the tear between their planes. Especially now he had proven he could affect its size.

Two thoughts collided in him: *I have to get out of here* and *I have to do what I've always wanted to do.*

One part of him, the moral and more human side, knew he had to leave. The other part, more base and more primal, writhed under his skin, craving change. He'd survived entry into the astral sea. Whether that was luck or something else, it didn't matter. He would never have this opportunity again.

Saba was still staring at the preserved version of Maksid, who said nothing.

"Did you ever love me?" Saba asked quietly. He thought of his brother in the sentinel mask, standing with his sword drawn toward Moss. Had Maksid reacted after Hirunz had pushed Saba into the breach? Did he care? Did he care at all?

This memory of Maksid certainly didn't. It blinked, eyes blank like a ragdoll's, and said nothing.

Agitated, unable to stand still, Saba cursed and started tearing at the dress. It was a particular bit of evil, dressing him up like this. Why had the astral sea sent him back to this? He tugged at the dress and began to pull it over his head, only to realize he'd then have to contend with the girlish childlike body he had been reverted to. He felt ill and pulled the dress back down.

"I thought you would seek me out instantly," a voice said.

Saba spun, and in the act of spinning, the world reformed itself. It could only have been a second or less, but in the moment Saba's vision blurred, Maksid disappeared. The grassy hinterland he'd encountered on his escape from Kerinsk went too. For a moment there was nothing but black, like Saba had closed his eyes, and then a fine red mist settled over the world like he was inside flesh, like he had been made into blood itself. Every part of the scene came together, every tree and blade of grass, and all of it was reformed into something else. That preserved little hell of his had been replaced—

—by a gedrok.

Saba's heart had never beat so hard.

The gedrok loomed tall. Saba had to crane his neck to see all of it. He had seen sketches and illicit materials harvested from their bodies before, but never an intact creature. Faintly, Saba could see the pulse of organs deep in the gedrok's body, the thick, impenetrable bone shadowed inside it. The scales were osseous material, and all of them glowed with life and arcane power. It opened its maw and huffed at him; a spray of salt, misted ichor, and unidentifiable red mist showered him. Saba smelled nothing, as if the astral sea preserved the creature's freshness long after it had gone extinct in Saba's plane. as if a mildewed rot was spreading infinitesimally slowly across the undead gedrok bodies scattered through his world.

His stomach dropped as it towered over him, this colossal and ancient beast. Looking at it generated a sense of unease in him almost immediately; something in his mind activated, unnerved him, upset him. Saba found himself stepping backwards instinctively. The gedrok had a distinctly human presence to it, or at least a sentience, and when the gedrok creaked and moved, the whole sea shook with the shift. Saba nearly toppled over as the gedrok lowered itself. Its jaw cracked as if opening for the first time in eons, and briny water spewed out from the fat pink roll of its tongue, which lolled out over its teeth at Saba's feet.

"I will show you," the gedrok said, voice resonating deep in Saba's skull, "what you have wondered for years."

The gedrok exhaled a warm, thick breath, and it enveloped Saba's body. His vision blurred, and the scene around him shifted once more.

He saw gedroks, dozens of them, more than he had ever conceived of being alive. Colossal beasts slouched across the ground, lurching across land that resembled Kerinsk, the empire, and further east. They were running—from something, or to somewhere, he couldn't be sure. Saba caught glimpses of eyes straining in their sockets and muffled inhuman noises. Fleshy feet hit the ground, a thumping vibration he could feel in his body like he was part of this stampede. Then Saba could smell the strange odor of their bodies, redolent not of death but of moss and rain.

An umbral dread took root in his bones. He couldn't tell if it was his own or a remembered, referred fear, given to him by the thousands of terrified beasts. The vision shifted to an earlier time, and Saba saw a tear form between their worlds in which a new memory unfolded. He watched as a natural breach cracked open in some snowy region. Countless bodies of colossal gedroks fell through and hit the ground. In a panic, they all stumbled, picked a direction, and ran. Saba knew with intimate knowledge that this took place long ago, long before humans. The gedroks had fallen through. It was as simple as that. They had fallen through, and, cut off from the astral sea, had struggled to survive in Saba's world.

So they had run, scattered—and died.

Saba didn't understand. He shook his head, and the vision cleared, returning him to his audience with the gedrok.

Saba's research had been answered, his hypothesis confirmed. Here was the origin of the gedroks, creatures formed in the astral sea.

In a voice that resonated in Saba's mind, the beast said, "Gedroks are vessels. Empty. They are made of ichor, formed from the ebb and flow of the astral sea. They have no sentience until the astral sea slips into them."

Saba sucked in a few breaths. He was beginning to understand. "Gedroks are your agents."

"Not mine," the voice told him. "Its."

The astral sea's, finished Saba. Just as he had theorized all this time. Power and potential, the astral sea was a force—one he had felt himself connect to when those first flares of the breach had skimmed across his hand. But the certainty of sentience here sent a chill through his mortal body. The human—the animal, the fearful creature he was—shivered at the thought this place was alive.

But then Saba thought of ichor, and what it really was: Infinite possibility. Infinite potential. The gedrok had gifted him this vision to settle him—had appealed to his scholarly mind . . . but for what reason?

After a beat it said, "Ask your questions."

Saba had hundreds, but standing before this creature, he struggled to form even one.

"Alright," he said from the ground. He looked up at the gedrok, which still sat with its mouth gaping. "Are you Suoduny?"

"Yes, but also more," it said. "I am one grain of sand in the entirety of the astral sea. I am you refracted and reflected at the source. I hold multitudes."

Unhelpful, really. Not quite an answer. But Saba had an innate understanding settle in him: the vastness of this place, the power in it, could not relate to humanity. What Saba spoke to now was barely more than a sliver of this plane given voice through Saba himself, and it would speak to him in his language, with his words, for his understanding.

"What—" he said, and then laughed. He went to his knees and stared at the ground, which consisted of nothing but blackness. Very politely, the gedrok said nothing. Saba stayed like that for a time as his brain struggled to catch up.

In among all this existential talk, Saba had to wonder what it meant that he had spent so long worried about how he could have been. Worried about potential, focused on change, and never once giving himself the credit for loving himself enough to change in the first place.

He looked up at the gedrok. He thought of his ideal self, thought of the young girl he looked like now, and of the body he had fought for back in the material plane.

"What is the true me?"

The gedrok did not so much answer as show him.

Saba had a brief and startling moment where he simply stopped existing. Then he returned, and midway through his scream, he saw everything and nothing, dozens of possibilities, hundreds of potentials unfolding around him. He saw them all at once, every possible version of himself, everything that had been and was and would be. He saw himself oscillating constantly, his hands grew and shrunk, his hands were male, female, old, young, injured, intact. When he blinked next, it all stopped. He was back to how he presently knew himself, back in the body he inhabited many years ago, when he still looked like *her*.

Which Saba thought must mean the gedrok—or Suoduny, or the astral sea—was granting him the grace of reality. It was keeping him sane. Right now, Saba concluded, whether he could feel it or not, he was oscillating through every potential in the many universes.

Every him was true here.

"Can I choose which one I want to be?"

Saba's ideal form came together suddenly.

Inexorably, the idealized Saba resolved, fully formed and perfect before him, with no bloody, viscous coming together of the body. Saba blinked, and then he was there.

That should have been the first sign that he and this Saba were different. Saba's body as he had lived it—that thing he had fought so long and so hard and so specifically for—was all bound up in ways of the flesh. In pleasure and in pain, sure, but also in blood. In surgery, in growth, in fat, in larger muscles pulling against stiff, brittle tendons. It was all in the body. It was all in the flesh. And this man standing before Saba now, if he could be called such, was too perfect to be real.

This did not stop Saba craving him.

This apparition looked like the carved marble likeness of a relative of Saba's. He had the same hair, he had Saba's nose, but then every minute change beyond that gathered and made an entirely new man—which surprised Saba. Even with his eternal desire to be different, it had proven difficult over the years to fully comprehend the holistic vision he sought to become. This version was born from all of Saba's insecurities. He had thought: *I have a weak jaw,* and so had envisioned a stronger one. He had thought: *My cheeks are round and ill-defined*, and so he had given himself prominent cheekbones. The result was a lengthened face, one that was slightly unapproachable; sharp features made him thorny, his expression pinched in a natural look of superiority.

The body itself was difficult to look at it because it was so perfect. This version of Saba had definition, lean muscle rippling beneath a healthy amount of fat. The arms were large, strong, well-defined, and the shoulders bulged with a firmness. The upper body was beautifully broad, and it tapered into a small waist unburdened by sizable hips. The serratus rippled and caught some imagined light that probably only existed for Saba to see exactly how defined the muscles were.

And then there was the matter of the cock, which Saba glanced at once, before an anxious and upset laugh expelled from his throat. There it was! There it was.

He had never seen a man quite that perfect—so perfect, in fact, that the apparition slipped slightly into the uncanny. Saba didn't care. Ethereal, untouchable beauty—who wouldn't want that?

But somehow, it didn't look quite right. Or rather, in looking right, the apparition's perfection made him so aware of how wrong he felt that he was moved close to tears within seconds. Because he should have been this body. If not this, then close to it. If not the muscle, then the height. The width. The cock. The *potential.*

It should have been. And it wasn't.

A lumpen, convoluted feeling grew tumor-like in his stomach. He locked eyes with himself—him as he had imagined himself for years—and felt urgently lustful, and afraid, and sad, and overwhelmingly joyous. Each feeling layered on top of itself, undulating over the percussive beat of his anxious heart, and the urge to wail bubbled up like vomit in his throat.

"You," he said.

"You," the apparition replied.

Saba's heart fluttered. He had thought of this for years, only much, much differently. He'd had years to think about the outside of this form and what he would look like, what he might do when he finally looked like this. Always, though, Saba had been occupying the vessel. Whatever or whoever operated it now was—Saba at least hoped—not him, and thus, even after years of imagining a moment akin to this, Saba had absolutely nothing prepared to say to it.

"I don't. . ." He swallowed pitifully. The apparition looked at him, not unkindly, but neither wholly impressed either. "I don't know what I'm meant to do."

"You're not *meant* to do anything," the apparition said.

"Then why are you here?" Saba said. He was surprised at how angry he sounded. How angry he *felt*. This was a taunting and ridiculous theatre. If the apparition was Suoduny, or the astral sea itself, or even just a reflection of Saba, he wanted to know why. Why must he be confronted by this perfection? Before the apparition could reply to his question, Saba continued, "And why did you force me to look like this instead of like you?"

Because there was something doubly evil about having to face his own idealized masculinity in the body of preteen girl.

"I would never force you," the apparition said. "You chose that form for yourself."

Which made no sense. Saba balked, choking halfway through his scoff. He rolled his eyes and crossed his arms, pressing them against the squish of his chest. "I would never."

"But of course, you would," the apparition said. His voice curled high into a laugh that felt mocking to hear. "To punish yourself."

Saba's stomach dropped. *Was* this a punishment? A punishment for what?

"For having had that body in the first place," the apparition answered unprompted. "For being born that way at all."

It was then that Saba understood it could hear him, that perhaps every thought that ran through Saba's mind echoed out into the astral sea. Saba had said no, had tried to reject so forcefully the idea of accepting himself.

How can you possibly understand, he wanted to say. *You, who are perfect. After everything I've fought for, longed for, dreamed of, and you want me to just—accept this?*

How close that felt to giving up.

He said none of this aloud, but it didn't matter. The apparition cocked its head. "It is never going to be that simple," it said. "You have lauded your version of perfection for years. You have made it your crutch. You have loved it and prayed to it and worshipped it the way one might a god. But it's not real—not beyond the torment your love has made it into. It can't save you. It can't protect you. It cannot love you back. All it can do is drain you, sap you of joy. It can thieve your peace and twist your mind, and that is all. It cannot grant you happiness."

"And if I managed to become it?" Saba spat angrily. "If I managed to look like that; if you just gave me what I wanted—"

"Would it be enough?"

"Yes!" Saba shouted automatically. But there was no confidence in the sound. It came out pathetic, a half-choking scream, like desperation manifest. He tried again and whimpered. "Yes."

His chest ached. He wondered if it was the pressure from this plane, or if he was dying. Somehow, he preferred these possibilities to the most obvious reasoning: he was more broken than he'd thought. He'd disliked his body so intensely that his own hatred had started to rot the rest of him.

"What happens to you if you can't let go?" the apparition said.

"Am I just meant to fall in love with *this*?" He gestured at himself, the preteen, girlish body, and aborted an accusatory gesture back at the clean-cut perfection staring back at him. He closed his eyes. He didn't want to give up.

"What you want, Saba, is legitimacy," the apparition said. "I never said you couldn't better yourself. I never said you couldn't change how you look. All I want you to consider is that who you are now—regardless of who you might have been before or might become later—is still worthy."

It wasn't news to Saba, not really. He had a decent logical mind that could tease through the anxiety and the loathing and the despair, and usually he pieced together a mostly coherent thought about his self-worth. This felt different, though, because someone else—something else—was saying it to him. Saba had to take it, and it might have been easier for him to take a blow.

The apparition continued, "Would it help if it wasn't random? If you were not an error of nature? If you were deliberate? Saba, you would not be able to exist here if you weren't exactly what you are."

"What do you mean?" Saba turned to the gedrok. "What is he talking about?"

"You have been dosing yourself with ichor for years," the gedrok told him, as he was still recovering from this latest shock. "If you had been anyone else, Saba Vasili, you would have ceased to exist the moment you were pushed inside the breach. But your decoction—that which you use to urge your body toward the masculine—has true power in it. And in dosing, you have shielded yourself."

Saba laughed. It was the first time in his life he'd ever been grateful to be born the way he had. But he also laughed at the irony. If he hadn't been dissatisfied with who he was, he wouldn't have dreamed of entering the astral sea in the first place. It made Saba think of the vision of the gedrok horde, the way they had run and floundered, terrified.

Hearing him, the gedrok said, "They were corrupted when they fell through. They stopped feeling nothing and instead felt everything. They stopped being empty. Ichor leaked into the lands, they ran, their minds opened and were overwhelmed, and many of them died like that. Not dead the way humans die, but dead all the same."

The gedroks had run east. They had died in the empire and bled ichor into the land there. But many of their corpses had ended up as far east as you could go: Usleth. Perhaps others had run off into the Prauv Ocean; perhaps gedrok bodies littered the ocean floor.

Everything he was now, Saba felt he owed to those gedroks. To their fear. Their suffering had eased his.

They had slipped through a breach, and now a breach was open again. Without really knowing why he did it, he went down on his knees, as if in worship. He let his body beg prostrate before an unknowable entity.

"My being here may mean nothing to you. It may be a blip in your existence, or in time, and I know I'm nothing really—I know none of us are. But if I think like that in truth, then my being here also means nothing, and I don't think that can be right. I think I'm here not only for myself. I think I'm here for Loefka Ward."

Suddenly, like Saba had spoken an invocation, all those ghosts in his head manifested into existence behind the gedrok. The shock of it made him jolt and sit back on his haunches. Unnatural umbral shadow draped them all so that he could see none of their faces, nor anything distinct about them.

Being here wasn't just about his body. It was about his duty.

The gedrok cocked its head. "Are you petitioning me for something?"

Saba made a decision then. Eagerly, he said, "Yes. I want to see how the breach opened."

He readied himself to make a bargain. Indeed, he expected it—but that was a human way of thinking. The gedrok exhaled without another word, and a cloud of misted ichor was expelled from its nostrils, thick as fog and just as opaque.

CHAPTER SEVENTEEN

He fell together through nothingness.

Wind and panic made Saba's scream edge out of him silently. His throat burned, and his breath was stolen. Then as suddenly as it happened, it stopped, and all the fog and indistinct shapes resolved with extreme clarity until he was seeing Byrengrad—as it had been a month before.

He knew this because Loefka Ward was alive and well.

A pang of something volatile shot through his heart: Guilt, maybe. Relief. Shame. Grief. A shuddering cocktail of every weighted feeling.

He heard a laugh go up, and the tinny sound of a Kerish wind pipe. He heard bartering, someone shouting, and the answering wail of a child being reprimanded. No blood. No limbs. No bodies. No ash. No death.

Kerinsk's legacy.

So many of his people were alive.

But that was the background to this scene, and not what he had been called to witness.

Two men stood out on an outcrop above Loefka Ward. One he recognized immediately as Judge Hirunz, given the ugly mask, many layered purple robe, and the distinct way he held himself—an ingrained haughtiness, a clear assumption of his own superiority.

Somehow, the man beside him had even more impudence. Lordly disdain dripped off him like sweat, and it had a scent to it, too, a lingering malodor that made Saba's nose wrinkle up. His blond hair had been pulled back into a ponytail and the very end of it grazed his shoulder blades. Saba's eyes were drawn to his nose, which was oddly small and dainty when compared to the rest of him. He had an average bulk, the kind of lord who likely spent more time on horseback, hunting, than other bodily exploits.

"And how do you feel," Lord Doric of Veprak drawled, "finding common ground with a Rezwyn?"

His accent was unique and sharp; he made Zvensian sound as jagged as the rocks of Byrengrad. He spoke slowly, no doubt in his attempt not to butcher his meaning, but he also seemed to speak without hesitation, giving him the air of control.

Hirunz kicked a stone off the cliffside. He threw his arms out so dramatically that the long sleeves of his gown made a whipping noise as they thrust into the air. "How do you think I feel?" Hirunz spat. He sighed disdainfully and gestured down. "But what else can be done. You are, sadly, right."

Lord Doric shrugged and wrinkled his nose. "It's not because they're Kers. Really, they could be from anywhere. It's because they're refugees. Stragglers without a home. As soon as you grant them citizenship"—he spat over his shoulder, in that Rezwyn way, and dusted his hands off—"Zvensia's power is diluted."

Hirunz muttered something to himself, and then said, "Berif has to go, too."

Berif? He must mean Judge Berif.

She had been the judge who had died in the event. Had Hirunz organized her murder, too?

"You are changing the terms," Lord Doric said with a click of his tongue.

"She has too much support," Hirunz continued. "She's always doting on these Kers, anyway. Like they're her pets. Promising them this and that on Byrengrad's coin—and she can't fulfill any of it. Not without Triad permission. But she does it anyway to put strain on us. And this vote—I mean—" He paused and looked up at the sky. Saba had never seen him quite so frenzied. He turned his gaze back to Lord Doric. "If it comes down to it, it's just her and I now, what with the old bugger Vilix dead. But if she's *gone*. . ."

Judge Vilix. The old judge that had died just weeks before Saba's imprisonment.

Lord Doric considered this all with a smarmy smile. Something that could have been lust filled his eyes. He shrugged and looked out at Loefka Ward.

"What did you have in mind in return, my good judge?" he asked.

"I'll fix the price of grain," Hirunz practically begged. "If we keep access to staple foods dependent on citizenship, the Kerish refugees will have no other choice. Either survivors can stay here and struggle, or they can flock to the kind lord who has opened his fields to refugees. You'll get a workforce to tend to your harvest, and I'll be rid of my fucking pests."

"I'll provide all the grain needed to feed your remaining refugees—in exchange for a fee."

Saba jolted just as Hirunz did.

"What?" Hirunz said. And then immediately, with a great deal of ire, "Why?"

"Why do you think, Judge Hirunz? The Kers will need you. But *you* need *me*."

It was the most honest and straightforward thing Saba had ever heard, and Hirunz must have thought the same for he responded with a broken, tired laugh.

"Fine," he said, like a coward. "Fine! You get a workforce of the remaining Kers in Loefka Ward, hopefully a handful at most. They will be dependent on you. It's a good deal," he said, clearly ignoring what Zvensian dependence on any part of the empire could mean for the country's future. "But you assured me that this device would do the job."

"I'm Rezwyn," the Lord of Veprak said, like that was an answer. He sighed and gnawed on his thumbnail, spitting once more over the edge of the cliff. "I know my way around ichor. You know what you're getting into, Hirunz. You know I want a foothold in Zvensia. Do this, and you get rid of your pests. Simple as that."

Saba understood what he was seeing slowly. A deal had been made.

Hirunz and Doric shook on it, and the scene shifted; it was the same place, the same people, only at dawn, some days later.

"What did you tell her?" Lord Doric asked. He had shucked his outer jacket and stood only in a flowing white shirt over his trousers. He looked like a dashing commoner, and if it wasn't for his attitude, which seemed impossible for him to excise from himself, he might have passed as one. He stretched his arm across his chest.

Hirunz seemed so young in that moment. He was squatting on the edge of the cliff. Loefka Ward was just waking up. Saba's insides filled with a knowing dread, an innate horror.

This was the day it happened.

"Not much," Hirunz admitted. He didn't look back at Doric, just kept staring down at the ward below. "But, then again, she didn't need much prompting. Berif believes in the cause, you know. In the people."

"And?"

"I had the sentinel set up the Eye in the center as instructed," Hirunz said. "That mechanism had already been pulled out. And the mark—the sigil—I've had it etched into the metal, like you said." His voice shifted and went flat, devoid of all emotion. His eyes flicked down to Lord Doric's hand. He held Saba's notes. "Are you sure. . .?"

"Positive," Lord Doric said. "This little scholar has quite the brain on him, and his notes are surprisingly clear. It will work."

Saba bit his lip, seething. Hirunz had handed his notes to a Rezwyn. Unabashedly, Lord Doric had read them with the intention of destroying Loefka Ward. They knew what the sigil would do. They knew what removing the failsafe would do. All of this was intentional.

Both wanted the Kers to die.

Lord Doric turned his gaze to Loefka Ward. "How did you get the device out of the basilica?"

"The sentinel took it in. Whilst that happened, I reported it missing, and I summoned the scholar Giste before I came here. Told her to return to the Scholar's Building and sweep it in case Vasili was stowed away there."

Lord Doric made a happy noise. "How astute of you to cover all bases, Judge Hirunz. And your colleague?"

Hirunz sighed. He gestured to Loefka Ward, where chatter was growing. "I told Berif it was a gift. That she'd see when she turned it on, as soon as she flicked the switch."

Lord Doric snorted derisively. "She's that gullible?"

"Not gullible," Hirunz murmured. He shifted, looked back at the lord over his shoulder. His eyes had darkened through the slits in his mask. "She is kind. Compassionate. Trusting."

"Oh, Hirunz." Lord Doric laughed. He ran a hand through his hair and squatted down beside Hirunz, smiling. "Is that regret I'm hearing?"

Hirunz thought for a moment, and then shifted. He turned back to look at Loefka Ward. Saba heard chatter, the sounds of people rising to start the day. Someone laughed. A bell rang out. The first calls of merchants wound their way up to the cliffside.

"No," Hirunz said, with a strange finality, given his previous concession. "Never."

Hirunz sighed and got to his feet. "We should get moving," he said.

Lord Doric laughed. "Whatever for?"

Hirunz flinched and stepped forward as if he'd misheard. "To get in position. We can't possibly stabilize the breach from up here."

"Surely you want this breach to do maximum damage," Lord Doric said.

The moment stretched out between them, silent and heavy. The Lord of Veprak tilted his head. He didn't have to say a single word. Saba knew, and it was clear that Hirunz did too.

Lord Doric had no intention of stabilizing it.

Hirunz laughed, short and flat. "Stop this," he said, though Lord Doric was doing precisely nothing.

In answer, the lord stretched out his arms and shrugged. "It's too late to stop it now, isn't it? Your kind and compassionate Judge Berif will activate the Eye. With the failsafe missing, your addition of that mad scholar's sigil, and the ichor I've provided, hopefully you'll have your convenient disaster."

Saba froze. The ichor Lord Doric had provided? The ichor flowers had come from him?

Had Hirunz been planning this from the instant the scholars submitted the grant?

"Well," Hirunz said stiffly. "Surely, we'll need to stop it at some point."

Another moment passed. Lord Doric smiled rather sweetly. "Well . . . that seems like your problem. It's been a pleasure doing business."

He turned to walk away. Hirunz didn't move, and Saba wanted to know what was happening in his head. Had he realized it yet? Had he truly thought Lord Doric, whose provincial hold was the closest Rezwyn territory to Zvensia, would allow their deal to be mutually beneficial?

Saba recalled Zek saying: *Lord Doric deserved to die.*

"He was an old relic—a threat to Dziove's rule, and an expansionist. He wanted to annex Zvensia. He wanted to reignite the war with Usleth. And he could have kept his life if he'd minded his own business. But he didn't."

Perhaps Hirunz hadn't had such a direct confirmation of Lord Doric's intentions, but the thought of willfully opening a breach in Byrengrad to eliminate the Kers—to do so even when other people, other city dwellers, would very well be caught up in the blast—horrified Saba. To rely entirely on Lord Doric to close or stabilize the breach after the fact . . .

"Wait," Hirunz said. "The notes. Vasili's notes. Give them to me."

"Oh, I think not." Lord Doric patted his chest. "I think I'll be taking these with me."

"Doric, you'll destroy the whole city!"

"Perhaps the whole country if we're lucky." Veprak waved over his shoulder. "Oh, don't worry, Hirunz! Whether you stole the notes or not, I was always going to find a way to do this."

And perhaps that confirmation was what made Hirunz finally snap to his senses. He lunged forward after Lord Doric, grabbed that ponytail of his, and wrenched him backwards.

Lord Doric choked. His voice came out like a bark as he stumbled and all the air struggled out of his lungs. Hirunz wheezed from the exertion and landed a sloppy blow to Doric's face. The lord's head snapped over his shoulder, and he laughed, hand shaking as he touched his lip and found it bloody.

"Is that the best you can do?" Lord Doric spoke with surprising calm. Hirunz's outburst obviously hadn't registered as anything serious to him, not yet. He was a Rezwyn, and clearly one spoiling for a fight—not, as Saba had expected, some dandy lord who had never been in a scrap before. Lord Doric's pupils dilated, and he quickly regained his footing.

Hirunz howled in anger and kicked him in the chest. Doric stumbled back, surprised. Despite his age, Hirunz grappled Doric, and the pair of them struggled back toward the cliff. Unceremoniously, Hirunz managed to punch the lord in the soft jugular. Doric's hands scrambled to his throat. He let go of his purchase on Hirunz's robes—a mistake.

Hirunz only had to give him one good shove.

Lord Doric screamed as he fell. A wet crack sounded distantly, and then the commotion below suggested the fall had been witnessed. Hirunz peered over the edge.

Saba followed, looking down at the familiar part of his city, knowing it was about to be unmade and knowing there was nothing he could do.

In his periphery, he caught more movement. A young man slid down an incline and hastily climbed down the cliffside. Saba watched him pilfer the notes off Doric's corpse and realized this must have been Hulik, Zek's agent. He dashed away and began scrambling back up the cliffside the way he had come. Saba wondered if Hulik had known what was about to happen to Loefka Ward—but how could he?

The breach was not born easily.

It tore into the world, ripped at the seams, and screamed its way into Byrengrad. Prismatic light burned away all detail and left the world a blinding white. A circular omission appeared in the earth, a perfect sphere punched out in an instant. An eerie and impossible silence crowded the space, and briefly everyone was suffocating as everything, even the air, ceased to exist. Then it all rushed back in, and a thunderous boom crashed back into the world.

Saba couldn't see the Eye. He couldn't yet see the breach. But he heard it, as he had that day, the sound of the astral sea opening.

Berif had turned it on.

Hulik abruptly stopped his ascent. He swung his head over his shoulder, staring at the ripple of prismatic energy surging toward him. His eyes went wide. Saba saw him mouth something under his breath. But he reacted quickly.

Transferring the notes to his mouth, Hulik scrabbled up the cliff face, and then kicked up the incline to high ground.

And just in time.

The shockwave reached the cliff. Hulik was now out of sight, but Judge Hirunz flew back as the force reached him, throwing him a good thirty paces from the edge of the cliff. For a moment Hirunz lay completely prone in the dust, groaning. Then he sat up and screamed, a high pitched, frustrated sound, and balled both hands into fists, which he used to beat the sides of his head. He was saying something, but Saba quickly realized he was crying, too, sobbing so hard the words were drowned out.

To think that Hirunz had the nerve to feel guilt, after everything the man had done, after his many attempts to shift the blame, enraged Saba so severely it burned off every other feeling and emptied him completely.

To think that this was it—that Hirunz had colluded with a renegade Rezwyn and doomed the whole of Loefka Ward, possibly the whole city, because . . . because the Kers had dared to survive a war?

Buildings at the fringe of the clean circular destruction began to crumble and shift, made unsteady by the parts of their foundations that had been obliterated. The site itself looked as it did when Saba was last there: clean, razed, flattened, with only the bubbling rift beneath where the Eye had stood before the earth had been unmade. The device rotated at eye level. Saba stared at it.

He rubbed his hands over his face and collected himself, and when he pulled his fingers free of his eyes he was once again standing before the open mouth of the gedrok, which wheezed slowly at him.

He gasped and caught his breath. What he needed to do wasn't about clearing his name, not really. It was about—justice? Recompense? No word sounded strong enough for what Saba hoped for.

"How can I prove Hirunz did this?" Saba asked immediately. His voice shook. "How do I—I need to—"

"The lens," the gedrok said, and Saba thought immediately about his device. "You are astral-touched. Let it see what you saw."

Saba didn't know what that meant, but his heart was racing, and he had been here, probably, for too long. He had the anxiety that he'd leave here and find Byrengrad destroyed.

"If I leave now," Saba said, "and close the breach from my side—"

He cut himself off because he wasn't sure of the precise nature of his question.

Can I come back?

Can I reactivate the Eye?

Do I run the risk of this happening again if I ever think about opening another hole between our worlds?

And the final thought came with clarity: *I don't want to let go.*

But the gedrok said nothing, and Saba realized, sadly, there was nothing left to say. He couldn't leave Byrengrad to this force. He couldn't leave Moss. Silvana. Not even Giste. Not even *Maksid*.

And he couldn't leave Zek.

Saba let himself remember that perfect apparition of who he had always wished to be. If he left the astral sea, he would be abandoning that perfection.

The sickness in his gut felt innate, like he would always feel vaguely ill. Something flickered into existence, hovering transparently in the gedrok's mouth. He saw an apparition of himself as he was now, in his own world—not the Saba he had built up and worshipped and fed into, not the perfect apparition shown to him earlier—but how he was. Him. The body he had made his own. The body he had built and would continue to build. The body that deserved to live and to love and to be joyful even if it was by no stretch of the imagination perfect.

Saba still had the urge to change. He might always feel it, as a grain of sand that grated softly on his skin, or a loose stone that found its way into his boot. He might always be aware of it; it might always shadow him.

But maybe that was alright.

He had chosen himself years ago and fought to become this. This body deserved acknowledgement. Celebration. Joy.

But first, before he could do any of that, Saba had to save his city.

"How do I go back?" Saba asked, but as if his legs were no longer under his own control he was already walking into the wet open mouth of the colossal beast. The apparition—him—smiled and held out his hand. Saba took it without hesitation, and he felt all the power in the astral sea thrumming through his fingers, lighting up his heart and his mind, and he cried. Without reserve, without shame.

Is this what it felt to love yourself? To have the whole power of the astral sea in his flesh?

The ribbed throat of the gedrok opened for him, and the apparition guided him down the pink and undulating flesh. Saba let himself be swallowed whole.

CHAPTER EIGHTEEN

Saba's heart rate increased and slowed and sped again within seconds. His body tingled, both the skin and the muscles, and exhaustion and hunger hit him simultaneously. He felt weaker than just a few moments ago, but perhaps that was gravity reclaiming him, reminding his bones and his flesh that they were of earth and did not, in fact, belong to the infinite magic of the astral plane.

Saba fell to his knees and made himself catch his breath.

He blinked up at the bright sky, disoriented first by the sun—it had been night not an hour ago—and then by the bright circular flashes in his periphery. He ignored those and tried to remind himself about his body, to reform his connection with this material plane. The dusty ground felt warm against his skin, and a cool breeze wicked sweat from his cheeks. His heart rate still sped, and his stomach roiled with nausea—a body panicking about a sudden deluge of physical feelings after existing in a space without such sensations. It made everything feel foreign, and Saba reintroduced himself to Byrengrad slowly. The weather felt slightly cooler than before he'd left. The sun flared proudly above him—was it midday? Or later? And the noise. The noise of the city horrified him, because no one screamed. No one laughed. There was no chatter, no music, no haggling—nothing but this warbling crackling in the air.

When he finally gained the strength to move, Saba rolled onto his side. He blinked rapidly. Byrengrad stretched below him—a thought that briefly caught on something in his brain before it slipped away into nothing—and a fire burned in the distance, large enough that he could see the flame rising into the sky.

Saba had no idea how many days had passed. He couldn't be sure if anyone was still alive, or if they'd fled the city.

Saba slowly pushed himself to an upright position and squinted.

He was nowhere near the breach. Or rather, nowhere near the breach that someone had shoved him into. His city was being destroyed.

Struck by sudden clarity, Saba shakily got to his feet and surveyed the city.

His city—his home.

Byrengrad yawned open like a wound. Buildings had crumbled over themselves, or stood, tilted in half ruins and clinging to verticality. A prismatic light leached into the rocky outcrops and spanned the whole municipality, crawling over the buildings that spurted up from the tooth-like rocks. Dozens of minute, flickering lights danced in the sky and reminded Saba of tight swarms of insects madly bunched together.

These were iridescent cuts, wounds that seemed to be torn into the very fabric of existence, the astral sea splitting open at various points and pulsing with its unmaking power. Prismatic tongues of astral energy licked out in spasms at the surrounding city, and everything they touched evaporated, either slowly turning to ash the way the victims of Loefka Ward had, or simply—disappearing.

Saba's mind slowed at that. He stared unblinking at the horizon, trying to understand. The fire Saba had seen in his periphery popped in and out of existence at random, jolting intervals.

Houses and shops did too.

He watched it happen to some of the trees and foliage that had burst defiantly up the city's stairwells and to the fuchsia that had made its beds on flat rooftops. Half of a building shuddered out of existence and destabilized the rest of it. A great rumble sounded as the lower half crumbled away, only for the original half to appear a second later, and promptly fall twenty feet into the rubble below.

Fuck!

His heartbeat pounded in his ears. Saba doubled over and screamed into the city below.

Where were the people? The animals? Moss, Giste—*Zek?*

They're fine. They must be fine, but that was anxiety and hope talking. He willed it to be true.

Calm down, he told himself, but his breathing remained erratic and sharp. He could stop this, surely. He had a bond with the tear—the original one. Surely that counted for something. Saba closed his eyes and tried to find the rage and the fear and funnel it like he had before. But the connection was gone.

Saba had held hands with the apparition and had made his peace with it—with himself.

After that, Saba had been cut off.

As he surveyed the injured city, it took him a while to spot Loefka Ward. From here, the original site sat to the west, a flattened circle. But that signature wound where the Eye had caused the first breach was gone, which was perfect and could only mean good things. Right?

If that had closed, why had so many others opened?

Where was the Eye? Hirunz had said something about building a casing, though he and the others had only been able to find enough gedrok material for the failsafe. Had Hirunz managed to move it? Or had something else happened to it?

Saba controlled his breathing and looked around. The astral sea had deposited him in the upper administrative ward, on the cliff where the Triad basilica overlooked the city. The basilica rose to his left, nearly three hundred paces away.

Its curling stone columns and dark grey exterior still intimidated him, mostly now because the building looked intact save for one of the windows, which kept disappearing and then splintering, dancing, or changing colors. The window seemed to oscillate between every possibility, and astral light bloomed from behind the glass.

There must be a breach inside.

Saba glanced away from the building toward a smaller tear. It was about the size of his forearm and had appeared near a tall cypress tree. Part of its branches were engulfed in the small breach. Saba watched them catch alight, fall to ash, and spiral in a fractal infinity as dozens of the same branch appeared over and over again and bloomed on top of one another.

He approached the thing slowly. He'd like to believe the apparition in the astral sea had been telling him the truth, and that his immunity to the ichor was a consequence of his decoction, but he had learned his lesson about sticking his fingers into astral wounds and wasn't willing to test it again.

He could hear the scratchy noise of the astral sea—like a hum that would occasionally drone and shudder like distant thunder—like how he imagined the cry of an ancient gedrok might sound. The animal part of Saba's brain flinched away from it.

The sound came from every popping, thrashing breach, and it took everything he had to resist the instinctual fear and move his feet forward.

Why does my body know to fear it, he wondered vaguely. This was the only good news Saba had encountered in a while: his scholarly mind was intact. But Saba had no time for that. He approached the closest tear and exhaled, forcing himself to look up.

It hurt to look at. Either it was because of the innate dread at seeing a breach and knowing its infinite power, or perhaps because his heart hurt over the knowledge that he had left the astral sea—and his bodily potential—for Byrengrad. Whatever the reason, Saba spent a good minute slowing his breathing and steeling himself before he could look at the breach and see anything of merit.

The leaves went purple, yellow, green. The branch grew bulbous and then shattered or disappeared, so the leaves quickly fell to the ground—infinite possibility. He tried to look over the breach with new eyes, but it was so like the one he'd been pushed into. It maintained the same, bright color, the same spitting of flares.

How could it be here?

How could any of them be here? There had only been a single breach, made possible by a single gedrok lens.

But Saba had warned the others about this possibility, hadn't he? He'd preferred the idea of a failsafe over building a casing, because of how fragile the gedrok lens was.

He squinted at this smaller breach and moved around it, tilting his head to a right angle. Now he could see how a gossamer beam emerged glinting from it and shot off toward the basilica. He turned his head perpendicular to the ground and started at the basilica, and at this angle, with the sun lighting them up, he could see that dozens of threads from the dozens of small tears were all interlocked and shooting toward the building.

Which could mean only one thing.

The gedrok lens that focused the power of the Eye had shattered, and now the light of the astral plane was refracting across the city, just as Saba had feared.

But at least he knew the device was in the basilica, and going inside was, for now, the only thing to do.

Saba approached the building with care, even though he could see no sentinels guarding the entrance. He had seen this building plenty of times from afar, and enough times up close, and always—always—had been struck by the majesty of it. By its presence.

The near organic, bony exterior had intimidated him, especially the way it loomed over the rest of the city.

Now, though, he felt nothing for it. Indeed, he found it lacking. It was only a building, as vulnerable to disaster as any other place.

Light and spectral energy glowed from within the windows, and parts of the basilica's exterior crackled and changed from the influence of the astral sea. Saba craned his neck to look at the spires, the tips of which disappeared into grey cloud. Something that might have been a bird—and the first sign of life he'd seen since his return—circled the spire ominously.

You're scared. But you have to go in there. You have to.

Saba pulled away and, shaking, walked up the cobbled road toward the door.

As he came around to the entrance, Saba expected to see two doors the size of three men stacked high, made of wood and black iron, and set back against a semicircular arch and triangular lintel that had TRIAD BASILICA engraved into it. He saw instead a sprawling epidemic of crystals that had ruptured through Byrengrad's natural rock and an archway that appeared to have been eaten by time. The lintel had cracked in half; indeed, the entire right side of the entrance appeared to have collapsed in on itself.

If he wanted to approach the Eye, there was little else to do but enter.

And if your immunity no longer works?

Well. Perhaps death would happen too quickly for Saba to even notice.

A plea for a quick oblivion. After everything, after all this—at least a painless death was still the one thing he could reasonably wish for.

Saba held his breath as he picked his way through the jumble of crystals. He had an awful fear in him that the sharp edges of the overlapping entanglement would cut his ankles, but he managed to pick his way through without issue.

No light spilled out from the basilica except those pulsing prismatic flares.

He understood, then—not in the way of a scholar, but in the way of one experiencing a kind of spiritual awakening—how the Rezwyns had come to worship the astral sea. How they had found gods in the indifferent, immeasurable power of a plane of existence that, if it had any thought at all, must have looked upon humanity as humans did ants. Saba understood how the Paladin Order of Usleth made their own rituals around the gedroks, how they made meaning of it all.

Saba had spoken to part of the astral sea—but that wasn't like he knew the plane itself.

It wasn't how he wanted to make meaning of this.

Saba stepped over the crystals and into the basilica's foyer. The red marble floor had fractured from the strain of the crystals in the natural bedrock. Crystals broke through in fissures, though as Saba looked, he realized this was the least of the damage. He looked up—and froze.

The Eye now spun in the center of the basilica's grand atrium. Suspended in a net of ichor threads, it rotated at head height around its own center of gravity.

Someone must have moved it.

The cube-like structure remained unchanged. Light refracted off the iron, and the mechanical underbelly whirred happily, still churning through ichor.

However, like a shattered mirror, the gedrok lens now floated in countless pieces, spread throughout the air as if paused in the moment of its splintering. The beam of ichor pierced through each piece and shot out in all directions beyond the basilica, feeding the many tears and breaches now scattered throughout the city, but the largest piece of the gedrok's lens sat directly above the device. The ichor bloomed into a deformed and rippling breach that cast all the basilica in unnatural prismatic light.

Beneath it, cracked pieces of gedrokbone and ceramic lay destroyed and scattered.

Saba thought about throwing up but found that a tired numbness had settled into his bones. He was so beyond shock now, he barely noticed the undulating red veins that shot through the white marble columns, pulsing as if alive. He made himself move and stepped over part of the red marble that had melted into gelatinous, writhing flesh.

Saba put his head in his hands. Sweat made his forehead slick. His breaths were rapid and hot against his palms.

Breathe. Breathe. But he couldn't. There were too many things to do.

He made himself move forward into the basilica, careful to avoid the spitting flares of ichor in case they forced him to learn where his immunity ended.

He wanted to see Zek; he wanted to be held by Zek. He wanted a different time, a different place. But had Zek even survived this? There seemed to be no one left.

How pathetic he was to worry about a near stranger when Byrengrad was crumbling. Guilt—years old, inherited guilt—swarmed him, because Saba had left Kerinsk to fall, and then his hubris had let its refugees die, and now he was in a position where he could run again. He could go to Usleth, to the far edges of the Ashmon Range, and pretend none of this had ever happened. Or he could try to fix it. He could make amends for his earlier failings.

Saba moved through the empty building. He pushed open doors into administrative rooms and smaller court rooms and found nobody. Abandoned work lay strewn on desks. An upended ink bottle had stained a red rug black. Someone had abandoned their plain-faced steward mask in the rush to leave. Saba closed the door and kept looking.

He went toward the large courtroom used for the more serious issues debated by the Triad. As he rounded the corner, he froze.

Someone was propped up against the wall.

Saba pulled himself from the corner and flattened his back. Carefully, he peered around to assess.

A sentinel.

Saba paused. They usually went in pairs, yet this sentinel was alone.

They wore their screaming bronze mask over the black cowl but otherwise appeared only partly dressed. Their heavy one-shouldered cloak had been unclasped from their shoulder and now piled in a black-and-yellow heap at their feet. As for their armor, they still wore the single decorated pauldron and gorget, but they'd abandoned the intimidating cuirass and greaves. Their gambeson was open and exposed the sweat-stained white shirt beneath it. They looked finished. Defeated. But they clung to the hilt of their scabbard, ready to draw at any time, even though their arms were shaking.

Oh, my heart.

Saba would know his brother anywhere.

CHAPTER NINETEEN

Perhaps it was the memory he'd relived in the astral sea, but upon recognizing Maksid, the only thing Saba wanted was to fling himself around the corner and walk into his brother's arms. Only he didn't do this, because of the niggling fear that on the night he'd been shoved into the breach, he couldn't be sure Maksid hadn't been the one to do it.

He's still wearing the sentinel mask, an angry part of Saba's mind said, as if that was proof enough of Maksid's betrayal. Call it the bond of blood or the desperation felt when there's no one else left, but in the end, Saba walked around the corner.

Maksid was slow to react. It was how Saba knew days must have passed—all the energy he'd had standing by the breach in Loefka Ward no longer existed. Maksid didn't even see Saba approaching until he was ten paces out. Then the sentinel lurched upward as if he was a marionette, strings yanked violently by some unseeable power. He scrambled and pulled his sword free with a sharp scrape, and this motion alone had Maksid panting. His hands shook. His back foot began to slip, caught in the tangle of his heavy cloak, which slid along the marble floor.

When had he last eaten? When had he last slept?

"Maksid—"

"No," Maksid said. His voice came out hoarse and thick from days of disuse. "No, get away."

Saba put both his hands up. His stomach twisted; it felt like Zek and his notes again, only more intimate, the wound deeper.

"Brother," he said. His voice cracked.

Maksid made a low, upset noise and shifted his hand on the hilt. He brought it up and slammed the pommel into the side of his mask three times, voice guttural and broken. "No, no, no. Go away."

Saba ran to him. He tore Maksid's arms away from his head and was surprised at the lack of resistance. Then Saba slipped his hands beneath his brother's mask, knowing he was overstepping, ignoring the brief catch of breath uttered before the gnarled bronze was pulled free of Maksid's face. Saba carefully put the mask on the ground, out of respect to his brother, but when he looked up and saw Maksid's bare face for the first time in years, he felt some long iced-over part of his heart crack open. And it hurt. It hurt. He saw in his mind Maksid pressing over him in the long grass, shielding him from view. He saw Maksid grabbing his hand, eyes wide, cheek splattered in their mother's blood. Where had his brother gone? For so long now, Maksid had been someone else.

How could anyone not realize they were brothers?

His brother was freckled. His auburn hair was shorn, cropped close to his skull. His big green eyes had a dullness to them, like all the luster had died, and the skin underneath them had thinned so much that a lattice of green veins showed through his dark circles. His lips were cracked, and an uneven down of stubble had grown over his cheeks.

He looked at Saba, but he wasn't seeing him. His gaze was distant and sad.

"I'm sorry," Maksid was saying. "I'm sorry, I'm sorry."

"You protected me the way you could," Saba said, because his brother *had*, in his own way. Even as sentinel, even ignoring Kerinsk and his blood connection to it.

"I'm sorry," Maksid whispered. He closed his eyes and a tear escaped, flowing slowly down his cheek. "I didn't stop him. He killed you."

Saba froze.

So, it had been Hirunz. Of course. Saba was a problem and what better way to solve it then to make him disappear for good. Oh, he could barely muster his anger—it was just another shitty thing Hirunz had done.

But Maksid seemed broken. Seeing his brother react like this reminded him too much of Kerinsk.

"Maksid," Saba said, taking his brother's face in both hands and shaking him. "Look at me. Look. I'm alive."

"You can't be," he whispered.

"Tell me what's happened here," Saba said, because as much as he wanted to coax Maksid out of this fugue state, he needed to find Hirunz. Or Moss. Or *Zek*.

"You can't be," Maksid said again, shaking his head. "Oh. *Oh*. I should have—I should have told you."

He was close to slipping into panic, and he wasn't making sense. Saba reached to touch him, and Maksid spun suddenly, both hands on Saba's shoulders.

"It was me," Maksid whispered. His lip curled off his teeth, and he shook his head in a shameful fear. "It was me . . ."

A sob cut him off. Maksid doubled forward and leaned his head on Saba's shoulder. This level of intimacy . . . they simply hadn't held each other like this in years. A lifetime ago. Maksid's shoulder shifted, and when he stood up again, he'd recovered enough to stop crying, though his breathing was still jagged. He held something in the palm of his hand.

"What is it?" Saba said, but his stomach was thick and churning.

No, no, no, not again—

Not after Zek. He couldn't handle this again.

Maksid opened his hand. Sitting there, shattered in half, was the original failsafe mechanism from the Eye.

Saba's stomach plummeted. For a time—perhaps a full minute—he could do nothing but stare.

When the betrayal hit, Saba had to go to his knees. He could say nothing except a strained and broken, "*Why?*"

"Because I was told to," Maksid said.

Pathetic.

Saba snapped his gaze up to his brother, but Maksid had squeezed his own eyes shut. He was saying, "Because I trusted Judge Hirunz when he told me your device was dangerous and that removing this part would render it inoperable. Because he said taking and destroying that would be enough. Persistence Sage had brought it to the basilica after you were suspended from the Scholar's Guild, and I removed the mechanism and split it in half. He told me to take it to Loefka Ward, where Judge Berif had organized transport out of the city. I thought she was in on it. I reported back to Judge Hirunz and—"

"—and did he pet you and call you a good dog?" Saba spat. He stood back up, tense with fury. "I inspected the device. I told you the failsafe was missing! I told you that was the cause of the continued breach, and you said nothing!"

Maksid snapped out of his upset. "I didn't know what I had taken! I followed instructions, and when Loefka Ward was destroyed, part of me thought—that you had activated it from afar!"

"You trusted Hirunz over me! Over your own brother!"

"*Yes!*" Maksid screamed.

Saba panted. He pawed at his eyes, pressed firmly against his temples. He felt mad, jittering with useless, reckless energy that had nowhere to go. "After everything. Our whole lives, the war, coming here, fighting for everything we've ever had—*why?*"

Maksid's lip curled. He glanced away, and in that beat of silence Saba could innately feel the answer. It grew fast, cracked the very core of him the way the crystal fault lines at the front of the basilica had cracked the façade. He knew, and hated what he knew, but he needed Maksid to say it.

To finally admit it.

"Because I was angry at you," Maksid said. "For changing."

Saba sucked in a breath and held it until his lungs burned. He tried to stretch the moment as much as possible, so he wouldn't have to speak. His heart hurt. Maksid was dredging up a pain Saba had long ago tried to bury: the insidious knowledge that the remains of his family would always laud a dead girl. That Maksid would never make room for Saba as he was.

Maksid wasn't looking at him or couldn't look at him. Either way he said, "I know. I know that isn't fair. And I know you didn't *mean* anything by it—I know you didn't do it just because you wanted to. But my whole life I was second to you. I was meant to serve you, as my Queen. But suddenly you were denying that. Denying you were even a girl. And we distanced ourselves from the Kers, but you refused to assimilate properly into Zvensia as well. You tried, but you weren't doing it seriously. Not like me. I tried. I'm still trying. I never—I never *thought* . . ."

It wasn't Saba's job to fix Maksid's opinion of him, nor should he hold his brother's shame at what he'd done; Maksid's guilt was his own. But *shit,* it ached to know Maksid saw Saba's decision as arrogant choice. As an inconvenience. As if his decision was related in any way to Maksid at all.

"Like I did this to upstage you somehow," Saba muttered under his breath. He glanced past Maksid's shoulder at the door behind him, to grand oak, the largest court room in the basilica. If Maksid was standing here, then surely he was protecting something—probably Hirunz himself.

"Did you tell Hirunz who I was?"

"No," Maksid said quickly, but his voice wavered. The truth broke through quickly. "But . . . I told Diligence Inquisitor who *I* was. Who I had been. She worked it out."

Diligence had acted so strangely around Saba. If she'd known, then her opinion of him—her acting as if he was a coward, or a relic of a dead kingdom, or something else—made sense.

But Saba shook his head.

"I don't have time for this, actually. I have to deactivate the Eye."

He tried to pass his brother, but Maksid snapped to attention and grabbed his arm, yanking him back.

Saba stiffened immediately. "Let go of me."

"Saba," Maksid said, with staggering sobriety. "You can't. There are four more sentinels in there. Diligence Inquisitor, Hirunz, Persistence Sage, too. They'll overwhelm you."

You, Saba's mind caught on his choice of words. *You. Not us.*

When perhaps he should have been lamenting Giste's betrayal—however predictable it was—he said instead, "They're all that's left?" He was momentarily struck by the magnitude of the apparent losses; the sentinels had numbered in the hundreds. But Maksid shook his head and loosened his grip on Saba's arm.

"Most of the sentinels evacuated the city. That's where a lot of people are—they're escaping. And the sentinels, they're protecting them, leading them away. Until . . . well, until whatever happens here . . . happens."

He sounded resigned to the possible fates of Byrengrad: whether the strange effects of the astral sea would lick out and shift the city's makeup—or erase it entirely.

"Evacuating where?" Saba asked. They couldn't go east into the empire without starting a new diplomatic issue. Saba didn't even know where the Rezwyn ambassador was, but if he thought about Zek—fuck, if he *asked* about Zek, and found out something he didn't want to know—then he might lose his grip on his sanity. And Saba had only just wrangled himself from the grip of his own bodily distress; he hadn't even had a proper chance to digest how he felt about himself or how he'd move through the world now.

It was all becoming too much.

"Towns to the west," Maksid offered weakly. "There wasn't . . . there wasn't a set plan. It happened too fast. People were trying to flee on their own. The roads got clogged. Diligence Inquisitor was the one who ordered the sentinels to move—Hirunz didn't try to stop her, but—" He then made a confusing gesture Saba took to mean: *But Hirunz didn't try to help, either.*

Was this what it looked like when faith was shaken in real time?

"I need to get the new failsafe," Saba said. "Mossinne had made it. I saw it on the table at the original breach site, made according to my design. Maksid, look at me. Do you know where it is?"

Maksid visibly swallowed. "Hirunz has it."

"Then I need to get it and deactivate the Eye."

Maksid balked, eyes glancing in the direction of the Eye in the other room. "It—something shattered. The lens, maybe. You must have seen it, it's spilling out everywhere."

Saba ground his teeth together. "Yes, but. . ." He suspected he already knew, but if Maksid could confirm the truth, he would make him. "How did it happen?"

"Hirunz wanted to move the Eye. He cleaned out the underdark, got every scrap of gedrok material left. It wasn't enough. He made the paladin try to forge something—a box—something to move it in."

Saba recalled the mess of gedrokbone and ceramic that lay scattered beneath the Eye in the central atrium. It was obvious what had happened, but he told Maksid to continue.

"They made it up here," Maksid said. "Sentinels put the device on a cart and drove it up. They think the lens was already weakened by the jostling, but when they brought it in here, they dropped it. And half the container was made of ceramic. I don't know. They dropped it, and ichor shot through the weak part of the container, and suddenly the device became exposed, and the lens shattered, and now the fucking astral sea is bleeding through every which way, and—"

"Breathe," Saba said sharply. It was as he'd expected. Hirunz had no idea what he was doing, and he couldn't fathom that Saba really was an expert or he wouldn't have shoved him into the astral sea. Saba pinched the bridge of his nose and tried to slow his breathing, to regain some control. "I will close it. I just need to convince Hirunz to give me the failsafe. Then I'll just. . . put it in."

Maksid flinched. "You've cheated death once. Can you survive it again?"

Saba shrugged. "Maybe."

He walked away without further comment. He'd wrench open the door, even if all of them drew their blades to him. He'd march up to Hirunz and demand the failsafe.

And then what? You can't prove anything. You can't convince the others Hirunz is behind all this. All you have is memory.

Unless he used the lens, as the gedrok had told him. *You are astral-touched. Let it see what you saw.*

Maksid said, "Wait," and Saba slowed, because his own mind was formulating something.

"What is it?" Saba muttered, half-distracted.

Maksid hesitated. "Before you maybe die—don't you want to . . ."

Saba turned around, frowning. "What?"

Maksid stared at him like he was insane. He stepped forward and gestured back the way Saba had come.

"Don't you want to free Luan Zek first?"

Saba was able to say, "Oh, fuck," which was a wholly underwhelming response that barely captured the nightmarish conglomeration of emotion currently flooding his body. Maksid's words cracked something in him: the smattering of control he'd had over himself, which was a tangential hold he'd been clinging to since emerging from the astral sea.

To know Zek was alive was one thing. To know Zek was here, in the building—that Zek was likely in the very same jail he had rescued Saba from—carried too much weight. Like this moment had a significance to it that couldn't be overlooked. Like everything that had happened was meant to happen—everything, as far back as Saba's birth. He exhaled and caught a wild sob in his throat, clasped both hands over his mouth, and whisked the hysteria away before it had a chance to catch hold.

Maksid said, "He was arrested for attacking Judge Hirunz after you were pushed into the breach. He's in the prison now. Mossinne and the paladin are in there too. Hirunz claims what happened to the lens is their fault. I think he just wanted to get them out of his way. Though no one has been down there in a day or so."

Saba walked forward and slapped his brother across the face. "You're a coward, Maksid."

"I know."

Saba sniffed and wiped his eyes. He wasn't crying—if he started, he wouldn't stop. But looking at Maksid felt painful, as if sand was being poured into his eyes, and so he looked away and put his hand out. Maksid understood intrinsically. He scooped the ring of keys from his belt and showed Saba which one would open the jail.

Then Saba had given his brother a very particular set of instructions, which Maksid had agreed to, either because he felt guilty or because he had truly turned from Hirunz.

When he was done, Saba said, "Tell me which cell," and Maksid told him.

Chapter Twenty

There was a muck to the jail that hadn't been there when Saba had been imprisoned—or perhaps he had grown so used to the scent of filth during his stay that he no longer noticed it by the time he left. But this, combined with his heart rate and the wild little animal in his head screaming about Luan Zek, forced Saba to let the quiet, logical portion of his mind take over.

Saba walked down the wide stone steps to the jail like a puppeted cadaver. Every movement grated him; every joint in his body rubbed against the bones, every step clicked something in his hip. He became overly aware of the way his body moved, and usually this only happened when he considered what type of man he was. But this was different.

If Saba thought too much about where he was going, he knew that hysteria would wrangle control of his body. He couldn't allow that. Not yet.

Now, here he was.

In the sweaty palm of Saba's hand, he held the key to the jail, which Maksid had silently relinquished to him. The corridor was empty like most of the basilica. The walls were a ruddy brown stone, and a few torches sat in sconces along the wall, but they'd all burned down to nothing. He had taken one from the upper levels, lit by Maksid before they parted ways, and this was the only source of light he had. The firelight glinted prismatic as it passed over bits of paladin armor that had been placed outside. Silvana.

This was it, then.

Saba slipped the key into the lock. It slotted in without protest, and then he turned it, and the lock clicked open. Simple. Except the air changed as soon as the door was unlocked. The weight of expectation crowded down on Saba's neck. Pinpricks of sweat began to itch at the back of Saba's head, and a chaotic ball of emotion rumbled inside him.

What are you doing? Just open it.

Saba breathed in deep and pushed open the door.

The first thing to hit him was the intensity of the smell. His nose wrinkled in immediate protest, and he probably let out a noise of disgust, which was unfair—there were three people down here. But some deep-seated emotion flared to life in him, and for a moment he felt briefly as he had in the astral sea—human, but beyond his body, or like all the impurities that weakened emotion through the body and the mind were gone, and what was left was undiluted joy. Undiluted rage. Undiluted want. Saba stepped over the threshold and into the dark.

And it was *dark*. The sentinels had left the three of them in complete darkness. He raised the torch in front of him and tried to chase some shadows away, but the blackness was so thick the torchlight barely made a dent. Saba heard the skittering of bodies pressing back against dirt, and the clink of chains, though he quickly realized the clanking wasn't static. They hadn't been chained to the walls. He could just make out the shift of a body moving out of shadow toward the light.

He heard a voice, thick with disuse and croaky like dust had coated her vocal cords, cry out, "*Now!*" Suddenly a heavy weight knocked Saba to the side. He collapsed immediately, landing badly on his shoulder. He made a noise of pain and wriggled backwards in the dust, but two sets of hands grabbed his ankles and began to drag him further into the jail. The torch was knocked from his hand and yanked up by another.

It was too much—too absurd, too wonderful; all three of them were alive. Saba ended up laughing. He felt sorry for it, almost didn't want them to feel bad for their efforts. If he had been a sentinel, they'd have done a very good job.

"It's me!" he cried sharply. "It's me." The torch crackled as it was brought low and waved over him.

"It's too dark. Use that torch to light the others," someone—Moss?—said. Footfalls sounded, and then light slowly filled the room as torches in sconces were lit.

And then he laughed again as his eyes adjusted, and he saw two figures looming over him, staring wide-eyed at his face as they realized who he was.

He first saw Silvana, who had been mostly stripped of her gedrokbone paladin armor. She stood over him with her long brown hair out, slick with grease and dirt, and somehow still looking beautiful. But she looked a little wild and unwell, and Saba registered distantly that paladins could not be out of their armor for long. She wore the greaves, and that was all. She flashed a look somewhere behind Saba's head and said, "Moss? This may be difficult to believe—"

But Zek spoke over her.

"Saba?"

He spoke Saba's name like a prayer. In fact, he lowered himself to the ground, but not like in worship—not how Saba had made himself prostrate before the gedrok. Zek looked like he was in a dream, eyes glazed over with a sort of rapturous joy so intense it softened every feature in his face. His smile was small, in awe; it pushed the side of his beard up. His fingers reached out and very gently grazed the side of Saba's jaw.

And Saba thought about all the things he could say—all the things he wanted to say:

Have you ever sat before someone you felt safe with and realized, very suddenly, exactly how much you care about them? Have you ever felt the absurd certainty of a near-stranger's importance in your life? Would you believe me, Zek, if I said I wanted to know you more and better, or that I felt excited by the idea of knowing you and caring for you, that I can see how easy it would be to fall in love with you?

Do you know what it means when a person like me feels secure around someone?

Saba said none of this. He opened his mouth with one intention, and instead his heart imploded. He let out one racking sob and scrambled onto his knees, looked Zek in the eyes, and failed to say anything coherent.

Together, at the same time, they both said, "I thought—" with the same pained inflection, and Saba sucked in a shuddering breath and crawled close enough for Zek to embrace him. Two large arms wrapped around him. Saba buried his face in the rise of Zek's chest, felt the curl of hair against his cheek and Zek's rough beard pressing onto his scalp. Zek's arms came around Saba's ears and the world muffled; there was only the two of them, locked in a moment of physical touch, of sweat and hair and breath and humanity, both their hearts thudding loudly against their chests.

Zek smelled like himself and the earth, an intense concoction of sweat and muck. It felt so human to be wrapped up in Zek's arms and squeezed until his ribs ached. Zek held him so tightly they might have slipped into one another. And Saba wanted to occupy him, to crawl inside for the closeness, so intense was his desire to hold Zek and not let go.

How long had it been? Saba had forgotten to ask Maksid how much time had passed since he had been pushed into the breach. He pulled away from Zek to ask, but Zek's big hand laced through Saba's hair and drew him forward into a firm, deep kiss. Saba's fists balled up in Zek's grime-covered shirt. Zek pulled away first and cupped both of Saba's cheeks. He tilted Saba's head, and even in the low light, Saba could see how Zek's eyes glinted watery. Zek inspected him, tilted his face this way and that, making sure he was intact. Then he pulled Saba close again.

"You were dead," Zek whispered against Saba's forehead. "And I felt it. I felt it."

"I'm sorry," Saba said. He shook his head; all of this was his fault.

"How are you alive?" Zek asked. They pulled away from one another, and Zek's eyes were wide, as though he was confused and surprised and relieved all at once. He shifted his gaze over to Silvana and Moss, who hadn't moved from where they stood somewhere behind Saba's head. "We thought—I mean . . . everything the astral sea touches is unmade." Zek frowned for a moment. "If you're here, then Hulik . . . ?"

Saba gritted his teeth. There was no way Zek's agent was still alive. Stiffly, he shook his head, and Zek nodded like he'd expected this.

"It's because it's you, isn't it?" Zek said. This was such an ambiguous sentence that Saba's stomach dropped in sudden worry: what new blame would he have to bear? But Zek brushed Saba's hair behind his ear and tilted his head. "Because there's ichor in your blood."

How Zek had come to this conclusion, Saba didn't know. It had been a shock to him, but Zek spoke as if it was obvious.

"I hoped so," Zek whispered after a moment. "I hoped it would be enough for Suoduny to accept you."

"You hoped?" Saba murmured.

Zek pulled farther away to consider him, frown buckling his brows. "Saba," he said seriously, "of course."

The sentiment felt nice but unwarranted—undeserved. Saba squirmed, suddenly filled with a guilt as thick as mud. "I need to fix this. I need your help. But we have to get out of here. Get your things—let's go."

Quickly, Saba took the ring of keys and unlocked the chains from everyone's wrists. Silvana put a hand on Moss's shoulder and whispered something. Saba looked at her, really looked at her.

With only the greaves left on her to mitigate it, ichor sickness must have been wracking her body.

Paladins ingested such large amounts of raw ichor that the body and mind rejected it immediately. Gedrokbone armor was the only mitigation proven to reduce the effects. Saba couldn't imagine what she was feeling now, with her armor outside this room. He couldn't imagine what she was feeling at all—the ichor in his bloodstream was diluted and miniscule by comparison.

"Your armor is outside. Take a few minutes to recover," he murmured to Silvana. Her eyes widened a little, and she nodded. Both women moved out and farther into the hall. Moss lit the other torches. Zek struggled to his feet in the cell and limped toward the door.

Saba looked back at him. "Your cane?"

"The corner," Zek nodded to Saba's right, to the corner near the door.

Saba went to retrieve it. "I'm surprised they let you keep it," he said, as he handed it to Zek, attempting a conversational tone as if that would help any of them forget the misery of this jail. The longer he stayed in here, the more the memories of his own wonderful imprisonment surfaced, and Saba couldn't handle yet more emotional turbulence.

No one said anything. No one answered.

Zek took it and walked badly out into the hall. Silvana and Moss looked at them in silence. Something about it—how far Saba stood from the rest of them, maybe—made him feel distinctly distant. And he'd never really believed in intuition, but his gut roiled in him then; like a full-bodied scream, it tore through him painfully.

Something had happened. He wanted to press Zek on what, but first he asked, "How long has it been?"

Zek stiffened. It was Moss who spoke.

"Three weeks," she whispered. "I think."

Three weeks. *Weeks*! He'd suspected time might move differently between the planes, but not like this.

"Why?" Moss asked at the look on his face. "How long has it been for you?"

"An hour?" Saba said. "Maybe two? What's the last thing you remember?"

"They made me make a bad casing," Silvana said. "It did not go well."

Saba shook his head. "No. It shattered, and the lens shattered. Breaches are everywhere."

Saba told them everything Maksid had told them: about the evacuations, who was left, and where Hirunz was.

By the time he was done, Silvana looked markedly improved; ichor sickness whisked away by time now that she had been returned to her armor.

Saba turned his attention to Moss, whose eyes had filled with tears.

She stood stiffly. Saba knew the fine skin around her wrist would be welts by now. She didn't look like she'd lost much weight, and her skin, though pale, didn't have the pallid sick sheen Silvana's had. But the light in her eyes had been snuffed out, and that was somehow worse.

He put out his hand like she was a wild animal, and Moss walked forward, ignoring the outstretched hand until she was close enough to lean her head on Saba's collarbone. Then, almost on impact, she began to cry. Not sobbing, but quietly, almost gently weeping, she balled her fists up in his shirt.

"You scared me," she said.

Saba wrapped his arms around her and squeezed. Moss didn't deserve this. None of them did. But Moss—Moss was the sweetest of them all. "I'm so sorry this happened to you."

"Stop it," she said sharply, and lightly beat her fist on his chest. "If it meant you'd live again, I would have stayed in that cell for months."

He pulled back to look at her face. Her hair clung to her cheek in wet clumps, and her tears had made clear tracks along her dirty face. Saba looked up to Silvana. "But she's been taking care of you, hasn't she?"

Moss's eyes started to well again, but she nodded, stepped away, and said, "Ugh," like it was its own sentence.

"Thank you," Saba said to Silvana, who frowned at him strangely.

"Thank *you*," she responded, and gestured to the open door.

"Right," he said. "Right, yes—we need to go."

Moss and Silvana began to climb up the stairs, and Zek rested against the wall before attempting to climb the first step out of the jail. He made a deep, throated noise, which had Saba rushing up beside him. "What is it? Did they hurt you? What hurts?"

"Saba," Zek said gently. He put up a staying hand with a look that said, *I live in pain. Please don't get hysterical.*

Saba deflated. "Sorry—sorry." He cupped Zek's cheek, the pressure in his fingertips needlessly firm, like he was trying to find purchase in the bristles of Zek's beard. "I just . . . they *did* hurt you, didn't they?"

When Zek said nothing, Saba touched the back of his knuckles, squeezing lightly.

"You don't have to tell me," Saba said. "I just want to know you're alright."

Zek flashed a pained look up at him and sighed. "It's nothing. I mean it isn't, but it's nothing, in the grand scheme of things."

Saba wished Zek was less stoic in that moment, but he didn't press him further. He stroked the back of Zek's hand and hoped that simple touch communicated enough. *I'm here. However you need me to be.* It must have said what Saba wanted it to, because Zek visibly relaxed.

"Oh, Saba, we both know Hirunz is a bastard," Zek began, like that could forgive whatever had been done. He hauled himself up the stairs. "It's quite simple, really. Very basic tenet of torture, which is that I think they did it for the fun of it."

Saba's mind snagged on the word. *Torture?* His hands started moving of their own accord, pressing against Zek's body like he might find the wounds and cure them through touch alone. His mind, somehow, managed to be horrified by another implication: if Hirunz was torturing the Rezwyn ambassador, he had truly lost it.

"What?" Saba hissed. "Why would Hirunz risk war with the empire?"

"Because he suspects the Rezwyns won't invade when Byrengrad is on the brink of being unmade. Because he thinks he can negotiate somehow—give the Rezwyns a way into the astral sea. Perhaps he's right. What that means for the rest of Zvensia, I'm not sure he's thought that through. But also . . . he believes I'm involved in the opening of the breach," Zek said. "The narrative has shifted while you've been away. He's still making it about your device, and yes, your negligence. But Hirunz is now claiming—to us, his prisoners, to his sentinels, to any paragon or, gods, anyone who will listen—that agents of the Rezwyn Empire deliberately opened the breach."

"Well, they did—or at least one did," Saba said. Surprise tinged his tone. Hirunz had actually spoken the truth—or at least part of it? Zek's eyes shot up to meet his, and Saba shifted, walking slowly. "The Lord of Veprak told Hirunz to destroy the failsafe and etch the expansion sigil. They overloaded the Eye on purpose to kill the Kerish refugees, and Judge Berif, who would have voted for the Kers to gain citizenship. For whatever reason, Hirunz trusted Lord Doric."

"And then was surprised when he turned out to be a cunning prat, I presume?"

"Hulik's report was accurate," Saba said. "Hirunz killed Lord Doric. I saw it in the astral sea."

Zek nodded. He smiled a bit, as if proud of Hulik. The conversation dwindled, but Saba wasn't satisfied. Judge Hirunz had hurt Luan Zek.

He would fucking pay for that.

"What did they do with your cane?" Saba whispered. They wound up the steps to the main floor slowly, and Silvana and Moss gave them the space.

Zek ground his jaw. He looked unhappy that the conversation had returned to this and seemed to be considering whether or not to tell Saba to fuck off. Fair enough—it wasn't Saba's business. But Saba wanted it to be. He wanted Zek to trust him with this, to let him care for him.

So when Zek spoke, Saba felt a range of conflicting emotions: joy at the trust, and horror at the truth revealed.

"In the war," Zek began, and then stopped. "Before Kerinsk, I was stationed in Usleth. When I became Squadron Leader, they shipped me over to the invasion of Kerinsk. But at thirteen, before I'd proved myself, they started me out as a runner. I'd be the messenger for critical information between commands, sometimes between camp and the battles themselves. Because I was quick. Really fucking fast, despite my size. And the word Zaj means hare in Doskorian, and they'd call me that—because I was too fucking big even at thirteen to be called a rabbit, and because it sounds like Zek. I was Zaj for years. Funny now, maybe. I'm too big to be a hare, and I won't ever run again. Anyway, I don't think Hirunz knew this, but it's all I could think about when he . . . he had them beat my buggered leg with it."

All the warmth drained from Saba's face. "What?"

"Not for long. They didn't break anything, either. But they did enough—I can feel it's more fucked up than it was.

They wanted me to confess, you see, and I couldn't do that. I couldn't give them what he wanted, not after what Hirunz did to you."

How could he speak so calmly? How was he not raging and crying? How dare they—how dare any of them touch Luan Zek. Everything felt—inconsequential. Every touch or word he could offer Zek in that moment wouldn't be enough.

But Saba found himself whispering, "For me?"

Zek looked over with the kind of vulnerable sweetness he seemed to keep locked up with his most unpleasant memories. He paused and leaned against the wall, beckoned Saba closer, ran his hand over Saba's cheek, and kissed him gently.

"Of course, for you," Zek murmured against Saba's lips. "But of course, for me, too. I won't be beaten into submission. I won't—my convictions are stronger than my bones."

A gruffness came into his voice, and Saba nodded. Fury burned beneath his skin, and he was sure it must have hurt to touch. But Zek smiled at him like he was the sun.

"Maksid," Saba said slowly. "Did he participate?"

Zek shook his head—but to Saba that only meant that Maksid hadn't stopped it, either.

He wanted to apologize to Zek, but he couldn't. It wasn't his apology to give. He wanted to say: *nothing like this will ever happen to you again.* But that was a promise he couldn't be sure he'd be able to keep.

But the one thing he could promise, he said with a rasping, angered voice. "I'm going to make Hirunz pay for touching you."

Zek's expression didn't change. He didn't look disbelieving, nor joyful about Saba's proclamation. His rough hands rubbed over Saba's knuckles, and Zek kissed the back of Saba's hand. "Then lead the way."

Before they reached the final corner and flight of stairs, Saba stopped them all. "I need a favor."

They turned to him, but Saba was looking at Silvana in particular. "I know you've barely recovered. But I need the three of you to split Silvana's Paladin armor among yourselves before we move through the foyer. In case part of the breach touches Moss or Zek—something is better than nothing. I don't want any part of the breach touching any one of you."

They accepted this at face value, which was the kind of trust that made Saba's heart swell with happiness. Silvana slipped off her gauntlets and gave one each to Zek and Moss. It wasn't much, but Saba wanted them to have at least some shield against the light emanating from the fractured breach.

He led them the rest of the way up, nervous about what was to come next.

It's fine. It's going to be fine.

But was it?

Because an audience was waiting for them at the top of the stairs:

Persistence Sage. Diligence Inquisitor. Four sentinels. His brother.

And Judge Hirunz.

CHAPTER TWENTY-ONE

"Arrest them!"

Hirunz's hand shook as he pointed at Saba, but his voice resounded clearly around the foyer, overcoming the spitting background noise of the breaches. At some point in the last three weeks, part of the judge's golden mask had shattered, exposing the pale chin beneath, dotted with rough, wiry stubble and the edges of a turned down sneer.

Persistence Sage and Diligence Inquisitor flanked him on either side, and four sentinels fanned out from behind them to enact Hirunz's orders. The fifth sentinel Saba recognized to be Maksid.

"Vasili?" Giste whispered. Her head jolted at the sight of the others, and her hand flew up to her sage mask at the sight of Moss. To Saba's shock, she removed it—flung the thing off and darted ahead of the sentinels just as they were drawing their swords.

Her oval face was tinged yellow with an old bruise, but her eyes were red and puffy from what was unmistakably a recent bout of crying. Long black hair fell in wisps around her face. Her lips were drained of all color, and she only had eyes for Moss.

"No," she was saying, "Mossinne? Moss!"

Moss stepped back behind Saba's periphery, and Silvana intercepted Giste's approach. She had no sword, nothing really except her own bulk and a considerably dark gaze, but it was enough to make Giste halt. Her lip seemed to wobble and then that brief show of weakness disappeared, replaced by a blinding fury as she rounded on Hirunz.

"*You!*" Giste hissed. "You told me they were working on getting close to the breach! A sealed suit of gedrokbone armor to safely place the failsafe—but look at them. You've kept them in *jail?*"

The sentinels were ignoring this exchange, ignoring Giste completely as they seized the former prisoners. They began to pull everyone's arms behind their backs. Maksid grabbed Saba.

As much as Saba wanted to watch as Giste's understanding bloomed and she broke from Hirunz, from her title as a sage, from Hirunz's Byrengrad altogether—he couldn't quite let her steal the show.

Flashing a look to Maksid, Saba stepped forward, angling himself so he could stare down Hirunz directly. He called loud enough that his voice echoed slightly around the foyer. "How long have you known about me?"

Maksid moved quickly. He was the one to take Saba's arms and pull them behind his back, firmly but far more gently than Hirunz would probably have liked.

"Whatever you are," Hirunz seethed, "you are monstrous. Nothing survives the astral sea. But you knew that—you knew that when you opened it!"

Saba flinched. Hirunz's story was ever-changing at this point—lies compounded on lies—the judge would say anything but the truth.

He's deflecting your fucking question. Make him talk, Vasili.

"Answer me, Hirunz. You owe me at least that much!"

A dry, flat laugh responded. Hirunz's posture changed. All the height and lank of his body extended suddenly, like he'd been carrying a great burden on his shoulders and only now had he thrown it off. Hirunz swung back to face him. The pink curve of his mouth had stretched open to show Saba his teeth.

He sneered, "I owe you nothing." His usual tone—grandiose and precise—had been replaced by a petulant sort of rage. By his side, his white-knuckled fist shook, and

Saba remembered Hirunz signing him over to Zek weeks ago—nearly a month, in truth—and the way Hirunz had shuddered in embarrassment at the sight of Saba Vasili.

You owe me nothing? Saba gritted his teeth. *What a lie. What a lie!*

Saba rolled back his shoulders. "You owe me my reputation, which you stole and tarnished. You owe me weeks of my life kept in your prison for something I didn't do. And you owe me the truth. How long have you known exactly who I am?"

Hirunz laughed. "I don't—"

Enough of this. Loudly and with confidence, Saba said, "Justice Sentinel Maksid, I order you to let me go."

Maksid hesitated. Saba could feel the pressure on his wrists tighten and loosen in the span of seconds. His brother leaned close and whispered back, "What are you doing?"

They hadn't discussed the plan this far. Saba hadn't really known for sure this was how it would go—that this was what he would do. But now it felt natural—needed. He turned as much as he could in Maksid's grip, until his right eye could take in his brother's wide-eyed stare through the slits of the mask. Saba stared at him, stared in the way a prince would, in a way he never got to practice. He stared with certainty and the definitive expectation of nobility, with the confidence of someone who could see the future and knew his orders would be enacted.

Maksid loosened his grip.

Saba pulled free of him and walked forward.

This triggered something in Hirunz. He stepped back, but he'd already sent his sentinels to apprehend the other three of Saba's party, and so he backed up into nobody's protection. Diligence Inquisitor stepped away from him like he was a bad smell. Her focus was on Saba, her eyes narrowed, intrigued, and waiting.

"What are you doing?" Hirunz asked. Nerves seemed to crack through him; his voice shook. "Justice Sentinel, apprehend him!"

"He won't," Saba said. "He knows who I am. And so do you."

Now, he could feel everyone's eyes on him. Zek and Maksid and even Diligence Inquisitor knew the truth, though Saba couldn't understand what she thought. An eagerness laced the air. Giste flashed her attention back and forth between Hirunz and Saba. Everyone waited.

Saba swallowed and turned to his left. The basilica's atrium opened like a grand cavity. Saba recalled thinking it looked like a body, a rib cage cracked open, as if he was sitting in the belly of the beast. The gedrokeye lens, shattered and hovering midair, still refracted the breach's endless potential. Pink webbing and flesh pulsed occasionally in the marble whenever the flares of ichor licked at the stone. The veins in the columns twitched with blood. Saba breathed deep and stepped further into the atrium. Hirunz and the others stood paralyzed, watching him closely.

"Judge Hirunz attempted to frame me for his own fuck up," Saba said. He jabbed a finger in the judge's direction. "I know you're responsible for the breach."

Loudly, Hirunz scoffed. "I never opened the breach."

"Worse," Saba said.

Saba was close to the breach now. Something in him—in the very core of him, in his gut, perhaps in his soul—responded to the ichor. He could feel the tiniest flecks of it in his blood and his flesh. He could feel the magic that had deepened his voice, changed the way his body grew, grown hair where he hadn't had prior. He could feel it like a primal ancient memory—it had a depth to it that he couldn't shake loose from his flesh or his existence. In a way, he had been made from the astral sea; it recognized him as a son the way his own mother had never had the opportunity.

Resonating with power, Saba said, "You gave the order to activate the Eye. You let it happen. You let Lord Doric, a foreign agent of the Rezwyn Empire, use my machine to—deliberately—open a tear into the astral sea in Loefka Ward. You had the failsafe mechanism removed, and you changed the runes on the casing so that turning on the device would cause a massive rupture instead of a pinprick. And when you were duped, when Lord Doric turned out to be a snake, you panicked. You couldn't close the breach, and neither could he. So you killed him."

Tense silence stretched between them. Diligence Inquisitor shifted, her heels clacking over the marble as she walked away from the judge and toward an undulating column between both parties, as if trying to remove herself from the equation. Hirunz stared after her, and then to the others, while the four sentinels stood lost, their gauntleted hands seeming to grip their charges delicately. All four of them had turned to Justice Sentinel for guidance, and he was staring straight at Saba.

Hirunz looked frightened for just a moment. Then he scoffed. Saba knew what he was thinking: So far, there had been no proof. Only talk.

"You're insane, Vasili."

Saba wanted to say all of it first, so he continued. "You had Judge Berif visit Loefka Ward, so she was caught in the shock wave and unmade, thus removing your only remaining political opponent. You had her turn the device on. You did it all to rid yourself of your Kerish problem, but if you want a damn problem, Hirunz, here you have one—me. You already know who I am, or you wouldn't have tried to have me extradited to the empire. You know who I am, or you wouldn't have pushed me into the fucking breach!"

Saba turned to the shattered gedrokeye lens. He reached up. Someone shouted—Moss, he thought—and Zek wrestled free of his sentinel and staggered forward. Saba shot his hand up to stay him.

Trust me, he urged Zek through the look in his eye. Zek's shoulders slackened, and he nodded, stepping back out of range of the breach's flares.

Hirunz's eyes were wide. His body had seemed to understand before the rest of him, because he was saying, "No, no," over and over again, though he'd slackened like a ragdoll.

"Here is your greatest fear realized," Saba said. "People will know who I am. *My* people will know who I am. And people will know you, too. Exactly what you did. Exactly the kind of person you are."

Saba spun away just as Hirunz made a noise of protest—and he touched the piece of gedrok lens closest to him.

A sharp, crackling light. A booming wave of power that shuddered through Saba's whole body. Momentarily, he was deafened, and then he realized the very nature of sound had changed for him. He felt a tugging sensation in his stomach, and then pain—pain like something sharp had dug into his clavicle and was rummaging around beneath the skin. Something was pulled from him, dragged out of a tiny, near inconsequential hole in his breastbone.

It joined the stream of ichor and was pulled through the gedrok lens where it split apart—not sharply the way glass would, but like liquid splitting into streams. Then it bubbled up and over, forming a foggy wall, and when the fog cleared, they were all watching the scene that Saba had been shown in the astral sea.

Hirunz and Lord Doric meeting. Hirunz and Lord Doric discussing the deaths of the Kers. Hirunz and Lord Doric later, when the device was already in Loefka Ward, rigged to tear the astral sea open. The struggle between the two of them. Lord Doric's scream as he was thrown over the edge, and then the shockwave itself, obliterating everything in its path.

Everyone was silent. Only the crackle of the breach echoed around the basilica as Saba pulled his hand free. He turned to face them; everyone was transfixed and stared, mouths agape. One of the sentinels let go of his charge—Silvana—and stepped unsteadily backwards, until he was close to Diligence Inquisitor.

Giste seemed to realize her part in this: she had been instructed to bring the device to the basilica and had done so, days before the event.

She stepped forward and said, "Judge Hirunz summoned me the morning before the event to say the device had been stolen from the basilica. He has the replacement failsafe mechanism on his person. For some reason, he refused to use it. He instead had Paladin Silvana make a casing out of scrap material and moved the Eye—against the expert advice of myself, Mossinne, and the paladin. Now it's shattered and it's worse than before. Whether you believe what you have just seen or not, Hirunz's decision to move the device, and the resulting multitude of breaches is resolutely his fault. Justice Sentinel, get the mechanism."

Hirunz flinched and his frozen stupor was broken. He stepped backwards. "What are you doing? Justice Sentinel—*listen to me!*"

But Maksid wouldn't. Saba felt certain of that. Maksid felt it as Saba did: the truth of his lineage was in his blood. There would be no more denying the Prince of Kerinsk.

Saba announced, "I am Saba Vasili, born Princess Sabina Vasyiluki of Kerinsk, child of Queen Deinah Vasyiluki of Kerinsk, and heir to the Kerish throne. My claim can be verified by the brand on the back of my neck. And I never really was their *princess*, but I can and will be their representative here. By the Zvensian-Kerish Treaty signed by Queen Deinah and Zvensia's Grand Council, you are required to render aid and assistance to me and my people in time of need."

Hirunz yelled, frustrated. "You don't belong here. You don't! You people—you should be going back to your own fucking country. You should be fighting the Rezwyns, not burdening Zvensia."

"You should have honored your agreement," Saba murmured, "because Zvensia promised to help us. But have no fear, Hirunz. I do plan to petition the new emperor about the occupation of Kerinsk. He's a close friend of Zek's, you know."

Zek nodded happily.

"What nonsense," Hirunz said. "Justice Sentinel, *get your hands off me!*"

Maksid took Hirunz's hands behind his back and forced him to the ground. He began to rummage in Hirunz's pockets until he found the failsafe mechanism, which he pulled free triumphantly and held above his head. Silvana took the risk of stepping forward, but none of the other sentinels stopped her. Maksid relinquished the mechanism to her.

Zek walked forward calmly, with far more poise and control than Saba could have had when seeing Hirunz again. "Before the occupation," he began, "Kerinsk had a treaty with the Rezwyn Empire. Nio Beumeut breached the treaty when Queen Deinah died. But Emperor Dziove has promised to make good on many of the empire's old promises—as the first gesture to repair the damages Nio Beumeut's reign has caused. As the last heir of the sovereign line, Vasili is able to negotiate directly with the Rezwyn Empire, and to ask for aid or assistance from us. But Queen Deinah was a diplomat, and she had a treaty with Zvensia, too. You knew that Saba would have the legal right to ask for the Kerish refugees to be given citizenship. That's why you defamed him. That's why you wanted him to die."

Maksid did the unthinkable in that moment and dislodged Hirunz's mask from his head. Where Giste had chosen this for herself, Hirunz paled to the point of looking ill—it was a disgrace for a judge to show his face. Hirunz's face seemed unnaturally pale, the way many Rezwyns' did, though without much exposure to sun his eyes had a sunken quality to them; the skin looked vaguely transparent the way gedrok skin did, and he seemed haunted. Barely human. He had a neat nose and a mouth that drooped naturally, only it had dropped farther now given his despair.

Zek walked over to inspect him. Hirunz glanced away, which clearly wouldn't do. Zek's eyes were searing as he cocked his head and, slipping his hand down the cane, gently knocked Hirunz's head back toward him. "The irony is that before you attacked him, Hirunz, Saba Vasili had no intention whatsoever of revealing his former identity. You brought this on yourself."

Hirunz looked up. And then he scrambled up suddenly. The motion was so quick and fluid it shocked both Maksid and Zek, their surprise slowing them down long enough that Hirunz ran past them. He threw himself toward the door at the end of the basilica, and Saba stepped away from the gedrok lens and the device to intercept him. Which is when Hirunz saw his opportunity.

Who knew what he was thinking. Whether it was a general self-destructive impulse, or something manic and cruel; whether he hoped to take all of them with him, or whether it was just a wild vagary.

Hirunz pivoted, changing course suddenly. He moved close to the Eye, screaming.

And he hit it.

The breach reacted. The basilica shook; a dry crunch echoed throughout the large chamber as something broke in the foundations. An enormous clap of thunder threw

Saba off his feet. Both he and Hirunz were thrown back into the belly of the basilica, thrown so hard neither could even scream upon impact.

Everything was muffled, and a high-pitched ringing shrieked through Saba's head. Distantly, someone was screaming, but after a moment his muffled hearing cleared, and he could hear the bloodcurdling cries of Hirunz. Saba turned over and saw the man cradling his hand. Three fingers had been degloved, the skin unmade by a quick brush with one of the breach's flares. Creamy bone stared out from a puckered hollow of flesh, and the red viscous remains of the finger hung in thin ropes from the finger bones. Hirunz was whimpering now, cradling the hand and shaking with the distant stare of a man losing himself to shock.

Raging, Saba shouted, "As you fucking deserve, you *idiot!*"

He knew that he should leave Hirunz here and let the breach have him. He should push Hirunz into the astral sea, taking revenge for himself. He should definitely not waste any time or energy on saving the bastard that had murdered so many Kers for his own comfort.

Saba pushed himself up but staggered. The gedrok lens—already in many pieces—had shattered further. A dozen more pieces now floated in the basilica's atrium.

The Eye jerked violently as the beam of ichor rumbled out of it. An ear-piercing bang sounded as the beam split an additional twelve times to reach each new lens target. Saba's stomach dropped, and he exploded into action before he'd even fully registered what was happening.

The Eye wasn't made for this. In truth, it was a miracle it had survived this long at all. Opening the breach wide enough for a person to step through had always been a risk—a pipe dream—a hypothesis he had never been able to test. But splitting that power source into so many pieces?

Destabilizing it, each piece of the gedrok lens demanding enough power to form its own breach and sustain the opening?

Saba knew in his gut it was going to keep fracturing and kill them all.

As if hearing its maker worry, a high-pitch whirr squealed out of the Eye. It began to shake, and then the whole basilica shook with it. Dust and rock shifted and rained down in crumbs from the ceiling, and a resounding crack whipped across the ground as the sturdy marble floor split open.

A bright light seared through the atrium—and then the whirring grew in earnest.

All of the breaches erupted. They came together in a horrific, glowing, stitching of power; gaping wounds bled into one another to form a single blinding cavity.

Diligence Inquisitor moved first. Her sand-colored dress whipped around her as unnatural wind howled through the basilica's chamber.

"*Evacuate!*" she shouted, her attention turned toward the sentinels. "Help the scholars!"

Silvana, Moss, and Giste raised their arms to shield their faces as another gust of wind blew over them. The sentinels moved as one, and it was perhaps the first time Saba was grateful they were named for virtues; all of them moved without question to aid the scholars.

Hirunz struggled to his feet. Saba turned to him.

"You have killed all of us, you bastard!"

Hirunz's eyes were wild, wide, and wet. "No," he was saying. "No, I—"

"Every chance you've had to stop this, you've squandered. You don't get to be scared now!"

Hirunz started at Saba, turned on his heel, and ran. Which was stupid and risky—the breaches were uncontained, and seams of power flashed out into the atrium randomly and violently. It didn't take long. It was like the flares were drawn to him. Three licked out at once as Hirunz hobbled between the sea of astral breaches, and as they touched him, he was unmade.

Hirunz screamed. The sound stopped abruptly as all of his flesh disintegrated, and the ash that fell ceased to exist.

Saba stared, heart racing. *That was deliberate. That was Suoduny.*

Saba felt nothing but a pinprick of relief at the sight. Who was he to question the astral sea?

Now Saba had to close it.

He spun back to the others. The scholars and sentinels had made it to the door. Diligence Inquisitor followed suit. It was Saba, Maksid, and Zek still in immediate danger. Without question, Maksid ran forward toward the breach. No—toward Saba.

No. No. It would be pure luck if he survived. Too many breaches had opened between the Eye and Maksid's location. Saba knew what was happening—Maksid had the failsafe mechanism.

But only Saba could fix this.

Saba dashed forward to meet him, sidestepping flares and crackling tears. He shouted, "Maksid, *no!* Throw it!"

Maksid skidded to a halt and hesitated. Perhaps he thought Saba couldn't catch it—that he wouldn't be able to. That he'd drop it and crack it on the hard marble. He paused and—finally—trusted his little brother.

Maksid threw the failsafe. It loped through the air three times. Saba rushed forward, lowered his body, and caught the small part gently. His body rolled over it. He tumbled and landed hard on the marble, but he had used his own body to cradle the failsafe, and it survived without a scratch. Saba pushed himself to standing and screamed over the wind, "*Get out of here!*"

Everyone started to peel away. The main entrance was blocked, but they'd find some other way out. They had to.

Saba's heart was racing. He didn't know if he could survive this. It was worse now, worse than it had been, because he wanted to live. He wanted a chance to love himself. But this—everything that had happened—was due to his own negligence and leaving the astral sea open and bleeding was simply not an option. Saba turned to face the Eye.

He stepped forward.

"*Saba!*"

Saba spun around. Zek was there—like an idiot, like a fool!—running as best he could toward Saba. He winced as pain flared up through his knee, but the adrenaline must have kept him going. He looked up at Saba, face twisting darkly, and pushed forward.

"Stop!" Saba hissed. "You can't be this close. You can't—*go!*"

Zek got close enough to Saba to drop his cane. He crashed forward, hands pressed to either side of Saba's cheeks, and he knocked their foreheads together. "Not a chance."

Saba's heart lurched. "Please," he said, reaching up to stroke one of Zek's hands. "Get out of here. I don't know what will happen when I close it—we're right at the center. And you shouldn't have to bear this. It's my mess. I'm cleaning it up."

The basilica creaked. The great weight of the astral sea bore down on them; the intangible becoming tangible, impossibility ebbing and flowing through the atrium. Zek grabbed Saba's shoulder to steady himself, and with his other hand, he raised up Saba's chin.

Zek said, "Look at me. *Look at me.* You saved me. From that dungeon, and from . . ." Zek hesitated, then cried out, "Don't martyr yourself for this. Come back with me."

Idealism, again. Zek had offered to whisk Saba away

from Byrengrad. He had offered to go with him. Here he was again, offering the same salvation, promising Saba that it was alright to live and to live for himself.

Zek was so much sweeter than he realized.

But Saba couldn't, and Zek must have known that, because his face shifted. The light faded from his eyes.

Saba murmured, "I have to close it. I must . . . close it for good."

"I'm not letting you do it alone," Zek said, and there was no further discussion—no time for Saba to debate him. Zek was wearing parts of Silvana's armor. That would have to be enough.

He took Zek by the hand and pushed against the screaming wind. The device pulsed and spun on its own axis, floating and whirring. Saba went to his knees and, after a beat of hesitation, put his hands up against the metal casing. He pulled it. With a crack, the outer casing dislodged itself, exposing the inner belly of the device with its cogs and mechanisms. The spot where the failsafe should have been sat empty, a dark hollow. The beam of ichor shot up. Saba craned his neck—and jolted.

The dozens of shards of the gedrok lens had been transformed; tiny living gedrok eyes rolled around and stared at him.

"What the fuck," Zek muttered.

Saba shivered. He felt the weight of all of them looking at him, and part of him felt them—these vessels of the astral sea, the confusion they had felt when they crashed into the material plane and felt everything all at once.

Saba looked upon all the eyes and said, "I'm sending you back. The Eye, the ichor, all of it. I will not make another tear."

Zek's eyes flickered down to the device as if he was seeing it for the first time. Surprise flashed across his face; he must have registered Saba's words slowly. "You would destroy it?"

"What's the alternative? Letting it consume Zvensia? The world?"

Zek gestured down at it. "It's your life's work."

Saba exhaled, reached out, and stroked Zek's cheek. "Still so idealistic," he bellowed over the noise. Then he turned back and took a deep breath. "That life ended the moment hundreds died. I won't be so selfish as to do that again."

Zek grimaced. Saba opened his palm and looked down at the failsafe mechanism. Its weight shone iridescently in the palm of his hand.

"What happens when you touch it?" Zek yelled.

"I don't know."

Zek nodded and wrapped his gauntleted hand beneath Saba's. "Then you're not touching it alone."

Saba looked at him, nodded, and together they reached in: Saba's bare flesh and Zek with his gauntlet-covered hand. Together they pressed the failsafe mechanism into place, and it clicked. Flares of astral energy licked out at them, and Saba moved to shield Zek as best he could. The ichor licked along Saba's arm with an almost gentle caress, and with his other hand, Saba reached back into the device and clicked the failsafe on.

At once, the Eye reacted. The whirring lessened, the wind calmed. All the many, many gedrok eyes closed and disappeared.

The quiet was instantaneous. All howling wind ceased. The crackling energy of the astral sea had dispersed, and the pressure in the atrium had lightened. Saba exhaled and closed his eyes and let himself feel. He let himself feel it all: The disappointment. The fear. The raggedy, raging guilt inside him. And then the release of pressure, the forgiveness he could allow himself, the joy that it was done.

The hope, too, of whatever was to come.

Light flooded the atrium through the formerly lovely back window that had imploded, been unmade.

"Are you alright?" Zek asked.

Saba turned to him. Zek had retrieved his cane. He stood half-bent over it, in obvious pain, and extraordinarily beautiful. His beard caught the afternoon light and glowed blond and orange. Sweat-dampened, grime-covered, and gorgeous.

Saba let out a little laugh in answer, and Zek came forward and slipped his free hand into Saba's. They squeezed each other's fingers.

The last struggle of the astral sea had transformed the basilica. Out of the crumbled archways and that destroyed back window, they could see the broken city of Byrengrad. But before that, much of the basilica itself had already been changed by the touch of the astral sea. Accelerated plant life grew across the building, ichor-infused flowers glowing and pulsing. Saba knew that cajudsan sometimes grew where ichor had touched. He wondered if Byrengrad would have a sea of them. Crystals, too, blossomed in running ridges along the inside. The whole interior looked like a reclaimed shrine.

Saba sighed. "This place is a wreck."

Zek squeezed Saba's hand and exhaled, almost with longing. "No," he whispered. "It's beautiful."

Saba rolled his eyes and scoffed. He turned to Zek, pushed up onto his toes, and kissed him on the cheek.

And Saba said, "You'll doom us, you know, with that optimism of yours."

EPILOGUE

Two Months Later

A month into winter, when the flat gray sky hung over everything and everyone like a funeral shroud, and the only plant life to survive the cold were purple flowering weeds, Legacy Sage examined himself in the etched looking glass mounted on the wall in his quarters at the Scholar's Building.

This evaluation used to be a habit—a bad one, closer to an interrogation, where he would stare and criticize and pull at parts of his body. One where he would see those iridescent crescent moon scars along his chest and find them ugly. He used to look and see, helplessly, the wrongness of his flesh; like everything else that might be considered good or attractive had been muted or hidden behind fog, and a beacon-like focus was given to everything else: The shape and sharpness of his hip bones. The lack of muscle, the softness of his lower belly, the thickness of his thighs. He had years of a dense memory, a tome of these inspections he could flip through in his mind. Every time he had ever looked at himself, he had othered his body.

And now, Saba stood there seeing all the same things. Only now he could look and feel—fine.

Good, even.

First had come the neutrality. He hadn't been certain he could trust that feeling, because it straddled apathy, and that type of numbness often gave way to pained hysteria when he ignored it for too long. But days passed when Saba could look at himself without disgust or upset or craving or grief for something he never had.

But then came this new feeling. Saba had woken up, stood in front of the mirror to ready himself for the day, and had the thought that he looked quite striking.

Which had stopped him in his tracks. The moment rendered him practically incapacitated for minutes, had even pushed him close to the verge of tears, because the voice that sat in his mind had never said something so kind to him.

He had his hair in a ponytail over one shoulder. It was long enough now to graze the top of his left pec, where his scars were dazzling, reflected in the mirror. A sheen of silver and pink iridescence like perfectly placed paint. A finishing touch on a work of art—ah, there that voice went again, feeling good about what it saw.

The most surprising, or the best thing, was realizing that voice belonged to him. At first it had sounded somewhat like Luan Zek's—with the same lilt and cadence and confidence. But sure enough, over time, it had become Saba's own voice.

He looked at himself. He looked at his shoulders, the way his collarbones pressed up through his skin. He looked at the way the light hit him, and the way shadows fell, carving out his pecs, his jawline, his stomach. He looked and sadness welled up in him, because he had spent so long wishing horrible things to happen to this body—to him. Who does that? Who spends so long letting hatred fester?

"Legacy Sage?" A muffled voice sounded through the closed door a half second before someone knocked.

It still spooked him, sometimes, to hear that title. He had chosen Legacy not just for Kerinsk and his new role, but for himself. The totality of his experiences, his beliefs, his values, his knowledge. His body, too, carried a legacy—and one he should be proud of.

"Just a minute!" he called back.

"It's . . . well, it's rather urgent," the voice said again, and this time Saba caught the tinge of fear laced in their words. "Persistence Sage has asked for you personally."

Not a good sign.

After everything that had happened, and with the dissolution of Byrengrad's Triad, the city had been granted a temporary, proxy council led by Diligence Inquisitor and a paragon representative from each discipline. Giste, of course, represented the scholars. But Saba had been granted a role, too—or rather, he had dug it out with force. Kerinsk was represented, now. First in Byrengrad City, with hopes to appeal to the Zvensian Council for further Kerish rights and eventually to the empire itself.

Saba hadn't visited the land that was once Kerinsk in a long while. Perhaps he soon could.

But if Persistence Sage had asked for him personally—given the fact that her attitude toward him had barely shifted toward the positive—Saba knew whatever was happening was not good.

A breach, Saba's mind thought instantly. Some slip in time and space, a little tear in the astral sea, his fault—*stop it.* That wasn't possible.

Saba threw on a shirt and opened the door. "What is it?"

The scholar, a stout young man, gave him a fearful look. "Better if you see it for yourself, Sage."

"Just tell me," Saba whispered.

Another fearful look, something of an apologetic smile. "The Rezwyns are attacking, sir."

A beat later and the alarm sounded throughout Byrengrad, a cacophony of noise as horn after horn began to blare and echo out the warning from the sentinels at the wall. The whole city screamed with the sound, and Saba's own head took up that droning wail, because surely not.

Zek wouldn't do that to him. Zek wouldn't.

But the emperor might.

You asked for too much. You demanded an audience to speak on Kerinsk's behalf, and now they'll sack Byrengrad, too. Damn the treaty. The Rezwyns had already broken it once. Why not again?

Saba sped out of his quarters, following the scholar to Giste's position.

The last letter Saba received from Ambassador Luan Zek could hardly be called a letter. It was barely a sad excuse for a note.

Busy here, it read. *Will find time to speak to you properly, soon.*

That was it. No sweet nothings. Nothing he'd wanted to hear. Saba walked past it only a moment before, laid open on his desk, sitting where it had sat for the past month. And he had been so desperate to receive it and whatever potential promise might be tied up in those words that he'd kept it open next to a treatise on the astral sea, next to quantum ichor studies and complex research and impossible theorems—all of which made more sense to Saba than the dry, insubstantial note Luan Zek had sent. Was Saba supposed to accept it? After everything, after the open wound of the astral sea, after feeling that power course through them together . . .

Busy here. Will find time to speak to you properly, soon.

And now: to war?

What brewed in Saba as he faced this sudden development was a particular kind of loneliness. Zek wouldn't do this—Saba had just told himself that—but what if he had? Saba, who had spent so much of his life guarded and angry around Rezwyns, had let down his guard for one—and still longed after him. He had thought there was something substantial between them, despite how short a time frame they'd known each other, and their cultural differences, and the huge physical expanse between them, and—*shit*, he had been naive, hadn't he?

Saba and the scholar moved in silence through the building, Saba trying in vain to keep that anxious gnawing locked away. But by the time the scholar had led him to the top of the Scholar's Building, a cold sweat dewed in the small of his back. He wanted to amputate the feeling, carve out around his heart, pop it out of his body. He wanted to control it, the way he used to be able to before he'd let his guard down—before he'd let Zek in.

The top of the Scholar's Building—not the small room Saba and Zek had visited before their trip to the underdark, but a tower that led to the roof—had been forever changed by the breach. Fractal glass curled impossibly around sunbeams, and columns warped at odd angles, though the pillars somehow still supported the building structurally. Saba loved this spillover effect of the astral sea. He loved that these things had been touched and then changed. He loved it almost ridiculously.

It scared most of the other paragons. It scared most everyone in Byrengrad, really. Every shift in architecture, or plant life, or animals reeked of chaos to them—inherently impossible to control through bureaucracy. They craved the inertia of a life curtailed by piles of paperwork. But Saba had grown to understand the joylessness in that control, the hopelessness of it. Against something like the astral sea, what could humanity hope to control?

And against something like the Rezwyn army?

At the top of the stairs, beside the bowled roof, was a raised flat terrace that overlooked the city of Byrengrad, namely the northern gate to the city. The sun bore down in a comforting way, melting the top layer of snow packed onto the parapet. Persistence Sage stood silently away from Saba, staring out at the horizon. Her bronze mask drooped from her hand, glinting in the sunlight—and the sight made Saba feel ill, because Giste might as well have been fused to that mask; she glorified it and let it glorify her in return. The only time Saba had seen her take it off was upon discovering that Hirunz had imprisoned Mossinne, and since then, she'd worn it constantly again. She let it become her true face. But to use the telescope easily, one had to press one's eye close against the lens.

And whatever she had seen seemed to prevent her from replacing the mask.

No one else was on the terrace, and Giste wasn't speaking, and only the scholar had told Saba what was happening. So he walked over to the telescope, bent down, and peered into it.

He saw nothing immediately, nothing save for the snow swaddling the rolling hills and naked trees slanting haphazardly, protrusions like bony fingers reaching for the sky. But when he shifted the scope for a more distant view, he saw it all. A horde was indeed moving toward Byrengrad.

What looked like signal fires smoked in the distance, a long line of them puffing up into the sky until they were snuffed out by the horizon line. A dozen Zvensian settlements must have seen this procession. Why had no one stopped them? Why was there no organized effort to drive them back?

"I estimate an hour, maybe two," Giste whispered. She cleared her throat and put her mask back on before she turned, but Saba still caught the look in her eyes: the fear sitting in the glint of her iris.

"Those are signal fires," Saba said carefully. "Right? Not . . ."

Saba considered the possibility that perhaps the reason no Zvensian sentinels had ridden out to attack was simply because every settlement had already been razed. But then Giste nodded, and Saba's frown deepened.

"I can't see any detail. Just a mass of bodies moving toward us," Giste said. "The sentinels will have to wait for orders until they get closer."

"They can't wait," the scholar said quickly. His voice was high and strained, and he was practically shivering as he stood. "The Triad—or, I mean, Byrengrad's council—must send the sentinels out."

Giste folded her arms and sniffed, staring out over the city with a grimace. "I need a drink."

"Have one," Saba murmured. "You say we only have a few hours before they raze the city. No point in appearing virtuous if we're all going to die."

Saba's leg wouldn't stop shaking. He moved to the parapet and leaned his bodyweight against it, letting the thing bounce wildly if only to expel some of the energy that had suddenly manifested itself.

Giste sighed. Whenever she spoke to Saba, she always managed to sound like she was teaching a small child some very valuable life lesson. "I guess it's time to let hope for your little tryst die."

It barely counts as a tryst, Saba wanted to say. *I hardly touched the man.* Which wasn't at all how he'd wanted his time with Zek to end, but the aftermath of the breach hadn't lent itself to the kind of atmosphere required to take off one's clothes. The questioning, the cleanup, the very boring political mess both Byrengrad and Zek had found themselves in had all meant returning to Doskor, the empire capital, was the smartest move on Zek's part. Saba couldn't fault him that. He could, however, be frustrated—with himself, his body and his wandering mind.

Giste stalked down the stairs past him, and the scholar went with her. Saba pretended like he wasn't glad to be alone for all of three seconds before he sprang up and pushed his eye against the scope once more. He scoured the dotted ranks as if some great amount of detail would somehow be visible only minutes after his last look. As if he might squint hard enough and see the strong, fat body of Luan Zek leading the charge, or up on horseback, or staring into the distance toward Byrengrad. Toward *him*.

Pathetic. Saba pulled away. Two months, and he was pining. Two months, for a man he'd known for such a short while, and yet every corner of Saba's mind centered around Zek as its gravity. He often found himself falling toward thoughts of him, no matter where he started. This was happening again now. Giste thought there might be an invasion, and Saba's mind fell toward Zek as if falling into the bigger man's embrace. He remembered the warmth of him first, but then the truth of him. Luan Zek had values he would uphold even in the face of powerful foreign officials. Even when the astral sea was bleeding into this reality. Zek had said Emperor Dziove was different—or at least trying to be—and perhaps Saba ought to trust that.

Perhaps he ought to trust Zek.

Saba calmly walked back to his quarters, closed and locked the door, and pulled everything he had to wear from his closet. If he was right—and it was a big if—he needed to look at least slightly better than a sleep-deprived rat. And if he was wrong—well.

He'd at least die pretty.

But in truth, a sense of possibility was taking root in him, a gut feeling where the anxiety, though present, wasn't dread. He was almost hopeful.

An hour later, as Saba fussed with his hair—which suddenly couldn't sit right no matter what he did with it—another knock sounded on his door.

"Yes?" he called.

Moss opened it with a sigh. "I suppose you know, then. Oh. You're all dressed up."

They stared at each other. Silvana poked her head over Moss's, looked Saba up and down, and clicked her tongue disapprovingly.

Unlike Zek, Silvana had managed, somehow, to stay in Byrengrad. Saba had heard several terms thrown about—"ichor residue" and "astral haunting" and the like—which apparently required a lot of testing and sometimes for Moss and Silvana to dedicate their afternoons to quiet, private study in one of the Scholar's Buildings many rooms.

"What?" Saba asked. He smoothed down his tunic, but he could feel the small ponytail tickling his neck, and he grunted. "It's the hair, isn't it? I can't get it to sit right."

"It's not the outfit," Silvana said smoothly, "but the attitude."

When Saba didn't reply, she wiggled her armored finger at him. The plates creaked together as she moved. "You are not dressed for war."

This was true. Saba had picked out a beautiful high-necked tunic with layered frilly sleeves that kissed at his wrists. The trousers were simple and pressed, cinching at the ankle and disappearing into his ankle boots.

"Well, neither are you, technically," he said to Silvana, and began fiddling with his ponytail once more. "You must wear that armor all the time or you'll go insane. Maybe I need to have good hair all the time or the same thing will happen to me."

Silvana scoffed, but Moss made a concerned noise.

"No, she's right," Moss said quietly. She put a foot over the threshold and placed a gentle hand on his shoulder. "Saba. They say an armed force is bearing down on us. Any moment—"

"No bells have rung," Saba said.

Moss blinked at him. "What?"

He took his eyes off his own reflection—he'd gone red in the cheeks like he'd been running, and sweat had already pooled at his lower back—and looked her in the eye. "No war bells, Moss."

Moss tilted her head and stared at Saba in awe. The realization dawned slowly. "No alarm . . . only warning of an approaching force," she said. And then she looked at him and saw exactly who he was dressing for. Her hand flew out to Silvana's arm, and Moss *squealed*—a bright, shrill sound Saba couldn't help but smile at.

"Oh!" Moss said. She waved her hand through the air with quick, excitable motions, her other hand gripped around Silvana's forearm. The paladin shored Moss up, standing stock-still with one eyebrow raised at Saba.

"Has someone come back for you, then?" Silvana asked, not unkindly. She had a teasing smile curling at her lip

"You know," Saba murmured, "that you shouldn't be using your new skills in Zvensian just to tease me, right?"

This only made Silvana shrug. "Your hair looks fine, Vasili. Stop touching it."

Saba exhaled and put his hands down. He turned bodily to face the two of them. Both their eyes had a weighted gleam in them, anticipatory excitement on his behalf.

How nice was that?

"Go," Moss said. Her knuckles had gone bone-white where she gripped Silvana's vambrace. They moved as one unit and stepped out of the doorway for Saba to pass. "Hurry up and go and meet them at the gate."

Saba stared. Anxiety bubbled in him; what if he was wrong? Or worse: what if he was only partly right? What if Zek had returned, but for politics or diplomacy, and not for Saba?

Moss raised a brow at him and snapped her fingers in front of his eyes. "Saba. Whatever you're thinking—"

Saba sighed, "I know. I know."

He had to trust Zek. He had to trust himself. He had to let himself feel and do what he wanted; and what he wanted was to meet Zek at the gate like a lovestruck fool.

"Wish me luck?" Saba said as he shuffled past the two women.

"You don't need it," Moss told him, but she squeezed his shoulder all the same.

Saba took a gig through Byrengrad. The driver pushed the horse fast, partly because he didn't want to be anywhere near the northern gate, and partly because he could—most of Byrengrad's citizens had retreated indoors, leaving the roads empty and easily navigable. Saba didn't mind it. Since the revelation of his identity—and his awkward, amalgamated role in Zvensian society as a sage—he had found it difficult to traverse Byrengrad as he used to.

The driver took them past the painted mural of Kerinsk's long-lost princess, and Saba nearly fell off the gig—because they'd changed it. Someone had gone back in and repainted it. Not perfectly, but they had swapped out the ideal feminine for his actual likeness, for his curls, his nose, his hair. The mauve, yellow, and blue of Kerinsk was smeared in the background, and the words KERINSK'S LEGACY were now painted over the cry for the princess' return.

Seeing it made him feel, in a way, insane. There was so much weight to an image like that, and so much responsibility. Saba occupied a unique and tentative position among other Kers, but when the truth came out, plenty of them had rallied, somewhat unexpectedly, to his side. Sometimes quite literally. Almost anytime he stepped out of the Scholar's Guild, a Ker or two would appear to shadow him: people with the blood of the old guard, folk who claimed to have met his mother at one point or another, people petitioning him, people eager to hear his plans for the return to Kerinsk. He met Kers who brought criticism, too, on occasion—but that he couldn't fault.

Shameful and hesitant, Saba had returned to his people—and he listened to them.

His old avoidance felt symptomatic of other things, really; he realized that in many ways, he had avoided the truth of himself out of shame. But from the Kers who had made their lives in Byrengrad, he found old guards, administrators, officials. He found farmers and artisans and merchants. He found people who had been even younger than himself when they'd fled their country, too young to remember what any of it looked like.

Naturally, then, he found among them people who

were willing—happy, honored, grateful, even—to help him. And so, Saba had appointed his own guards from the Kerish ranks.

Now, materializing by the gig, an older Kerish woman named Osera rode to join him on horseback. She had the Kerish flag stitched into the shoulders of her tunic and a sword at her hip, and she'd been part of the army that had escorted Kerish civilians from the country. On his other side rode a soldier named Xalah, whom the Triad had once jailed for stealing grain. These were two of his guards, but many Kers looked out for him, and Saba needed to look out for them, too.

What would Zek think of that, he wondered.

They arrived at the oddly deserted northern gates just as the Rezwyns did. There was a beautiful symmetry to their arrival, and if Saba was less scholarly, he might have called it fate—only that kind of talk would get his hopes up.

And if it's an army come to sack Byrengrad?

Well, he had to hope it would be quick. The northern gates were closed, and the sentinels along the battlements readied themselves. Diligence Inquisitor's squadron lined the streets, swords drawn. Archers had set up on the rooftops, many of them lying flat to avoid potential enemy arrows.

Every civilian had rushed inside. The news of the impending Rezwyn arrival had spread, and half the city—who in truth had only recently returned to their homes following the mass evacuation—had begun to prepare themselves to leave.

"I wouldn't be out here, if I were you," a sentinel called out to Saba from their place on the parapet. Another turned and bowed on sight, a Kerish sentry. Diligence Inquisitor had allowed Kerish refugees to join the city guard.

"It's quite alright," Saba called back, as he climbed out of the gig. He let the driver return to the upper ward, and nodded at both Osera and Xalah, who continued to flank him. "I don't believe there's—"

But the rest of his words were promptly drowned beneath the trumpeting wail of Rezwyn horns. A call went out on the parapet, and boots thundered on the stone as the sentinels prepared themselves.

Saba heard the scrape of steel and turned to find Xalah had pulled their sword free; a sentinel was attempting to negotiate an approach from behind—Maksid.

"Let him," Saba called, and Xalah relented. Maksid slipped forward, eyes wide behind his mask.

"What are you doing?" he hissed. "Please. You can't negotiate with them."

"No alarms have sounded. No other city has sent a warning. This isn't an army, Maksid."

His brother looked at him in a way that made Saba's heart crumple. Maksid gently shook his head. "Then what is it?"

The gates opened with a resonant groan before Saba could say anything. Reflexively, he took a step back. The road out of Byrengrad was clogged with Rezwyns. A beautifully gilded carriage sat as the centerpiece of the procession, and six armed guards flanked it. More guards were positioned farther down the line at various intervals, protecting wagons overflowing with goods. Wagons packed with bags of grain caught his eye.

Saba looked closer and saw that at least fifty rolls of fabrics had been loaded into their own carts. Liquor, too. And there were about a hundred fucking sheep.

"What," Saba said with a laugh.

A wiry woman rushed forward ahead of the procession into Byrengrad and blew her horn again. The sentinels turned on the parapet, unsure where to aim their swords. The archers had their arrows knocked and ready, but the tension was fading, given the absurdity of the situation.

The bleating sheep made it difficult to imagine any kind of attack.

From the top of her lungs the crier shouted, "On behalf of Emperor Izra Dziove and the Emperor Consort Oren Radek, I humbly present the Ambassador Luan Zek of the Rezwyn Empire, who requests an audience with Prince Saba Vasili of Kerinsk!"

Saba flushed immediately. It was the first time he'd been announced with his title before. Osera looked to him for confirmation, which he gave—a jolting, anxious wave that made her walk forward toward the crier and announce Saba right back.

"See?" Saba murmured to Maksid, who was standing stock-still. "Under that mask, I bet you're furious."

"Not furious," Maksid said. "Not even surprised, actually. I saw the way he looked at you."

This shocked Saba enough he turned to face him—Maksid was usually never so forthcoming with his emotions or observations.

"You deserve it, you know. After everything," Maksid murmured. He was backing up now, allowing Saba space.

"Deserve what?" Saba asked loudly.

"Someone that will do this just to see you," Maksid said, before he slipped back into the sentinel ranks.

After some quiet discussion between the crier and Osera, Saba was given a wide berth. His guards still flanked him, but they moved well away, allowing the Rezwyn carriage to roll inside the gates.

Saba's heart ached. His breathing came in short and fast, and he could feel the sweat cooling at the back of his neck beneath his hair. None of this felt real. Saba moved with dreamlike slowness, drifting out of the way as the carriage rolled up to him. Its exterior was blue and silver in the Rezwyn colors, inlayed with filigree and patterned with the likeness of Borviet and Suoduny. It had none of Zek's personality, none of his soft power. This was a show of the emperor; this legitimized Zek's visit—and that just made Saba more nervous.

The carriage rolled up right next to him. Saba flexed his hands and exhaled. He waited and waited, hand itching to wrench the door open, and eventually he was rewarded when the Rezwyn groom—the very same who had accompanied Zek and Saba around Byrengrad—hopped off to open the door. She smiled brightly at Saba like they were old friends and even bowed her head to him slightly.

"Prince Saba," she said.

She sounded entirely genuine, and Saba had a pang of guilt for not even knowing her name.

"It's good to see you again," he said, and then paused.

"Ursezka," she supplied.

"Ursezka," Saba repeated. "Thank you for taking such care of Ambassador Zek."

She smiled and turned back to the door, pulling until she heard the quiet click of the latch.

Someone inside pushed back.

The door swung wide with more force than was strictly necessarily—by someone perhaps unused to the delicate interiors of gilded empire carriages, or someone so eager to get out he'd forgotten the role of the groom. The door slipped from the Ursezka's hands and hit the side of the carriage with a dull whack. From inside, Saba heard someone say, "Shit."

Luan Zek sat inside.

He wore the most elaborate finery Saba had ever seen on a man, let alone a man like Zek: A fabric cuirass in velvet, detailed in silver embroidery and beaded along the collar. Trousers that did nothing but accentuate the pillowy muscle of Zek's thighs. Long laced boots up to his knees, calves bulging against the leather, which had been tooled with hares, a dozen of them up and down his legs. He had his usual cane balanced against the empty seat beside him.

He looked at Saba softly, smile warm and inviting, teeth gleaming beneath the blond fur of his moustache and beard. Saba's heart jolted. Heat rushed to his face—and elsewhere—and he grinned back, grinned like a fool, so intensely his cheeks instantly ached.

But dumbstruck by the sight of Zek, instead of anything beautiful or intelligent, Saba blurted out, "What are you wearing?"

Zek blinked at him and laughed—a full-bellied sound that filled up the interior of the carriage. He smoothed down the outfit, which had the clear handiwork of a master, and said, "Well, when I told the Emperor Consort what my intentions were, he refused to let me cross the border unless I promised to wear this to meet you."

"Is that why you took so long?" Saba murmured.

Zek raised a brow. "Been impatient, have you? All things considered, I've practically run to the empire and back."

Saba looked at him and considered that; reality settled slowly. Two weeks to reach the empire, and two weeks here: a month's worth of travel. Zek had needed to report to the emperor, needed to explain and convince said emperor that Saba Vasili and his grand interest in the astral sea posed the empire no threat, and then . . . well, he must have mentioned returning to Zvensia almost immediately.

Almost immediately.

"What have you done?" Saba said cautiously. "You haven't . . . completely uprooted your life to come here, have you?"

"Why?" Luan asked with a chuckle as he pulled himself out of the cart. "Found someone else in the last months you like better?

How could I, Saba almost said. *How could I when you look like* **that***? When you make me laugh, when you make me feel safe?* He said none of it and let Zek step down off the carriage.

"I hope you don't mind, though," Zek said, gesturing to the carts with the grain. "I owed you, you see, for your good will regarding your notes."

Saba didn't want to think about that. It put a sour taste in his mouth. Zek nodded at him now, acknowledging that feeling.

"I betrayed your trust," Zek said. "And I didn't apologize then, but I wanted to—I wanted you to know that—well, I am sorry."

Saba said, "Thank you. I actually . . . it means a lot that you said that."

Zek leaned on his cane and looked out at the procession. "I hope you don't mind, but I . . . I discussed it with the emperor. He read your notes, and, well . . . You'll say no to this, but I promised I would pass on the message."

"Which is?"

"The empire would always accept your counsel in the matters of the astral sea. Should you ever wish to settle there."

Saba raised his brow as high as it would go, and Zek nodded. "I know. I know you wouldn't—not now, anyway. Perhaps not ever. But if you're ever at a loss for what to do with your life . . ."

Saba laughed. "Oh, is that before or after I figure out what being Prince of Kerinsk means for a prince with no country?"

"Before," Zek said instantly with his own smile. "That other thing sounds much too difficult."

Saba smiled and nodded; it was a near impossible thing to sort out. But he had years, he supposed. He had his life.

"Anyway," Zek said, "another thing. The reason for all this—I did remind the emperor that his predecessor had undermined the treaty between the Rezwyns and Kerinsk,"—how fucking bold of Zek—"And that it might be a show of good faith for him to send some material aid."

Saba blinked, not understanding. "For us? The Kers?"

"Of course," Zek said.

Saba considered this. He looked back at the grain and all the rest of it: fine gifts, rich bolts of fabric. It might take the edge off, perhaps helping Kers step into their citizenship, the terms of which he would be negotiating in the coming days. He flashed a look back to Zek. "And the rest? The sheep?"

Zek leaned close and whispered against Saba's ear, "Consider them part of my dowry."

He pulled back, and Saba stared at him. What?

When Saba couldn't speak, Zek added, "You are a prince after all."

This was—simply put—ridiculous. Saba made a panicked noise, and then he laughed. He pressed his hand against his mouth and stepped back, taking it all in. "You're mad. We hardly know each other."

"I want to know you," Zek said, extremely seriously. The look on his face made Saba flinch—not because of its intensity, but because of the heat beneath it. Chalk it up to the time apart or the distance, but Saba could feel a sudden tension swarm the two of them. Gone was the quiet and happy reunion. An immense and aching want interrupted every soft and gentle thought in Saba's mind.

Even with the eyes of the Rezwyns, the sentinels, the archers, his own guards, his own *brother* on them, Saba found himself saying, "How, exactly, do you want to know me?"

Zek's eyes fluttered closed. "I'm headed to the embassy. Same room as last time. And I do recall we, uh—"

"Had some unfinished business there," Saba supplied for him.

"Yes," Zek said, opening his eyes once more. His smile was airy, his breathing heavy. "Quite right."

Saba said quickly, "Get back in the carriage."

Zek laughed. "What, *now*?"

"Yes, *now*," Saba said. There was time for the other things. Years and years of diplomacy and negotiations and politics. But now? After months? After relentless interruptions? "Diligence Inquisitor will be expecting you at some point, and I'd rather no one suggest we go and have that conversation before we *finish* that business of ours. Alright?"

Zek looked around. A few people had begun to walk out of their houses. Chatter had started up. People were excited or questioning the arrival of the Rezwyns—or the sheep. The archers descended from the city wall. Osera and Xalah were discussing logistics for the animals, which would be helpful to some of the Kerish farmers, if Saba could negotiate the land and the—

Zek stepped forward, in front of everyone, and kissed him.

A collective gasp went up, and it must have finally hit the crowd that the Rezwyns weren't at all here for war. No matter what anyone thought of Saba Vasili, this relief was enough to get everyone cheering.

Saba flushed. His eyes fluttered, and he exhaled against Zek. Without even realizing it, he had pushed their bodies close. Something stirred in him—something hot and desperate.

"Get in the fucking carriage," Saba said roughly, and Zek snorted against his lips. With a short wave, and with a nod to his guards to work out the logistics of Zek's so-called dowry, they clambered into the carriage and were off.

The ride was tense. Their thighs touched the entire time, which took a great deal of Saba's focus. The rest of his mind was split between looking intensely at Zek, and then attempting to listen to Zek's rundown of what had happened in the last two months, and his intention now.

Zek said, "You'll be moving around, you know. Between the empire, Kerinsk, here. Negotiating for a very long time—but that's quite alright. I don't particularly enjoy staying in one place for too long."

Saba wanted to get up and straddle him, but he said, "So, you—mean to stay with me?"

"You'll need a Rezwyn in Kerinsk. For the negotiations. And no doubt someone will try to kill you, since the empire is still full of expansionist fanatics.

"So you're my guard now, are you?"

"I'm a man of many talents, Saba," Zek grinned. "I'd rather you didn't limit my potential."

"I'm sure you'll prove your talents," Saba said, "in due course."

Which only made the tension much, much worse.

Zek smiled at him, like a tease, and then it was just all too much. Or not enough. Whatever—Saba pushed up and kissed Zek hard.

Zek welcomed him with a low, hearty chuckle, and Saba climbed over and slid his legs around either side of Zek's hips. The soft rise of Zek's belly was warm beneath his tunic. Saba ground his hips down, ruttish and animalistic, and Zek grabbed his hips, hands pressing firmly as he pressed their bodies together and thrust impotently. They kissed messily, hands in each other's hair, fingers roaming. Zek slipped his calloused palm up Saba's tunic and along his back—fuck. Warmth flooded Saba's cunt, which twitched; he needed friction. Pressure. Saba made a low noise and kissed down Zek's neck, slowing his desperate thrusts to a more intentional grinding.

And then Zek said, "Off."

Saba froze and pulled back. "What?"

"You heard me," Zek said. "Get off."

Stunned, Saba slipped off Zek's lap. He could feel how wet he was, and Zek's pants were tenting with the bulge of his cock, but Zek's expression was calm and focused. He stared at Saba for a few seconds before he raised a finger to his lips and said, "Don't say another word until we get there—or I'll have to have you right here."

Saba breathed deep as Zek dragged his cane over his lap and stared stoically out the window. What kind of a threat was that? Yes, the carriage was cramped. Yes, the Rezwyn satin roofing and the plush cushions would probably be stained beyond repair, but so what?

You forget you're a prince. Everyone knows who you are.

It was a foreign concern to have, but important—and it was all the worse that Zek had realized this before Saba had. Zek was more of a diplomat than he cared to admit.

Saba balled his fists at his side and slowed his breathing, but every time he closed his eyes he thought of Zek naked, and eventually he had to stare unblinking out the carriage window as it wound up to the embassy.

Ursezka opened the carriage door, winked at Saba, and then it was another half an hour before they were alone. Zek had brought luggage, and everyone seemed determined to get it to his room before he settled. Saba waited and watched him, his back pressed against the cool wall of the embassy as the Rezwyn guards and servants lifted a trunk up the stairs. Zek made a very good show of being completely normal and not driven to the point of breaking by his desire, so good Saba wondered if he himself simply had an abnormal amount of lust. He watched Zek chat and laugh and give directions, and then the guards saluted him, and the servants bowed, and the embassy officials peeled away and left them both, finally, alone.

Zek turned to look at him and smiled. "Coming?"

Saba practically jumped off the wall. "Lead the way."

Zek did, ascending with extra care. At the top, he led them to the room he'd occupied two months before, and everything hit Saba the instant he crossed the threshold. Zek went to the bed and began to unlace his boots. Saba did the same. He couldn't look away from Zek. His eyes caught every detail: the way he was breathing, the careful way he placed the boots. Zek stood and groaned, beginning to unlace his tunic at the neck. He half turned toward the stand where the drinks were, and Saba pushed off toward him before he got there.

Zek asked, "Do you want a drink?" and turned for Saba's response—but Saba was there already, pushing up against him on the tips of his toes. He pressed forward, looped his arms around Zek, and kissed him.

"No," Saba breathed. "Don't make me wait any longer."

This apparently was the wrong thing to say. Firmly, slowly, Zek's hand pulled Saba's head back by his neck. He searched Saba's face. Those piercing blue eyes studied his expression; concern and something else flashed there. What now? Impatience bubbled in Saba's stomach. Was it—Saba's body? Did they need to have this conversation again?

Zek tilted Saba's head and made a soft noise. "Now, where have your manners gone, Vasili?"

Saba frowned, his comprehension slow and stilted by the heat of desire throbbing at the base of his skull, where Zek's thick fingers touched him.

"You have lost all your patience," Zek whispered. A smile ghosted at his lips, but the rough tone to his voice overshadowed it. Saba exhaled so heavily he went dizzy.

"Yes," he whispered. "Yes, I have." Zek nodded, his gaze unknowable and cryptic. He slipped his hand out of Saba's hair and stepped back to inspect him, shifting his weight more heavily onto his cane. As he nodded, Saba half expected Zek to ask for an apology, and perhaps Saba would have given one to him, without even knowing what for, if it meant Zek would touch him again.

"Sit down," Zek ordered. There was no doubt that it was an order—Saba's body reacted not with the indignation of a prince being told what to do, but with a thrilled shiver. Saba sat on the edge of the bed without question, willing, anticipation hot and thick in his stomach. But it all froze when Zek walked close and, hand leaning against one of the posts of the canopy, raised the carved wooden hare of his cane and positioned its ears beneath the soft submental of Saba's chin.

Saba gulped.

Zek looked down at him unaffected; his eyes were heavy and heated, but there was an immense feeling of authority to all of Zek's movements. Everything was measured, considered. Luan Zek was in control.

"Take off your clothes," Zek said. He dragged the hare head away, scraping those pointed ears along Saba's mouth.

The request had a surprisingly sobering effect on Saba. Some sense crawled back to him, and he froze anxiously, questioning Zek with a quirked brow. The big man said nothing, made no attempt to assist him, and did not care to repeat himself. So, what else was there to do?

Slowly, fingers shaking, Saba moved to undo the button on his high-necked tunic. He regretted wearing something with such long sleeves. Even in winter, he'd gotten too sweaty—too overstimulated before he'd even started. Saba made sure to maintain eye contact as he undid the buttons, each loping release slow and as sensual as he could make it. He teased Zek, exposing one nipple and then the other, and then let the tunic slip from his shoulders.

The gedrokbone necklace sat nicely in his clavicle. Zek smiled at the sight of it and stepped forward. They stared at each other. Saba's skin was itchy, hot—something quivered, a tingle in his groin. He wanted Zek already. He wanted him now.

Zek ran his hand over Saba's shoulder and dipped it lower, forefinger and thumb grazing over a sensitive pink nipple. Saba jumped close to Zek's touch with a hoarse grunt. Surgery had done nothing to dampen the effect any sensation had on his nipples; the touch sent a jolt of anticipatory pleasure to Saba's groin.

Saba moaned and looked up at Zek from beneath his brows. The big man glided his forefinger along Saba's chest, along his scars, thumbing them gently with an awed sound.

"They're beautiful," he murmured. "They suit you."

Zek shifted out of the window's light, so the sun refracted through the glass and set the iridescence of Saba's scars ablaze; those flaming colors danced beneath his chest.

"Ichor infused," Zek said knowingly. "Selvik truly is a master."

Saba was briefly torn away from the intense heat pooling in his belly—just long enough to be surprised by how much Zek knew of the techniques involved in what was, really, quite a rare surgery. But then they made eye contact, and every thought evacuated. Zek leaned down. Saba extended his neck, expecting a kiss, but Zek only moved lower. Wet warmth covered Saba's right nipple as Zek took it in his mouth.

"Fuck," Saba hissed. Zek's tongue stroked the nipple in flat, teasing motions—fuck, fuck, Saba was probably drenching the sheets already. He snaked his fingers up into Zek's hair and pushed Zek closer. The ambassador sucked and bit. Saba hissed but pushed him closer.

Then Zek roughly pulled away, teeth and all, dragging Saba's nipple with him. Powerless to do anything, Saba groaned, having to jolt forward with a weak, desperate sound to keep himself from crying out.

Zek stood and made an appreciative noise. "Go on," he said, gesturing for Saba to continue undressing. Saba stared at him defiantly. He didn't say no so much as thought about saying it; thought about what Zek might do to him if he teasingly refused to follow through. Zek's trousers were tenting—his cock must have been straining, aching beneath the fabric. So, Saba spread his legs and calmly put his hands on either side of his thighs, flat on the bed.

Zek tutted.

The cane came up again and slipped beneath Saba's chin, then knocked his cheek to the side. Saba grunted, trying to keep their eyes locked.

"Vasili," Zek said.

"Yes?"

"I told you to take off your clothes."

This wasn't enough—certainly not all Zek wanted to see. Saba's heart rate quickened in his chest, but any anxiety was being suffocated by the eager throb of his groin. He wanted friction—he wanted pressure there. More than a simple touch—a lot more. Zek stepped forward, sliding the cane off Saba's cheek, and replacing the pressure there with his own hand, which he used to anchor Saba's chin.

"Well?" he asked.

Saba once again said nothing, and Zek's cane whipped out again, tapping lightly beneath Saba's chin.

"I promise you, I can find many uses for this cane."

Saba did not move.

Zek stepped back. A simple movement. The cane came whacking down across the outside of Saba's thigh.

Saba yelped and shivered and grinned despite himself. Everything throbbed in delight.

Teasing was fun, but not worth the delay. In answer, Saba slid his hands down his own body. He slipped his forefinger between the band of the trousers and worked to unlace them, hands gently tugging and pulling until they loosened. Zek's breathing was so heavy now that Saba half expected him to give up this teasing game, to wrench the trousers free and have his way. But all Zek did was watch intensely, and it was up to Saba to sit up on his haunches and wiggle out of the trousers. At the underclothes, he hesitated and looked up to Zek, who reflexively pulled back. His erection was straining against his own trousers, but Zek didn't move his hand up his own laces. He didn't attempt to relieve his mounting pressure at all.

Saba closed his eyes and slipped out of his underclothes.

He lowered himself to the sheets, which became slick immediately. Zek made an appreciative noise and cocked his head. He brought the cane up and pulled it up Saba's inner thigh—slowly, intently, so every second dragged. Saba felt insane. He was panting, rolling his hips.

Then the bottom of Zek's cane grazed lightly across his clit.

Saba groaned and thrust up toward the feeling, but Zek snatched the cane away.

"Touch yourself," he said.

Saba pulled his gaze away from the bulging pants and blinked at him. "What?"

"I want to know how you like to be touched," Zek said. He watched Saba's expression carefully, and Saba realized very suddenly that no one had ever asked him that. No one had ever cared. His pleasure had always been secondary, and he was used to that. He wasn't used to—whatever this was.

"Vasili?" Zek prompted, his voice low, and Saba rose on his knees again. Zek's gaze dropped immediately to the exposed pink between his thighs; Saba's clit throbbed just from that attention—just from Zek looking at him with obvious lust. Then Zek stood up straight, and his cane slapped the inside of Saba's thighs. "Wider," Zek said.

Saba moaned as he sank down, legs spreading so Zek might get a better view. And then he leaned back on one hand and used the other to show Zek what he liked. He couldn't really focus, though; Zek's gaze was too intense, and Saba's impatience was mounting. He put two fingers inside himself.

"Oh, Gods," Zek groaned, leaning heavily on his cane. He started to touch himself over his trousers, grinding up into the palm of his hand. Saba felt nothing but good about his body in that moment. He showed Zek how to touch him, how he was allowed to touch him, and every groan from Zek's lips only made him more confident. When Saba wanted more, he teased Zek—moaning and grunting and biting his lip—and he was satisfied when Zek was the first to break.

"Get over here," Zek grunted, and Saba pushed himself up and crawled forward, up onto his knees, so he was at head height with Zek. He leaned in for a kiss which was summarily denied—Zek ghosted his lips away with a breathy laugh—and this frustrated Saba so extensively that he firmly gripped Zek's wrist and pulled his hand close, angling those big fingers down. Zek's hand slicked over Saba's arousal; he was already drenched. They both moaned; Saba airy, pleasured, and Zek roughly, possessively— his vocals matching his movements. Saba moved his legs apart and leaned his head against Luan's neck. They were pressed up against one another, Zek's fingers rubbing up and down, mouth on Saba's neck. Zek's cane clattered to the ground as he put all his weight against the edge of the bed and used his other hand to thumb Saba's nipple.

Saba couldn't control the noises he was making. He ground down like he was trying to get Zek inside him. He squeezed Zek's chest, which filled out both his hands, and his mouth was sloppy against Zek's neck, half kissing and half panting through open-mouthed moans. And then Zek slipped two fingers inside Saba, who roughly jerked down with a loud, pleasured moan. He laced an arm around Zek's neck and looked down now to see the big man's cock straining through his trousers. Saba's fingers roamed to Zek's laces. Usually he was better at this—better at concentrating, at following the steps in this little dance—but Zek's touch had softened the sharpness of his mind. He felt himself grinding impotently, knew he was making all kinds of noises, but it just felt so good. Zek watched him carefully, twisting the fingers he had inside Saba, and angling in a way he could simultaneously thumb Saba's clit.

Saba groaned through a reflexive spasm, rolling his hips with more intention than before. Then he looked up and locked eyes with Zek.

"Fuck," Zek moaned, and this deep-bellied sound of pleasure emboldened Saba enough that he started to fuck himself on Zek's fingers, up and down, rutting against the insufficient pressure of Zek's thumb until his thighs burned.

Then Saba gently pulled Zek's fingers out of him.

"Clothes," Saba said, and Zek at least agreed with him on this. He pulled away slightly, just enough that he could free himself of the very impressive finery one-handedly, the other dutifully continuing to rub against Saba until it came time to slip the sleeves free. As soon as his shirt was off, Saba was done with the laces on Zek's trousers. He tugged until the band slackened around Zek's waist, and he slipped off the bed and went down on his knees. He met the hard flooring and looked up at Zek from under his lashes, and as he tugged Zek's trousers free, his cock twitched.

Zek's fingers wove gently into Saba's hair. He put his weight there, the other hand gripping the canopy's poster.

Saba opened his mouth.

"Ah," Zek said, smiling down at him. His touch was gentle as he ghosted his finger under Saba's jaw. "Good boy."

Saba gave a breathy moan. Then he leaned in to take as much of Zek down his throat as he could, eyes fluttering closed as the other man pushed over his tongue.

Zek's groan was inarticulate, and he half crumpled over Saba, grip on his hair tightening as that big hand hooked for a greater grip. Zek let Saba set the tempo, so Saba teased him, tongue grazing up around the swollen head, his right hand curling around the slick hilt to work up and down Zek's length. But this only proved Zek was just as desperate as him. He repositioned his grip on the back of Saba's head and angled himself, pushing deeper into the warm sheath of Saba's mouth. Saba grunted and choked. And Zek was eager; he was thrusting, grunting, clearly having to hold himself back from fucking Saba's throat too deeply. Saba was moaning and choking, and he looked up at Luan through half-closed lids, tears brimming, with the sunlight of the city at his back. He could just see Zek's pleasured face over the big man's belly. Saba felt small, but not in a bad way—small, and controlled, and it made him wet.

Zek pulled his cock out of Saba's mouth and pressed it close to Saba's lips.

"Is this what you want?" Zek rasped.

Saba nodded eagerly. His eyes were heavy-lidded, and he was panting; shit, he wanted Zek to fuck him already.

As if hearing this, Zek cocked his head, tongue poised on the edge of his teeth. "Tell me."

Saba bit his lip and keened out, "Please." His fingers slid between his own legs. "Please, I want you—inside me."

Satisfied, Zek released his grip on Saba's hair. He reached down and tugged Saba up before shoving him onto the bed. Saba went sprawling, scrambling to reposition himself against the pillows. But he kept his legs open, watching as Zek took in the sight of him.

"Please," Saba said again, but Zek shook his head. He climbed on and nudged Saba's legs further apart.

"Not just yet," Zek murmured.

Then he lowered himself carefully, eyes searching for Saba's reaction as he leaned slowly toward Saba's exposed cunt, mouth yawned open and tongue perched at the edge of his teeth. Saba's breath hitched. He wasn't—he was not used to people wanting to do this. He was certainly not used to seeing such an open display of lust. Zek tugged Saba down the bed, closer to his mouth, and raised a brow. *Can I?* his expression seemed to ask, and Saba nodded emphatically.

Zek exhaled, thumbs carefully gliding in the slick. "Oh, fuck," Zek groaned at the sight of him. "Your cunt is so. . ."

Whatever he was going to say, he didn't manage it. Saba impatiently laced his fingers through Zek's hair and pulled him down. Zek's tongue flicked out over his clit, and Saba squirmed, thighs squeezing close to Zek's head as the other man slowly dragged the flat of his tongue up and down, licking Saba with a slow, careful intention. His tongue dipped low and slid up inside Saba, making him spasm, his eyes rolling back into his skull with a deep moan. He pushed up on the heels of his feet, rolling his hips eagerly against the grazing friction of Zek's beard.

"Please," Saba keened, "Damn it, Zek, please."

Zek pulled back. Saba's arousal coated his beard; he wiped it away with the palm of his hand and dragged his big body up between Saba's legs. His cock jumped against Saba's thigh, and the weight of Zek's belly pressed firmly down on him as Zek leaned in—finally—for a kiss.

They were all messy tongues, moaning into each other's mouths. Saba tasted himself on Zek's tongue—the tang, the salt, the sweat—and made a noise caught somewhere between embarrassment and intense, rushing arousal.

"I love the way you taste," Zek whispered against Saba's lips. He was grinding slowly, his cock rubbing against the wetness of Saba's inner thighs, and then it slipped over his mound, and Zek rutted against Saba's clit, pressing more firmly each time Saba's moan deepened. Saba's hands made a wild, desperate search of Zek's back, his chest, his nipples poking out from the soft down of hair—a selfish roaming of hands that ended when Saba laced them around Zek's head and pulled him down for another deep kiss. They groaned together, moans answering each other, and this time when Saba panted out a please, Zek nodded against the side of his head. He took Saba's legs and brought them up to rest on either shoulder, his stomach pressing into Saba's, and he planted his hands on Saba's hips. With his fingertips gripping firmly, Zek dug close to the entrance of Saba's cunt, and Saba's shoulders rose: an anticipatory tensing, silent desperation for Zek to finally *fuck him*.

Zek nudged closer and pressed in, eyes raised to watch Saba as he took him to the hilt. He slipped easily inside; Saba's moan was rapturous and guttural. One hand fumbled up to the nape of Zek's neck, the other twisting in the sheets, and Zek's blue eyes flared wide before his head arched back as if pulled toward his tailbone. Zek thrust out of rhythm, rolling his hips, getting a feel for Saba's body and the way it throbbed around him, and in turn, Saba moaned and moved with him, eager for a rougher motion but loving the feel of Zek's length pulsing inside him. Zek rolled forward and bestowed a long kiss upon his lips, his mouth moving lazily as he slowly fucked forward. But with their mouths still locked together, Zek suddenly shifted, pulling out with his hips so his cock slipped out most of the way. Then he drove it all the way back into Saba with a single, forceful thrust.

Saba threw his head back with a cry, both hands clutching desperately at the sheets as Zek began to work him in earnest. The big man had no trouble keeping Saba in place; the pressure on Saba's hips kept him from jerking back from the slow, deep strokes. The pressure was hard and deep; in the curve of Saba's lower belly, he felt a pleasured pain recoiling through his body with every move. It was like Zek couldn't quite help but scrape as deep as possible with every thrust.

Saba's moans were airy, staccato cries, and suddenly Zek pulled out of him all the way, dragged him back on the bed, and flipped him. It took no effort at all, just those strong hands maneuvering Saba's legs over until his belly was pressing into the sheets. He arched his lower back, and another appreciative noise came out of Zek's lips.

"Gods, look at you," he murmured, spreading Saba's ass apart and taking in the view, and Saba was so long past embarrassment now that he squirmed insistently, back arched, wordlessly begging for Zek to take him again.

He didn't, of course; he seemed to be enjoying this obvious display of desperation. Saba turned to look at him over his shoulder to find Zek stroking himself, teasing, a self-satisfied smile stretching his lips apart. Zek reached out and thumbed lazily over the sloppy warmth between Saba's legs, pushing inside, teasing the entrance, grazing over the clit.

Saba flushed and turned, but Zek reached out with his other hand and pushed on the small of Saba's back. He sprawled, utterly unable to resist the pressure of the bigger man.

"Don't make me beg," Saba whispered, straining to catch Zek's expression.

Zek smiled at this, cocking his head. A wolfish grin Saba had never seen before rushed across his face.

"But Your Highness," Zek said, in the same voice he used to diplomatically ruin people, "you haven't told me what to do."

Saba exhaled and closed his eyes. "I want your cock."

"You're a prince, aren't you?" Zek said, and Saba met his playful gaze with one of his own. He felt so empty—so desperate—he wanted to drive backward onto Zek's cock then and there.

But Zek clearly had other plans. His firm hand moved back and squeezed Saba's ass, finger gliding over the hole, and he said, "Tell me what you want the way a prince would."

An order. Zek wanted an order.

Saba's lips twitched. "And here I thought I was the dog," he whispered.

Zek exhaled. Saba settled himself, turning on his side and gazing at Zek over the rise of his hip.

"You like taking orders, Zek?" Saba asked him.

Zek didn't answer, save for the near imperceptible squeeze he gave his own cock. That soldier training had another impact on Zek's development, it seemed, because when Saba shifted, grazing his leg up the sheets to allow Zek a better view, and said, "I order you to fuck me. Without restraint," a lusty haze swept over Zek's eyes.

The big man groaned roughly, grabbed Saba's legs, and pulled him back. Saba shouted, and then shouted again with deep, heavy pleasure as Zek surged into him. Saba's eyes rolled back. He could feel the rough thatch at the base of Zek's cock as it pounded into him—roughly—and every thrust felt deeper and more purposeful. When Zek pushed Saba's head into the bed, his loud, protracted moan was muffled by the sheets. And finally, when Zek started to really fuck him, every noise escaping Saba's throat was an amalgamation of sobbing relief, unrestrained pleasure, and that blissful scraping pain in his belly.

"Don't move," Zek said. "Just enjoy taking it."

Saba angled his hips forward and relaxed, letting Zek plunge down in vigorous thrusts. Zek gripped Saba's hips tightly enough to bruise, and Saba's submission to the force was absolute; he lay there at the edge of ecstasy as Zek fucked him again and again, until the recoil had him bouncing off Zek's cock in slick, wet motions. Their bodies slid together, a mixture of arousal, precum, and sweat, and Zek kept the rhythm going until Saba felt a slight pulsing of the cock inside him. Zek groaned low and gripped Saba so hard he ached. Then he thrust faster, harder, breaths short and heavy and building. Saba gave a full-throated cry, swearing and screaming into the sheets, and then suddenly Zek pulled out of him, and a pleasured cry was wrenched from his throat as he came over Saba's back.

Saba lay there panting, fingers clenched in the sweat-covered sheets. Behind him, he heard the heavy gasping of Zek, felt the man twitch as the aftershocks pulsed through him. Which Saba had to see: he pulled himself up and looked at Zek over his shoulder. The ambassador was watching him, hairy midriff rising and falling in rapid breaths as he tried to catch his breath.

"Fuck," Zek said. "Fuck. You feel so…"

He trailed off, watching Saba carefully—trailed off, Saba presumed, because he'd been distracted by Saba sliding his finger through the string of cum on his back and sucking that finger into his mouth.

Zek's cock wobbled as he sighed and shifted and laughed, biting his lip and shaking his head. "Look at you," he said.

"Look at me," Saba echoed. Zek, seemingly undeterred by the mess he'd made on Saba's back, spun him again. Saba was pulled down along the bed, so his legs were above his head, and Zek's thumb pads pressed into the soft meat of his thigh. Then Zek put his mouth on Saba again and slowly moved over Saba's clit. Saba was so turned on he could feel himself throbbing; he buried Zek's head between his thighs with both hands and rolled his hips. Zek moaned with him, eyes shifting between Saba's expression and rolling back into his head—which drove Saba insane. His tongue moved from flat and wide to a point, the tip flicking over Saba before it flattened again like he was kissing Saba's mouth. And then he sucked.

"Fuck, *fuck*," Saba moaned breathlessly, grinding up into Zek's mouth with all the force he could muster. Zek devoured him sloppily, determined, focused, and it started to push Saba's body to the edge. He jolted compulsively, barreling toward his ecstasy, and all the blood was in his ears, so all he could hear was the rapid beat of his own heart over the background noise of his incessant cries and Zek's moans against him.

Saba knew he was babbling now: saying Zek's name, begging, inarticulate cries all overlapping. His body started to tremble. That tell-tale twitch became a tremor, a building flow, and then he cried out as his orgasm hit in a pulsing wave. He rode it as long as he could, fingers desperate in Zek's hair or the sheets, or gripping nothing in the air; he moaned, and Zek moaned with him, a satisfied, guttural sound from the depths of his belly.

And Zek didn't stop. Saba shook and whined against Zek's mouth until the sensation was too much, and only then did Zek release Saba's clit.

Saba sprawled and panted. It took half a minute for him to open his eyes. He pushed up to find Zek still down there, chin resting on Saba's stomach. Stringy saliva and arousal coated his mouth—he was a mess. Saba didn't care. He reached down and pulled Zek up into a kiss.

Within seconds, they were laced in each other's arms, breathing slowly into a comfortable rhythm. Then they looked up at each other and smiled, both of their lips splitting apart into wide, happy grins. Saba laughed and buried his head in the crook of Zek's neck just as the ambassador repositioned his hand and squeezed Saba's body against him.

They lay like that, basking in their afterglow for a long stretch of minutes. Lazily, their fingers stroked along one another's backs, heads, bodies in gentle, affectionate touches. Zek pressed his lips against the sweat of Saba's forehead. How perfect it all felt then. Saba closed his arms and rolled close against Zek's chest.

Everything felt right. Everything felt good.

Nearly a quarter of an hour later, Zek finally shifted, inhaling deeply to speak.

"As I was saying," Zek whispered, "I plan to accompany you when you leave Zvensia."

Saba snorted and kissed his cheek. "Enjoyed yourself, then?"

"Eh," Zek said. He made sure Saba was looking at him when he said, "So-so."

It was an echo of their first meeting. Saba smiled at him, thought about hitting him, but the brevity slipped away. His mind sobered, and he pushed up to really look at Zek, delicately tucking the ambassador's hair out of his face.

"You have no idea what it means," Saba said. "That you would come with me. I imagine the logistics will be nightmarish. We might move around a lot, or spend weeks in one place before shifting again. And once it's all said and done—once I've gotten the best I can for Kerinsk—we can settle. If, you know. If you're still interested by that time."

Zek was still smiling at him. "*We* can figure that out eventually," he whispered.

We. Zek had made sure to say it. *We.*

"That would be nice, wouldn't it?" Saba whispered.

"Yes," Zek said, fingers gliding up and down Saba's back.

And Saba found he felt, for the first time in a long time, nothing but hope for his future.

ACKNOWLEDGEMENTS

It feels fitting that this is the book I leave the world of *Reforged* on for now.

Reclaimed has been a true labor of love. I wrote it during a difficult time in my life, a period of transition, as it were, and I sometimes found it difficult to maintain the hope, self-love, and kindness that I wanted the book itself to reach. There were things I had to overcome to write it, and sometimes the things I was writing about felt extremely on the nose—tensions of the self, tensions between others, and the difficulties of self-love—were suddenly things I had to contend with in my life beyond writing. The process for writing Reclaimed involved a lot of upfront work, not only in terms of plot, balancing the mystery, or developing the characters, but on myself.

All that to say: Saba Vasili and his story mean a lot to me.

I must thank my editor Nicole Kimberling and publisher Blind Eye Books for encouraging the vision for this book and helping me wade through the complexities of writing a genre I'd never tackled before. Thank you for all your mystery advice! Of course, thank you to Nicole for your mentorship over the years.

To my agent Maeve MacLysaght, thank you always for your support. The advice you gave me years before you signed me has helped me become the author I am today, and I'm excited to keep growing and pitching new projects to you!

To Hilary Hensley, you have been an excellent copy editor. Thank you for engaging with my work so holistically and genuinely. You found things I'd overlooked, and this story wouldn't be as tight as it is without your help.

To Julie Dillon, you have blessed me with three beautiful covers now, but *Reclaimed's* made me tear up. Thank you for such unabashed queer and trans love.

To my friends, in a very particular order (if you know, you know): Chrissie Hague and Ellie Taylor, you keep me sane. Thank you for reminding me of who I am and for never judging me, except for all the times you do.

To Gemma Driscoll, for the general friendship you provide me. We are united in our suffering.

To Bex Deveau, I'm endlessly proud of you. You are the best writing partner I could hope for. Thanks for everything!

To my parents: as always, thank you for believing in me. Especially this last year!

To Aleks: a quiet thank you. You saved me last year.

To Shaz, my eighteen-year-old deaf, scrunkly cat. We grew up together and I'm so glad I could come back for the last few years of your life. You sat curled up next to me or sitting on a stool by my desk as I've written this. Thank you for your emotional support and foul-smelling breath.

To Zek and Saba: your relationship formed a bit slower than the other couples, but I felt you both had walls that needed to come down before you could be ready for love. I needed to tell your story and I'm happy I could do it.

To someone very special: you'll know who you are. I'm not sure if you'll read this, ever, but if you do, know that the way you support my creative career, the way you engage with it, and the way you take me and my work seriously is the greatest blessing. Grateful to have you in my life.

ABOUT THE AUTHOR

Seth Haddon is a queer Australian writer of fantasy. He is a video game designer and producer, has a degree in Ancient History, and previously worked with cats. He lives in Sydney with a deaf 18-year-old cat. Some of his previous adventures include exploring Pompeii with a famous archaeologist and being chased through a train station by a nun.

Photo by Minna Sophia Manu

REFORGED

Since time immemorial the warriors of the Paladin Order have harnessed arcane powers to protect their rulers. For Balen, who has given up his chance at love and fought his way to the top of the Paladin Order, there can be no greater honor than to serve his king. But when assassins annihilate the royal family, Balen suddenly finds himself sworn to serve the very man he abandoned.

Reborn

Izra Dziove, visionary advisor to the Rezwyn Emperor, is struggling to hold the turbulent court together while being plagued by dreams if his fated man—a man who strongly resembles the newly arrived Usleth diplomat, Oren Radek.

But when Izra's adversaries launch an attack he finds himself and Oren surrounded by enemies and battling not only to save their nations but to uncover the ancient secret that forged their destiny.